"You're not leaving yet."

"Like hell I'm not. You've got no reason to keep me here," Cass said.

Once more her words set off his body's alarms. "I've got reason," he growled, not explaining his double meaning.

Cass needed to get away from this man. She jerked hard on her arm, but felt him counter her movement by pulling her toward him, throwing her off-balance. The anger in her eyes turned to shock as she found herself leaning flush against his strong, muscular body.

Brett's heart exploded in his chest as Cass fell against him. All his nerves jumped to life, and his manhood pulsed with a need so great he was nearly dizzy with it. Locking her gaze with his, he saw the startled passion that blazed to life in the blue depths. Hesitating only a second, he lowered his head and claimed her lips in a devouring kiss, branding her with the fire that flashed between them. . . .

Books by Faye Adams

Lady of the Gun
The Goodnight Loving Trail
Rosebud

Published by POCKET BOOKS

FAYE ADAMS

LADY of the GUN

POCKET BOOKS
New York   London   Toronto   Sydney   Tokyo   Singapore

This book is a work of fiction. Names, characters, places and incidents are products of the author's imagination or are used fictitiously. Any resemblance to actual events or locales or persons, living or dead, is entirely coincidental.

An *Original* Publication of POCKET BOOKS

POCKET BOOKS, a division of Simon & Schuster Inc.
1230 Avenue of the Americas, New York, NY 10020

Copyright © 1996 by Faye Swoboda

All rights reserved, including the right to reproduce this book or portions thereof in any form whatsoever. For information address Pocket Books, 1230 Avenue of the Americas, New York, NY 10020

ISBN: 0-671-52723-1

First Pocket Books printing January 1996

10 9 8 7 6 5 4 3 2 1

POCKET and colophon are registered trademarks of Simon & Schuster Inc.

Cover art by Elaine Gignilliat

Printed in the U.S.A.

This book is dedicated to Dr. Barry Markman and his wonderful staff. All doctors and medical personnel should strive to be what you already are; not only professional, but caring, sympathetic, and compassionate. Thank you for everything you've done for me.

Chapter 1

"*U*ncle Darby, wake up," Cassidy whispered as she shook the old man's shoulder.

"What? Cass? It's still dark out. What are you doing up already?" Darby peered up through bleary eyes at his niece.

"I'm going into town and I didn't want you to worry if I wasn't back before you got up."

Darby sat up quickly and looked suspiciously at Cass. "What are you going into town so early for?"

"I've got business."

"What kind of business?"

Cass scowled in the semidarkness of her uncle's room. She'd been sure he'd be too sleepy to question her. He was dead set against her continued quest for revenge, and she didn't want to hear another lecture. "I just have things to do."

Darby swung his spindly long-john-clad legs over the edge of the bed. "What things?" he somberly.

Cass clenched her jaw and breathed a heavy sigh through her nose. "I'm going to talk to Sheriff Jackson," she finally said.

"Damn it, Cass. Can't you let it be? Your ma and pa

1

would want it to end. They wouldn't have wanted you to do what you've done so far."

Cass turned and started to leave the room, tired of the same conversation they'd been having since she returned to her home in Twisted Creek.

"Cass, don't walk away from me, girl. You know I'm right. Just let it be," Darby insisted, wrapping a blanket around his waist as he followed her from the bedroom.

Cass stopped in the main room of their small home and turned to face him. "No!" she hissed. "I won't let it be. I saw those bastards murder my entire family. I can't just let it be!" She crossed to the pegs beside the door and pulled her guns from their place. Wrapping the twin gun belts low on her hips, she strapped them tightly to her thighs. Turning to once more face her uncle, she saw the sadness in his eyes as he watched her. "I can't let it be," she whispered.

"But you already killed four of them fellas. Ain't that enough?" Darby tried again.

"It won't be enough until I get the man who was behind the killings," she answered.

"So why the trip to see the sheriff? He's already done all he can."

"Jackson never did half enough. I had to go find those killers myself. I'm only hoping he can do one thing for me."

"What?"

"I want him to talk to Mr. Tylo."

"Tylo? Are you crazy, girl?"

"Why the hell is everyone so afraid to talk to Hunt Tylo? He isn't God," Cass said disgustedly.

"No, he ain't God. But he might as well be in these parts. He's got the biggest spread around. Hell, his ranch keeps Twisted Creek on the map."

"And he's the one man who had something to gain from my family's destruction," Cass argued.

"What? Tell me what did he gain from their deaths?"

Cass narrowed her eyes. "His cattle have been running across our land with free access to the Losee River ever since Pa and Ma and the kids were murdered."

Darby rubbed his hand over his eyes. "I need a drink," he sighed. Cass had been on a one-horse track since her family had been slaughtered. Actually, she'd been exacting her own kind of justice ever since she'd taught herself how to shoot. Darby crossed to the fireplace and took a bottle of whiskey from the mantel. Tugging out the cork, he raised the bottle to his lips and let the fiery liquid slide down his throat. "You really think Hunt Tylo had something to do with your pa's murder? You think he had your ma and the kids killed? He was your pa's friend, Cass. He even courted your ma for a while when they were kids. Hell, with the kind of money and power he has, do you really believe he'd wipe out a whole family just so's his cows could get to water a little quicker and easier?"

Cass had wondered for the past five years why her family had been massacred. She'd lain awake at night reliving the horror of returning home to see the murderers finishing their handiwork. When she did sleep, she would wake in a cold sweat remembering details of the scene. "I know it wasn't a random act by passing outlaws, as Sheriff Jackson was so quick to assume. Someone wanted my family dead. I'm just trying to figure out who."

Darby lowered himself onto one of the rickety chairs next to the table. "Well, it wasn't Hunt Tylo, Cass." He took another swig from the bottle. "You're getting desperate and grasping at straws."

Cass clenched her fists. "Maybe. But I can't let it go. And Tylo is the only person I can think of who gained anything after my family was killed. I just want Jackson to question him a little."

"So you're going to go bother the sheriff at this god-awful hour to nag him about this again," Darby grumbled.

"I should think you'd be grateful that I want this settled," she said. "Pa was your younger brother, remember?" She tried to keep the accusation from her voice, but couldn't entirely.

Darby lowered his eyes. He'd felt the hurt of losing his baby brother and his family. What happened was horrible and senseless, and he'd cried and drunk himself into oblivion for several days, but a body had to go on. He looked up at his beautiful niece. If only Cass could let it go. She was hanging on to her anger with a vengeance, and he was terrified it was going to get her killed. Killed, or so eaten up by emotion that she'd rather be dead. "Cass honey, it ain't gonna bring 'em back. Even if you find and kill every last one of those bastards, it ain't gonna bring 'em back," he said quietly.

Tears stung Cass's eyes, but she refused to let them fall. "I know that, but I have to finish this," she said with resolve. She crossed the room and put her arm around her uncle's shoulders. Bending over, she kissed the top of his hairless head. "I'm going to talk to the sheriff and check on the saddle I left to be repaired at the livery. Is there anything you need from town?"

Darby eyeballed the whiskey bottle. " 'Nother one of these wouldn't hurt," he said.

"You shouldn't drink so early in the morning," she admonished gently.

"And you shouldn't wear your guns to town so much. Folks are already afraid of you."

Straightening her back, she walked toward the door. "I don't care if folks are afraid of me," she said over her shoulder. "I'll be back in a few hours, and I'll bring you your whiskey." Just before going through the door she turned back around. "Tell Soony when he gets up that his damned chicken pecked the crap out of Mirabelle again."

"You'd think that cat'd have enough sense to stay out of that chicken's way," remarked Darby.

"Well, she doesn't."

"You want Soony to fix anything special for dinner tonight?"

Cass thought for a moment. It was Sunday. There'd been a time in her life when that meant something. "No, anything he feels like cooking is fine with me." Sighing, she pulled open the door and went outside into the stillness of the early morning.

Riding to town, Cass thought about what Darby had said about the townspeople being afraid of her. She did care, but it couldn't be helped. She couldn't take the chance of going anywhere without her guns. Not yet, anyway. Someday she would hang up her guns for good. When she'd finally rid the world of the scum that had destroyed her family.

Adjusting her seat, she couldn't keep her mind from wandering back to the day she'd come home to find her family being murdered. She'd been visiting Darby that morning at his mine, Darby's Dream, had brought him biscuits her mother'd baked special. That early morning visit had kept her from being murdered too.

She couldn't stop the shudder that coursed through her at the memories. Her father and mother, both shot through the head. Her brothers also shot, but several times. And her little sister burned to death in the fire that engulfed their home. No. She couldn't let it go, no matter what Darby said.

She squirmed a bit in the saddle as the memories became foggy in her mind. There was much she remembered about the massacre. Details that had led her on her search for the murderers. Details that had pinpointed the men when she'd found them. Men she'd bested in gunfights and seen fall to their deaths at her hand. But there were things she couldn't remember. Important facts that, try as she might, she could't force to the front of her memory. Her head would ache from the strain of trying to remember. "Damn," she fumed, as once again she felt that something was eluding her.

"But I do remember the gun," she whispered.

As the murderers had finished their work and begun to ride away, she'd seen their leader wave his gun in the air. The image of the sun glinting off the silver handle had burned its way into her memory like a fiery brand. Throughout the years she'd searched for the men and exacted her revenge. But no one could tell her about the man with the silver gun.

"Someday I'll find you," she promised the faceless killer. "Someday you'll find yourself in the sights of my gun. And when I pull the trigger you'll know you're on your way to hell," she whispered.

Cass entered Twisted Creek the way she always did, checking the horses at the livery on the outskirts of town for strange mounts and looking to see if any horses she didn't recognize were tied to the hitching posts. Frowning, she saw a strange palomino tethered outside the Best Bet Saloon. "Might be trouble," she mouthed as she passed.

Banging on the back door of the jail a few minutes later, she was greeted by a grumpy sheriff still in his long-handle underwear.

"What the hell do you want this early in the morning, Cassidy?" he barked when he saw who'd awakened him.

Cass didn't let his gruff greeting sway her. Instead, she pushed past him into the jail and picked up the coffee pot. "You go put on your pants while I get some water for the coffee," she told him. She headed out to the pump and was soon back inside, measuring coffee into the pot and setting it on the woodstove. After stirring up the coals, she slid a log into the fire.

Sheriff Jackson shook his head as he pulled on his pants, then stomped his feet into his boots. He would never get used to Cassidy's abrupt ways. As he tucked in his shirt, he stepped to the doorway that divided his living area from the jail, and watched her waiting impatiently in front of the stove.

Cassidy Wayne was a beautiful woman. She was tall and slender, though curved in the right places, and had long dark chestnut hair and deep blue eyes. Her skin glowed with a creamy light, just touched by the sun, and her lips were full, perhaps a bit too full, which made her appear to be pouting slightly, like a woman who had just been properly kissed, which led a man to thinking all sorts of things he shouldn't. Jackson cleared his throat as he left his living quarters. "Now, what do you want, Cassidy?"

Cass looked at the sheriff as he entered the jail. She smiled when she noticed he'd buttoned his shirt wrong. "Long night, Sheriff?" she teased, letting her gaze linger on his shirt.

Jackson looked down. Damn, he thought. He'd been looking at Cassidy so intently that he'd messed up dressing himself. "A man has a right to make a mistake now and then," he grumbled, beginning the rebuttoning process.

Cass watched him adjusting his shirt and waited. She wanted his full attention when she spoke to him about Tylo. Crossing to a chair opposite the sheriff's desk, she sat down, pulling one booted foot up to rest on her knee.

Sheriff Jackson finished with his shirt and looked up to find Cassidy sitting, waiting for him. "All right, what can I do for you, Cassidy?" He stepped behind his desk and sat down.

"I want you to question Hunt Tylo about the murders," she said bluntly.

Jackson heaved a heavy sigh. "Damn, Cassidy. You don't want much do you? Can't you just let it go?"

Cass's nerves screamed at hearing the same question her uncle had asked her earlier. "No, I can't let it go," she answered, her voice a threatening monotone.

"But why Tylo? There wasn't any evidence that pointed to Mr. Tylo five years ago. And you've already killed almost everyone who had anything to do with it."

"Almost," she repeated his word. "And almost isn't good enough. I want the man responsible. The one who planned the murder and paid those guns to carry it out."

Jackson rubbed his hand over his forehead, then looked toward the coffee pot, wishing it was finished brewing. "Look, Cassidy, I did all I could when your family was killed. The posse lost the gunmen's trail. In all the years you went searching for the killers, you've never found one piece of evidence to prove it was more than what I said it was from the start—just some drunken bastards that got carried away during a robbery."

A shutter had fallen over Cass's eyes. "They didn't take anything," she said stonily.

"They got scared."

"They weren't scared, Sheriff. I was there, remember?"

Jackson let his eyes meet hers. "I remember, Cassidy. And I'm sorry you had to see something so horrible. But it's over."

Cass stood up abruptly and slammed her hands on his desk. "It's not over. It won't be over until the last man is dead. The man with the silver gun."

Jackson leaned back in his chair. "You think Tylo's the man with the silver gun?" he asked, tired of fighting this fight with her.

"I don't know, but he's the only person who benefited from my parents' death."

"How?"

"He's been letting his cattle use our land to get to the Losee."

Jackson stood and crossed to the coffee pot, grateful the liquid had become dark and hot while he and Cassidy had been talking. Pouring himself a cup, he thought about what she'd said. "Didn't he use your father's land before?"

Cass looked down. "Yes, but . . ."

"Then why on earth would Tylo kill your family for something he was already doing?"

"Pa wanted him to stop. I heard them arguing about it."

"Did he stop?"

"No."

Jackson raised his shoulders.

"You don't think Tylo had anything to do with it, do you?" Cass asked.

"No, Cassidy, I don't. The man was using your father's land, so they'd obviously come to an agreement before your father's death." He sipped his coffee and watched her over the rim of the cup.

Cass wasn't convinced. But she had no proof. When she'd taught herself how to shoot, she'd vowed to rid the earth of every man who'd had anything to do with her family's death. She'd searched them out one by one and killed them, legally, in gunfights. And until she'd found herself close to Twisted Creek, it hadn't struck her that her search had brought her back home. There had to be a reason for it. "Darby says I'm grasping at straws," she said quietly.

"I agree with him," Jackson confirmed. "You've been through hell these past years, Cassidy. Maybe you're not seeing things clearly anymore. You need to take it easy. Start over."

Cass met the older man's eyes. Jackson was barely as tall as she was. He was pushing sixty, thick through the middle, and had gray running through his dark hair and mustache. He was older than her father would have been. "I can't stop," she said. "Will you talk to Tylo?"

"I'd rather not get folks riled up about the murders again, Cassidy. It's bad enough you came back wearing those damned guns and carrying a reputation a mile wide."

"If you don't talk to him, I will," she said bluntly.

"Now, Cassidy . . ."

"I mean it, Sheriff. If you don't ask him a few questions, I'll be glad to do it. But I won't be as polite as you."

Jackson set his cup roughly on his desk, sloshing coffee over the rim. "Damn it, Cassidy. I don't want you starting any trouble."

"Then talk to Tylo for me. Just get a feeling from what he tells you. If he seems nervous, let me know."

Jackson shook his head. "You think I'd tell you if I thought he was guilty? I wouldn't. You'd ride over there and shoot him before I could arrest him and the circuit judge could get here to hold a trial."

"Then you believe there's a chance he's guilty?"

"Damn it, Cassidy, I didn't say that. Quit putting words in my mouth. I'll go talk to him. That's all I'll do for now."

Cass let her breath out slowly. She was relieved she'd been able to talk Jackson into going out to see Tylo. "All right, Sheriff. Thank you."

"You get along now and let me drink the rest of my coffee in peace."

Cass nodded. "When . . ."

"This afternoon. I'll go this afternoon. Now get!" Jackson waved his arm at her, shooing her from his office.

Federal Marshal Brett Ryder narrowed his eyes as he neared the town of Twisted Creek. He was still angry with his superiors for sending him on this wild-goose chase. It didn't matter that they thought they had good reason. Turning to stretch out the kinks that the last twenty-four hours in the saddle had put in his back, he scanned the buildings of the town as he rode closer and let his mind wander to the reason he'd been banished from investigating the murder of his best friend and colleague, Gerald Ivers. He could remember them telling him he was too close to the case, too personally involved. "Hell yes, I was involved," he grumbled between tight lips. Gerald was my friend, and I'm the one who found him with a bullet in his head, he finished in thought. Anger and the desire for revenge surged through his veins. Clenching his jaw, he knew his anger was what prompted his captain to send him to Twisted Creek, Wyoming.

Riding into the small dusty town, he checked out the buildings as he looked for the sheriff's office. He once more pulled his thoughts to his mission here. "Lady of the Gun, my eye," he muttered a few minutes later as he pulled his mount to a stop in front of the jail. Whoever started the ridiculous stories about a lady gunfighter had to be drunk or crazy, he thought. "Or just plain bored," he added out loud, letting his gaze wander down the quiet main street.

After swinging down from the saddle, he tethered his horse and brushed at the dust clinging to his clothes. Clouds of the stuff billowed from the fabric and caused him to grimace. "As soon as I put this thing to rest, I'm getting a bath and heading home," he muttered. Stepping up on the wooden sidewalk, he reached for the doorknob, only to have it pulled from his grasp as a woman nearly ran into him.

Cass stopped dead just before running headlong into the cowboy standing on the sidewalk in front of her. He was tall, and covered with dust from head to toe, an indication that he'd just come in from the trail. Years of experience in sizing men up had her instantly searching his eyes, eyes that had a cold edge to them when they met hers. Stepping back, she let her arms fall to her sides, waiting.

Marshal Ryder's cross mood showed on his face as he sized up the woman standing in the doorway of the jail, but he couldn't help it. He was tired, hot, and thirsty. And fuming over the assignment to find the Lady of the Gun. "Sorry, miss," he said, lowering the brim of his hat respectfully.

Cass let her eyes travel over the stranger's body. He wore his gun low and strapped to his thigh. His stance was easy, giving the impression that he was relaxed, but she could see by his eyes, nearly hidden beneath the brim of his dark hat, that he was anything but relaxed. "That's all right," she returned. "I didn't think anyone would be coming into the sheriff's office so early. I should have been more careful." She backed several steps away from him, watching to see what move he'd make before she turned her back on him.

Ryder could see the woman was nervous. He also noticed she was beautiful, and was surprised it had taken him even a few seconds to realize it. *I must be more tired than I thought*, he mused. As he stepped toward the door of the jail, he saw her finally turn away from him and walk down the street. He leaned back from the door slightly to inspect the way the fabric of her trousers molded itself to her bottom and thighs. Raising a dark brow, he felt his body heat up at the sight of her round behind moving gracefully with her steps.

Jackson cleared his throat. "What can I do for you, young fella?" he asked, feeling a pang of jealousy he had no right to feel.

Ryder pulled his eyes away from the woman's curves and swung around to face the sheriff. Stepping into the office and holding out his hand, he introduced himself. "Marshal Brett Ryder, sir. You're Sheriff Jackson?"

Jackson took the offered hand. "Yeah. You here on business?" he asked, wondering who the marshal was after.

"Yes," he answered, feeling a little sheepish about divulging the ridiculous nature of his assignment.

"Well, then, come on in and sit down. Would you like some coffee?" Jackson offered.

Cass thought about the man she'd just encountered at the jail and felt her heart rate increase slightly. He was tall, much taller than she, which was unusual, and despite the dirt and dust that covered him, she could tell he was startlingly attractive. His body was hard and muscular, dark hair curled softly from under his hat, and his steely gray eyes had pierced hers when he spoke to her. The one descriptive word that kept coming to mind as she remembered him was "dangerous."

Marshal Ryder sipped the strong brew Sheriff Jackson had poured him and leaned back in his chair. His mind kept flitting back to the woman he'd nearly run into. He was still surprised it had hit him after the fact that she was beautiful. Her thick, long hair had hung around her shoulders and down her back with just a slight curl turning it under. The blue of her eyes was a color to rival the sky on a clear day, and her mouth—he let himself relish the memory—her mouth was something a man could fantasize about.

"You were going to tell me why you're here?" Sheriff Jackson asked.

Ryder brought his thoughts back to the sheriff. "Yes." He sighed. "I was sent here to check out the stories about a lady gunfighter. The Lady of the Gun, to be exact. Rumor has it she's killed four men. So far, the information indicates the gunfights were fair, but I'm supposed to determine if they were, and whether or not the lady should be brought up on charges of murder."

"Really?" Jackson asked, his bushy brows drawn up in surprise.

Ryder read disbelief on the sheriff's face. "Between you and me, I don't really believe any of it, either. It's probably a case of a woman getting a lucky shot off at someone who deserved it, and the story getting blown out of proportion every time it's retold. I've found most gunfighters are more fiction than fact."

"Lady of the Gun, heh?" Jackson repeated the epithet with a little awe. He knew Cassidy had a reputation. He knew how she got it. But he'd had no idea she was becoming a legend.

"Can you believe it? Someone named her." Ryder laughed lightly. "She's probably some poor old woman who shot some fool who'd made the mistake of getting a little too drunk, then a little too fresh." He smiled into his cup as he sipped his coffee.

Jackson leaned back in his chair and grinned at the younger man. "I wouldn't call her 'old' to her face, Marshal. I have a feeling Cassidy'd take it personal."

Brett lowered his cup and sat up straighter. "Cassidy?"

"Yep. Cassidy Wayne."

"You know this woman?"

Jackson nodded his head and grinned once again. "Seen her nearly every day for most of her life. Except, of course, the last few years ..." He trailed off, thinking about what she'd been doing during those years.

Brett couldn't believe there was any validity to the stories he'd heard about the woman. Jackson must have misunderstood him. "I'm talking about a female gunfighter, Sheriff, not some little girl who grew up here."

Jackson raised one thick brow. "I know exactly who you were sent here to find. Fact is, you already found her."

It took a second for Brett to realize what the sheriff was saying. "The woman . . . That was her at the door?" he asked.

Jackson nodded. "Cassidy Wayne. Lady of the Gun, according to you." He took a deep drink of his coffee, draining his cup. "You want more?" he asked as he stood to get himself some more of the strong liquid.

Brett shook his head. His eyes were narrowed as he remembered the beautiful woman he'd nearly run into. She had been wearing guns. Twin Colts slung low on her hips and tied to her thighs. "Can she really shoot?" he asked.

Jackson finished filling his cup and turned back to the marshal. "Well, Marshal, I haven't actually seen it for myself, but the stories you heard weren't just stories. Cassidy's killed four men that I know of. I've heard rumors there were more, but those were just rumors. She's an honest person and owns up to the four."

"And you haven't arrested her?"

"The killings didn't happen here in Twisted Creek. Besides, I haven't received any wanted posters on her. From what I understand, she bested the men in fair fights."

"Four of them?"

Jackson sighed. "She has her reasons," he said.

"Has?" Brett wondered at the tense.

Jackson crossed to sit at his desk again. "Yeah. I'm afraid Cassidy isn't done killing yet."

Brett sat back slightly, surprised. "And you're just going to let her?"

Jackson narrowed his gaze a little as he looked at the younger man. "You don't know Cassidy, Marshal. I do."

"What difference does that make? You have a known killer in your midst—hell, in your office—and you just let her walk out to kill again? Are you the sheriff or aren't you?"

Jackson wouldn't let himself take offense at the marshal's question. He didn't know what led Cassidy to kill. "What were you told about this Lady of the Gun, Marshall?" he asked, ignoring Brett's words.

Brett sized up the sheriff as he evaded his question. He could tell the older man wasn't afraid of confrontation; he was merely avoiding it for his own reasons. Deciding to let it go, he answered, "Not much. My superiors got wind of a story spreading across the West about a lady gunfighter. There were rumors of the four killings. I was sent to investigate the story's validity, to see if there were grounds to make an arrest."

Jackson summed up Ryder's explanation. "I'm sorry you came so far for nothing, Marshal. Cassidy does exist, but there's no reason to arrest her. If there was, she'd already be warming one of those cells," he said, tipping his head back in the direction of the jail cells down the hall.

Brett sipped the last bit of coffee from his cup. There was more to this story and he found himself wanting to know what it was. "Why'd she do it—turn gunfighter, I mean?"

"Why do most folks?"

"Money?" Brett knew that wasn't the answer before he got the word out. When Jackson didn't respond, he tried again. "I've found most gunfighters want the fame and glory they think goes with the reputation, but I doubt that's her reason. You wouldn't be so ready to defend her if those were her motives."

"I haven't exactly defended her," said Jackson.

"No, but you haven't exactly been jumping up and down to have me arrest her, either."

Jackson shrugged. "You still haven't hit on the reason a sweet girl like Cassidy would turn gunfighter."

Brett remembered the woman again. He forced his mind's eye away from the curve of her butt and the way she'd filled out the shirt she wore, and remembered the way she'd looked at him. Yes, she was beautiful. But sweet? No. "Sweet" was the last word Brett would have used to describe her. Her eyes were hard. The clear blue had penetrated his with a challenge. She'd even taken a defensive stance, which he should have noticed, and would have if he'd been looking for a man. Shaking his head slightly, he wondered what had put the hard edge into her expression. "Revenge?" he finally asked.

Chapter 2

*R*eyenge can be a powerful motivator," Jackson said, looking over the rim of his cup at the young marshal.

"And she has reason enough to kill four men, maybe more?"

"One more, at least. She's determined to kill the man who was responsible for the destruction of her family."

" 'Destruction'? Isn't that a strange word to use about people?"

Jackson lowered his eyes as he remembered what he'd found the day he'd been summoned out to the Waynes' place. "No, Marshal. Cassidy was the first to use that word, and it couldn't be more right. Her ma and pa, two brothers, and her little sister were all murdered while she watched."

Brett sat very still while what he'd just heard sank in. "Why?" he asked softly.

Jackson raised his brows in question.

"Why were they murdered? Why was she spared?" asked Brett.

Jackson pushed his lips together tightly for a moment before speaking. "It was plain dumb luck that kept her alive, and sometimes I think she wishes she'd died with her folks.

She wasn't at home early that morning. She'd gone to visit her uncle. She came back in time, though, to see the last of the killing. She hid and watched." Jackson looked at the top of his desk without seeing it. "Never saw nothin' like it, myself. And I never saw the likes of Cassidy after it happened. She didn't cry. At least not in front of folks. She just bought those two guns she always wears and started practicing. Darby—that's her uncle—he once told me he had to massage her hands every night because of the cramps she'd get from shooting for hours without stopping." Jackson looked up at Brett then. "I hear she shoots equally well with either hand."

Brett digested Jackson's story and found himself pitying the girl she must have been. "You still haven't told me why her people were killed."

Jackson heaved a heavy sigh. "Wish I could. Nobody knows why."

Brett leaned forward, his curiosity truly piqued at this point. "Weren't there any clues? How did Cassidy find four of the men? Didn't you get a posse—"

"Whoa, Marshal," Jackson said, raising a hand to the younger man. "Hell, yes, I rounded up a posse to go after the bastards, but we lost their trail. As for clues, they were mostly in Cassidy's head. Still are." He rubbed his face tiredly. "And now, after all this time, she's got me goin' out to question a man I know had nothing to do with those murders." He stood up. "Hell, I might as well get going now and get it over with."

Brett stood up with the sheriff. "You say you know the man had nothing to do with the murders?"

Jackson nodded.

"Then why does Cassidy think he did?"

"She's got some fool notion Mr. Tylo benefited from her family's death."

"Tylo?" Brett repeated the name, making a mental note to remember it.

"Yeah. Hunt Tylo. He owns the Lazy T, the largest ranch in the area. Anyway, I'm going out there more to protect

Tylo from Cassidy than to ask him questions. She said she'd question him if I didn't, and I hate to think of the way she'd do it." He reached for his hat, hanging behind his desk, and placed it levelly on his head. "So, Marshal, can I do anything for you before you leave?"

"I don't think so, Sheriff. I'll want to speak briefly to Cassidy before I go, of course," Brett said as he walked toward the door, Jackson close behind him.

"Sure, sure. I understand. She didn't tell me where she was going when she left my office, but I could swing by her place on my way back from the Lazy T. If she's not there I can leave word that you want to talk to her." Jackson opened the door and stepped out onto the sidewalk.

"No, thanks, Sheriff. I appreciate the offer, but I'd like the advantage of surprise, if you don't mind. It helps to get straight answers. I'm sure you understand." Brett's steely eyes met Jackson's. He was certain the man had no understanding at all of proper questioning procedures or of murder investigations. His botched job on the Wayne murders and Cassidy's subsequent killings were proof of that. Brett softened his gaze slightly and forced a smile.

Jackson nodded and returned the marshal's smile, though for a moment the younger man's expression had unnerved him a bit.

"I think I'll have breakfast and get a hot bath before I look for Cassidy," Brett informed Jackson, still with the feigned smile. He stretched, trying to appear casual, and let his gaze slide quickly down the street in the direction Cassidy had gone. No sign of her, he noticed. "I guess I'll see you later, Sheriff," he said as he began walking away.

Jackson raised a hand in farewell to the retreating marshal. "Yeah, Marshal. I should only be gone a couple of hours."

Brett heard the sheriff mount and ride away. He then turned slowly and watched the man in the distance. Five-year-old unsolved murders. A woman who'd already killed at least four men and then announced to the local sheriff that she wasn't done killing yet. What had he ridden into?

He felt a familiar tightening in his gut—the tension that always preceded his getting involved in something big. "It seems this wild-goose chase might in fact get pretty wild before it's over," he breathed.

Cass was disappointed; her saddle wouldn't be ready until later that day. She'd wanted to head straight home, but because of the delay she decided to get some breakfast in the hotel restaurant. Sitting safely with her back to the wall, and with a clear view of the room, she sopped up the last of the thick sausage gravy with a chunk of buttermilk biscuit. Scanning her surroundings, she found herself thinking about the stranger she'd nearly run into at the sheriff's office. His eyes bothered her. The way he'd met her stare. The more she thought about it, the more certain she was that her first assumption was correct: he was dangerous. But what would a dangerous man be doing at the sheriff's office? Usually his kind of man avoided the law.

She glanced down at her empty plate, then drained the last of her coffee. Who was he? And what was he doing in Twisted Creek?

"You done here, Cassidy?" the waitress, Rosie Shafer, asked.

Cass smiled up at the young woman and noticed the weak smile she received in return. Almost sighing out loud, she set her empty cup down and softly touched the rim. "A little more, please?" she asked.

Rosie nodded and turned away from the table, but not before glancing down at the guns strapped to Cass's sides.

Cass did sigh after Rosie left. It was too bad her uncle Darby was right about the townspeople being a little afraid of her. She'd known Rosie most of her life, had gone to school with the chubby redhead, had even been to several of her birthday parties. Now Rosie would barely speak to her, only did because she was a waitress and Cass was a customer. Cass watched as she returned with the coffee pot. "Thanks," she offered.

Rosie only nodded and left the table quickly.

Cass shrugged off the snub. I should be used to it, she thought.

Once again scanning the room, she felt her pulse take a giant leap as the stranger entered the restaurant.

It took Brett less than a second to see Cassidy sitting across the restaurant watching him. His nerves jumped, and the hair along the back of his neck and arms stood on end. Here was the infamous Lady of the Gun, the woman he'd been sent to find. He narrowed his eyes as he studied her.

This time it didn't take him seconds to see her beauty. She'd removed her hat, and thick waves of chestnut hair glistened in the sunlight pouring through a window not far away. Her features were even and lovely. Her eyes were startlingly blue and surrounded by thick black lashes. Then his gaze dropped to her mouth. The moist curve of her full, pouty lips caused him to swallow as a rush of blood began the trail to his loins. It was then he realized she was staring just as intently at him and her eyes had never left his. She was waiting. Waiting to see what kind of a threat he'd be to her. She doesn't know I'm a marshal, he realized with surprise. Taking a step in her direction, he noticed her right hand slip beneath the table.

"Mister, you alone?" asked Rosie, holding a menu toward the stranger.

Brett blinked as he was distracted. "What?"

"You sittin' alone, or are you waitin' for someone?" Rosie explained.

Cass took this opportunity to leave her table. She'd seen the stranger start her way, and she didn't want any trouble today. Especially not in town. Leaving two dollars on the table, she slipped quickly down the hallway that led to a back way out of the hotel, grateful she'd chosen a table close enough to it to allow her escape.

Brett cursed under his breath as he saw Cassidy leave the restaurant via a hallway at the back of the room. "I'm not going to be staying," he answered Rosie, and walked past her to follow Cassidy.

"Suit yourself," said Rosie, tossing the menu back on the

counter. She turned to another waitress and grimaced. "As if it wasn't bad enough having Cassidy Wayne in here, now we get strangers that just come in to look around and leave."

Cass breathed a sigh of relief as she closed the hotel door behind her. She'd made her getaway and didn't have to confront the stranger. All she had to do now was get back to the sheriff's office, where she'd left her horse. She admonished herself for not bringing the animal to the hotel in case she needed to leave quickly, and promised herself she wouldn't let her guard down even that much again.

Walking the length of the alley toward the street, she wondered what the stranger had wanted. Just trouble? She remembered the way his eyes had traveled over her features. She remembered the hard appearance of his body as he stood so still, examining her with his gaze. Her pulse beat rapidly at the memory, and she felt a strange heat growing deep within her. She wondered briefly what it would feel like to run her fingers through the dark curls at the back of his neck, then shook herself mentally. She had never let herself get sidetracked by her lust for a man in her life. She wouldn't now.

Brett was angry. He'd discovered that the hallway Cassidy had taken didn't simply lead straight to a back door. It led first to a side door that opened onto a closed courtyard, then turned and ended abruptly, flanked by three doors that all looked exactly the same. He'd found out the hard way, by startling guests, that two of the doors opened into hotel rooms. He finally found the door that led outside, but by then Cassidy was nowhere in sight. Heading quickly toward the street, he was relieved to see her walking determinedly in the direction of the sheriff's office.

Cass was still thinking about the stranger when she heard someone call her name from across the street. When she looked up, she saw another man walking toward her. Behind him was tethered the palomino she'd seen outside the Best Bet Saloon. "What can I do for you?" she asked in a monotone.

"You Cassidy Wayne?" the man asked.

Cass instantly sized up the man before her. Gun tied low. Hands nervous at his sides. Eyes blinking quickly. Her heart seemed to stop beating as a calm came over her. "I know Cassidy. I'll be happy to give her a message for you," she said.

The man blinked several times in rapid succession. "The bartender said you were Cassidy Wayne. Are you or aren't you?" he demanded.

Cass stepped forward to face him squarely. "That depends."

"On what?" he asked impatiently.

"The reason you're looking for her." Cass sidestepped slowly, moving so the sun was no longer in her eyes.

"I heard she's fast. I want to see how fast," the man answered snidely, sure of his superior speed.

"She's not so fast," Cass offered. She'd been challenged before and had been able to talk her way out of having to kill. She hoped she could do the same now.

"You know that for sure? Or are you just trying to keep from gettin' killed, Miss Wayne?" the man asked, grinning now.

Cass stopped moving. "I never said who I was," she told him.

"Didn't have to. You're Cassidy Wayne, all right. I heard about those twin Colts," he said, glancing quickly at her guns.

"So?"

"So I want to see if you're as fast as I heard."

"Pick a target," she offered, her voice quiet.

The man took a step toward her, his eyes narrowed. "You makin' fun of me?" he asked.

"No. There's just no reason for us to shoot at each other. I can show you how fast I am without killing you," she explained, staring hard into his eyes.

The gunman blinked again. "You're pretty damned sure of yourself, for a woman," he said rudely.

"I'm very sure of myself. I've found that guns don't care who holds them and bullets kill just the same no matter who pulls the trigger. So let me ask you a question," she said softly.

The man nodded slightly.

"Do you really want to die today?"

"Why, you—"

"No need to lose your temper, mister. Just answer my question. The sun is shining in a blue sky, and there's a cool breeze blowing in from the range. Do you want to die on such a nice day?"

"You bitch," the gunman hissed. His left eye began to twitch as he blinked. Spreading his stance slightly, he poised his hand over his gun.

Cass sighed inwardly. "I'm serious, mister. I'm not trying to be funny. I'm faster than you are, I guarantee it, and you're going to die if your gun clears leather. Do you want to die today?"

The man clenched his jaw as she spoke. He stood stone still except for his incessant blinking. He was going to draw.

Time stopped, and Cass waited. But only for a second. She saw the jerk of his shoulder muscles and pulled her guns with lightning speed, sending bullets to explode in his chest before he even got his weapon completely out of the holster. She watched as he fell to the dirt, a look of surprise on his face.

"Jesus Christ!" cursed Brett from a short distance away. He'd never seen anyone so fast in his life. He wasn't even sure he could beat her himself. And he couldn't believe it had happened while he watched. Running the last few steps to reach Cassidy, he grabbed her by the shoulder and jerked her to face him.

Cass felt the strong hand take hold of her, and she was ready to fire again as she was spun around. Only her quick reflexes kept her from shooting the stranger. Instead, she found herself staring up into the hard gray eyes that seemed to pierce her to her soul.

"What the hell was this all about?" demanded Brett.

Cass didn't answer. She just looked up at the handsome face above her. Her heart had started beating again, and now raced wildly in her chest. It took her only seconds to realize he still held her shoulder in his firm grasp, his strong fingers biting into her flesh. Stepping back, she tried to jerk herself free of his grip. "It's none of your business," she informed him stiffly.

"Like hell it's not," warned Brett, holding tight to her shoulder. "You better give me an answer, fast."

Cass pinpointed the aim of her guns. "And you better let go of me," she threatened.

Brett glanced down at the guns almost touching his stomach. All she had to do was pull the triggers on the deadly weapons and his life would be over, but something in her eyes told him she wouldn't do it. "Miss Wayne, I'm a federal marshal, and unless you want to spend the rest of your life in prison, I suggest you drop those Colts." He looked hard into the blue of her eyes and kept his tight grip on her.

Cass blinked once. Federal marshal? Was he telling her the truth, or was he a friend of the dead man, trying to get the better of her? "I don't think so. Not without proof," she challenged.

Brett kept his eyes level with hers. She wanted proof, eh? Reaching slowly inside his shirt beneath his vest, he pulled out a tarnished silver badge. Letting it lie in his palm so she could see it, he waited.

Cass lowered her eyes to inspect the badge. It could have been a fake or stolen, but her senses told her he was telling her the truth. Looking back up into his eyes, she kept the guns trained on his stomach. "What are you going to do with me, Marshal?" she asked quietly.

Brett felt his pulse take a small jump as her words brought some startling pictures to mind. His body instantly reminded him of some very interesting things he'd like to do to her. He narrowed his eyes. "I'm taking you to the jail for questioning," he told her, his voice stern. "Now bury those guns."

Cass slowly lowered the Colts. A group of people had started to gather, and murmured gasps traveled through the crowd as they inspected, with relish, the wound her two bullets had made over the gunman's heart. She glanced at the body of the dead man, then back to the marshal.

Brett saw the crowd gathering just as Cass had, and he didn't like the expressions on some of the faces. "You people go on about your business," he said loudly to the group.

Nobody moved.

Releasing his hold on Cass's shoulder now that she had lowered her guns to a relaxed angle, he took a step toward the crowd. "I said to disperse," he told them.

"And who are you to tell us what to do?" a belligerent voice demanded defiantly from the back of the crowd.

"Marshal Brett Ryder," he responded with authority. Pinning his badge to his vest, he took a step toward the crowd. "One of you go get the undertaker. The rest of you go on about your business."

"You're a marshal? Where's Sheriff Jackson?" asked a tall heavyset man as he disengaged himself from the group.

Brett raised a brow slightly in Cass's direction.

"Jaybird Johnson," she whispered crossly. She had her own bone to pick with this man. She knew he had to be the bartender who'd identified her to the gunman.

Brett noticed Cassidy's hostility and felt an inward tension as he stepped between her and the man. "Mr. Johnson, Sheriff Jackson had business out of town this morning. He'll be back in a couple of hours. Until he get's back, I'm the law. And I want this crowd to disperse before it gets out of hand. You seem to be one of the community leaders"—he heard Cassidy snort behind him—"so I wonder if you could assist me in getting folks to go on home."

Jaybird didn't like anyone telling him what to do, even under the guise of a compliment, but this marshal didn't know him, so maybe, just maybe, he'd let it slide this once. He looked past the lawman to where Cass stood just behind him. "What about her? She just murdered a man in the street. You gonna do something about it?" he demanded.

Cass threw down the gauntlet. "It wasn't murder, Jaybird. You know that better than anyone else."

"How would I know? You gunned him down, didn't you?

I was in the bar when it happened," answered Jaybird, his voice full of the animosity he felt toward Cass.

"You're the one who told him who I was. You're the one who sent him out here knowing full well what he had in mind. And don't think I don't know you were hoping I'd be the one bleeding all over the street now."

Jaybird took a step closer.

Brett held up his hand. "That's enough," he ordered. Looking directly at Jaybird, he asked, "Do you know who he was?" indicating the dead man.

Jaybird smiled then. A smug, evil smile. "Yeah, I know who he was." He looked at Cass, and his smile widened. "You just killed Bobby Fleet's kid brother," he announced with relish.

Brett's eyes flashed to the dead man. "Henry Fleet?" he said amazed.

Cass narrowed her eyes at the news. She felt the weight of what Jaybird had just said, but she refused to let him see he'd affected her.

"You gonna run?" Jaybird taunted.

"Shut up," ordered Brett.

"Hey—" said Jaybird angrily.

"I said shut up," repeated Brett, walking toward him.

Jaybird looked at the black scowl on the marshal's face and backed up a step. "What the ..." He stopped when the man passed him and paused to look at the body of Henry Fleet.

Brett had a hard time believing this was one of the Fleet brothers. They were reputed to be among the fastest guns in the West, and Cassidy had beaten him with seconds to spare. Stooping down, he picked up the dead man's gun. His scowl deepened when he saw, carved into the handle, the trademark initials and notches showing the number of men he'd killed. Looking up sideways at Cassidy, he suddenly wondered if she, too, had notches on her guns.

Cass looked into the marshal's eyes and knew what he was thinking. She was as nonplussed that she'd guessed his thoughts as she was at what he was wondering. Her heart skipped several beats, and the blood raced through her veins at an alarming rate. Opening her hands slightly, and turning her palms upward, she showed him the unmarked handles of her twin Colts.

Surprise registered in Brett's gray eyes when Cass showed him her guns. He felt as though she'd been inside his head, had read his mind, and it bothered him somehow. But he couldn't deny the feeling of . . . what? Joy? No, that was too strong a word, but he was definitely relieved to see that she hadn't marked her kills on the weapons.

"What are you going to do about this, Marshal?" Jaybird demanded belligerently, hoping the hushed crowd would rally around him. "Cassidy just murdered this man."

Brett stood up and faced the burly bartender. "I'll see to it she receives the reward," he answered smartly.

"What?" fussed Jaybird.

"I'm sure there's a reward for this man, dead or alive. I'm going to see to it that Cassidy receives it. Unless you think you should get part of it for setting him up?" he challenged.

"I never . . . You're crazy," Jaybird argued.

Cass couldn't believe she'd heard right. A reward? She didn't want any reward for killing a man. Maybe Jaybird was right. Maybe the marshal *was* crazy. Watching his back, she wondered about him. What was he doing here in Twisted Creek? Why had he followed her out of the restaurant?

Brett turned away from Jaybird's flushed countenance. "Would one of you people go get the undertaker, please?" he asked.

"I'll do it," offered the town barber, Bill Conroy.

"Thanks," said Brett as the man left, heading toward the funeral parlor. He then eyed Jaybird once again. "Was Fleet alone?" he asked.

"Yeah," Jaybird answered gruffly.

"Are you sure?" He was worried that Henry's brother Bobby might have been traveling with him, or was somewhere in the area.

27

"Of course I'm sure," groused Jaybird.

"Good," said Brett. He scanned the crowd of people staring at the body or watching the scene between Jaybird and himself. "You all go on home or back to your businesses now," he told them.

Cass saw that a few people started leaving right away, with most meandering off a few seconds later. Jaybird stood his ground until he saw there was no longer an audience to watch his bluster. Then he too started back toward the Best Bet Saloon, but not before throwing the marshal a few very challenging looks. Cass let out her breath slowly. "What now?" she asked as the marshal turned toward her.

"Now we go to the sheriff's office so I can ask you a few questions," he explained.

"About this?" she gestured toward the body.

Brett glanced over his shoulder, then back at her. "No."

Cass's eyes narrowed. "About what, then?"

"I'll get to it in the jail. Why don't you holster those?" Brett looked down at the guns she still held.

Cass shrugged and slipped the Colts into their resting places. "Whatever you say, Marshal," she agreed.

Brett's nerves jumped at her words, and he frowned at the way his body had begun reacting to innocent statements she made. Swallowing, he gestured toward the jail and let her lead the way to the small building. As she walked in front of him, he couldn't keep his eyes from inspecting the sweet curve of her bottom.

Minutes later Cass sat in front of the sheriff's desk as she had earlier that morning. Only this time it wasn't the familiar, older face of the sheriff she watched. It was the handsome face of the marshal that held her attention as he searched through wanted posters he'd found in a drawer. "I don't want the reward," she stated firmly.

Brett looked up at her briefly. She'd already told him this once, but he kept on looking.

"I mean it, Marshal. I don't want a reward for taking a man's life," she insisted.

Brett dropped the stack of posters on the desk. "Then

why did you kill four men before today?" he asked. He knew what the sheriff had told him. He wanted her answer.

Cass felt the cold hand of hate close over her heart as she remembered the murders as if they'd happened yesterday. "I had my reasons," she said through clenched teeth.

"I want to know what those reasons were."

Cass met his gray eyes with the cool blue of her own. "Did the sheriff tell you?" she asked.

"Yes."

"Then why . . ."

"I want to hear it from you." His voice was a deceptive monotone.

As calmly as though she felt nothing, Cass spoke. "The men I killed murdered my family."

The calmness in her voice sent a chill through his heart. Brett knew that emotion, had seen it in others, had felt it himself. "Revenge," he said quietly, his eyes taking on a faraway glaze.

Cass didn't answer. Something in his voice touched her oddly. He knew. He knew what she was feeling as though he'd crawled inside her.

"And you're not through yet," Brett continued.

Cass shrugged slightly.

"Can't you let it go?" He had no way of knowing he'd chosen exactly the wrong words to use. Not until he saw the clenching of her jaw and the tightening of her fists did he realize his mistake.

"I think I'll be going now, Marshal," Cass said coldly, standing abruptly.

"Not yet, Cassidy."

Cass ignored his request. Intent on leaving, she started toward the door.

Brett rose and quickly stepped around the desk. "Cassidy, wait," he ordered, reaching out to grab her arm.

Cass felt the strength of his fingers as he grabbed her. Sparks of awareness jolted up her arm. Trying to pull away, she met his gaze. "I told you once today to let me go. I'm telling you again."

Brett didn't lessen the tension of his grasp. "You're not leaving yet."

"Like hell I'm not. You've got no reason to keep me here."

Once more her words set off his body's alarms. "I've got reason," he growled, not explaining his double meaning.

Cass needed to get away from this man. She jerked hard on her arm, but felt him counter her movement by pulling her toward him, throwing her off-balance. The anger in her eyes turned to shock as she found herself leaning flush against his strong, muscular body.

Brett's heart exploded in his chest as Cass fell against him. All his nerves jumped to life, and his manhood pulsed with a need so great he was nearly dizzy with it. Locking her gaze with his, he saw the startled passion that blazed to life in the blue depths. Hesitating only a second, he lowered his head and claimed her lips in a devouring kiss, branding her with the fire that flashed between them.

Chapter 3

Cass had no experience on this battlefield. As Brett's lips opened over hers she found herself responding in ways she never had before. Blood pounded in her ears and behind her eyes, heat pulsed through her to her most secret places, and her flesh burned where it met the hard firmness of his body. She felt as though she were about to faint, and as she attempted to take a breath, she moaned in surprise as his tongue entered her mouth and began a mating ritual against the soft tissue of her own tongue. Again she responded blindly, following his lead, learning as she went.

Brett was stunned by Cassidy's immediate surrender to his desires. He marveled at the way she molded herself to him and moaned against his kiss, meeting his exploring tongue with her own. He allowed this tender touching to go on as he slid his hands behind her, lowering them to cup the bottom that had intrigued him earlier in the day. The firmness of her flesh under his fingers excited him further, causing him to pull her closer to him, pressing his engorged manhood against her abdomen, wanting her to feel how badly he needed her.

Cass felt the desire that blazed between them. She felt

the pressure of Brett's body, rhythmically pulsing against her, and she felt her own body changing inside to accommodate him. But she'd never been with a man before. She'd never met one she'd wanted like this. A fog seemed to cloud her thinking as she matched his motion with her own and opened her mouth more, allowing a deepening of their kiss.

Brett tasted Cassidy's sweet kiss. He let his tongue tease hers, then retreated to nibble on her beautiful full lips. He licked gently across her lower lip and pulled it into his mouth for a moment, then kissed her fully again, savoring every second of their union. Bringing one hand up between them, he found her breast, the nipple hardened with desire. He brushed his palm across it and felt her shudder as sensation shot through her.

Cass nearly groaned out loud as she felt white-hot ripples flowing from where Brett massaged her breast. She pushed herself deeper into his hand and knew that he could give her even more pleasure. The pressure of his arousal was increasing with each moment, and the feel of his strong body against hers was drugging her. Her knees felt week and she wasn't sure she could remain standing without the support of his well-muscled arm around her. So this is sex, she thought. But deep inside her she knew she'd only just begun the journey toward true passion.

"Oh! Excuse me . . . I mean . . . I'll come back later," Bill Conroy stammered as he entered the office. "I'll just go . . . I . . ."

Cass jerked away from Brett at the sound of Bill's voice, horror and embarrassment turning her face blood red.

Brett glanced up at the flustered man and tried to stand straighter, but his still evident arousal made moving nearly impossible. He looked at Cassidy, blushing, embarrassed, her beautiful lips swollen from his kisses, and felt a new surge of passion's blood rushing to his loins. The quick slamming of the door as the barber made a hurried retreat brought his attention back to the interruption. "Who was that?" he asked, his voice coming out in a raspy groan.

Cass heard Brett's question, but she couldn't force herself

to make eye contact with him. She was more embarrassed than she'd ever been in her life, and she couldn't understand her own actions. She'd never responded to a man in this fashion before, never lost control, or felt that reality had ceased to exist. What power did Brett Ryder have that other men didn't?

"Cass?" he prodded.

Cass tentatively raised her eyes to meet his. When she did, she felt herself being pulled into their gray depths, the whirling fires of desire rising up to claim her once more.

Brett felt Cass's gaze as though she touched him still. The inferno of passion that burned between them stunned him, causing him to open his lips and take a deep breath. This woman was under investigation, he'd just seen her gun down a man in the street, and yet all he wanted to do was pull her down across the sheriff's desk and bury himself in her, to plunder her body until she cried out his name in ecstasy. The picture in his mind's eye sent a shocking jolt of blood to pulse deep within his loins. Leaning slightly forward, he began to reach out for her once more, slowly.

Cass saw Brett's gesture and realized what it meant. She wouldn't be able to resist him if he touched her again, and she didn't want to be found in an even more embarrassing position should someone else come along. The thought that Bill Conroy had walked in on them, was probably spreading the gossip over at the saloon right now, gave her the strength to pull back. "No," she whispered.

Brett lowered his hand, but continued to watch the emotions that played over her beautiful face. She wanted him as badly as he wanted her. "Why not?" he asked.

"It isn't right. I won't . . . I can't . . ." she stammered, not sure how to turn him down. "I won't be the subject of gossip." She paused a moment, realizing how ridiculous that sounded, when she'd just killed a man in a gunfight in the middle of the main street. "I won't have people talking about who I . . . or when . . . like that," she lowered her eyes, blushing at the reference to their sexual behavior.

Brett saw her redden as she spoke and was surprised she

could act so demure when the way she'd responded to him proved she was no innocent. And the fact the lady was a gunfighter made her pretense of modesty nearly laughable. One didn't search out and kill four murderers without learning a few facts of life along the way. Brett's mouth turned up into a slow smile of amusement. "Then when and where can we continue this? You've started a fire in me that needs to be put out, and soon. I'm pretty uncomfortable right now," he said, allowing his glance to fall briefly to the bulge in his trousers before fixing her with a purposeful stare.

Cass's eyes opened wide. Responding to a man's unexpected kiss was one thing; arranging a time and place to have sex was quite another. "Never!" she burst out. "How dare you!"

"How dare I?" Brett asked incredulously.

"Yes. How dare you assume I'd be willing to plan . . . it," she finished.

"'It'?" Brett almost laughed out loud at her. "Who do you think you're going to fool with this shocked-virgin routine?"

Cass's mouth opened, but no sound came out. She was shocked. She was mortified. "I'm not trying to fool anyone," she finally managed.

"Good." Brett's voice became seductive. "Because you took to me like cream on fresh milk. I'd hate to think all that passion was going to go to waste."

"You pompous ass," Cass hissed, backing away from him. "You think just because you kissed me that I'm ready to fall into bed with you?"

Brett shook his head. "You're one confusing lady, Cass. I wasn't the only one doing the kissing. It takes two, you know. And since you seem to have forgotten, you responded to me with more heat than an August brushfire."

Had she? Cass didn't know what a man expected from a woman.

Brett continued. "If that character hadn't blundered in here we'd be on the floor right now, and I promise you, you'd be forgetting all the men who came before me."

Cass just stood in stunned silence, blood staining her face with embarrassed shock. All the men who came before him, he'd said? Did he think she was a slut? Obviously. Clenching her jaw tightly, she breathed through her nose in deep, self-righteous puffs.

"Come on, honey," Brett urged, ignoring her indignant stare. Maybe he shouldn't have been so blunt. He knew most women couldn't handle the truth unless it was sugar coated, but damn it, she'd participated in their kiss like a cat in heat, and for her to pretend such innocence now just rubbed him the wrong way. "You know I'm telling the truth. Next time I'll plan things better so we won't be interrupted."

"Marshal Ryder, ponies will fly before you touch me again," she spat between clenched teeth as she turned abruptly and headed for the door. As she jerked it open, she turned back toward him briefly, ready to sling a foul insult in his direction, only to be caught short by the steel gray of his eyes as he returned her glare. "I . . . never mind," she finished. Turning her back on him, she stepped outside and slammed the door behind her. "What a conceited jerk," she breathed as she stood in the brilliant sunlight that beat unmercifully on the wooden sidewalk. Pausing there a moment while she decided which way to go, she welcomed the sun's heat as a much-needed poultice to her wounded pride.

Brett watched Cass leave in a huff and couldn't figure out why she'd gotten so damned mad. Okay, he'd already admitted to himself he'd been too abrupt and straightforward, but that didn't really warrant her behaving like an insulted schoolmarm. She was, after all, a gunfighter, and she had responded to him in a way that even now sent his blood racing at the memory. "Damn it," he cursed as he took a deep breath to clear his head.

Straightening, he walked around the sheriff's desk and sat down. Leaning forward on his elbows, he rested his head in his hands. What the hell am I doing getting involved with the Lady of the Gun, anyway? I'm supposed to be investigating her, not making love to her, he thought disgustedly. But even as he admonished himself he remembered the softness of her full lips beneath his, the way she'd leaned into his touch and pressed her firm curves against his feverish body. "Holy shit," he grumbled.

Cass glanced quickly to the place where she'd gunned down Henry Fleet. She was relieved to see that his body had been removed and the crowd had dispersed, though the dark red stain marking the dusty ground like an old puddle still showed where he'd fallen. Somewhere deep inside her she felt a pang of remorse. She hadn't wanted to fight him. She'd tried to talk her way out of it, just as she'd done twice before when young gunfighters had challenged her, but he wouldn't listen to her.

Looking at his blood, drying quickly in the hot sun, she pushed the remorse from her heart. That could have been her blood. Henry Fleet was no better than the men who had killed her family, and his big brother Bobby was said to be even worse.

Sighing heavily, she let her eyes scan the street and noticed that it was unusually quiet. Everyone had apparently taken the marshal's advice and gone home. Shaking her head with disgust, she knew that, what with the gunfight and the scene with Brett that Bill Conroy had walked in on, she'd given the townfolk ample fodder for at least a month's worth of gossip. "Wait until Uncle Darby hears about all this," she groaned.

Stepping off the sidewalk, she headed in the direction of the livery, hoping her saddle was now finished. As she walked along the deserted street, she couldn't stop the wash of emotions that flooded her senses at the memory of what Brett's mouth and hands had done to her. Was what she'd felt normal? she wondered. Did all women feel this way? She'd never felt like this with any other man, and God knew there were men who'd tried to have their way with her. Up until now she'd felt only mild interest at best, and powerful disgust and revulsion at worst. And why Brett Ryder? She didn't even know him, or like him. She pictured his tall form, his dark hair, and haunting gray eyes, and swallowed hard. No, she didn't like him at all, she decided. And she sure as hell wouldn't give him the opportunity to touch her again.

A cloud of dust, the loud creak of wood and leather, the jingle of harness chains, and a stream of colorful expletives from Jed Higgens, the driver, announced the arrival of the noon stage. Cass glanced upward to confirm the time, surprised so much of the day had already passed. "I guess when you're having fun ..." she murmured sarcastically.

Slowing her walk to the livery, she saw the coach pull up in front of the stage office next to the jail, wondering who, if anyone, had found reason to visit the small town of Twisted Creek. It wasn't exactly a social metropolis.

She watched Jed's movements as he climbed to the top of the coach and tossed the mailbag down to the waiting stage agent. She knew there would be nothing in the bag for her or Darby. They had no family left other than each other.

The stage door opened slowly then, catching her eye, and she saw the long fingers and manicured nails of a man's hand as he grasped the door to steady his descent from the coach. Once he was outside the stage, she could see he was young and tall, with blond hair and a golden mustache. She let her eyes search his frame from boots to hair, and though his suit was obviously expensive and tailored to perfection, it couldn't hide his too thin physique. She thought about how perfect Brett's body was in comparison, then frowned angrily at her own observation. Why on earth would she compare anyone to the marshal? Just then the man turned in her direction and let his gaze fall directly on her, a smile creasing his face. He looked familiar, but she couldn't quite place him. A few puzzled seconds later it hit her: the man was Ramsey Tylo, Hunt Tylo's son.

Ramsey was only three years her senior, but she barely knew him. He'd traveled in a different circle than she had. Being the son of the richest man in town had gone to his head, and though they'd been neighbors, he'd never noticed the tall, skinny, gawky kid she'd been. She remembered he'd left for college shortly before her family was murdered. So the big-city boy has come home, she mused, wondering why he was grinning at her now.

Brett heard the stage outside and decided to see who might be arriving. He was still concerned that Bobby Fleet could be in the area. The chance that the gunfighter would enter town on the stage was slim, but Brett couldn't gamble with Cass's life, no matter how sure she was that she could take care of herself. Leaving the office, he went to watch the unloading of mail, luggage, and passengers.

Cass narrowed her eyes when she saw Brett leave the sheriff's office to stand and watch the stage unloading. Seeing him again, even at this distance, did strange things to her heart. Grimacing, she was about to turn away when she heard her name being called from the stage.

"Cass? Cassidy Wayne, is that you?"

Cass did a double take, not sure that she'd heard right. She would have bet good money that Ramsey didn't even know her name, yet here he was calling to her as though they were old friends. Tilting her head slightly in curiosity, she began a slow walk in his direction. "Ramsey?" she said when she was close enough to speak.

"Yes, Cass, it's me. And look at you, all grown up," he said smiling down at her, reaching out to take her hands in his.

Cass nearly pulled away. She didn't know this Ramsey. His golden hair and light blue eyes shone as though he'd been touched by the sun, and he was smiling down at her as if he'd been waiting all these years just to see her. "Ramsey?" she repeated a little incredulously.

"Yes, Cass." He nearly laughed. "I didn't know I'd changed that much," he commented.

Cass blinked several times. He did seem to have changed. As a child there'd been a hardness to him that had made him seem a little cold and cruel. She remembered him teasing Rosie, the waitress, when they were kids. His teasing had gone beyond the normal childish taunts, sending her running home in tears. To this day Rosie paled whenever Ramsey's name was mentioned.

But the Ramsey standing before Cass now, beaming down at her with an angelic smile, seemed softer, kinder, somehow. Cass looked up into his eyes. Maybe he's just grown up, she thought. Finally returning his smile, she allowed him to hold her hands familiarly. "Hello, Ramsey," she offered. "I hadn't heard you were coming back."

Brett watched Cass and the stranger standing close, talking. He looked at them curiously. Was this man a special friend of Cass's? He squinted speculatively as he sized up the fancy man in the expensive suit. Tightening his jaw, he waited and watched.

"Dad knew I was coming for a visit, but I didn't tell him when. I wanted to surprise him," Ramsey explained, letting his eyes roam over the curves that had appeared on Cass's figure in the last few years. The Cass he remembered had been thin and awkward. What a pleasant surprise to see that the weed had blossomed into a rose. "Have you seen my father lately? How does he look?"

Cass lowered her eyes. "No, I haven't seen him in a while," she explained. "I've been very busy." She couldn't add that she'd sent the sheriff out to the Lazy T to ask questions about his father's possible part in her family's murders. Now, with Ramsey looking down on her, all golden hair and friendly smiles, she felt a little guilty.

Ramsey watched the color rising in her cheeks. He'd heard the stories about Cassidy's revenge. His father had written him about it. But even the twin Colts strapped to her thighs couldn't convince him she was as dangerous as Hunt had claimed. Stepping even closer to her, he leaned over slightly, creating a feeling of privacy. "You've become a very beautiful woman, Cass," he breathed intimately.

Cass glanced up into his eyes, startled by such a revelation from a man she hardly knew. "I—don't know what to—to say," she stammered.

"Don't say anything. Just accept the truth when it's told to you." He squeezed her hands.

Warning bells went off in Cass's head as he tightened his grip on her. Why would Ramsey Tylo get down off a stage, after not having seen her for five years, and not even knowing her that well to begin with, and act as if they'd been close friends before he left town? This was too much, too quick. And it was making her uncomfortable. "I . . . ah . . ." she started to pull her hands from his grasp.

"Excuse me, Cass." Brett spoke coldly as he stepped closer to the couple. "I don't mean to interrupt your reunion, but I'd like to meet your friend."

Ramsey looked up from Cass's face to see a tall, dark man with steel-gray eyes sizing him up. He instantly stiffened. "Yes?" he said coolly.

Cass looked from Ramsey's golden countenance to the dark, attractive features of the marshal and could feel the tension between them. Opposites, she thought. Taking her hands from Ramsey's, she stepped back. "Marshal Brett Ryder, meet Ramsey Tylo," she stated simply.

"Tylo?"

"Yes," Ramsey affirmed. "Of the Lazy T. You probably know my father."

"No. I only just arrived in Twisted Creek this morning."

"Then that would explain why my father never mentioned you in his letters."

Cass watched this seemingly innocent exchange and felt the animosity between the two men grow with every word. She looked from one to the other and could see no reason they'd be at odds when they'd just met. Then Ramsey took a small step in her direction and placed his hand softly at the base of her spine. Raising her brow in surprise, she glanced up at him, then at Brett.

Brett's gray eyes had taken on the color of storm clouds, and she could see the anger behind them, ready to explode like a summer deluge. Ramsey's eyes now glowed with the fire of his temper, a temper she remembered from childhood.

"Does Twisted Creek have need of a marshal, or are you just snooping around?" Ramsey asked, an innocent tone barely masking the rudeness of his question.

Brett smiled, a feral stretching of his lips. "I'm here on business," he answered.

"Really? Do tell. I love small-town gossip. What dangerous criminal are you chasing down?"

Brett transferred his gaze purposefully to Cass. "Actually, I'm here to investigate the Lady of the Gun," he explained softly.

Cass's eyes widened. He couldn't mean her, could he?

"The Lady of the Gun?" inquired Ramsey.

"Yes," answered Brett, not taking his eyes from Cass's face. "And what I've found so far has me very intrigued."

Ramsey looked suspiciously from Brett to Cass. His father had never told him she'd acquired a title to go with her reputation. "You don't mean . . ."

Brett glanced only briefly at Ramsey. "Yes. Cass is the woman I was sent here to find. Now that I've found her, I'll be sticking very close to her for a while."

Cass could feel Ramsey's fingers stiffen at her back.

"I do hope you're not planning on being a nuisance when I take her to dinner this evening," Ramsey murmured.

Cass's eyes jerked upward as she fixed Ramsey with a startled glare. "Dinner?"

Ramsey met her expression with a confident smile. "Yes, Cass. As soon as I saw you again, I realized I'd made a terrible mistake in not getting to know you better when we were children. I intend to correct the oversight—that is, if you'll do me the honor of accompanying me to dinner."

Brett scowled blackly as Ramsey held Cass's attention. "I don't think it would be a good idea for Cass to spend the evening in town," he interjected.

Ramsey raised one blond brow in Brett's direction. "I didn't ask you what you thought about it. I'm inviting the lady to dinner, and I don't think she needs your approval."

"She needs my permission," answered Brett, his voice dropping threateningly.

Cass looked from one man to the other with exasperation. This verbal parrying over her was ridiculous. Had something happened to the air in Twisted Creek to cause men she barely knew to argue over her? she wondered. "Excuse me, gentlemen," she interrupted coldly. "I have business to attend to today"—she turned toward Ramsey—"and though I'm flattered by your invitation, I'm afraid I'll have to make it another time." She then leveled her gaze on the marshal. "And I ask no man's permission to do anything."

"I'm merely concerned about Bobby Fleet's whereabouts," Brett told her firmly "As a marshal I have the authority to protect anyone in any way I see fit."

"I think I proved this morning that I don't need anyone's protection."

"Bobby Fleet is more dangerous than Henry was," Brett informed her. "I don't think you could best him."

"I'll take my chances," Cass stated flatly.

"Henry Fleet?" Ramsey asked, not understanding the conversation he was hearing.

Brett fixed the blond man with a hard glare. "Cass here killed Henry in a gunfight this morning. I'm concerned Bobby may be in the area. If he is, he'll come looking for her when he hears what happened."

Ramsey raised a brow in fascination. Looking over Cass's very feminine form, the fullness of her breasts, the rounded hips and long legs, he found it hard to believe she was capable of committing the cold-blooded killings his father had written him about. It was even harder to believe she'd bested a professional gunslinger in a showdown. The others she'd killed had drawn down on her, but none had been very good with a gun. A surge of excitement coursed through his veins. Cass had become more interesting than he'd have imagined possible. "I'm certain, if what you say is true, that Cass can take care of herself." He smiled warmly at her. "And I would be close by to protect her. I'm not entirely ignorant of the use of pistols."

"I don't need anyone's protection," Cass insisted, glaring at Ramsey. "Not anyone's," she added, switching the direction of her angry gaze to Brett. "Good day, gentlemen," she finished with exasperation. Turning on her heel, she left the two standing next to the stage and headed toward the livery once more.

Brett tightened his fists at his sides as he watched her leave.

Ramsey smiled to himself. Cassidy Wayne had grown into quite a woman. This trip home could prove to be much more interesting than he or his father had bargained for.

Chapter 4

Cass rode toward home some time later, her newly repaired saddle tied on behind her. She laughed softly to herself, remembering the way the smithy had fallen all over himself apologizing for being late with the work on the saddle. There were some advantages in having people feel a little afraid of her, she decided.

Her mirth was short-lived when she saw movement out of the corner of her eye and looked to see a riderless horse heading in her general direction. Stopping her mount, she waited briefly to be sure it wasn't some sort of trap, then nudged her animal toward the loose horse. As she neared the animal she blew a curse from between her teeth. "Damn, you're the sheriff's mount, aren't you, boy?"

The horse shied away nervously as she reached for the trailing reins. "Whoa, fella. I'm not going to hurt you," she cooed. Leaning toward the animal again, she grabbed the reins before he could veer off. "Whoa, boy. Where's Sheriff Jackson? What's happened to him?" she questioned softly, trying to calm the frightened animal with her tone.

Pulling the reins in slowly, she tugged the horse nearer, feeling pity for the animal as he rolled his eyes in fear and tried to rear against her control. "It's okay, boy. I'm not going to hurt you," she soothed.

After a few more moments of quiet talking and very gentle pressure on the reins, she was able to bring the horse abreast of her own. Inspecting the sheriff's saddle caused her to narrow her eyes in concern. Smeared across the right latigo, stirrup leather, and fender was a streak of blood. Feeling the hair along the back of her neck rise, she gazed at the horizon in the direction from which the sheriff's horse had come. "The Lazy T," she breathed. Looking back at the horse, she gently rubbed his muzzle. "Sheriff Jackson's dead, isn't he, boy?" she asked.

Letting out the length of the reins, she tied the ends to her own saddle horn. Then, leading the sheriff's horse behind her, she gave her mount a gentle prod and guided him toward the Lazy T.

Brett had tracked Cass's movements around Twisted Creek, then watched her ride out of town. He'd been tempted to follow her but had decided against it, the opportunity to talk to Ramsey Tylo posing an even greater temptation. After securing a room at the hotel and taking a much-needed bath, he went in search of the blond man.

It didn't take him long to find Ramsey. He'd taken root at one of the card tables in the Best Bet Saloon, a red-haired prostitute at his shoulder, a bottle of whiskey at his elbow, and a hand of five cards gripped tightly between his fingers. "I'll see your fifty and raise you another twenty," he told his fellow players.

"Too rich for my blood," grumbled one of the players, dropping his cards disgustedly on the table and pushing his chair back loudly, signifying his departure from the game. Two other players merely laid their hands face down in defeat, but remained at the table. The remaining player, an old gentleman, stood his ground, glaring over the top of his hand. "You think you got a winner there, kid?" he challenged.

"I'm sure of it," Ramsey announced smugly.

Brett walked quietly to the bar and leaned against it as he watched the scene at the poker table.

"Are you going to call my additional wager, old man?" Ramsey asked.

"Just hold on there, young fella. You should let a man savor his victory a bit." The man grinned at his opponent, wrinkling a face already marred by the folds of time.

Ramsey snorted inelegantly. "Really, sir. Do get on with it. I doubt you have a hand to beat mine, but if so . . ." He sighed. "I do have things to do with what's left of this day."

"I'll call yer bet, sonny. There's no law against a man taking some time to do it." He reached into his coat pocket, pulled out the necessary twenty dollars, and laid it gingerly on the pile of money already making up the pot. "Now let's see whatcha got."

Brett grinned to himself at the old man's attitude. He enjoyed a good poker game now and then, and it would be fun to play against this old character. He straightened a bit in order to see the cards as the men laid them on the table.

Ramsey eyed his aged opponent. He was confident his king high straight flush would beat any hand the old man had managed to put together, and it would serve the old fool right to see his money enter someone else's pockets. "I'll certainly oblige you," he said derisively. Laying his cards face up on the table with one hand, he reached for the pot with the other. "I'm sure you'll understand if I don't let you win back your losses. I really must be getting out to the Lazy T now."

Brett heard the soft groan of several people in the room as Ramsey's cards were shown. He even felt himself sigh at the old man's apparent loss. He didn't look as if he could afford it.

"Not so fast, young fella," the old man announced, reaching out to stop Ramsey from taking the pot. "You're pretty fast with your hands there, don'tcha think? Hadn't you ought to wait and see if you won before you go grabbing money that don't belong to you?"

Ramsey stiffened at the touch of the old man's hand on

his own. He raised one eyebrow threateningly. "I don't like an uninvited touch," he warned.

"And I don't like no one stealing my money," the old man answered, laying his cards on the table for all to see.

Brett's eyes opened wider when he saw the royal flush staring up from the green felt tabletop. "Holy cow," he whispered. The old man had produced the only hand capable of beating Ramsey's.

Ramsey stiffened. Not an eyelash moved as he digested what had just happened. Seconds ticked by as his anger raged silently within him. He hated losing. He hated the old man for winning. And he hated the fact that he'd been bested in front of a crowd. Finally he released his hold on the pot and slowly pulled back. "It seems Lady Luck was favoring you today," he practically whispered.

"It weren't luck, sonny. It was just plain better poker playing that did it," the old man boasted while scooping up the money from the table.

Ramsey lowered his eyelids at the old man's words. "What's your name, if I might ask?" he inquired.

The old man straightened proudly. "Stanley Draper's the name, young fella, but folks just call me Sharky."

Brett bit his lower lip to stifle a laugh at the sound of the old man's moniker. It had been years since he'd heard the name Sharky Draper. He'd figured the old man was dead. Apparently not. Ramsey'd been taken by one of the best poker players in the West.

Laughter and whispers filled the room. The two other participants in the poker game chuckled at their misfortune and left the table.

Ramsey's rage grew when he realized he'd been taken so completely by the old man. He'd have bet everything—in fact, he had—that the old man was nothing more than some itinerate fool. He clenched his jaw as he rose from the table. "Perhaps we'll meet again," he rasped as he placed his hat levelly on his head.

"Maybe, maybe not," answered Sharky. "Not too many fellas want to play poker with me more than once." He started to laugh quietly as he scraped the last of the money off the table and into his dusty, tattered hat.

Brett was still grinning as he watched Ramsey head toward the door of the saloon. He wanted to ask him some questions about the murder of Cass's family, but this was not the time to do it. Ramsey would need some time to cool off before he'd want to talk to anyone about anything.

The marshal crossed the room instead and stopped at the table where Sharky was counting his winnings. "You already know how much is there, don't you?" he asked.

Sharky didn't look up. "To the penny, Marshal. To the penny."

Brett's grin widened. "Then why count it?"

Sharky raised his gaze for just a second. "To make sure that young fella didn't palm any of it before he left."

Brett stood still and pondered the old man's words. He didn't think Ramsey was the type to steal a man's poker winnings, but there was something about Hunt Tylo's son that he didn't like, something about the stifled anger that had been so apparent in his stance as he'd left the saloon. "You'd better be careful around here for a while," he advised.

"Have a seat, Marshal," Sharky offered, pushing a chair out with his boot. "You think I should be worried about that one?" he asked, tipping his head in the direction of the door.

Brett turned the chair around and straddled it, his arms resting on the back of it. "Maybe."

"You think he'd do something to me to get even?"

"Maybe," Brett repeated.

Sharky leaned back, putting his winnings deep inside his trouser pocket. Meeting the marshal's gaze, he shook his head. "I don't think I have too much to worry about. That one doesn't usually do his own dirty work. Leastways, not when there's a chance of getting caught."

Brett was surprised. "You know Ramsey?"

"Yep. He just doesn't remember me. I've been in and out of this town off and on for the last twenty years or so. That boy didn't gamble much before he left town, mostly just drank himself into oblivion and spent his daddy's money on whores." He shook his head in memory. "Never did see a boy set so much store on spending time with whores. Randy as a young bull, he was." He glanced back briefly toward the door. "He's been gone a long time. Didn't remember me at all, and he didn't spend any money on the whores."

Brett looked at the women, who were standing against the bar, waiting for their next customers. "I guess he's changed," he offered.

"Guess so."

"Which is why I think you should be a little careful for a while."

"Aw hell. I didn't get this old by bein' careless."

Brett grinned again. "All right, Sharky. I won't pester you about it anymore."

Sharky smiled his wrinkled smile at the younger man. "You don't feel like a game, do you?"

"I don't think so," Brett declined. "I don't make enough money at this job that I can afford to give some of it to you."

Sharky chuckled and began picking up the cards still lying across the table. "Too bad. I reckon you'd be a real challenge. I doubt I could beat you."

"Don't try to hustle me," Brett warned in a friendly tone. "By the way, how'd you know I was a marshal when I walked over? You didn't look up."

"I make it my business to know the law before the law knows me."

Brett raised his eyebrows.

"I was in here earlier, when that gunfighter, Henry Fleet, was looking for Cass. Went outside in time to see the whole thing," Sharky explained. "I ain't never seen anyone as fast as that girl. 'Course, I can't blame her. Not after what happened to her family."

"You know about that?"

Sharky gave the marshal an incredulous stare. "Everybody around here knows about it."

"Were you here when the family was murdered?" Brett questioned.

Sharky remembered for a moment and nodded. "Yeah, I was here. I was even part of the posse that went out looking for the murderin' bastards that did it," he said, his eyes vacant with the memory. "It was real strange," he mumbled.

"What was?" Brett asked, grasping at the old man's words.

"The way we lost 'em." He raised his eyes to meet the marshal's. "They all scattered, every one of 'em. You'd think some of 'em would have stuck together. Criminals usually do have partners. But these fellas just went their separate ways. It was almost as if they'd come together just to commit the one crime, then went off about their business." He shook his head again. "And poor Cass was left behind. Terrible thing. Never saw her cry, though."

Brett remembered that Sheriff Jackson had said the same thing. It was odd she'd never cried. Instead, she had strapped on the twin Colts and become one of the deadliest shots in the West. She'd managed to track down four of the killers and was now back in Twisted Creek, hoping to find the last one. And she thought it might be Hunt Tylo, the father of the man Sharky had just beaten badly in a poker game. The man who'd just come home after a five-year absence. Was his return a coincidence? Suddenly Brett wanted very badly to see Cass, to see if she was all right. Pushing himself up from the chair, he looked down at Sharky. "I've got a few things I need to take care of. Are you planning on being in town for long?"

"You asking me to leave, Marshal?"

Brett smiled down at him. "Just the opposite. I was hoping you'd stay around for a while, in case I start feeling like I need to play a hand or two."

"Sure thing, Marshal. I'll be here when you want me. I've got a room at the hotel."

Brett nodded good-bye quickly and headed out of the saloon. As he walked toward the sheriff's office, his thoughts continued to focus on Cass. Was she on the right track with

Tylo? Did Ramsey's coming home now have anything to do with her? His gut tightened with dread. "Damn it," he fumed, realizing he had no idea where the Wayne ranch was.

Cass followed the fresh horse tracks down a wash along the base of a ridge. The sheriff's horse was getting more and more skittish by the minute, and her own mount had begun sidestepping nervously. "Calm down, boy," she soothed. "Just keep going a little farther. I think we're about to find something." Nudging her horse to increase his gait, she felt the sheriff's horse pulling on the lead.

"You had a real scare, didn't you?" she asked, turning in the saddle. The horse's eyes rolled wildly, seemingly in response.

The tracks led Cass up out of the wash and along a narrow path at the very base of the ridge. She was definitely on a course leading to the Lazy T. Her blue eyes narrowed as the path widened and turned away from the ridge, curving into a more open area of the range. Ahead of her was a dark bump on the landscape. A bump that looked, sadly, as if it could be the curled-up body of a man. "Come on, boys," she urged as she spurred her mount, leading the sheriff's horse along behind.

Cass's heart sank as she neared the form. It was Sheriff Jackson, and the whole right side of his head was caved in. "Oh, no," she breathed, swinging herself out of the saddle and ground tethering her horse. Rushing to the body, she knelt beside it and pressed her fingers against the sheriff's throat in a frantic and hopeful search for a pulse. Closing her eyes, she sighed sadly at the firm, cool feel of his skin. "Damn, damn, damn, this is all my fault," she breathed. "If I'd gone to talk to Tylo myself, you'd still be alive." She straightened a bit, more certain now of Tylo's involvement in the massacre of her family. "You must have asked the right questions, Sheriff," she whispered. "If I'd done the asking, maybe it'd be Mr. Hunt Tylo's body cooling under the late afternoon sun right now," she said through clenched teeth.

It took some doing to get the heavy, stiffening body of the sheriff over the back of his horse, especially since the animal kept shying away from the smell of blood. "Whoa, boy," she kept coaxing until the job was done.

Finally, with her saddle blanket tied over the upper half of Jackson's body as he hung across the saddle, she started back toward town. The sound of the horse's hooves behind her, plodding heavily with the body, pounded against the earth like a steady heartbeat, a heartbeat that matched her own and caused the anger and need for revenge to burn hotter in her chest. "I'll finish this yet," she vowed quietly as she rode.

Brett had found out where the Wayne ranch was by asking the blacksmith, and was readying his horse to make the trip when he saw Cass riding into town leading a horse behind her. It took him a second to realize the horse she led was carrying a body.

A few of the townspeople also saw Cass and ran to see who she was bringing in. Brett heard Sheriff Jackson's name being spoken in hushed, saddened tones as he walked to meet her in the street. "Cass, what happened?" he asked when he neared.

Cass pulled her horse to a stop and looked down into the gray eyes of the marshal. "He's dead . . . and it's my fault," she told him stonily.

A murmur of disapproval and anger floated through the crowd of people growing larger by the second. "Wasn't killing one man already today enough for you?" a voice from the crowd asked.

Cass turned her head only slightly in the direction of the voice. This was what her life had become since the murder of her family. This was what it would be until she finished what she'd started. So be it.

Brett watched Cass's reaction to the words. He could see the stern set to her jaw, the stiffness in her neck as she turned a bit. He could see the way her hands gripped the reins of her horse so tightly her knuckles turned white. But the thing that bothered him most was the death in her eyes.

Eyes so beautiful the sky should have been envious of their color. Eyes that should have been turned up in sparkling laughter or drooping slightly in the loss of a tear. But he saw no possibility of those emotions in the eyes of the woman before him on horseback. He saw only the death there. The cold, harsh reality of human mortality and the frustration and anger that went along with it. "Bring him to the office, Cass," he told her. "We'll take care of things there."

Cass glanced back down at the marshal. Was it possible she'd been kissed by this man earlier that same day? Had Ramsey Tylo really surprised her with his attentions? She'd been confused by the feelings Brett had caused in her. She'd been startled and a bit unnerved by Ramsey's unexpected behavior, but she had at least felt something. Now she felt nothing. Only a cold, stony emptiness and the need to finish the job she'd started. "All right," she answered, nudging her horse in the right direction.

"Aren't you going to do something about this Marshal?" Jaybird Johnson asked from the crowd.

Brett found the bartender among the onlookers. "Yes," he answered. "I'm going to find out what happened." He looked around at the people of Twisted Creek. For the second time in one day he was going to have to send one of them after the undertaker. Cass had been the direct cause of the first killing, and by her own admission, she was somehow involved in the second. No wonder some of these people didn't seem particularly fond of her.

Finding a familiar face in the midst of the crowd, Brett singed him out. "Would you mind getting the undertaker?" he asked quietly.

Bill Conroy nodded and turned away.

Brett then scanned the crowd once more. "Go on about your business, please. I promise I'll get to the bottom of this."

"Yeah, unless you're too busy getting to the bottom of Cass," another anonymous voice called from the back of the group.

Brett suppressed the urge to rebut the statement. Obviously his behavior with Cass earlier had been quickly reported from neighbor to neighbor. Ignoring the whispers that floated through the crowd, he turned and headed toward the sheriff's office. "I deserved that," he told himself when he was out of earshot of the crowd.

He was still mentally kicking himself when he reached the office. Cass had left the sheriff's body tied to his horse and gone inside. He took a look at the body before heading inside. When he opened the door he saw her standing in front of the woodstove staring down at the coffee pot.

"I made him his coffee this morning," she said softly when she heard the door open and close behind her.

Brett crossed the room to stand next to her. "What happened?"

Cass turned slowly to face the marshal. "It's my fault he's dead," she said in a monotone.

"You didn't kill him," Brett told her.

"No, but I might as well have. I sent him out to the Lazy T to question Hunt Tylo." She turned abruptly and slammed a clenched fist against her gun belt. "Damn it, I should have gone out there myself. This is all my fault."

Brett took a step closer to her. "Would you stop being so quick to accept the blame for this? We don't know what happened, but from what I could see, he died of a severe head wound, not a bullet."

"So?"

"So his horse could have been spooked by something. He could have fallen and hit his head on a rock."

"There were no bloody rocks where he fell."

"His horse might have kicked him. I've seen it happen before."

Cass snorted in disbelief. "After questioning Tylo about the massacre of my family, Jackson just happens to fall off his horse on his way back to town?"

"Maybe. And how do you know he ever made it to the Lazy T?"

"I know."

"Cass, listen to me. Even if you're right there's no proof."

"So you're going to do nothing?" she asked snidely.

Brett straightened at her tone. "I'm going out to the Lazy T first thing in the morning to question Hunt Tylo myself. And I'll have you show me where you found Jackson's body. After that, I'll decide what else needs to be done."

Cass snorted again. "You can wait until morning to talk to Tylo if you want to. I'm going to go talk to him now."

"Like hell you are," Brett told her. "It'll be dark soon, and you're going nowhere but home."

"Hah," Cass argued. "I'll go where I want, when I want, and no one can stop me."

"I can," stated Brett in a quiet, threatening tone. "In case you've forgotten, I'm the law around here. You will do as I say."

Cass took a step back. She waited to see if he'd make a move toward her.

"You're going home," he told her. "Nowhere else."

Cass raised her chin slightly in defiance.

Brett knew that as soon as she left his office she'd go directly to the Lazy T, ignoring completely his order to go home. "I'm taking you home," he finally said.

Cass closed her mouth and clenched her jaw. This marshal, this man, was proving to be an irritating obstacle. "Fine," she answered shortly.

"Fine," Brett repeated.

The ride to the Wayne ranch would have been almost pleasant for Brett if Cassidy had chosen to be friendlier. He knew she was completely aware of his reasons for accompanying her. Her safety was his uppermost concern. But despite this, she rode silently beside him, looking neither left nor right, giving no explanation of their surroundings. Nor did she let him know when they'd crossed over onto Wayne land.

"Is that a river in the distance?" Brett made an attempt at conversation.

Cass turned her eyes toward the aspen and willows that

lined the river and indicated its location. "Yes," she answered.

"The Losee?" he tried again.

She nodded.

"Is it a boundary to your property?"

Cass turned her head slightly to look at him out of the corner of her eye. "No."

Brett grimaced at her one-word answer and gave up trying to talk. Her demeanor left no room for doubt about how she felt about his presence at her side.

Soon a little house, a barn, and some outbuildings were visible in the distance. As they grew closer, Brett could also see the remains of a burned-out structure. A stone fireplace and foundation were barely discernible in a stand of trees not far from the small house that now existed. He felt a wash of pity flow through him as he realized it had to be the home that the murderers had burned down during their raid. His eyes darted to Cass's profile as she rode closer to her home. Not once did her eyes stray to the burned remains of what had once been her home.

"We're almost there. You can go back to town now," Cass said without looking at the man she'd felt next to her every step of the way home. Some time since she'd seen him in the morning, he'd bathed and put on clean clothes. His dark hair glistened in the sunlight that crept under the brim of his hat, and the fresh, clean, manly scent of his body had assaulted her nostrils during the entire ride.

Brett continued along beside her. "I'll see you safely to your door."

Cass let out her breath slowly. "Fine," she answered.

As they neared the house, Cass heard a commotion coming from the backyard. "What the . . . ?" Speeding up her mount, she steered him toward the noise, Brett following close behind.

The sight that met them as they rounded the corner of the house took Brett completely by surprise. A small Chinese man in a long garment was chasing a huge chicken, which seemed to be chasing a large yellow cat. The man shouted at the top of his lungs in a foreign tongue, his long pigtail flapping behind him as he ran. The cat kept running around in large circles, stopping briefly beside trees, bushes, and fence posts, only to have the chicken catch up and begin pecking him fiercely on the head. The entire scene was being watched, and cheered on, by an old balding man who hopped barefoot in the dirt outside the back door of the house.

"Soony, catch that damn chicken!" shouted Cass when she saw the melee.

"I'm trying, Missy Cass. Pork Chop won't leave Mirabelle alone!" the Chinese man shouted back.

"Uncle Darby, don't just stand there. Do something!" Cass yelled at the old man.

"I am. I'm bettin' on the chicken," the old man answered gleefully.

"Uncle Darby!" Cass shouted threateningly as she jumped from her horse and joined the chase.

"Oh, all right," grumbled the man, and he took up the rear.

Brett watched the ensuing scene with laughter bubbling up inside him. Cass took the lead, trying to catch either the chicken or the cat, chasing them around and around a tree in the center of the yard. The old man rounded the tree once, then stopped to catch his breath.

"Climb the tree, Mirabelle!" Cass shouted at the cat. "Soony, grab that chicken! I swear I'm going to fry him for dinner!"

Brett felt himself start to laugh out loud. He hadn't seen anything so funny in a long long time.

Cass heard Brett laughing and glowered at him. "You big jerk, get down and help!" she yelled in his direction.

Brett pointed innocently at himself. "Me?" he answered.

Cass rolled her eyes and took off again after the two wayward pets.

Brett jumped down from his horse but didn't really know where to enter the chase. The cat, darting haphazardly from one spot to another, didn't give much clue to the course the chase was going to take from one moment to the next. It was all Brett could do to stay out of the way and hold his sides laughing. Mirabelle chose that moment to get acquainted. Taking a flying leap, she threw herself onto Brett's chest, clawing furiously for a good grip of his shirt and taking a large amount of flesh along with it.

"Ouch!" yelped Brett, trying to pull the frightened cat from his chest. Then before he could save himself, his vision was blocked by flapping wings and chicken feathers. The cat released its death grip on his chest and jumped to the ground in terror. Pork Chop tried to follow, but Brett managed to grab her by one leg. She began to furiously peck his hand trying to escape. "Ow! Somebody come get this chicken before I wring its neck," he threatened.

Soony ran as fast as his legs could carry him and grabbed his precious pet from the fingers of the stranger. "Don't kill Pork Chop. She's a good chicken. She just doesn't like cats," he explained.

Brett rubbed the tiny peck wounds on his fingers and looked down at his bloody shirt. The cat had done worse damage than the chicken.

Cass had stopped running when Mirabelle leaped onto Brett's chest, and she now found herself in the center of the yard, staring at the wounded marshal. The whole thing suddenly seemed hilarious to her. Her face split into a grin, and her chest started to heave with laughter. Soon she was guffawing loudly, tears filling her eyes and running freely down her cheeks. Finally she had to sit right down in the dirt, she was so weak with laughter.

Brett looked indignantly at the hysterical young woman. "I don't see what's so funny," he told her, pointing to the bloody marks on the front of his shirt. "That damn cat nearly tore me in half. And look at my fingers!" He held his hand up for Cass to see the angry red marks along his knuckles.

Cass just kept on laughing. The more put out Brett looked, the funnier the situation became. She didn't know or care whether or not anything was truly funny. Right now it seemed hilarious, and she needed this. After the horrific day she'd had, she needed to sit in the dirt of her own back yard and laugh until she cried. She let herself fall backwards to lie flat, staring up at the sky as she laughed. Oh, how she needed this.

Brett walked over to where Cass lay and looked down at her. "I'm certainly glad you're enjoying this," he said, which sent Cass into another fit of choking giggles.

Darby took hopping steps to Cass's side. "She's always been a bit strange," he said to Brett, as though in explanation.

Cass laughed even harder.

Brett shook his head and held out his hand to Darby. "Brett Ryder," he offered.

Darby shook the proffered hand. "I'm Darby Wayne, Cass's uncle."

"Nice to meet you, Mr. Wayne."

"Just call me Darby, Marshal. Everybody does."

"Yes, sir, Darby."

Cass's fit had begun to subside a bit as the two men made their introductions. She felt as though a huge knot of tension had started to relax in her chest, and knowing what she still had to finish, she relished this momentary respite. Taking a deep breath, she closed her eyes and listened to the sounds around her as hiccups jerked her frame every few seconds and the remnants of a giggle escaped her lips now and then. A few peaceful moments passed before she sat up.

"Where's Mirabelle?" she asked, looking around the yard.

Brett glanced around them. "There she is." He pointed toward the barn where the cat had stretched out lazily in the doorway, looking none the worse for wear despite her ordeal. "Damn cat," he fumed.

Cass smiled widely. "Mmmm," she murmured noncommittally. "Looks like Pork Chop has calmed down too," she said. Pushing herself up to her feet, she brushed the dirt and dust from her trousers. "Is dinner almost ready, Soony?" she asked.

"Just about, Missy Cass."

"What are we having?" Cass was suddenly famished.

"Roast chicken."

Cass turned to Brett and surprised him by smiling. "Sounds good, don't you think? Why don't you stay for dinner, and we'll see what we can do about cleaning up those scratches for you," she said as she turned toward the house.

Chapter 5

"Those aren't so bad," commented Cass as she watched Brett washing off the scratches Mirabelle had planted on his chest. "You're nothing more than a big baby, complaining the way you did," she finished.

Brett had been standing with his back to her, watching her reflection in the mirror. Turning to face her, he smiled. "You really think so?"

Something in Brett's smile caught Cass off guard. She'd been teasing him, unaffected by the fact that he'd removed his shirt to minister to his wounds, but now, in the breadth of a second, something had changed. Her gaze traveled a path over his chest, taking in the strong curve of muscle covered by a shadow of softly curling hair that narrowed as it trailed downward, seeming to point to a different, lower part of his body. Letting her eyes fall, she stared at the floor. "Dinner's nearly on the table," she told him quickly.

Brett read the thoughts flitting through Cass's mind and felt a rush of desire course through his body with the force of a tidal wave. Standing perfectly still, the damp washcloth hanging limp in his hand, he whispered roughly, "Cass?"

Cass couldn't raise her eyes to meet his. He made her

feel things that were unfamiliar to her. Just the sound of her name on his breath sent sizzling little tingles skittering along her flesh. She remembered the way his kiss had felt and tasted earlier that day and wondered why this man had managed to start a wild fire inside her as no other male had ever done. "Come and eat . . . as soon as . . . you're through here," she told him without looking up. Turning on her heel, she left the doorway of her uncle's room, not giving Brett another chance to speak.

Brett felt confused by Cass's reaction to him. Sighing, he turned back to the mirror and dropped the washcloth into the basin, glancing up at his reflection as he did. She's a strange one, he decided, remembering the way she'd responded to him in the sheriff's office. She'd poured herself into his kiss, giving back as much as she'd received, yet, now she blushed and stammered because he'd faced her with no shirt. Shaking his head in wonder, he reached for the clean shirt Darby had left for him; his own was snagged and spotted with blood from the cat scratches. Pulling Darby's shirt on over his shoulders, he headed from the bedroom to eat dinner.

Cass saw Brett enter the room and busied herself with making sure the silverware was straight on the table. She caught her Uncle Darby watching her and stepped back from the table, stuffing her hands in her trouser pockets.

"How are those scratches?" Darby asked as Brett neared the table.

Brett tore his gaze from Cass's blushing face and looked at the older man. "I'll live," he answered, smiling. "Thanks again for the shirt."

Darby raised his hand to brush off the thank-you. "Aw, that's okay. I got lots of shirts. Never do wear them all." Standing, he crossed to the mantel and took down some glasses and the fresh bottle of whiskey Cass had brought him from town. "You want a drink?" he offered Brett.

"Sure. Sounds good."

"Cass?" Darby offered.

"No, thank you, Uncle." She rarely drank, and when she

did, it wasn't whiskey that passed her lips. Her uncle knew this, so his offer of the drink was unusual.

"Come eat, please," said Soony as he carried a platter of chicken into the room from the kitchen. Setting the heavy platter in the center of the table, he addressed Cass. "Pork Chop is very sorry for today," he told her sincerely.

"She is, eh?" Cass asked.

"Yes, Missy Cass. She says she'll never do it again."

Brett grinned at the man's words. "That chicken talks to you?" he couldn't help asking.

Soony looked at Brett. "Yes, sir, Mr. Brett. She tells me many things."

Brett walked to the table and waited to find out where he should sit. "What kinds of things does she tell you?" he coaxed.

Soony looked sideways at the new man in their midst. "She tells me when it's going to rain," he explained.

"Anything else?" Brett urged.

"Don't encourage him," Cass said lightly as she took her seat at the head of the table. "If you get him started he'll never be quiet." She smiled fondly at Soony while she spoke.

Soony returned her smile and left the room to fetch the rest of the meal.

Darby sat in the seat opposite Cass, indicating Brett should sit to his right, Cass's left.

Brett took his place and waited while Soony made two more trips with serving dishes. Soony then sat at the table across from him, and it was Soony who lowered his head first for prayers. Brett did likewise and listened while Darby said grace. It was only when he raised his eyes that he noticed Cass didn't join in this ritual. She sat instead with her head level, her eyes open, and her mouth set in a grim line. When he met her gaze, she didn't look away, only stared blankly at him until Darby was finished with the prayer.

"Amen," Darby and Soony said in unison.

Cass continued to stare at Brett as though she expected

him to say something about her nonparticipation in the saying of grace.

Brett saw the glint of a challenge in Cass's blue eyes and chose to not to comment. Along with the challenge, deep within her beautiful eyes he saw the look of death once again. Saying grace with her uncle and Soony reminded her of her family and what she'd set out to do. Instead, he let his eyes talk to her, sadly, quietly. He let her know he felt her thoughts.

Cass tilted her jaw slightly at the look she received from Brett. She knew what he was thinking, and she didn't like it. She didn't want to be inside his head, and she sure as hell didn't want him inside hers. Tearing her gaze from his, she grabbed a bowl of biscuits and tossed two of them on her plate. "Biscuits?" she offered Soony. Soony was busy picking over the chicken and barely looked up.

"May I have some biscuits, please?" Brett asked.

Cass looked back into the gray eyes of the dark-haired man watching her so intently. Handing him the bowl, she glared at him, hoping to make him understand that she didn't want his sympathy, or his interference.

After dinner, when Soony was finishing up the dishes and talking to Pork Chop, who pecked the ground just outside the open kitchen door, Darby sat in his chair beside the cold fireplace. "This is a toasty spot in the winter," he thought out loud.

"I'll bet it is," Brett commented, leaning against the mantel with his elbow. Cass had disappeared right after excusing herself from the table, and Brett assumed it was to take a discreet trip to the outhouse. She'd been gone quite a while, though, and he was beginning to worry about her.

Leaving the fireplace and covering the distance to the front door, he peered out, searching the yard for her form.

"She usually takes walks after dinner. Been doin' it since her family was killed. I think she visits their graves."

"I didn't see a cemetery as we rode in."

Darby shook his head and swallowed the last drop of whiskey in his glass, his third since dinner. "You wouldn't.

It's over the hill behind the barn. Closer to the Losee. It's where she wanted them buried."

Brett nodded, uncertain of an appropriate comment. He hated to picture Cass kneeling over her family's graves. He was surprised at the pity and sadness he felt for her. He usually didn't get so involved with the people he came in contact with. At least not this quickly.

Darby filled his glass again and held up the bottle toward Brett, lowering it when the marshal declined another drink. "Sometimes this is all I can do to forget."

Brett nodded again. "And Cass?" he asked softly.

"She doesn't want to forget. It's been five years. You'd think she'd be ready to put it to rest, but she hangs on to her anger. She lets it fester inside her. Sometimes I can see the hurt and the anger just burnin' to get out." He shook his head sadly. "Then she smiles and kisses my old head and tells me everything will be all right." He took another long drink. "I sure do love that gal. It's been torture watchin' what she's done and gone through. And now Sheriff Jackson's dead. It'll be worse than ever now."

Brett knew that the old man spoke the truth. The look in Cass's eyes was convincing as nothing else would have been, and after seeing her take down Henry Fleet, he knew she had the ability to carry out her plans. He just wished she could be talked out of this mission she'd set herself.

Some people were meant to be killers, and others weren't. Cass was the latter. He knew that each time she killed, it took a little more out of her. Each death she witnessed left its mark on her. Soon, he felt, she would reach her limit, and he hoped when she did she wouldn't completely crack under the pressure.

"Come sit down and have another drink, Marshal," urged Darby. "Have several. She'll be a while."

Brett shrugged and walked away from the door. Accepting the offered drink and sinking down into the soft chair opposite Darby, he realized how exhausted he was. He needed to get back to town to his hotel room, but he wanted to see Cass again before he left.

* * *

It was dark before Cass came walking into the house once more. Raising her eyebrows at the sight of Brett sitting across from her uncle, she walked between the two men. "I thought you'd have left for town by now," she said to Brett, taking in the relaxed way he sat back the chair, his long legs stretched out in front of him.

"I wanted to make sure you were safe inside before I left," he explained.

"I'm not a child. I am perfectly safe walking around my own property."

Brett shrugged one shoulder. "Maybe." He pushed himself forward, preparing to stand up. "Now that I know for sure that you're safe, I'll be going."

Cass frowned as she detected a slight slurring of his words. "You're drunk," she accused.

Brett grinned up at her. "Not drunk, just relaxed."

Cass shook her head and glanced to where her uncle smiled into the empty fireplace. "You did this. You got him this way."

Brett chuckled slightly, and Darby looked away from the fireplace. "He's a big boy, Cass. I didn't force him to drink."

Cass looked from her uncle to Brett. He was indeed a big boy. "Fine," she mumbled.

"Fine," Brett mimicked. "Then I'll be on my way." Pushing himself up from the chair, he staggered as he put his weight on his feet.

Grabbing Brett's arm to steady him, Cass glared up at him. "You can't ride like this. You'll fall flat on your face."

Brett was surprised the whiskey had affected him so strongly. It was probably because of his lack of sleep in the last two days. "I'll be fine," he tried to assure her, slurring his words even worse than before and swaying slightly.

Cass stepped forward and wrapped his arm over her shoulders. For just a second she was aware of the feel of his muscled chest against hers as she turned to accept his weight. She hurriedly twisted around to a less suggestive angle. "You're staying here tonight," she told him. "I'll help you to the bed."

Brett still felt the warmth of Cass's breasts against his chest where she'd touched him so briefly. Blood pounded in his ears as he leaned over to smell the sweet fragrance of her hair. "To bed?" he asked softly, his head swimming with the heady scent of her.

Cass's gaze shot up to meet Brett's. "The bed right here in the living room." She led him around behind Darby's chair. "This bed," she told him, indicating the small daybed pushed against the wall and covered with pillows and folded quilts.

Brett looked at the bed and frowned. "I don't think I'll fit," he grumbled. Then, stepping slightly away from Cass, he looked her up and down. "I don't think you'd fit, either."

"Well, I don't have to sleep here. You do. And whether or not you fit is no concern of mine. You're the one who got too drunk to ride back to town. Now sit down and I'll help you off with your boots," she ordered.

Brett lowered himself to sit on the edge of the bed, grinning at her gruff tone. "You can sure get bossy when you want to," he accused teasingly.

"Ain't that the truth," interjected Darby. "And she pouts, too."

Brett laughed at Darby's remark. "I believe it," he agreed.

Cass looked with irritation at one man and then the other. "Well, then, to hell with the both of you. You, Marshal, can just sleep with your boots on. And, Uncle Darby, you can sit in that chair and swill whiskey until you drown yourself. I'm not going to stand here and be insulted by the likes of you two. I'm going to bed." She turned with a haughty air and stomped from the room.

"Told you she pouted," said Darby when he felt Cass was safely out of earshot.

"I'll bet she threw temper tantrums when she was a little girl," commented Brett.

"Still would if she thought she could get away with it," added Darby quietly, yawning.

Brett pushed some of the pillows and quilts out of the way and lay down. His whole body ached with the exhaustion he felt as he closed his eyes. It was only seconds before he began to dream. In his dreams Cass was smiling up at him with no fear or anger in her beautiful blue eyes.

Cass couldn't sleep. Her insomnia was nothing new. Since the loss of her family, no matter how tired and sleepy she was, as soon as she laid her head on her pillow she was wide awake. And tonight was no different. Sighing heavily, she forced her eyes to close and tried to lie perfectly still, hoping she'd nod off if she thought pleasant thoughts. The only thoughts that filled her head on this night, though, were of Henry Fleet as he fell dead in the dusty street of Twisted Creek. Brett wondered if Henry's brother Bobby would come looking for her. He probably would. "Let him come," she murmured into the warm night air.

Sighing heavily, she turned over onto her stomach and propped herself up on her pillows. She could see out her window in this position, and sometimes staring out into the darkness helped her clear her mind. This night it didn't. Sheriff Jackson's death—she was sure he'd been murdered— Ramsey Tylo's return and strange behavior toward her, and Marshal Brett Ryder's entrance into her life kept her head swimming with thoughts that threatened to keep her awake all night.

Finally, after what felt like several hours of lying awake, she decided she needed to take a walk. It was the only thing that truly helped when the insomnia got this bad.

After tiptoeing from her room, she made her way down the short hallway to the living room. Stopping before she entered, she listened for Brett's breathing. She didn't want to awaken him. "Fat chance of waking a drunk," she whispered to herself. Proceeding quietly to the front door, she was soon outside and walking toward the burned-out ruin of her family home.

Brett heard a sound and opened his eyes, instantly wide awake. It took him several seconds to remember where he was, and then he relaxed only slightly. There were too many possibilities for trouble in Cass's life for him to be sure the sound he'd heard didn't mean danger. Sitting up, he grimaced at the pounding that began in his head. Damned whiskey, he thought. Holding his temples, he listened. There was no other sound. The house was silent. Had he really heard something? Was his mind playing tricks on him? He didn't think so.

Standing up, he walked quietly to the window and looked around the yard, wanting to make sure no one was snooping around. The moon was bright and illuminated the night very well. He could see the barn and other outbuildings clearly. He could see his horse in the corral, along with Cass's and several others. They were calm. No sign of any trouble. He then looked toward the trees beyond the yard. The trees where Cass's family had been murdered. A shiver of apprehension brushed his soul. Something moved out there. Something ethereal seemed to float through the shadows of the trees.

Brett blinked several times, then squinted, trying to make out what he was seeing. A voice somewhere inside his head said ghosts, but his common sense argued otherwise. Reaching for the doorknob, he turned it silently, determined to find out who or what was moving around outside in the middle of the night.

Cass sat on a little stone pile in front of what was left of the fireplace in her family's burned-out home. She let her mind wander back to the days before the murders. Back to the days before she'd held a gun for any reason other than to hunt game with her father and brothers. Back to the days when she could still let her tears fall freely because she wasn't afraid she'd never stop crying if she got started.

Taking a deep breath of the wonderful fresh night air, she remembered her mother and how she'd laughed at her children's antics when they were up to mischief. She remembered one particular incident when she was about ten. Her brothers had bet her she couldn't get their new bull into her bedroom and back out to the barn without either of her parents finding out about it. She'd managed to get the bull through the house without doing too much damage, but the stubborn animal refused to leave her room once he got there. She chuckled as she remembered the panic she'd felt as she pushed with all of her ten-year-old strength against the huge back end of the smelly animal, and the look on her mother's face when she walked in and saw what was going on.

Her mother had stood stock-still for a moment, horror registering on her pretty face, then calmly told her that if she didn't get the bull out of her room before bedtime she'd have to sleep with it. Cass laughed softly again in remembrance.

Brett stepped softly through the trees, peering around them one at a time to ensure his concealment. He didn't want whatever was out here in the dark to know he was coming. When he finally reached the edge of the stand of tall pines, he could see the burned-out remains of what had once been a large house. Scanning the broken, charred timbers, the blackened stones of the foundation, and the precariously leaning chimney, he searched the area. Then he saw it. Huddled near the fireplace was something small and white. He remembered Sheriff Jackson telling him that Cass's little sister had burned to death in the house, and an eerie shiver sliced through him. Just then he heard a sound. A soft whimper.

Stepping from his hiding place in the shadows, Brett moved toward the ghostly apparition. Moving stealthily over the bare ground, he made his way to the foundation and stepped silently over it. He heard another sound floating on the night air, and moved closer still. It wasn't until he was standing only a few feet from the specter that it moved and he realized with a jolt to his senses that it was Cass, curled up with her head on her knees. His heart rocked with pity as he heard her whimper once more. This is where she does her crying, he thought. No longer concerned about his silence, he took one more step toward her.

Cass jumped at the sound behind her. Damning herself for not bringing her guns along with her, she rose to face her attacker. "It's you," she let her breath out when she recognized Brett in the moonlight. "What the hell do you think you're doing sneaking around out here in the dark?" she demanded.

"I wasn't sneaking," Brett said defensively. "At least not once I saw it was you out here."

"Who did you think it would be?"

"I didn't know. I thought I heard a noise, and when I looked out the window to investigate, I saw something white moving through these trees." At his words, Brett looked more closely at Cass. She was wearing nothing more than a filmy cotton nightgown. It was what he'd seen in the moonlight, and now that he knew it was no ghostly apparition, it struck him hard that she was barely clothed.

Cass, too, responded to Brett's words about something white in the trees. She swallowed, suddenly self-conscious. "As you can see, it's only me. You can go back to the house now," she told him without meeting his gaze.

"I thought you were crying," he said softly.

Cass raised her eyes to his. "I don't cry," she stated simply.

"Never?"

"Never. Now please leave me alone."

Her insistence that she never cried bothered him more than if he'd found her weeping uncontrollably. He took a step closer to her and saw her cross her arms protectively in front of her, a move that pushed her breasts up against the soft cotton of her gown and caused his blood pressure to rise measurably. "I heard . . ." He was certain he'd heard her sobs.

"I was laughing," she explained. Standing so close to Brett with nothing but her nightgown covering her body was terribly unnerving. Why hadn't she grabbed her robe before she'd left her room? Because before tonight she'd never had a strange man around the place, she answered her own silent question. "Will you please go back to the house?" she asked him, shivering slightly.

"You're cold?" Brett took another step nearer, near enough to smell the sweet fragrance of her hair as a light breeze caught and lifted it in the moonlight. His senses reeled at her scent.

"I'm not cold," she answered quickly. How could she explain that it was his nearness that caused her to shiver, not the night air.

Brett studied the curve of her cheek in the soft, silvery light of the moon. He gazed into the blue of her eyes, made dark as sapphires by the night's shadows. He let his gaze fall to the fullness of her moist lips, and could feel his need for her grow as he indulged himself in her beauty. He saw her shiver again. "Cass?" he whispered.

Cass wanted to step back, but the rock pile was in her way and the hem of her gown had somehow wrapped itself around her ankles. She felt trapped. Trapped by a man who'd already made his intentions known earlier that day. "Marshal, I think we should both go in to bed now," she murmured. She was surprised at the timbre of her own voice as she spoke. Her tone was soft and husky, breathy, as though it took great effort to speak.

Brett knew her statement was innocent, but he also heard and felt the tone of her voice. He couldn't stop himself from thinking about what it would be like to fall into bed with her. To feel the soft, full curves of her body as she writhed beneath him. To pull her over to ride him astride and wild.

Cass could see Brett making no move to leave. If anything he'd managed to get even closer to her without even taking a step, and he was such a big man that looking up to see his face caused her to tilt her head back at a sharp angle. It was unusual for her to find a man who could look down on her the way he did. She was so tall herself that most men merely met her eye to eye or looked up at her. It was strange to feel small. Strange and somehow nice.

She found herself staring up at Brett's handsome face. His startling gray eyes seemed to glow with a silver light of their own as he looked down at her. His nose was straight, the nostrils slightly flared. His cheekbones were high and complemented the strength of his jaw. All of these things made him stunningly attractive, but his mouth drew her more than any other feature. The width suited her perfectly, his lips, smooth and firm, the lower just a bit fuller than the upper. She knew what those lips felt like. She knew how they demanded a response. She felt herself leaning toward him.

Brett's eyebrows rose slightly in surprise as Cass seemed to drift his way. He'd been fighting the urge to reach out and touch her; now she swayed into him. Surrounding her with both arms, he held her tightly against him, her head on his chest. His heart beat madly, shooting blood throughout his body in great gushing jolts, pulsing hotly in his desire.

Cass relished the feeling of being cocooned in the strong embrace of Brett's steely arms. She felt warm and protected. She felt safe. Something she hadn't felt in a long, long time. Then she began to feel something else: she felt the desire so evident in the hardness of Brett's body. Her own body responded passionately, heating up and becoming liquid, melting against him, molding itself to fit the strong planes of his body.

Brett sensed the change in Cass. He felt her breasts, full and ripe, crushed to his chest. He savored the feel of her smooth stomach muscles pressed close to his own. And he could feel the tilt of her hips and the push of her femininity where she nestled against him. He was nearly knocked to his knees when she began to swing her hips in a rhythmic motion over this manhood.

Cass didn't know what force was driving her to move against Brett. She could only feel the pulsating beat of their hearts, pounding together as they seemed to play a forbidden rhythm in her head, a rhythm her hips were matching. She swayed into him over and over again, the bulge between his legs growing larger with every rock of her body into his. Her pulse raced out of control. Her nipples hardened against the heat of his chest. She wound her arms around his back and pulled him even closer. The heat they produced seemed to engulf her very soul, swirling around them in a blazing fire of desire.

Brett could barely stand the sweet torture Cass was inflicting on him by merely moving slowly, methodically against him. He shivered with the need to complete their union, bringing one hand up to catch the heavy weight of one tender breast. Touching its firm, thrusting peak sent new spasms of desire spiraling through him, downward to center in that most heated part of him. "Cass . . ." He rasped her name. Lowering his head, he nuzzled her cheek, tasting the smooth skin there with the tip of his tongue. "Cass," he whispered again. As she turned her head, he claimed her lips in a fierce, possessive kiss.

Cass opened her mouth to Brett's kiss. She let him taste her, let him thrust his tongue against hers in a rhythm that mirrored the dance of their hips. She matched his exploration with her own, biting gently on the tip of his tongue, then not so gently on his lower lip. She heard him moan her name and felt his hands move down to her buttocks to pull her even closer to him. She stood on tiptoe, wantonly thrusting her femininity upward over the length of his manhood, then slowly lowering herself, shuddering with the wild sensations that pulsated through her. Her heart nearly stopped beating with the wonder of what she was feeling. She had to get closer. The fabric that separated their bodies was an obstruction she had to be rid of. She had to feel this man as she'd felt no other.

Chapter 6

S tepping away from Brett slightly, she brought her hands up between them and began to unbutton the bodice of her nightgown. She could see the heated glaze of passion in Brett's eyes as he watched her, and she gained a feeling of self-confident power as she opened the neckline of the gown very slowly, exposing herself to his gaze. As the night air caressed her heated flesh, she reveled in the coolness, but felt no cooler for its touch.

Brett watched Cass's fingers deftly unfastening her gown. He was mesmerized by her movements, captivated, as inch by inch, the luscious curves of her chest were revealed to him. As she neared the buttons still protecting the full mounds of her breasts, he reached up to assist her, needing to see the glorious globes of femininity that jutted upward to his touch.

Cass brushed his hands aside. She was enjoying this moment. She liked what she was doing to him. Carefully she held the gown up to cover her breasts as she eased her arms one at a time out of the long sleeves. Then, leaning forward, she rose up on her toes again to nibble gently on his lower lip, taking care not to let their bodies touch. Hearing him

75

groan sent a rush of liquid desire to her core. Stepping back once more, she dropped the nightgown, and stood before him nude, her skin glistening in the moonlight, her hair blowing gently in the soft breeze.

Brett gasped at the sight of her. She was glorious, beautiful beyond anything he'd ever seen before. She seemed to glow from the inside, warm and passionate. He had to have her, to possess her, body and soul. Reaching out with both hands, he cupped her breasts, marveling at their perfect size and shape, their rosy crests puckered and wanting, like two perfect rosebuds pouting in the morning dew. He stepped closer, lowering his head as he lifted her breasts to his mouth one at a time. He heard her gasps as he suckled her, gently at first, then more roughly, tugging each deep into his mouth in turn, tantalizing with his tongue.

Cass arched her back as Brett ravished her breasts. She'd had no idea such sensations were possible. Jagged spasms of delight danced through her, shooting from her nipples to the moist center of her being. She couldn't help but push herself against him again, her hips swaying in a search of the unknown. Brett thrust his hips forward to meet hers, his pulsing manhood huge inside his trousers. She wanted it. She wanted him.

Brett heard tortured groans coming from deep within Cass's chest. He shuddered against her as she continued moving her nude body over his. Lowering one hand, he found the curve of her bottom and cupped it, lifting her, pulling her into a sensual rhythm, forcing her to rock against the fiery tip of his manhood. His body vibrated with excitement. He was ablaze with the passion that engulfed them both. Sliding his hand from her buttocks, he caressed her hip, then the smooth plane of her abdomen. Letting his fingers slip downward, he touched the softly curling hair that decorated her feminine apex. Slipping his fingers lower still, he opened the tender folds to discover her womanly secrets.

Cass shuddered, breathing in suddenly as Brett's fingers touched that part of her that had never been touched by a man's hands. She gasped as he teased the sensitive bud of her desire with his thumb. "Oh, Brett . . ." She breathed his name, shaking from the sensations he was causing. "What are you doing to me?" she moaned.

Brett smiled at her passion. He took her nipple deep into his mouth again as he continued to tease her, feeling her body respond to his touch. Lower still did he explore. The moist heat of her body sent him reeling with the need to feel himself inside her. Taking his hand from her body, he began to unfasten his belt buckle, fumbling in his haste.

Cass reached out to help him. Pulling his hands away, she unbuckled his belt, then started to unbutton his trousers. Each button that gave way allowed more and more of his engorged manhood to push free. Finally the only thing between her hands and his throbbing shaft was the light fabric of his undergarment. She pushed the garment downward, then waited, suddenly timid, afraid to touch what she'd never felt before.

Brett thrust his hips toward her, causing his manhood to jut proudly upward with his need. "Touch me, Cass." His words came out a rasping moan.

Cass looked up into his eyes, blazing with a silver fire of desire, and reached for his manhood. She touched the head first, finding a drop of liquid balanced over the tip. The responding spasms in the organ, and the guttural groan that shuddered from deep within Brett's body gave her a new sense of female awareness.

"Cass," Brett groaned. "Please." Placing his hand over hers, he guided her to grasp him wholly, wrapping her fingers tightly around his shaft. Then, moving with her, he slid their hands downward, stroking him to an even higher level of excitement.

Cass allowed Brett to guide her hand. She loved the feel of his manhood, steely hard with a silken skin. She'd had no idea a man would feel so incredible. She seemed to instinctively know the pressure and rhythm he enjoyed and was soon stroking him without his assistance. She glanced up to see that he'd thrown back his head and closed his eyes as she ministered to his desire. Leaning forward, she nibbled on his chin. Then, trailing kisses downward, she nipped and kissed his neck.

Brett knew what he needed. Cass's kisses only confirmed it. Pressing gently on her shoulders, he urged her to kneel before him. Watching the surprised look in her eyes, he leaned his hips toward her, letting the heated shaft of his passion now stroke her, first on one cheek and then the other.

Cass was stunned by the feel of Brett's manhood on her face, but was soon caressing it firmly with her hands, allowing him to thrust gently against her skin and into her hair. Then he did something that surprised her even more. He stopped the rhythmic motion of his hips and poised himself directly in front of her mouth. Tenderly he prodded forward against her lips, brushing her cheeks with his fingertips. "Taste me, Cass," he urged.

Cass's eyes opened wide at his request, but she was enthralled by the idea. Why not? she thought. Opening her mouth, she tentatively stuck out her tongue and licked the tip of his manhood. He shuddered violently at this simple contact. Opening her lips wider, she took him inside her mouth as far as she could, leaving much behind to be stroked by her fingers. Mirroring the motions she'd made with her hands, she began a suckling rhythm over his shaft that had him groaning out loud in seconds. Her own passion seemed to rise and build as she tasted, licked, and fondled him.

Brett was at the very brink of losing all control. He felt himself shuddering, ready to spill his seed, but he wanted to pleasure Cass first. He vowed he would pour himself into her womanly core only after he'd felt her reach her own wild release. "Cass, wait," he rasped. "Please stop."

Cass looked up at him with passion-drugged eyes. She didn't want to stop. She loved the taste and texture of him. Only when Brett pulled himself from her grasp did she begin to understand what he was saying. She watched as he began to remove his clothing.

Watching Brett undress was like watching the unveiling

of a great work of art. His body was well muscled, perfect in its proportions. His shoulders, chest, and arms were large and strong, his waist and hips narrow and firm. His legs were straight and long, masculine in line and form. Finally he stood totally nude before her. She felt in awe of his male beauty. Then she saw him begin to lower himself to her.

Brett bent to her, pushing her backward, cushioning her with his arms. Reaching for his shirt, he tucked it beneath her. "There, that should keep you comfortable for a while," he whispered.

Cass nodded and stared up starry-eyed at him. She smiled through her passion. "Touch me," she whispered.

Brett felt a new rush of blood to his loins at her simple plea. She was amazing. Never before had he been with a woman who was so abandoned, so willing to please and be pleased. Smoothing his hand over her breasts once more, he tantalized their peaks with his fingers, then followed with the touch of his lips and tongue. Rolling over to lie atop her, he kissed and nuzzled her breasts lovingly, relishing their fullness. He traced circles around them with his tongue, then began a trail lower, to the smooth plane of her stomach.

Cass shivered as the night air touched the moist patterns Brett drew with his tongue. She closed her eyes and sighed with pleasure as he gave his attention to kissing her navel. His lips were tender on her flesh, his hands caressing as he reached up to massage her breasts. He then began to kiss her lower still. Her eyes flew open in surprise as the wet tip of his tongue probed her body gently. "Brett?" she whispered.

"Relax, I'm only going to do for you what you did for me," he answered.

Cass had never even heard of doing the things they were doing to each other. Did everyone do this? No wonder some people thought of nothing but sex. This was incredible. She arched her back as his tongue found her passion's bud. She moaned his name again and again as he tantalized her beyond reason. Then she felt his fingers again, parting her, exploring her. She didn't think she could stand any more.

Brilliant lights began to dance behind her eyes. She soared. She floated. She cried, "Brett!"

Brett felt Cass's climax as it began and wanted to match her ecstasy with his own. Quickly poising himself above her, he placed his throbbing manhood at the tender opening of her sweet body. Then, in one mighty thrust, he pushed himself deep within her. Shock registered in his brain as he felt the tearing of her maidenhead. "Cass?" he asked, horrified.

Cass's head moved from side to side in her need for completion. "Don't stop, Brett. Please don't stop."

"But . . ."

Cass put her finger to his lips. "Shhh."

Brett looked down in amazement at this woman and wondered why she had just given him her greatest gift. Why him? Then Cass's clawing fingers on his buttocks, pulling him deeper inside her, chased all other thoughts temporarily from his mind. He pulled out slightly, then plunged deeper, claiming her as no other had done before. He began a slow, powerful rhythm, piercing her again and again, feeling her rising with him. She caressed his back. She moaned his name. She raised her hips and arched upward to meet his thrusts. She was everything he could have asked for in a lover, and more.

Cass was filled with him. She relished every thrust of his passion, every forceful move of his hips. She matched his lust with her own and felt her body melting into a huge dark puddle of sensation. At the center of that sensation was Brett, massive, potent, dominant. She felt her desire spiraling out of control.

Brett sensed that Cass's climax was near and let himself begin his release. His muscles began to grow tense. He pinned her tightly to him, crushing her breasts against his chest. Thrusting again and again, he pushed her upward, over the edge of a magical precipice, cradling her for the fall. As the molten eruption began, he called her name, shuddering with the mighty spasms that shook his very soul.

Cass was blinded by the brilliant bursts of light behind her eyes. She felt millions of tiny explosions emanating from her womanhood, shooting outward like the spokes of a wheel. Nothing could have prepared her for what she felt. Grasping and clawing at the strong muscles of Brett's back, she whimpered until the spasms began to subside, only to feel him move within her and to find herself riding upward again to another pinnacle of sensation.

After what seemed like an eternity, she lay replete beneath his warm, heavy body, listening to his heartbeat and the steady, even breathing that had replaced the gasping breaths of moments earlier. The night birds called overhead. The cool night air touched her once more. The moon dipped behind a slow-moving puff of a cloud. She began to think about what she'd done, and the gravity of her actions started to take hold of her.

Brett lay very still over Cass, supporting his weight with his arms. His mind whirled with the knowledge that she'd been a virgin. He'd never have guessed it, her passion and desire ran so high. And why, when they'd only met that morning, had she chosen him? She was beautiful and intelligent. She could have had anyone she wanted. Try as he might, he couldn't find a plausible reason for her actions. Then a single thought gripped him, a thought so powerful it made him weak: maybe she didn't have a plausible reason. Maybe . . . could it possibly be? Had she fallen in love with him in the span of a few hours? He lifted his head and gazed down at her beautiful face, so still as she lay resting beneath him. She'd spoken no words of love, and yet . . .

Cass felt Brett watching her. What should she do now? What should she say? Did a man expect a woman to talk about their lovemaking when they were through? Did he expect her to act as though it hadn't happened? And how did she feel about this man? She hardly knew him. She'd always been certain she'd save herself for marriage, yet the thought of marriage hadn't entered her mind when he touched her. Even now the feel of his sleek, muscled body over hers caused her temperature to rise. What was wrong with her? she wondered. Her thoughts and emotions spun out of control.

The moon played hide-and-seek with the clouds, leaving them in darkness one minute, illuminating them in a silvery glow the next. Brett waited for Cass to open her eyes. He wanted to see how she would react to him now that they'd made love. Lifting one hand, he traced the curve of her cheek with the tip of one finger. "Hey, lazybones," he teased, "you going to sleep out here tonight?"

Cass felt the deep, intimate growl in Brett's voice. It was the voice of a lover. She tried to smile, but didn't open her eyes. "I might," she attempted to tease back.

Brett let his finger graze the silken skin of her jaw. "You might get cold. Besides, isn't the ground getting awfully hard?"

Brett was right. The ground had ceased to be a comforting cradle for their lovemaking and had turned back into a cold, hard, rocky surface she usually wouldn't walk barefoot over, let alone lie down on. Drawing on all the courage she had inside her, she finally opened her eyes and looked up. Brett was smiling down at her, his gray eyes shining silvery in the moonlight, his dark, almost black hair illuminated from behind by the light. The sight of his handsome features began to melt her insides again. "I guess we'd better go in now," she said, her voice crackling nervously.

"I guess so," Brett agreed. Pushing himself up, he stood, unashamed of his nudity.

Cass blushed at the sight of him. She knew she was being foolish. She'd just made love with this man, yet the sight of his body before her caused the blood to rush to her face. His hand, reaching out to help her up, gave her something to focus her eyes on other than his nude form. She took it, grateful for the concealing darkness. Once standing, she hurriedly looked for her nightgown, bending to snatch it quickly from the ground.

Brett watched as Cass tugged the light gown over her head and down around her body, hiding her luscious curves from his sight. "I guess I'd better get dressed too," he commented.

Cass's gaze fell to the pile of clothes on the ground. "Yes, I think you should," she said quietly.

Brett pulled his clothes on quickly, not bothering to tuck in his shirt or put on his boots.

"Don't you think you should finish dressing before we go back to the house?" Cass asked nervously.

Brett raised an eyebrow at her words. "I am finished. We're just going to go to bed when we get back."

"I beg your pardon?" asked Cass.

Brett took a step backwards. He studied her quietly. "You are going to go to bed in your room, and I am going to go to bed on that awful thing you put me on in the living room," he explained.

Cass lowered her eyes again. "Yes. Yes, of course," she mumbled. "I just didn't want you to think . . ." She let her voice trail off.

"I didn't, Cass. Your uncle's in the house. I wouldn't compromise you by trying to climb into bed with you," he said.

"Of course," she stammered, embarrassed by her own assumption. "Then let's go," she said, taking off toward the house.

"Cass," Brett called softly. "Wait."

Cass sighed and stopped walking. "What?" She turned around to face him.

"Cass, we need to talk before we go into the house."

"About what?" she asked as nonchalantly as she could.

Brett glanced down at the site of their lovemaking. "This," he said pointedly. "What happened here."

Cass swallowed hard. This was a conversation she didn't want to have. She had no idea what he expected or wanted from her. Would he think he now had a say in her life? He didn't. Did he want her to absolve him of responsibility? She would; she was equally to blame. She just didn't want to discuss it. "I'm awfully tired now," she offered. "Besides, it wasn't that big a deal," she said, hoping this would appease him.

Brett let his breath out in a gust. "It wasn't that big a deal?" he said, repeating her words.

"No, so you don't have to worry about me blaming you."

"I don't have to worry about you blaming me?" His eyes widened with surprise.

"Would you please stop repeating what I say?" she asked. "I know men worry about things like this. You don't have to. I don't blame you for what happened."

Brett crossed his arms in front of him, his boots still dangling from one hand. "And just where did you learn that men worry about things like this? From all your vast experience with men, no doubt." He had answered his own question.

Cass clenched her jaw against the anger that began to grow in her middle. "Don't taunt me, Brett. I know what happened here tonight. I just don't want it to change things."

"Between us?" he asked incredulously. "It's too late for that. Things have changed, baby, and they're going to stay changed."

"Like hell they are," she argued. "I made a mistake tonight. I admit it, and now I want to get on with my life. My mistake doesn't have to affect you."

"And what if you're pregnant? I think that would affect me, don't you?"

Cass's heart stopped beating. Pregnant? She hadn't thought that far ahead yet. How could she have been so stupid? Breathing deeply to alleviate some of the shock she was feeling, she glared at him. "If I'm pregnant, which I doubt, you'll be the first to know. If not . . . we aren't obligated to one another."

"And what if you go and get yourself killed while you're on this ridiculous quest for revenge?" he demanded.

Cass's jaw jutted upward at his remark. "Then I'm dead, and you're none the worse for it," she hissed.

"Hah!" he nearly shouted.

"Shhhh! You want to wake up my uncle Darby and Soony?" she whispered.

"I don't care if I do. If you're killed while carrying my child I'll be a whole lot the worse for it, don't you think?"

It occurred to Brett while he was speaking how much he would care if she was killed, and it wouldn't matter whether she was pregnant or not. This woman had gotten completely under his skin in just a matter of hours. And if she was pregnant with his child, he'd be damned if he would let anything happen to her. "You might as well face it, Cass. What you did here tonight pretty much guaranteed that I'm going to be a part of your life for a while."

"You can't—"

"Just try to stop me. I'm going to see to it that you stay alive despite yourself. Now let's go to bed." He took a step toward her, raising his free hand to guide her to the house.

"Don't touch me," she warned. "Don't you ever touch me again.

"Whatever you say, sweetheart," he drawled sarcastically.

Cass jerked around and started for the house once more. She didn't hear Brett following her, and she didn't care if he did. "I don't care if you stay out here all night and freeze," she mumbled to herself, though she knew there was no chance of freezing on this lovely summer night.

Brett watched Cass stomp to the house. Once she was inside, he sank down on the same pile of stones she'd been using when he came upon her earlier. Dropping his boots, he rubbed his eyes hard with the heels of his hands. "How did this happen?" he asked himself. He was usually so careful about avoiding virgins. How did he not know Cass had been one? "Because she's hotter than a brush fire out of control," he grumbled.

As he sat and thought about Cass, he wondered if she would respond to other men's kisses the way she had to his. He doubted it. If she had, she'd have lost her virginity a lot sooner. Pulling on his boots, he started for the corral and barn. He needed to go for a ride. A long one.

Cass heard Brett ride out some time later. "Damn you," she whispered into the darkness of her room. She could see his handsome face as though he stood before her. What was it about him that had caused her to abandon her senses? Other men were as tall as he was. Other men had marvelous bodies, muscular from hard work. Other men had shiny dark hair that curled softly and begged to be touched. Other men even had gray eyes. What was it about Brett that set him apart from the others? "What?" she breathed. Turning over abruptly and punching her pillow, she cursed into the night. "Damn you, Brett Ryder. Damn you to hell."

Brett rode in frustrated circles for over an hour before he came upon the gate to Hunt Tylo's ranch, the Lazy T. All seemed quiet on the road to the house, and he could see no lights burning in any windows to indicate that anyone was losing sleep. He could hear the faint barking of a dog somewhere behind the house, and he could hear cattle low-ing softly in the distance. Then, just as he was about to turn away, he heard a gunshot. Pivoting in the saddle, he listened. The shot had come from far off, and he wasn't sure from exactly which direction. Relaxing a bit, he waited. Who would be shooing this late at night? he wondered. After quite some time had passed, he decided he wasn't going to hear anything else. With narrowed eyes, and a suspicious heart, he headed back toward the Wayne ranch, and Cass.

Cass forced herself out of bed the next morning. Knowing Brett had left in the night made it easier for her to face everyone, though neither her uncle nor Soony knew how foolish she'd been. As she crossed her room to the wash-stand, she noticed a tenderness between her legs and an extra sensitivity to her breasts. "Damn," she whispered. It wasn't until she looked at herself in the mirror that she really began to curse.

Facing her reflection, she studied the effects of Brett's lovemaking. Her lips were swollen, looking almost bruised, and her cheeks and neck bore red marks where his whisker stubble had scratched her skin. Uncle Darby and Soony would have to be blind not to notice how she looked.

Trudging back to her bed, she plopped down to sit on it. "What am I going to do?" she asked herself. What am I going to say if they ask what's wrong with me? she won-dered. Soony's noises in the kitchen told her breakfast would be ready in a minute, so she had to decide what to do if she was questioned. Finally, after frantically searching her mind for some plausible excuse, she gave up. "If they ask me any questions, I'll tell them it's none of their business," she announced. Hurriedly dressing, she was ready to eat when Soony called down the hall that breakfast was getting cold. She wasn't ready, however, to see Brett sitting at the table and helping himself to some eggs. Her first impulse was to run back and hide in her room.

"Good morning, Cass," called Darby when he saw her emerge from the hallway.

Cass knew she was trapped. "Good morning, Uncle. How are you this morning?" she asked as she continued into the room.

"Fine, fine. Slept like a baby," he told her. "Come sit down now. Soony says the breakfast's getting cold."

"Soony always says the breakfast's getting cold," she replied. As she crossed the room, her heart hammered out of control at the sight of Brett's broad back as he sat facing away from her. He hadn't said anything yet. He was probably waiting to say something scathing to her after she'd sat down. She decided she'd speak first and not give him the opportunity to make any smart remarks. "Good morning, Brett. Did you sleep well?" she asked innocently.

Brett eyed Cass as she sat down. "You know I didn't," he answered.

"Oh . . ." she stammered.

"You didn't sleep well?" asked Darby.

Brett didn't take his eyes off Cass as he spoke to her uncle. "No, so I went out for a ride."

"In the middle of the night?"

"Mmmm," answered Brett, still studying Cass. "That's when I saw Cass." He directed a question to Cass: "How are you feeling this morning?"

Cass's eyebrows went up in startled surprise at his question. Last night he'd said he wouldn't compromise her by trying to sleep with her, but that had been before she'd angered him. Apparently he felt the need to get even. "I'm fine," she said deliberately. "Why wouldn't I be fine?"

"Well, after the fall you took out there in the trees I'd have thought you'd be a little sore."

"Fall?" Darby questioned. "You took a fall out in them trees? I've told you and told you not to go walking around out there in the dark, but do you listen to me? Of course not. Now you've gone and taken a spill. Let me look at you. . . . Yes, I see you got scratched up some. Well, it's no more than you deserve. You're lucky you didn't break your stubborn neck. Now maybe you'll listen to me when I tell you something."

Cass only half heard Darby's tirade. It had taken her a second to realize that Brett had covered for her, giving her an excuse for the marks on her face, and then she couldn't tear her eyes from his. He winked at her as he raised a cup of coffee to his lips, and her heart did a little flutter. "Thank you," she mouthed.

"And you found her in the dark?" continued Darby.

"Yes. She'd just fallen as I rode back into the yard. I heard the sound and went to investigate. I have to say I was surprised to discover what Cass is capable of doing in the dark." He winked at her again, his eyes twinkling at the double meaning of his statement. He grinned when he saw her face redden.

"Well, yes. Cass is a capable person," agreed Darby. "But I still don't like the idea of you walking around in the middle of the night," he added, glaring at his niece.

"I have to agree with your uncle, Cass," Brett said solicitously. "I mean, if some other man had come along last night . . . you never know what might have happened."

Cass glowered at him. His barbed remarks hit her just as he intended, and she didn't like it one bit. "I suppose you're right," she said sweetly. "Anyone else might have taken advantage of me. I hate to think what might have happened if I'd been found by a cad, someone with no moral fiber. I daresay if that had happened I wouldn't be sitting here calmly eating breakfast. I'm sure I'd be in my room crying my eyes out at my lost innocence."

Brett choked on a bite of biscuit, red-faced in response to the meaning behind her words. Darby began pounding him on the back, and Soony rushed to help in the rescue. Cass grinned widely. Picking up two biscuits, she rose and sauntered to the door. Opening it, she turned her back on the scene. Brett continued choking, coughing loudly, tears streaming from his eyes. He tried to get up to follow her, but was pushed back down into his chair by Soony. Uncle Darby continued to beat him between the shoulder blades. "I think I'll go for walk," Cass informed them breezily. She giggled as she stepped outside into the early morning sunshine.

Chapter 7

ou're not going with me, Cass," Brett argued later that
morning. He tugged on his saddle cinch one last time and
turned to face her. "And that's final."

Cass glared up at him. "I'm going, and you can't stop me.
Tylo killed Sheriff Jackson, and I'm certain he had something to do with my family's death. If anyone has a right to
question him, I do."

Brett let out an exasperated breath. "You don't know that
Tylo had anything to do with either crime." He held up a
hand to silence the protest she was about to make. "You
have no evidence. Do you know what evidence is, Cass? It's
facts, facts that prove beyond a shadow of a doubt that the
accused actually committed a crime. All you have is a gut
feeling. Gut feelings might help in an investigation, but they
don't hold up in court. And if Hunt Tylo had anything to
do with Sheriff Jackson's death, or with your family's, then
I'll do my best to prove it and see that he's brought to
justice."

"And if you go out to the Lazy T and ask him if he's a
murderer, and he says no, then what? You just let him go?"
Cass demanded. "Do you think he's going to tell you he did

it? He might need some persuading." She rested her right hand over the butt of the gun at her right hip.

"That kind of persuading can only hurt your cause, not help it." He stepped closer to her. "Listen to me, Cass. If Hunt Tylo is the man you think he is, he's a lot more dangerous than the others you caught up with."

"A bullet won't think so," she stated firmly.

Brett shook his head. "You're not going with me."

Cass glowered defiantly up at him. "If I don't go with you, Marshal Ryder, I'll go by myself."

Brett turned away from her and let his head fall back, raising his arms in an exasperated arch. "Most damned stubborn woman I ever met," he growled to the sky. When he turned back around, she was staring hard at him.

"Well?" she asked.

"All right, fine," he groused. "But you listen to me." He took a threatening stance. "I'm in charge. I ask the questions. You just stand there and listen. And if you hear something you don't like, you wait until we're out of there before you tell me about it. You don't make assumptions, and you don't start shooting. Do you understand me?"

"But—"

"No buts, Cass. If you do anything to hamper this investigation I'll throw your pretty ass in jail. You got it?"

Cass clenched her teeth and squinted in anger at him. Moments passed while she decided whether or not to believe him. The look in his steely eyes gave her the answer. "I've got it," she finally grumbled.

"Good." Brett stepped over to his horse and swung up into the saddle in one smooth movement. He watched as Cass did the same.

The ride out to the Lazy T gave Cass time to think about what Brett had said. He was right about one thing. If Hunt Tylo did have her family killed and if he had something to do with Sheriff Jackson's death, as she believed, then he was more dangerous than the others she'd found and dealt with.

The men she'd caught up with had been common criminals. Too evil or stupid to do anything worthwhile with their lives, they'd turned to crime as a way of life. She'd caught one of them, a man named Slick Henry, outside a small town about three hundred miles north of Twisted Creek. He'd taken up with a whore named Lucy Mae and was pimping for her, an occupation he'd found most appealing, as Lucy Mae did all the real work and he kept all her money. Cass remembered the poor woman didn't seem too upset when Slick lay dead on the street. She didn't even blame Cassidy for shooting him. Slick had been a blight on society.

The other three men Cass had hunted down had fallen into similar categories. One was suspected of robbing a stage. She'd found him out on the range, camped for the night. He'd gone for his gun, and she'd sent him to meet his Maker.

Another of the remaining two had run to Mexico to hide. She'd called him out in a cantina just over the border. A blink of an eye later, he'd cursed her as he died.

The fourth man had been in jail in Denver. She'd paid his bail to get him released, then met him in the street in front of the sheriff's office. She'd been arrested that time, the sheriff there thinking Denver was too big and sophisticated a town to allow gunplay in the streets. It didn't matter; the murderer had fallen like his comrades before him, and she'd been released from jail with no charges filed.

It was there the trail had grown cold. Always before, she'd been able to glean information from the people the murderers had associated with. But at that point she had nothing further.

Realizing she wasn't too far from Twisted Creek, she'd decided to go home and check on Darby. It was while she traveled homeward that the idea had struck her: there were no further clues to the fifth man's whereabouts because he'd never left the area. He'd been in Twisted Creek all along.

She'd thought about the arguments she'd overheard between Hunt Tylo and her father. She remembered Tylo's warnings that Farley Wayne would regret his decision to keep Lazy T cows off his land. And she remembered her mother's concern over angering Tylo. She'd said Farley didn't know how cruel the rancher could be.

Now, riding beside Brett to the Lazy T, she could hear her mother's voice again. Cass remembered several occasions as a child when she'd seen Hunt Tylo and her father together. They'd been friends of a sort, though Tylo never let her father forget who was the wealthier, more successful of the two. Her eyes narrowed as she thought about how uncomfortable she'd always felt around him. Her mother's words rang once more in her head, and she believed she knew exactly how cruel Hunt Tylo could be. She was determined to prove what he'd done and to see him receive the justice he so richly deserved.

She glanced at Brett's straight back. He rode angrily, ignoring her. She took in the breadth of his shoulders and the strength of his thighs as he straddled his mount. She mentally measured the growth of the dark whiskers that still covered his chin, and she touched one of the tender spots on her neck where he'd nuzzled her. Feeling a wash of emotion flood through her at the memory, she noticed him shift slightly in the saddle. Cass knew that he doubted Tylo's involvement in the murders. That doubt made him vulnerable. She would have to protect him. She knew she could.

"We're here. Remember what I told you," Brett warned as they rode onto Lazy T land.

Cass just nodded, then looked around the ranch. A few hands were visible on the place. One man was cleaning out the barn. Another was working a horse in a circle in one of the corrals. Still another was sitting in a rocking chair on the huge porch that completely encircled Tylo's two-story home. The men watched them coming, but made no move in their direction.

"So far everything seems normal here," Brett stated quietly.

"Too normal," breathed Cass, seeing Brett raise an eyebrow at her comment. "Don't worry, I won't shoot first," she said.

Brett scowled in her direction.

As they neared the house, the front door opened and out stepped Hunt Tylo's son, Ramsey.

"Cass, how wonderful to see you," he said, ignoring Brett. "Please get down and come into the house."

"We've come to speak to your father, if we may," said Brett. "Is he at home?"

Ramsey turned icy eyes toward Brett. "Oh, yes. Hello, Marshal. My father's in his study."

Brett dismounted and tethered his horse to the rail running parallel to the porch. Cass began to dismount, only to find Ramsey standing below her as she swung herself to the ground.

"Let me to do that for you, Cass," Ramsey said softly, reaching for the reins.

"All right," she answered, perplexed by his attention. Scanning him with her eyes, she decided his looks hadn't changed much during the years he'd been gone. He'd always been a thin boy, although quite tall, and she was surprised to see he hadn't filled out much. His body was still youthfully angular, actually looking a little bony. She cringed slightly when he deliberately made contact with her fingers as he took the reins from her. Stepping back from him, she waited while he tethered her horse to the hitching rail.

"There now, that's done. Let's go into the house, shall we?" Ramsey spoke again, holding out his arm to Cass.

She let her gaze fall to his arm. Not wanting to offend him, she placed her hand over his forearm, and fought the urge to pull away when he covered her fingers with his own.

"This is such a pleasant surprise," he said, smiling down at Cass. "And a coincidence too. Father and I were just discussing you this morning."

"You were?" interjected Brett.

Ramsey glanced back at Brett over his shoulder. "Yes, Marshal. There's no law against discussing a beautiful woman, is there?"

"Of course not. Call it professional curiosity that makes me ask what was said."

Ramsey laughed out loud. "Really, Marshal, you don't

expect me to tell you that in front of the lady, do you?" he gave Cass a provocative grin as he spoke, and gently squeezed her hand.

"You said nothing to slander the lady, I hope," Brett said in a challenging tone.

Ramsey laughed again. "Certainly not. Relax, Marshal. I only told my father what a stunning woman Cass had grown into. Surely you can't find fault with that?" He looked at Cass for a moment. "Now we're in danger of the lady getting a swelled head, I think," he teased.

Cass felt awkward with Ramsey flirting so openly with her, but Brett's scowl and his rude remarks and attitude were causing her to bristle. If this was an example of what he was going to be like from now on, she decided he needed a good lesson. He didn't own her just because she'd made love with him. And he had no right to govern her actions just because he thought there was chance, however slight, that she might be pregnant. Turning to Ramsey, she smiled beautifully and tried to look interested. Squeezing his hand, she demurred. "You flatter me."

"Not at all. I only speak the truth," Ramsey assured her, his pulse taking a leap at her smile. He was going to have more fun with her than he'd hoped. "Shall we find Father?" he asked.

Cass nodded her agreement. The reminder that she and Brett were here to speak to Hunt Tylo gave Cass a small stab of guilt. She was allowing Ramsey to flirt with her even though she believed that his father was guilty of multiple murders. Looking up into his smiling blue eyes she felt pity for him. A person couldn't be held responsible for the actions of his parent, but he would undoubtedly be terribly hurt when the truth came out.

Brett followed Ramsey and Cass through the house toward the study. He noticed that Cass blushed at something Ramsey had whispered in her ear, and he saw Ramsey grin in return as she spoke softly to him. Brett clenched his jaw and controlled the urge to wipe the stupid grin from Ramsey's face with the heel of his boot.

As they neared a pair of ornately carved double doors standing ajar, he heard a booming voice coming from the room they protected. "Cassidy Wayne, as I live and breathe. I'd heard you'd come home. How are you, my dear?" the voice asked.

Cass entered the study at Ramsey's elbow and looked at the man she suspected of murder. Her blood ran cold, and the hair on the back of her neck stood on end. "Hello, Mr. Tylo," she said coolly.

"Now, now. You're all grown up, as my son pointed out to me this morning, so you can call me Hunt."

Brett stepped into the room and let his eyes do a quick inventory of the man called Hunt Tylo. He could have been Ramsey, only twenty years older and forty or fifty pounds heavier. He stood well over six feet, with a muscular build and a wide smile. His hair was nearly white, showing only the tiniest evidence that he'd once been blond. His skin was tanned and leathery with few lines to give away his age. Then Tylo looked in his direction and their eyes met. Brett suddenly felt a little of what Cass felt. Hunt Tylo had cold, hard eyes. Eyes that didn't match the friendly words he spoke.

"Is this a friend of yours, Cass?" Hunt asked.

Cass glanced quickly to Brett. "This is Marshal Brett Ryder. Brett, Mr. Hunt Tylo."

Brett stepped forward, his hand out.

"Marshal? Cass? Is there a problem I should know about?" he said, shaking Brett's hand, then stepping back. "Are you in trouble, Cass?"

"No, Mr. Tylo. Brett's here to talk to you."

"Me? What have I done?" he asked, surprised and innocent.

Brett spoke before Cass got a chance to reply. "Nothing, sir. At least nothing I'm ready to arrest you for, yet," he said in a teasing way, followed by a slight laugh.

"Well, that's good to hear. You had me going there for a minute. Please sit down, won't you?" He indicated the two chairs facing his huge mahogany desk. Moving behind the impressive piece of furniture, he sat down and rested his elbows on its surface. "Tell me how I can help you, Marshal."

Brett settled into one of the large leather chairs Tylo had pointed to. He watched Cass do the same. Ramsey leaned on the back of Cass's chair. "Did Sheriff Jackson pay you a visit yesterday?" he asked.

Tylo shook his head a bit. "No, Marshal. I haven't seen Jackson since the last time I was in town. Why? Is something wrong?"

"Yes, sir, there is. Cass found the sheriff's body out on the range yesterday."

"No," Tylo breathed. "How horrible."

"Yes. He was on his way to speak to you here at the Lazy T." He paused for a moment. "Apparently he never made it this far."

Tylo shook his head again. "No, he never showed up here. I'm sorry to hear he's dead. Jackson was a good man."

"Yes, I'm sure he was," agreed Brett. "Did any of your men report seeing anything out of the ordinary yesterday? Any strangers hanging around the place?"

"No, no one reported anything. Of course, one of them might have seen something and just not mentioned it. I can ask them all if you'd like."

"I'd appreciate that, Mr. Tylo. Let me know if you learn anything."

"Certainly, Marshal." He rubbed his forehead with the palm of his hand. "What did the sheriff want to talk to me about?" he asked.

Brett saw Cass tense up and willed her to keep silent. "Nothing much, really. He said he had a few follow-up questions to ask you about the Wayne murders. I'm **sure** it was all just routine stuff."

Tylo looked at Cass. "Really? I thought I'd answered all the sheriff's questions about that when it happened."

"What could my father possibly have told Sheriff Jackson now, after all these years?" asked Ramsey.

"I don't know. Maybe—" Cass started.

"I'm sure it was nothing," Brett interrupted. "He didn't say it was anything too important."

"It's important to me," said Cass.

"I'm sure it is," Tylo said solicitously. "It was a real tragedy. You're a lucky girl to have escaped."

"I don't feel so lucky, Mr. Tylo," she told him levelly. "You know, sometimes I wonder what would have happened to my family's land if I had been murdered with the rest. Would you have taken it over?"

"I don't know, Cassidy. I never thought about it. I hardly need any more land." He smiled at Brett.

"But you would like better access to the Losee," she pointed out.

"I have access to the Losee."

"But my father told you he wasn't going to let your cattle cross our land anymore."

Tylo looked from Cass to Brett, then back to Cass. "Your father and I discussed it. He decided to leave things the way they were." He glanced at Brett again. "You're not trying to implicate me in these five-year-old murders, are you?"

"It doesn't matter that they happened five years ago," answered Cass.

"Marshall?" Tylo questioned.

"No, sir, Mr. Tylo. No one is accusing you of anything. I don't know what the sheriff was going to ask you. As I said, he told me he just had some routine follow-up questions," explained Brett. "You'll have to forgive Cass for being so tenacious. I'm sure you understand her reasons."

Cass gritted her teeth at Brett's patronizing, apologetic tone. "I'm perfectly capable—"

"I do understand," Tylo interrupted. Letting his gaze fall on Cass, he continued, "I'm sure I'd act the same way in similar circumstances." He gave her a pitying smile. "I know I'd grasp at straws and make false assumptions."

Cass narrowed her eyes at the older man. She opened her mouth, but before she could speak, Brett touched her arm.

"Let's go, Cass. I'm sure Mr. Tylo has a lot of work to do running this place." He stood up. "Thank you for your time, sir. And I'll be waiting to hear whether or not any of your hands heard or saw anything strange yesterday."

Tylo pushed himself away from the desk. "Certainly, Marshal. If I come across anything I'll let you know. You'll be in town?"

"Yes. I'll be staying at the jail now that the sheriff's dead."

"You're planning on being here for a while, then?"

Brett looked at Cass. "For about a month, I guess," he answered.

Cass reddened at his meaning. Standing up, she started for the door.

"Cass, may I walk you out?" Ramsey asked.

Cass turned to face him. She'd all but forgotten about him, and she certainly didn't think he'd be interested in flirting with her after she'd implied his father might have had a motive to kill her family. "I—suppose so," she stammered.

"Good," he answered, crossing to take her arm once more.

Brett stepped behind them to follow, but before they left the room he turned back to Tylo. "Do you have a night watch?"

"Of course."

"And none of those men reported anything?"

"No. Why?" asked Tylo, his eyes narrowing.

"I was out riding last night—insomina—and I happened upon your place. Must have been about two in the morning. I could have sworn I heard a shot from somewhere on your property."

"Really? That's interesting," commented Tylo.

"Yes, it is," answered Brett. "You're sure no one saw or heard anything?"

"Not a word, Marshal. One of my boys probably just shot at a prairie dog or something."

"Yeah, probably," Brett agreed, turning back toward the door. "Your boys must have real good eyesight," he murmured.

Cass was perplexed. Brett had said nothing to her about

hearing a shot on Lazy T land last night. As she watched him leave the room, brushing past her and Ramsey, she tried to catch his eye, but he passed quickly, heading toward the front door.

"Shall we?" Ramsey suggested.

She nodded.

"Good-bye, Cassidy. Come visit me again sometime. I find your visits very interesting," Tylo said to her back.

Cass glanced back over her shoulder as Ramsey guided her through the door. "Good-bye" was all she could manage when she saw the evil glint in his eye. He did it, her heart told her. He had my family murdered, and he knows I know.

By the time her thoughts had coalesced, Ramsey had her out the front door and standing on the porch. "Please say you will," she heard him say to her.

"What? I'm sorry, Ramsey. I wasn't paying attention. What do you want?"

"I'm asking you to go to the Fourth of July festivities with me, Cass," he tried again.

Cass blinked in surprise. She hadn't even thought about the upcoming celebration, let alone considered going with anyone. "There's a parade, isn't there?" she asked.

"Yes. And a chicken dinner. And of course, the fireworks."

Cass thought about his offer for a moment. It would be fun to go to a parade and to see a fireworks display. It had been years since she'd done anything so lighthearted. Yet, looking up into Ramsey's expectant eyes, she wondered why he'd asked her. Hadn't he heard anything she'd said to his father? The Tylo men were a strange breed. Maybe, in their case, blood wasn't thicker than water. She wasn't sure she liked that aspect of their personalities, and she certainly didn't want to lead Ramsey on, but maybe she could gain some clues about his father without his knowing it. "I'd be happy to go with you, Ramsey."

"Wonderful! The parade begins at one o'clock, so I'll pick you up around noon. Will that do?"

She nodded. "I'll be waiting."

Brett watched the exchange between Cass and Ramsey

but couldn't make out what they were saying because he'd mounted his horse as soon as he left the house. When Cass swung up into her saddle a few minutes later, he gave her a scathing look. Turning his horse, he started them on their way home.

"What was that all about?" he asked as soon as they were out of earshot.

"None of your business," she retorted.

"Everything about you is my business for a while," he returned.

Cass let out an exasperated breath. "I accepted Ramsey's invitation to the Fourth of July celebration in town," she told him.

Brett's eyes widened in angry surprise. "Do you enjoy consorting with the enemy, or are you just plain stupid?" he demanded.

"How dare you! Ramsey wasn't even in Twisted Creek when the murders took place, and he certainly doesn't act like a man who knows his father is a murderer."

"Precisely."

"What's that supposed to mean?"

"He doesn't *act* like it. Hasn't it occurred to you that he might be acting?"

Cass thought about it for a moment. "If he knew anything, he certainly wouldn't want to have anything to do with me," she said.

Brett set his jaw as he looked Cass up and down for a moment. "You just don't get it, do you?"

"Enlighten me."

"What better way to keep abreast of any investigation into your family's massacre than to pretend to be interested in you?" he asked.

"Thank you very much for the compliment," she huffed.

"Don't get insulted. You know very well how attractive I think you are. I'm sure Ramsey thinks the same thing. Hell, any man with eyes in his head would want to take you to bed."

"Don't be crude."

"I'll be anything I have to be to get you to see what might be going on here. I'm sure Ramsey's tickled pink that you turned out to be beautiful. I just wouldn't set too much store in his being honest. If his father had something to do with the murders, Ramsey knows about it. I'd bet my last dollar on that."

"You won't have to. If he knows anything about the murders I'll find out about it."

"Oh, no. You don't think you can get information out of him by pretending to be attracted to him, do you?"

Cass wouldn't answer.

"Cass, please don't try this. I think you're in way over your head with Hunt and Ramsey Tylo."

Cass glared at him.

"I have little doubt you could beat either man in a fair gunfight, but I don't think these men play fair."

Cass glanced sideways at Brett. "Then you think I'm on the right track about Hunt Tylo?"

"Maybe. There's definitely something about the man I don't like. Whether or not he had anything to do with the killing of your family remains to be seen, but I think he knows more than he's saying."

Cass thought about what Brett said. "I know he did it," she said quietly.

"You *think* he did it."

"You should have seen the way he looked at me as I was leaving. He's evil. I can feel it."

"All the more reason for you to stay away from Ramsey."

"Too late. He's picking me up at noon on the Fourth."

"I'll be watching you."

"You can't follow us around all day."

"Why not?"

"He'll think you're crazy."

"I won't be that obvious. You could invite me to join you," he said, liking the thought of thwarting Ramsey's plans, whatever they might be.

"I don't think so," she replied. "If Ramsey knows his father is guilty, this outing could be a good opportunity for me to find out. If he doesn't ... well ..." She trailed off, spurring her mount to a faster gait, not wanting to take this conversation any further.

Brett glowered at her. How could she be so obstinate? She was deliberately putting herself in danger without regard to how he felt about it, or her. Speeding up his own horse, he spoke. "Didn't last night mean anything to you?"

Cass's gaze darted to Brett, her face reddening at the memory. "I know what it meant to you, a reason to stick your nose in my business," she accused.

"It gave me a reason to care about what happens to you," he said softly.

Cass didn't say a word in answer. She studied Brett's eyes until he turned away from her, then stole glances at his profile as they rode silently toward her home. He was devastatingly handsome. Dark and wild. Every time she thought about what they'd done together the night before, her blood pressure shot through the roof and her heart hammered in her chest like the hooves of wild horses. Her body grew hot and felt as if it were melting from the inside out. The problem with feeling this way was that it interfered with what she had to do. If flirting with Ramsey Tylo would bring her closer to finding out the truth about her family, and in the end help her find the last man, the man with the silver gun, it was worth it. She would do what she had to. If she hurt Brett in the process, so be it.

Her gaze skimmed his handsome features again, and her heart did a little flip, sending blood flooding through her veins with a jolt. She didn't really want to hurt him. "Brett, I'm sorry, but this is something I have to do."

"You don't have to put yourself in danger."

"I have to finish what I started."

"You don't have to kill the last man. I'll find out who he is and bring him to trial. You'll see your justice."

Cass met his eyes. "What if he gets off? What then?"

Brett couldn't answer. It happened sometimes, if there wasn't enough evidence to convince a judge and jury, or if the criminal could afford a tricky lawyer who knew all the loopholes. Sometimes the crook got away with his crime. "It won't happen," he promised.

"You can't say that for sure, Brett. My way finishes the job once and for all."

"And what about afterward?" he questioned her. "What do you do with your life after you've killed so many men?"

Cass lowered her eyes. "I haven't thought much about the future. I always knew there was a chance I'd lose one of those gunfights."

"Have you thought about what your death would do to your uncle?"

"He'd get over it," she said defensively.

"Do you really believe that?"

Cass took a deep breath. "He did fine while I was gone."

"Only because he could hope you'd come home again. If you were dead he'd be alone, Cass. You're all he's got left."

Her eyes filled with hatred. "I'm all he's got left because of Hunt Tylo. I'm going to finish this, Brett. If you don't want to help, just stay out my way." Pulling her horse to a stop, she glared at him, defying him to argue with her again.

"You may find that the price you ultimately pay isn't worth the revenge you seek," he said quietly.

"It'll be worth it," she said. "This is where you turn off to go to town. I guess I'll see you on the Fourth."

"Unless I can talk you out of your social engagement with Ramsey."

"You can't."

"Then I'll see you on the Fourth."

Chapter 8

Cass saw Brett before the Fourth. She saw him at Sheriff Jackson's funeral the next day. As they stared at each other across the open grave, she felt his thoughts, his desire for her to end her quest for revenge. She shook her head almost imperceptibly, only to have him frown at her. He then stared at her abdomen, reminding her that they could have created a baby together, as if she needed reminding.

When the minister had finished his graveside sermon, Brett crossed to where Cass stood waiting to toss a handful of dirt on the coffin. "He seemed to be a good man," he said softly.

"He was," she answered solemnly.

"It could have been an accident."

She looked up into his eyes. "It wasn't. There was blood on his saddle."

"I saw it."

"It was on the right side."

"I know. That doesn't prove anything."

Cass stopped the slow shuffling walk they'd been making in line to the grave. "Tell me, Brett. Do you mount a horse from its left or its right?"

"Cass . . ." he said exasperatedly.

"Tell me."

"So the blood was on the right side and horses are mounted from the left. That doesn't prove he was murdered."

"It proves he was struck while still on horseback. It proves he was already bleeding when he fell off the right side."

Brett sighed. "It looks that way, but since he was alone when it happened, we can't prove it. Look, Cass, anything could have happened."

"You and I both know what happened. There just isn't anything you can do about it. Isn't that right, Marshal?"

Sighing again, he responded, "For now."

"Well, I don't want to wait patiently until Tylo decides to write out a confession. I have a feeling it'd be a while," she said sarcastically.

Brett glanced at the people standing behind them. "Come on, we're holding up the line."

Cass stepped closer to the grave and dropped the warm dirt she'd been squeezing tightly in her fist. It hit the casket with a thud. Walking away with Brett at her side, she paused when they were far enough from the other mourners not to be heard. "Did you notice who's absent from this little gathering?"

Brett glanced back at the people paying their last respects over the grave. "The Tylos," he said, adding, "Both Tylos." He gave her a meaningful stare.

"And why, when practically everyone in town showed up for this funeral, do you think that they are so glaringly absent? And why are none of the Lazy T men here either?"

"You can't blame them for murder just because they don't show up for a funeral."

"You know something? When I was growing up, I thought it would be wonderful to be a sheriff or marshal. Lawmen always seemed to have so much power and control. But I've found out since then that you have almost no power. You tie yourselves so tightly in the law that you can barely move. I'll keep doing things my way. You do, or don't do, them your way. Good day, Marshal." She turned and left him standing alone.

Brett watched her go. Joining her uncle and Soony as they headed toward their wagon, she mounted her horse for the ride home. She was the most stubborn, and most beautiful, woman he'd ever known.

Walking from the cemetery back into town, Brett decided he needed a drink. Entering the Best Bet, he let his eyes adjust to the dim light of the saloon for a moment before he headed to the bar. Then, leaning on its shiny top, he called out, "Whiskey, please."

Jaybird turned toward the voice and scowled. "Just a minute."

Brett knew he'd wait longer than a minute. Jaybird didn't like him, and he had to admit there wasn't any love lost on his part for the big man. Turning his back to the bar, he scanned the room while he waited. Several girls, perched provocatively on chairs or on customers' laps, smiled in his direction, hoping for future business. Two poker games were in progress, and a man played the piano in a corner of the room.

Brett looked for Sharky. The old man was a character, and talking to him or losing some money to him might just take his mind off Cass and her trouble for an hour or two. Walking to one of the tables, he watched for a break between games. "Any of you boys seen Sharky around today?" he asked.

"Nope. Ain't seen him in a while," one man answered.

"Didn't show up for our game last night," another added.

"Thanks," Brett said, and headed back to the bar.

Once again leaning on the cool wood of the polished bar, he thought about what the second man had said. Sharky hadn't shown up for a poker game. His eyes narrowed as he pondered this. Sharky was a gambler, his chosen game, poker. He wouldn't have missed a scheduled game unless something was wrong.

"So what do you want?" Jaybird asked in a belligerent tone.

Brett looked up. He hadn't seen Jaybird approach him. "Nothing. I've changed my mind." Pushing himself quickly away from the bar, he turned and headed for the door, leaving Jaybird standing with his mouth open, pondering the wisdom of leaving a customer, even a customer he didn't particularly like, alone too long. He'd just missed a sale.

Brett walked to the hotel, his bootheels digging into the dusty street with each hurried step. Once inside, he approached the registration desk. "Did Sharky check out?" he asked.

The man sitting against the wall behind the counter looked up from his newspaper and blinked his surprise at the marshal's urgent tone. "What's that?"

"Did Sharky Draper check out?" Brett repeated.

The man stood up and met Brett at the counter. "Old Sharky? No, he's still registered," he answered.

"Have you seen him since the day before yesterday?" Brett asked.

The man scratched his forehead with his thumb. "No, can't stay as I have. But that don't mean nothin'. Sharky sometimes gets to drinkin' and don't come in for days."

"He's not at the saloon, and he missed a poker game last night."

The man frowned slightly. "Well, that don't sound like Sharky."

Brett scowled. "No, it doesn't. Does he have any hangouts other than the saloon?"

The man glanced past Brett to an old rocking chair in a corner beside a window. "Right there. If he ain't in his room or at the bar, that's where you'll find him."

"May I check his room?"

"It's a little out of the ordinary"—the man paused a second—"but Sharky's a good old bird. I reckon it'd be all right."

Brett took the key and was told which room was Sharky's. It seemed he'd been staying in the same room off and on for as long as he'd been coming through Twisted Creek.

Standing outside the door, Brett got a terrible feeling of dread. What if the old man was lying dead inside the room? Turning the key in the lock, he twisted the doorknob and pushed inward. The room was empty. It didn't even look as though anyone had been using it. Had Sharky left town?

Brett walked farther into the room. It was then he noticed the corner of a battered carpetbag sticking out from under the bed. Reaching down, he picked it up and opened it. It was empty. He tossed it on the bed and crossed to the armoire. Opening it, he found Sharky's few clothes hanging neatly on wire hangers. An extra pair of shoes had been placed side by side on the bottom shelf, his toiletries in a small leather case on the top shelf. Sharky was a neat man, and he definitely hadn't checked out. "Where are you?" Brett breathed, his chest filling with concern.

Back downstairs a little while later, he tossed the key on the counter.

"Well?" the desk clerk asked.

"His things are still up there," Brett answered.

"I didn't think Sharky would run out on us." The clerk sighed, obviously relieved. "Like I said, he probably just got drunk somewhere and is right now sleepin' it off."

"I hope you're right," Brett murmured as he left the hotel.

While eating dinner the previous night, Cass had felt herself getting anxious about going to the Fourth of July celebration with Ramsey.

"I'm glad to see you're starting to act like a normal woman, Cass," her uncle said as he passed the potatoes.

Cass laughed at his lack of tact, but couldn't help the pang of guilt she felt about deceiving her uncle about her motive for spending time with Ramsey.

"I have to say I'm disappointed you're going with Ramsey, though. I never did like that boy."

"He's grown up, Uncle," she offered in explanation.

"Maybe . . ." Darby let the word dangle between them.

Cass grimaced. "Well, I've already given him my word," she said. "It's too late to cancel now." She wouldn't if she could.

"I'd have thought you'd be going with that handsome young marshal."

"I don't want anything to do with the marshal," Cass replied, her eyes open wide with surprise at her uncle's comment.

"Really? I thought you two looked real good together. I think he thought so, too."

"You can both think what you like. It's what I think that counts, and I think he's an interfering busybody, and you should mind your own business, too." She smiled when she said this last.

"All right, all right. But if that marshal rides out of your life before you come to your senses, don't blame me," he said.

"Humph," she snorted.

"Most ladylike," Darby commented. "I'm sure Ramsey will love that particular noise."

Cass began to giggle. Darby joined in, and even Soony began to chuckle. "I love you, Uncle," Cass said through her laughter.

Darby suddenly got serious. "I love you too, Cassidy. I'm so glad you're back home where you belong."

Cass's mirth quickly dissipated. Brett's words about what Darby would do if she was killed came back in a flash. Angry that he could manage to ruin a wonderful moment when he wasn't even there, Cass frowned down at her plate.

"Something wrong with the food, Missy Cass?" Soony asked, noticing her expression.

Cass looked up quickly. "No, everything is wonderful. I was just thinking about something . . . someone," she amended.

"Someone?" inquired Darby.

"Someone who makes me very angry, Uncle Darby," she explained.

"Someone who makes you frown at your food? Someone who wears a marshal's badge, maybe?"

"Oh, shut up and eat your dinner," she groused goodnaturedly.

The following morning Cass rose early, nervous about the prospect of spending the day with Ramsey. Crossing to wash up at the basin, she stared hard at her reflection in the mirror. It suddenly occurred to her that she'd never been on an outing with a man before. She'd been so young when her family was killed that she hadn't started spending time with gentleman callers yet, and after that . . . well, she'd never been interested. Now here she was, getting ready to spend the day with Ramsey and it was no more than a ruse to gain information about his father.

Crossing to her bureau, she pulled out a chemise, pantaloons, and stockings. She so rarely wore dresses that her undergarments had actually gotten dusty sitting in a drawer. She shook them off and sniffed them to make sure they smelled fresh. The fragrant sachet she kept in the drawer had done its job, and the fabric smelled sweet. "Thank God," she murmured. She didn't have time to do laundry now.

Cass only owned two dresses—one that she wore to church, when she went, which wasn't often, and one that was a bit fancier. She'd seen it in a store window in Denver right after she'd been released from jail for killing one of the murderers. She'd needed something to make her feel alive again. The creamy creation hanging in the store window had done the trick. She'd purchased it, and the shoes and reticule to go with it, and brought it, still wrapped in the store paper, all the way home and hung it in her armoire. She'd never worn it. Today she pulled it out and laid it across the bed.

"It's so beautiful," she crooned, carefully fingering the soft crepe fabric. The neckline was high, but the lace bodice was lined only from the breasts down; the rest would let her skin show through behind it. The leg-o'-mutton sleeves were solid crepe on top and lace from the elbows down. The waistline was tight and fitted in front to just below her hips. A small bustle accentuated the back, and ribbons hung to the floor from gathered material. Sighing, she straightened up and began to dress.

After donning her undergarments, she lifted the dress over her head and let it slide down around her body. The soft feel of the fabric against her skin reminded her of the way Brett had touched her, sending a heated flush to light her body. She couldn't help but wonder what he would say if he saw her in such feminine attire. Then, shaking her head, she thought, "I don't give a damn what you'd think, Brett Ryder."

"Cass, my goodness, you're beautiful!" exclaimed Darby an hour later when she emerged from her room.

"Thank you," she replied, blushing at his compliment. She did feel pretty. She'd spent a long time on her hair, sweeping part of it up and catching it with a cream-colored ribbon that matched the dress. The rest flowed in chestnut curls down her back.

Soony came out of the kitchen at that precise moment and began to clap his hands. "Very pretty, Missy Cass. Very pretty."

She smiled shyly. So far, so good, she thought. Now if only Brett—no, Ramsey, she reminded herself, correcting her wayward thoughts—if he thinks I looked pretty, I should be able to ask him questions without his being any the wiser, she told herself.

Cass was sitting on a kitchen chair, afraid to move lest she get dirty, when Ramsey drove his buggy into her yard at exactly twelve o'clock. Walking out to meet him, she knew she'd done well by the look in his eyes.

Jumping down from the buggy, he took her hands and openly studied her figure. "Father told me after you left the other day that if he were twenty years younger he'd court

112

you himself. After seeing you today, I daresay I'd fight him for you. You're divine."

Sinking into a tiny curtsy, she smiled up at him and suffered the squeezing contact of his hands holding hers. "Thank you, sir. You look divine yourself," she said, attempting to flirt, letting her gaze take in his tall, thin physique. He'd worn a soft camel-hair coat and light wool trousers. His vest was gold brocade, his shirt, the finest starched linen, but none of his finery could compensate for what he lacked in stature. His body had none of the strong width of Brett's, and try as she might, Cass couldn't help comparing the two men.

He released her hands and bowed before her. "Thank you, Miss Wayne," he said formally, but with a teasing twinkle in his eye. "Shall we?" he said, pointing to the buggy.

"Certainly, sir. Just let me get my reticule from the house."

Ramsey followed Cass into the tiny house and looked around. She'd had the house built shortly after the murder of her family, and her uncle had lived there and tended the place while she was gone. All this he'd learned from his father's letters. "You have a lovely home, Cass," he ventured.

"Thank you, Ramsey. It's nowhere near as impressive as your home, but it's comfortable," she answered. "Ready?"

"Hello, Ramsey," said Darby as he entered from his bedroom.

"Hello, sir. You must be Cass's uncle Darby." Ramsey held out his hand.

"Yes, that's right. You don't remember me?" Darby shook his hand.

"Sorry. It's been a long time since I was home last. Before that, I have to admit, I was a little wild. I didn't set too much store on meeting or knowing anyone much older than I was. Childish pride, I suppose," Ramsey offered in explanation.

"I suppose," replied Darby. "Would you care for a drink before you two leave?"

"Uncle Darby, Ramsey does not want a drink now. It's barely past noon." She turned to Ramsey. "I'm sorry. My uncle has a habit of drinking much too early in the day." She then faced Darby. "And I certainly wish he'd stop it," she said meaningfully.

"Don't badger me, girl," said Darby. "When a man gets as old as I am, he has a right to drink whenever he chooses. Isn't that right, Ramsey?"

"Yes, sir. Whatever you say, sir," Ramsey said with a grin.

"But, Ramsey, don't you think—"

"I'm not getting in the middle of this," he interrupted, holding up his hands in surrender.

When he raised his arms, Cass noticed he was wearing a heavy chain around his wrist. "What's that?" she asked, pointing to the bracelet.

Ramsey looked down. "It's something my father gave me. See, here are my initials on the side." He turned his wrist so she could see the monogram RST.

"Very nice," she complimented him.

"I've always worn it," he responded quietly, smiling.

"Well, I guess we'd better get started to town, I don't want to miss anything."

Ramsey bowed again. "Your wish is my command, fair lady."

"Good-bye, you two," said Darby. "Have fun, and Ramsey, take good care of my girl, won't you?" He felt a little melancholy about Cass going off with a young man. He knew she would probably have been married and settled down with children of her own by now if she hadn't used up the last five years hunting down criminals, but seeing her like this, all dressed up and going out, made him realize it might not be long before she married and went to live in another man's house. He glanced at them and hoped it wouldn't be Ramsey she lost her heart to.

Cass glanced at her uncle and thought she read a little sadness in his eyes.

"I'll take excellent care of her, sir," Ramsey promised.

Cass still studied her uncle. "Would you like to join us, Uncle?" she asked.

"Not on your life. I'd only be in the way. Besides, Soony and I might come to town later ourselves. Soony doesn't like anyone else's cooking, but I know he'll like the fireworks," Darby told her, the momentary sadness gone.

"Good, then I hope we see you there. Maybe we can all sit together during the fireworks display." She turned to Ramsey. "Would that be all right?"

Ramsey hesitated only a second before answering. He had plans of his own for Miss Cassidy Wayne, and they didn't include chatting with her uncle, but if that was what it took to get what he wanted from her, so be it. "We'd love to have you join us, sir."

Darby felt the second of Ramsey's hesitation tick by slowly. He knew he couldn't blame the young man for not wanting him to butt in on his time with a pretty girl, but it made him just the tiniest bit angry, anyway. "We'll see," he answered. "Maybe Soony and I will find you in the crowd, and maybe we won't."

Cass leaned forward and put her hands on either side of Darby's face. Tilting his head down, she kissed him on the top of his head. "I hope you'll find us," she said quietly. She then turned to Ramsey, smiling. "Let's go."

The ride to town wasn't pleasant; Ramsey tried to be entertaining, relating what he thought were amusing stories about his life at college, but a few of his college pranks had bordered on cruelty. One in particular made her skin crawl.

It seemed one of his dormitory mates was unable, for whatever reason, to keep his room up to standards. The rules were such that if any room failed inspection, they all did, and the students lost privileges because of it. Ramsey's prank, or revenge, was to find out what frightened the young man most and to use it against him. It seemed he feared death and was very superstitious, having been raised in the Deep South by a nanny who practiced voodoo. One night Ramsey and a bunch of his cronies broke into the nearest funeral parlor and stole a corpse. Bringing it back to the dormitory, they placed it under the boy's bed. In a very short time the stench made the discovery imminent. A note was attached to the corpse, telling the young man to clean under his bed more often. He was so traumatized by the incident that he ended up leaving school.

Cass noticed the relish with which Ramsey told the story, and though she smiled for him when he told it, she was repulsed by the tale. After that, she could find no way to bring up the subject of her family's murder without adding to the gruesome mood Ramsey had set.

As they neared town, Cass could hear the music of a band. "The parade has started!" she exclaimed. "Hurry, Ramsey," she urged, hoping to lift the pall on her spirits a bit.

Ramsey pulled the horses to a stop just outside the livery and put on the hand brake. "We'll leave the horses here and walk. You don't mind, do you?"

Cass could see the street was crowded with buggies and wagons. It seemed everyone had come to town for the celebration. "Of course I don't mind."

"You're wonderful," Ramsey told her. Climbing down from the buggy, he held out his hands to assist her.

Cass glanced uncertainly at his hands before she gave him hers and stepped from the buggy. It was then he pulled her to him.

Ramsey bent his head and stole a kiss, pressing his lips firmly to hers.

Cass was so shocked by Ramsey's unexpected behavior that she didn't know what to do except stand there. His lips were dry and too hard, pressing roughly against hers. He pulled her to him swiftly and held her tightly, his thinness apparent in the sensation of his ribs pressing into her chest. "Don't!" she finally said, frowning, trying to step back from him, turning her head away from his mouth.

Ramsey released her reluctantly and looked at Cass. "You find my kiss distasteful?" he asked when he saw her frown.

Cass fumbled for an answer. She didn't want to offend him, as she hadn't yet found the moment to question him about his father, but she certainly wasn't a good enough actress to make him think she'd enjoyed his kiss. "Oh, no, Ramsey, I'm sorry. I was thinking of something else," she blurted.

"I don't know if that's any better," he said sardonically.

"No ... I mean ... I'm sorry. I can't explain it. I liked your kiss, really I did." She tried to lie. "It's just that you took me by surprise." She looked up into his pale eyes and smiled. Briefly, something in the cold depths of his eyes sent a shiver down her spine. Then he smiled back at her, his features softening boyishly. Had she imagined seeing that short moment of dark emotion?

"That's all right, my dear. I'll try to do better later," he promised, giving her a lecherous grin and holding out his arm to her.

Cass took his arm and let him lead her toward the music.

Brett scowled blackly from just inside the livery. He'd been looking for the smithy to tell him he'd found a will among Sheriff Jackson's things and that, according to the will, Jackson had left his horse and saddle to his sister. Since the horse had been taking up space in the livery, Brett wanted to let the smithy know about the will.

He hadn't found the smithy. Instead, he'd witnessed a scene that had made his blood boil. How dare Ramsey Tylo kiss Cass? And why the hell didn't she slap his face when he did it? Clenching both fists at his sides, he fought the impulse to rush out and beat the man to a pulp. Just as he was losing the battle, he saw them turn and walk away. "You don't want me to follow you, Cass? Too bad. I'm going to stick to you like a tick on a hound dog," he grumbled between clenched teeth.

Cass accepted the glass of lemonade Ramsey held out to her. Putting it to her lips, she sipped the cool liquid. "Mmmm, delicious," she murmured after she'd swallowed. It was hot standing in the sun watching the parade, and Ramsey had purchased the libation from a street stand.

"Almost as delicious as you are," he whispered, leaning closer. His first attempt to sway Cass in his favor hadn't turned out the way he'd hoped. She hadn't responded to his kiss as he'd wished. In fact, she'd acted slightly repulsed by it.

Cass blushed slightly at his suggestive statement. She was uncomfortable with Ramsey's sexual attentions, but she refused to admit that maybe she'd taken on more than she could handle. He was her best link to Hunt. Sipping her lemonade once more, she decided that not commenting on Ramsey's innuendo was the wisest move, so she turned her attention back to the parade.

A small circus had found its way to town that very morning, and some of its performers and their animals had joined the parade. A baby elephant was marching past, a tiny man riding on its back, and Cass laughed as the man lifted his hat to her. It was then she noticed Brett on the opposite side of the street, watching her through the crowd. When their eyes met, he winked and tipped his hat to her also. Feeling her pulse rate increase to a fevered tempo, she looked away. Why did he have such an effect on her? she wondered.

"There's the marshal, my dear," announced Ramsey. "Oh, damn, sorry, but he's coming our way."

Cass looked back across the street to the spot Brett had occupied. It was empty. As she turned to search the crowd, he appeared in front of her. "Hello, Cass," he said, ignoring Ramsey. "Your as pretty as a moonlit night," he said softly.

"How very poetic, Marshal. I didn't know you had it in you," drawled Ramsey.

Cass stared up into Brett's silver-gray eyes. She knew what he meant. He was reminding her of that night. Her heart beat wildly, and she was suddenly much hotter than she'd been moments before. She remembered the way he'd looked and felt. She remembered the way he'd tasted and the things they'd done together. "I, ah . . . My, it's warm out here," she finally stammered.

"Yes, it is," agreed Ramsey. "Quite unpleasant," he stated, staring hard at Brett. "Let's go into the hotel and rest for a while."

"That sounds like a good idea, Ramsey," Brett parried.

"I didn't mean for you to join us, Marshal," Ramsey said rudely, a cold edge to his voice.

"I didn't say I was joining you. I just agreed it might be a good idea to go inside to cool off."

Ramsey lowered his eyelids perceptibly. "Very well. Come, Cass." He touched her arm.

Cass saw the tense set to Ramsey's jaw, the way his eyes narrowed. It made her nervous to see such anger being held in check. She suddenly wished she'd worn her guns to town, but picturing herself in her beautiful dress with her guns strapped to her hips brought a cloud over her mood as swiftly as if someone had just blotted out the sun.

Brett noticed the change in her. "What's wrong, Cass?"

Lowering her eyes, she shook her head. "Nothing. I'm fine," she said, thinking about what she was becoming. It couldn't be helped, she reasoned. She had to finish what she'd started. She'd promised herself, and she'd promised her family. Raising her eyes again, she gazed at Brett. Yes, he understood her. "Would you like to join us in the hotel?" she asked.

Ramsey's hold on her arm tightened at her words, but she didn't care. "It would be rude not to invite the marshal to join us, Ramsey. He is, after all, a newcomer to Twisted Creek. We should make him feel welcome."

Ramsey gritted his teeth to hold in the words he wanted to say. After a moment he was able to speak civilly. "Of course, you're right, my dear." He couldn't bring himself to echo her invitation, though. He simply began walking toward the hotel, leading Cass by the arm.

Brett had to clench his fists once again at the sight of Ramsey touching Cass in such a possessive way.

Moments later, comfortably settled in the lobby of the hotel, Cass tried to recapture her earlier good mood. "So, gentlemen," she said, addressing them both, "what should we do with the rest of the afternoon?"

"We could go to the circus," suggested Brett.

"We?" asked Ramsey.

"I wouldn't want to impose ..." Brett left the comment open ended.

"You wouldn't be imposing, Brett," Cass offered. She remembered his warning about following her all day and stifled a smile. If he was going to be standing on every street corner, and lurking in every shadow, she might as well have him sitting next to her. She certainly wasn't going to get rid of him by being rude.

"Thank you. Then I vote for the circus," Brett announced.

Ramsey couldn't believe this day was turning out so badly. The last thing he wanted was to have the marshal tagging along with them everywhere they went. He was determined to kiss Cass again, maybe more than once, if he could manage it, but the marshal's presence would ruin any chance for a sexual encounter. He looked at Cass, sitting so coolly in her beautiful dress. He had to get closer to her. *I suppose,* he thought, *if the way to her heart is through ridiculous gestures, I can put up with it for a while.* He glared at Brett and wished her need to be generous didn't include this particular man. "If the circus sounds good to Cass, it sounds good to me," he said as convincingly as he was able.

Cass nodded. "Wonderful," she agreed. It was then she saw Rosie coming from the hotel restaurant with a tray of glasses. She smiled at the young woman, only to be snubbed once again.

"Rosie, is that you?" Ramsey called when his gaze followed where Cass's had led.

Rosie stopped dead in her tracks and turned slowly around. Her normally white complexion grew even whiter, and she dropped the tray of glasses. Shattered glass flew everywhere as the tumblers hit the hardwood floor of the hotel lobby.

Cass studied Rosie curiously. She seemed to be unaware of the broken glass at her feet or of the many people coming to her aid. She could only stand and stare at Ramsey. Cass frowned at her odd behavior. She knew Ramsey had teased Rosie unmercifully when they were children, but that had been years ago. They were adults now. It was hardly likely Ramsey would begin to taunt her today.

Ramsey rose from his chair and crossed to where the waitress still stood like a statue. "Rosie, are you all right?" he asked.

Rosie backed up without saying a word and headed toward the kitchen, leaving the mess behind.

"Odd," Ramsey said, turning back toward Cass and Brett.

Brett thought the same thing. Rosie was terrified of Ramsey, and he wanted to know why.

Chapter 9

*E*xcuse me for a moment, won't you?" Brett said as he rose from his chair.

"Of course," answered Ramsey, rejoining them. "Take your time."

Cass saw that Brett was staring intently at the door between the hotel lobby and the restaurant. "What are you going to do?" she asked.

"I'll only be a minute," he said, not answering her question. Leaving Cass and Ramsey sitting together in the lobby, he pushed open the swinging doors to the restaurant. The dining room was closed for the day, but the staff was serving cool drinks, cakes, pies, and sherbet to people in the lobby and on the long front porch of the building.

Brett stepped inside and scanned the room. He'd eaten most of his meals here in the last few days, and Rosie had waited on him many times. She was usually a jovial sort, ready with a friendly smile as she poured the coffee.

Spotting her behind the lunch counter, he noticed she was having a hard time composing herself. She was wringing her hands, visibly shaken. Her complexion was even whiter now than it had been before, and she was chewing on her lower lip.

"Rosie," he called, his voice echoing across the large dining room.

Rosie jumped at the sound and took several backward steps, as though she felt afraid.

"Rosie, I'm not going to hurt you," he offered. "I just wanted to see if you're all right. You looked pretty upset out there."

"I'm fine," she said quickly, still wringing her hands.

Brett's eyes narrowed imperceptibly. "Are you sure? You seemed upset to see Ramsey Tylo." He saw her breath catch when he spoke Ramsey's name. "Do you have reason to fear Tylo?"

Rosie dropped her hands to her sides and raised her jaw defensively. "No, sir," she answered. "Ramsey means nothing to me."

Brett could tell she was lying, but why? "You know, if he's threatened you in any way—"

"No, sir," Rosie interrupted. "Ramsey ain't ever threatened me."

"All right. But if he ever does, or if he gives you trouble of any kind, you can come to me with it. I'll handle it for you," he offered.

"Nobody can stop Ramsey from doing nothin'," she said solemnly. "Not when he sets his mind to it. His daddy raised him to be that way."

Brett frowned. "I'm the law, Rosie. I could stop him."

She snorted her disbelief. "Not likely. Sheriff Jackson couldn't."

"I'm not Jackson," he responded.

"No, sir, you're not. But you don't know Ramsey."

"Why don't you tell me about him? Start with why you're so afraid of him," he said.

"I ain't saying a word. Please just leave me alone. I don't want to talk about it."

Brett pondered her choice of words and the implication in them. "You don't want to talk about what, Rosie?"

"Nothin'. Just nothin'," she answered adamantly. "I've got to get back to work now, Marshal." She began to look around her for something to do.

Brett watched her for a couple of seconds. It was obvious that she was through talking to him, and whatever it was that frightened her about Ramsey was going to remain her secret. "Damn," he mouthed. Turning slowly, he left the restaurant.

"I can't imagine what got into Rosie," Ramsey commented to Cass.

Cass shrugged. "I wouldn't know. She's never very friendly to me."

"She's not?"

Cass shook her head. "It's all right. It's her right to like or not like whomever she wants."

Ramsey locked his hands together, then touched himself just under the chin with two fingers. "Perhaps I should speak to her about it," he reflected out loud.

Cass snickered. "I don't think that'd be a very good idea," she told him.

Turning to look at her, he asked, "Why not?"

"Because she doesn't seem to like you any better than she likes me," she explained.

"It did seem that way, didn't it? But Rosie has strange way about her. She rarely shows how she's really feeling," he answered.

Cass studied Ramsey's eyes as he spoke. "You know her well?" she inquired. She'd have been willing to bet otherwise.

"We've spent time together," he answered.

Cass raised her brows in surprise.

"I think I will speak to her." He seemed to be thinking out loud again. "But not today. I don't want to spoil today." He smiled down at Cass. "Are you about ready to go to the circus?"

"Just about," she answered. "Let me excuse myself for just a minute. By the time I get back, Brett will probably have returned."

"Oh, joy," Ramsey grumbled.

Cass ignored his comment and stood up, straightening her skirt. Leaving him sitting there, she headed through the hotel toward the rear entrance. The outhouses were behind the hotel. As she left the lobby she met Brett. The look on his face gave her some concern. "Is something wrong?" she asked.

"Not with me. I've got a feeling something is terribly wrong with Rosie, though."

"You followed her?"

"I wanted to know what spooked her so badly in the lobby."

"What was it?"

"I don't know; she wouldn't discuss it with me."

Cass shrugged.

"I'm sure it has something to do with Ramsey," Brett told her.

Cass remembered Ramsey had just told her he'd spent time with Rosie. "Maybe they quarreled," she offered.

"It's more than that," he said. "Much more."

"If it's important it'll come out."

"I suppose." He then looked her up and down. "Where were you going just now?"

"Out back. Go wait with Ramsey in the lobby. I'll hurry."

Brett grimaced.

Cass grinned. "Go on. And try to be nice," she told him as she walked away.

Brett sighed. She was so beautiful, so desirable. She'd given him her virginity in the most passionate bout of love-making he'd ever experienced, and now she was completely ignoring his wishes, keeping company with Ramsey Tylo in order to gain information about his father, the man she was certain had murdered her family. He clenched his jaw to tamp down the frustration that burned in his belly. He would never understand women if he lived to be a hundred.

Reentering the lobby, he sat down in a chair facing Ramsey. As he planned his next action, he stared at the blond man. "Rosie seems to be afraid of you. Do you know why?" he asked.

Ramsey lowered his eyelids a bit. "I couldn't tell you, Marshal. Women are strange creatures."

Brett had just had similar thoughts about Cass, but Rosie's case was different. "She wouldn't tell me anything when I asked her about it."

"That's because there's nothing to tell."

"I'm sure there is. She's just afraid to talk."

Ramsey shrugged. "You're letting your job go to your head, Marshal."

"Because I refuse to believe a lie?"

"Because you refuse to believe the truth."

Neither man spoke again.

"Are we ready?" asked Cass a few minutes later when she returned.

The circus proved to be quite entertaining, and the chicken dinner, served at long tables outside, was delicious. And as Cass tilted her head back to see the fireworks light up the night sky, she pondered the day behind her. She hadn't found an opportunity to question Ramsey, but there was still the ride home. Brett's presence during the afternoon had kept her senses on edge, his silver-gray eyes assessing her every move. And she hadn't been able to keep herself from stealing glances at him when he wasn't looking, his powerful body reminding her again and again of how he'd felt as he possessed her. The tension between Brett and Ramsey had been a palpable thing, but she'd managed to referee well enough to keep them from starting an all-out brawl, though if it came down to that, she doubted Ramsey would accept a challenge from Brett.

She stole a glance at each man, standing one on either side of her. They were both tall, but as different as night and day. It was strange that they were vying for her attention. She felt certain Brett had no ulterior motives behind his advances. He'd been very honest about his attraction to her. Ramsey, however, was another story. Her eyes narrowed as she studied his profile. She let her mind wander over the things that had happened in recent days: Jackson's murder—she was still certain it was murder—Ramsey's homecoming, and his remarks about his father's letters. Was his homecoming a coincidence? Or had her own arrival prompted Hunt to notify his son to come home?

She continued staring at Ramsey's profile in the reflected light of the fireworks. Did he know his father had something to do with murdering her family? Did he have something to do with it himself? No, she reminded herself, he wasn't even in town when the murders took place. She was just getting desperate. Sighing, she lowered her gaze. On the ride home perhaps she'd get some answers.

"The fireworks seem to be about over, my dear," observed Ramsey. "Perhaps we should start back to the buggy."

"I suppose. I just wish this day didn't have to end." She sighed.

Brett looked down at her, the colored reflections from the last burst of fire in the sky glistening on her shining hair. He'd spent the entire day with her, not the way he'd threatened, following her like a shadow, but at her invitation, and despite Ramsey's protests. But now it was time to let her go, and it was killing him to think Ramsey would be alone with her on the long ride back to her ranch. He didn't trust the man, and he was sure Cass had underestimated him. "It doesn't have to end. We could go to the hotel for a nightcap."

"I think we've had enough excitement for one day, Marshal," Ramsey said. "I'm sure Cass is getting tired. I know I am." He raised his arm and, taking her hand, placed it in the crook of his elbow. "It's time to go."

Brett scowled at him. "Then I'll walk you to your buggy."

"That won't be necessary," Ramsey said in a slightly threatening tone.

"I insist." Brett met the challenge.

Ramsey looked down at Cass for a second. "All right, Marshal," he said, giving in.

The walk to the spot where they'd left the buggy was pleasant. Passersby stopped to say hello and to welcome Ramsey home. Cass was even included in the salutations, and she enjoyed the momentary respite from their usual animosity.

"This is where I left the buggy," observed Ramsey. "Where the hell is it now?"

Cass looked around. The buggy was indeed missing.

"The smithy probably took care of it for you," Brett offered.

"I didn't ask him to," complained Ramsey.

Cass looked up at him. "He probably assumed you'd want him to take care of the horses. You did park right outside the livery, and it was an awfully hot day to leave the horses standing outside the way we did," she commented.

Ramsey let out an impatient sigh. "I'll go see if the horses are inside. You wait here."

Brett smiled to himself. This would be the first time today he'd had a chance to be alone with Cass. He watched as Ramsey stalked off in search of his buggy and team. Then, touching Cass gently on the arm, he motioned for her to follow him.

Cass was suspicious of Brett, but she followed him toward a small stand of trees not far from the livery. "I shouldn't go too far away. Ramsey will wonder where I went," she whispered as he stopped under the concealing shadow of several tall trees.

"Let him wonder," said Brett, his voice a soft growl.

Cass's pulse took a leap at the tone of his voice. "Brett, I should go back," she told him.

Brett could just make out her features in the dark. She was so beautiful. He'd wanted to touch her all day, had suffered every time Ramsey had claimed his right as her escort. But now was his chance. Stepping forward, he raised his hands to her shoulders and slowly began to pull her to him.

Cass's heart skittered in her chest. She knew she shouldn't let this happen. Ramsey would come looking for her at any moment. Yet she couldn't stop the tremendous attraction that gripped her every time Brett touched her. She felt drawn to him as to a magnet. Staring up into his gray eyes, she watched as he lowered his head to claim her lips. Closing her eyes at the last moment, she felt herself begin the slow burn that would turn her into a mass of liquid fire.

Brett kissed Cass possessively, opening his mouth over hers, slipping his tongue tenderly between her lips. He heard her moan against his kiss and felt his heartbeat become erratic, sending blood charging through his body, bringing his manhood to life with a surging force. Lowering his hands to her back, he pulled her closer, thrusting his hips forward, making her aware of what she did to him.

Cass groaned at the evidence of Brett's desire, so blatantly pushing against her abdomen. She knew from experience what Brett could make her feel. She knew that if she didn't end this kiss she'd be grasping and clawing at him, encouraging him to make love to her. Tearing her lips from his, she gasped for air. "I have to go, Brett."

"No, you don't. Don't let Ramsey take you home. Stay here with me. I'll see to it you get home safely." He said this while kissing her lightly all over her face.

Cass's breath caught in her chest. "No, Brett. I have to go with Ramsey. I have to . . ." Her words were stifled as his lips covered hers once more.

"Please, Cass?" he said against her mouth.

Cass could barely breathe. Her heart raced. Her senses reeled. It would be too easy to stay with Brett. Leaning away, she pushed against him with her hands. "No, I have to go. Ramsey will be looking for me soon."

As if to emphasize her words, Ramsey's voice carried on the night air. "Cass? Where are you?"

"I have to go, Brett," she told him again.

"Don't."

"I have to."

Brett slowly released her, his desire diminishing only slightly. "I don't trust him, Cass," he said.

"He got me to town safely enough."

"It was high noon, not ten o'clock at night. You'll be at his mercy, Cass. Remember what you're accusing his father of, and tell me you trust him completely."

Cass's eyes filled with storm clouds. "I know what his father did, Brett. And if Ramsey knows anything about it, I might be able to find that out. But only if I'm alone with him. He's certainly not going to confide in me, or let something slip accidentally, with you around. Wasn't today proof of that?"

"What if he tries something?"

Cass sighed. "All right. Let's say for the sake of argument that he knows his father's a murderer, and he knows I know it. Even if he wanted to do away with me, he's certainly smart enough not to try to hurt me after spending the entire day with me in front of the whole town."

"Cass!" Ramsey yelled louder.

"I'm coming," she called back. "Now I really have to go, Brett." She stepped back, seeing the frustration in his steely eyes.

"You're making a mistake, Cass."

"It's my mistake," she responded, then turned, leaving the shadows of the trees. "I'm over here, Ramsey," she called, walking quickly to join him once more.

"What were you doing over there?" he asked, looking around. "And where's the marshal?"

"He went back to his office," she answered.

Ramsey looked suspiciously at the dark shadows under the trees and repeated his first question: "What were you doing over there?"

"I just went for a little walk," she explained, then quickly asked, "Were the buggy and horses in the livery?"

Ramsey looked down at her, gauging her truthfulness. "Yes, the smithy is getting them ready now." He looked back at the stand of trees. "Shall we take a walk together while we wait? Perhaps we could walk back under those lovely trees."

"No," Cass answered hurriedly. "I'm really getting quite sleepy. Let's just wait here."

"All right," he agreed.

Cass nearly sighed her relief. She didn't know for sure whether or not Brett was still standing among the trees, but her woman's intuition told her he probably was.

Ramsey had studied the shadows under the trees and was certain he'd seen something, or someone, moving there. He felt it was reasonable to assume it was the marshal. Narrowing his eyes, he pondered what Cass was doing with him under those trees. He couldn't allow Cass to become romantically involved with another man. He needed her for himself.

The smithy guided the horses and buggy out of the livery doors and stopped in front of Ramsey. "That'll be one dollar, Mr. Tylo," he said.

"What for?" Ramsey asked.

"Why, for taking care of your horses and rig, sir."

Ramsey's expression darkened. He hadn't asked this man to take care of his rig. It was the fool's loss for doing something he hadn't been asked to do. He then glanced down at Cass's expectant face. Gritting his teeth, he reached into his pocket and pulled out a dollar. After tossing it to the smithy, he led Cass to the buggy. "Let's go, my dear," he murmured, keeping his temper under control.

Cass wondered why Ramsey seemed so cross. He was definitely given to strong mood swings.

The buggy creaked and jostled over the rutted road that led out of town. The night air had cooled slightly from the day's earlier heat, and tiny bats swooped and dipped around the vehicle in search of insects. Cass smiled as she listened to the sound of crickets calling their mates. She loved summer nights. Taking a deep breath, she sighed. "Mmmm, doesn't the sage smell wonderful?" she asked.

"I suppose so," commented Ramsey.

Cass closed her eyes, letting her head fall back in pure enjoyment of the moment. "Sometimes, during the summer, I walk for hours at night."

"Alone?"

"Yes," she answered, opening her eyes once more.

"Aren't you afraid?"

"Why would I be afraid on my own property?"

"Well ... a woman alone ..."

"I'm not afraid," she said firmly.

"You're a brave woman, Cass," he told her.

Cass thought about his words. She didn't feel particularly brave. She just saw no need to be afraid. She'd seen death. She'd stared it right in the face while waiting for an opponent to draw. She'd listened to the pounding of her own heart, knowing that each beat might be her last. She'd taken deep, slow breaths, savoring her precious existence. And she knew there were worse things by far than death. There was nothing more horrifying than watching the death of someone you loved. "After you've seen what I have, you find there's not too much out in the world that can frighten you anymore." she said quietly.

Ramsey glanced down at her. She'd lowered her head. "Your family?" he asked.

Cass raised her eyes and nodded. "Did your father write and tell you about it?"

"Yes."

"You'd only been gone for about a week when it happened," she said, remembering.

"I'd left for school."

"Yes. It was about two weeks after our fathers argued about the water access across our land," she said.

"I don't remember that."

"You were there, Ramsey," she reminded him. "You were with your father that day. How can you not remember the way your father threatened mine?"

Ramsey shrugged slightly. "I guess when you grow up with a man who threatens violence every other day, you get kind of used to it," he explained.

"Did your father ever threaten you?" she asked.

Ramsey looked down at her with a derisive expression. "All the time, Cass."

She looked at him with a condemning glint in her eye.

"But he never carried out his threats, Cass. I know what you're getting at. You practically accused my father of having something to do with murdering your family. Well, I know he didn't do it."

"But you weren't even here, Ramsey. How do you know for sure he wasn't involved?"

"I just know. My father is loud and overbearing at times. He raised me with a strict hand, and sometimes I thought he was cruel in his methods. But he doesn't have it in him to be a murderer, Cass. He doesn't have what it takes."

"And what's that?" she hissed.

"No conscience," he murmured, leaning closer to her.

Cass's skin crawled at his words. Someone with no conscience, she thought. Hunt Tylo still fit the bill as far as she was concerned. He did threaten her father, and Ramsey's telling her he never carried out his threats didn't change things. He'd protect his father the same as she would if her father were still alive. "I don't blame you for defending your father, Ramsey," she said softly.

"I'm not just defending him, Cass. I know my father didn't kill your family," he said.

Cass didn't answer. She'd taken her shot at questioning him about the murders. She'd accomplished nothing.

Ramsey watched her face in the moonlight. She'd grown into such a beautiful woman. The thought of having sex with her made his manhood begin to throb.

"Perhaps we could talk about something else for a while?" he asked.

Cass looked up. "I suppose," she said curiously.

He pulled on the reins, stopping the buggy. "I'd like to go on seeing you, Cass," he began. "I know how you feel about my father, but someday you'll learn how wrong you were about him. I don't want this ... misunderstanding to keep us apart."

Cass glanced around them in the dark. He'd stopped the buggy at a turn in the road, just next to a bluff, giving them the feeling of privacy. "It won't keep us apart—" she began to explain.

"I'm so glad," he interrupted, inching closer. "We could be so good together."

Cass frowned at his misinterpretation of her words. "That's not what I mean, Ramsey. The way I feel about your father has nothing to do with the way I feel about you."

"Good . . ." He slid his arm across the back of the buggy seat behind her.

"No. You're not letting me finish." She didn't want to deliberately hurt his feelings, but she added, "I don't feel we should keep seeing each other, Ramsey."

He lowered one eyebrow as he looked at her. "And why is that? Is there someone else?" he questioned. If he wasn't able to seduce her, he would have to kill her, as his father had originally wanted.

Cass shook her head. "There's no one else," she answered hurriedly. She wouldn't acknowledge Brett's claim on her.

Ramsey studied her face. She'd answered so quickly that he tended to believe her. "I'm glad to hear you say that. I was beginning to think you had an eye for that marshal."

"Brett?" she asked, the memory of his kiss under the trees causing her to blush.

"The way you let him tag along with us today had me wondering."

"I told you, we had to be polite to the man. He is a stranger to our area."

"Right you are. But I dislike the fellow."

"Why?" she asked.

"Because he's so obviously smitten with you, my dear. I'm not too ashamed to say that I'm jealous." He leaned a little closer to her.

"You barely know me, Ramsey," she said, beginning to feel very alone with him in the dark.

"A circumstance I intend to change." Leaning forward, he took his upper arms in his hands and drew her forward. Lowering his lips until they hovered a fraction of an inch above hers, he stared into her eyes. "We're going to try another kiss, and we'll see if we can do better than we did this afternoon." Before Cass could protest, Ramsey's mouth came down on hers hard, the pressure forcing her lips to part. He used his tongue to find hers, pushing against it in a rhythmic pattern.

Cass was immediately repulsed by Ramsey's kiss. His mouth was hard and demanding; his tongue gagged her as he attempted to be sexual. Trying to turn her head, she struggled against his embrace. Wishing she'd listened to Brett, she raised her arms to push against Ramsey's chest.

Ramsey fought to control her, pinning her arms behind her and securing them there with one of his own. She was going to be his. She had to be. As he struggled with her, he felt himself becoming more and more excited. Cass was one of the most beautiful women he'd ever been with. "Cass," he groaned, raising a hand to grip her breast.

Cass inhaled a shocked breath as his hand closed over her breast. He began to knead it roughly, hurting her in his haste. "No—" she protested, only to have his lips crush hers again.

Ramsey continued to stroke her despite her struggles. The fullness of her breast, the weight of it in his palm, had him groaning deep within his chest. He knew he needed to be touched also. Releasing her breast, he reached behind her and took one of her hands in his own. Pulling it forward, he placed it firmly over the bulge in his trousers and tried to make her stroke him through the fabric.

Cass jerked her hand back violently, horribly revolted by touching his erection. This was the opportunity she'd been hoping for. She was surprised to see a nearly drugged look in his eyes. "Ramsey, let go of me and take me home!" she demanded.

Ramsey was startled by the way she'd managed to pull her hand from his, but the few seconds he'd felt the pressure of her hand over his erection had his head spinning. Grappling for her hand again, he tried to place it over the front of his trousers once again. "Just a little bit more, Cass. Just a little—"

"No!" she nearly screamed, jerking her hand away once more, and this time bracing her feet against the footboards of the buggy and using leverage to heave her body upward. "Let go of me!"

Ramsey lunged against her, pinning her to the back of the buggy. "But I'm not finished yet." He gripped her breast tightly in his hand once more and turned his body so his manhood pressed against her thigh.

"No, Ramsey! No!" She pushed roughly against him. Fighting as hard as she could, she managed to put a little space between them. Bringing up one hand, she slapped him as hard as she could across the face, her palm throbbing from the stinging blow.

Ramsey sat back, stunned. Blinking rapidly, he put his hand to his cheek where the skin tingled painfully from her slap. He'd beaten women for less than this. Looking at her with narrowed eyes, he saw the look of fear on her face. It was a look that made him feel powerful. Maybe he'd just gone a little too fast. Maybe he'd gotten a little carried away because of her beauty. And maybe, with the right kind of persuasion, he could still have her without a fight. "I'm sorry, Cass. I don't know what got into me," he murmured apologetically.

"Just take me home," she told him, her breath coming in heaving gasps. She'd moved as far away from him on the buggy seat as she could, and yet she still felt as though she'd cringe if he so much as brushed against her.

"Please, Cass. "I'm truly sorry. You have to forgive me. You're so beautiful, I just got carried away."

Cass looked at his stricken expression. "Just take me home, Ramsey," she ordered him.

"Please, give me another chance. Say you forgive me."

Shaking her head, she stared straight ahead.

Ramsey leaned toward her. "Please, Cass. I'm not moving this buggy until you say you'll forgive me, that you'll give me another chance."

Cass glanced sideways at him from the corners of her eyes. She would never forgive him, but now was not the time to enlighten him. "All right, Ramsey. I'll forgive you. Now take me home."

Ramsey heard the insincerity in her voice. He knew she was treating him like a fool. Gritting his teeth, he thought about what he was going to tell his father. Hunt had told him he was a fool to think Cass would fall in love with him. He'd bragged and blustered that he'd have her in his bed in a fortnight. If he went home and confessed that he'd blundered so badly tonight he'd have to listen to one of Hunt's lectures until dawn. No, he would let Cass off the hook for tonight, and himself as well. "Thank you, Cass. I know I don't deserve it. I can only attribute my horrid behavior to your beauty . . . and the moonlight."

Cass glanced up at the night sky. The moonlight was beautiful, but it reminded her once again of Brett. Of his passionate kisses, of his strong but gentle hands, of his broad back, his muscular chest, his straight legs, his . . . She shuddered with the memories and felt her insides heating up to a liquid level. "Just take me home now, Ramsey," she repeated, sighing.

Ramsey nodded and picked up the reins. Tapping the animals' backs, he leaned against the seat as the buggy surged forward, rocking accordingly.

Cass relaxed a little once they were moving again. She continued thinking about Brett and watching Ramsey out of the corner of her eye.

Ramsey did some thinking of his own as he urged the horses toward the Wayne ranch. Cassidy was a very complex woman. He would have bet everything that she'd have moved away or married young after her family was murdered. But no, she'd strapped on guns and hunted down four of the men who'd done the killing. Now she was after the fifth man. "Cass, why can't you leave it be?" he suddenly asked, his voice breaking the silence between them. "You're only going to get killed yourself if you keep up this chase."

"I don't think so. I think I'm going to find out who the last man was. And when I do, I'm going to kill him."

"Or die trying," he said solemnly.

Chapter 10

*I*n the days that followed the fiasco with Ramsey, Cass became restless. She had to prove that Hunt Tylo had something to do with murdering her family, and the only way to do that was to give him a good enough reason to expose himself. She'd finally come up with plan, and she was saddling her horse, preparing to set it in motion, when she heard her name being called.

"Brett . . ." She turned, feeling the jolt of awareness his voice caused. "What brings you out this way?" she asked, noting the appreciative glint in his eyes as his gaze roamed over her body.

"I just thought I'd ride out and say hello, and maybe get myself invited to another one of Soony's delicious dinners," he said, grinning at her.

"Well . . ." She hesitated, knowing what his reaction to her plan would be.

"If it's a bad time . . ."

"No, of course not. It's just that I'm leaving for a while. You're welcome to stay and visit with Uncle Darby if you'd like," she offered.

Something in her tone put Brett on edge. "Where are you going?"

"Ah, just out for a ride."

"Where?"

"Just out," she answered, lowering her gaze.

"You're headed to the Lazy T, aren't you? Are you crazy?" he said, without giving her a chance to explain.

"Why the hell did you have to show up now?" she demanded.

"I'd say it's a good thing I did. You're not doing it, Cass."

"Doing what?"

"Whatever it is you're thinking of doing. Just get the idea out of your head. You can't shoot Hunt Tylo just because you suspect him of a crime."

Cass started laughing. "You actually think I'd just ride over there and shoot him?"

"If you're not planning on shooting him, what are you going there for—to see Ramsey?" he asked, his eyes narrowing at the idea.

"I'm going to the Lazy T to discuss something with Hunt, not Ramsey, though I can't see why it should make any difference to you whether I see Ramsey or not. The only reason I went out with him was to get information from him about his father."

"Humph," Brett grumbled. He knew what motivated Cass's pretended interest in Ramsey, but knowing didn't help. He still felt a terrific pang of jealousy every time the man's name was mentioned, and each time the possibility of Cass seeing him arose. "You may only have the murder investigation in mind, but Ramsey's got *you* in his mind. If you're not careful you'll bite off more than you can chew with him," he warned.

Cass glowered at him. If he knew how close he was to the truth he'd throw a bloody fit, but she would never give him an opportunity to say "I told you so." "To hell with you, Brett Ryder," she taunted, turning her back on him once more. She swung up into her saddle. "You can stay here and visit with Uncle Darby and Soony while I'm gone. I'll tell you all about my visit with Tylo when I get back."

"You won't have to. I'm going with you," he stated.

"You are not," she said.

Brett spurred his horse toward the Lazy T. Ignoring her protest completely, he glanced back over his shoulder at her. "Are you coming or not?"

"Damned stubborn man," she grumbled.

"I heard that," he called back to her.

Cass's eyes widened. There was no way he could have heard her. He was just goading her. "If you heard that, you'll hear this: you're a giant pain in the ass," she said in the same quiet grumbled tone. Brett never turned around. She stuck her tongue out at his back, then felt foolish for behaving so childishly. This man had the ability to completely discombobulate her emotions. "Damn," she whispered.

Ramsey was nowhere to be seen when they arrived at the Lazy T. Hunt, however, was sitting on a corral fence, watching some of his hands working a little mare. "Keep her going, boys. She's looking good," he instructed as he stepped down from the fence. Walking toward them, he smiled. "Cass, Marshal, it's good to see you again. Cass, if you've come to see Ramsey, I'm sorry to say he's in town."

"I didn't come here to see Ramsey. I came to speak to you about something. May we get down?"

"Certainly. What do you want to talk to me about?"

"Business," she told him as she dismounted. Brett followed suit.

Tylo raised his eyebrows. "What business do we have in common?"

Cass led her horse along behind her as she followed him toward the house. "The same business you had with my father."

"And what would that be?"

"I'm home to stay now, and I've decided to increase the size of my herd. I've come to tell you to stop running your cattle across my land to get to the Losee."

140

Tylo frowned threateningly. "You're father and I worked all this out between us years ago," he said.

"My father is no longer the owner of the Wayne ranch. I am. And I've made my decision. I want you to keep your cattle on your own land, Mr. Tylo, and I'm taking measures to see that it's done."

"Are you threatening me, girl?" Tylo asked, an evil glint sparkling in his eyes.

"Not at all," she said calmly. "I'm merely explaining our new arrangement. I'm putting up barbed wire at the end of this month."

"You can't do that."

"Yes, I can, Mr. Tylo, and I'm going to."

"You're starting something here, girl," Tylo said in a menacing tone.

Brett stepped forward. "I certainly hope you're not threatening her, Mr. Tylo."

Tylo scowled at the marshal. "Your badge doesn't intimidate me, so back off. Cass is asking for trouble, Marshal. I don't think she understands what she's doing."

"I know exactly what I'm doing."

"I'm not the only person who uses your land for easy access to the Losee. Do you think the other ranchers are just going to sit back and let you wire your land?"

"There's nothing they can do about it. It's my decision."

"And it's a bad one," he said.

Cass stood still for a moment. She had nothing more to say to Tylo. She'd set her plan in motion with the same ammunition her father had used. The difference between her father and her was that she knew she was starting a war; he'd never even known one was coming. "Good day, Mr. Tylo," she said, turning to mount her horse.

Brett shook his head as he swung up into the saddle. She'd definitely started trouble here. The smoldering look of hatred on Tylo's face was unmistakable.

After they'd ridden through the Lazy T gate, Cass began to chuckle.

"I don't see what's so funny," remarked Brett.

"The look on Tylo's face," she replied.

"The man would like to see you dead," he said.

"Exactly."

"Why did you do it, Cass?"

"You know why. I had to do something that would cause him to be careless. If he's angry, he might make a mistake. Then I'll have him."

Brett rubbed his face in frustration. "The man has—how many?—thirty or forty hands working for him? I'm sure within that number there are quite a few who'd have no qualms about hurting you if he asked them to."

"So?"

"So your family was murdered in a morning raid by a group of men who showed no mercy.".

"Yes," she murmured

"I read the reports, Cass. Your brothers were shot from behind. They left your little sister to die in a burning house."

"What's your point?" she demanded.

"The point is this. The men you killed, you faced down in gunfights. They were fair fights, Cass. The trouble you started today isn't going to come in the form of a gunman knocking on your door and announcing it's time for a confrontation. This kind of trouble comes without warning, and it doesn't play fair."

"Maybe not, but I'll be ready for it," she told him.

Brett shook his head again. "You're kidding yourself, Cass."

The sight of a rider coming toward them ended their conversation. Brett grimaced when they recognized Ramsey.

"Hello, Ramsey," Cass said as he approached, trying not to let any of the revulsion she felt show on her face. She didn't want Brett to suspect that anything untoward had happened between them.

"Hello, Cass. I've been meaning to call on you. I've just been very busy helping my father."

"Ramsey," said Brett, nodding at the man he so disliked. Ramsey glanced at the marshal. "Hello, Marshal," he replied stiffly, then turned to Cass again. "You're more beautiful every time I see you, Cass."

"Thank you, Ramsey," she answered, feeling a shiver run up her spine at the leering glint in his eye.

"What are you doing out this way? Were you perhaps coming to see me?" he asked.

"No. I needed to see your father," she told him. "I had something to tell him."

"Nothing about me, I hope," he said a little sheepishly, cocking his head boyishly.

Cass remembered his behavior in the buggy and swallowed hard. His slightly teasing demeanor showed how easily he'd turned a disgusting episode into something much less in his own mind. "No, nothing about you. I had to let him know that I'll be stringing barbed wire at the end of the month."

Ramsey's attitude changed immediately. "Barbed wire?"

"Yes. I'm going into town now to order it. It takes several weeks for shipments from back east to get here, so I figure by the end of the month I should be able to start putting it up."

"Why would you want to do such a thing, Cass?" he asked.

"It's my right. It's my land, and I want to protect it."

"From what?" he asked, his eyes narrowing.

"The lady doesn't have to explain herself to you, Tylo," Brett cut in.

"I wasn't talking to you, Marshal," Ramsey angrily returned.

"Ramsey, please," Cass interjected. "Brett, I don't mind telling him, or anyone else for that matter, why I'm stringing the wire. I've decided to take ranching seriously. I'm increasing the size of my herd, and I think the best way to protect my investment is with the wire."

"You're asking for trouble with such a fool move, Cass," Ramsey informed her, his voice a menacing monotone.

"From you, Ramsey?" she asked, her eyes meeting his in a challenge.

"No, of course not from me," he assured her unconvincingly. "But from the other ranchers in the area. If one rancher closes off a part of the range, others might want to follow suit."

"That'd be their business," Cass told him.

"An open range keeps everything even, Cass. Not everyone has easy access to water, as you do. Not everyone has access to good bottom grass. If you do this you'll be starting more trouble than it'll be worth in the long run."

"I'll be ready for it," she answered.

Ramsey sat very still for a moment. "I hope so," he finally told her quietly as his pale eyes did a battle with hers.

"We'd better be going, Cass," Brett said to break the tension.

Cass tore her gaze from Ramsey's. Something deep within their blue depths had made her uneasy. "Yes, I've got to get to town and order the wire," she said. "I'm sure we'll be seeing you around, Ramsey."

"Of course you will, my dear. I was hoping to call on you very soon."

"Oh, well ... ah, yes ..." she fumbled, uncertain why he would continue to pursue her when he was so angry about the wire.

Ramsey tipped his hat to her and rode away. He seethed inwardly, his fingers tightening on the reins, his jaw clenched almost painfully. He needed to discuss this new turn of events with his father. Instead of things getting better with Cass, they were definitely getting worse. He spurred his horse cruelly, urging the poor animal to a faster gait. He had to get home to see what damage had been done by Cass's visit. He'd lied to Hunt about the Fourth of July date. He'd implied that Cass was nearly ready to fall into bed with him. Now, with Cass showing up with that damned marshal at her side, announcing she was closing off the range, Hunt would know he'd exaggerated his progress with her. Ramsey thought about his father's anger.

"Well?" Cass asked as she rode alongside Brett.

"Well, what?"

"You're dying to say something. So go ahead."

Brett looked at her sideways. She sat her horse straight, her head high. The reins hung loose in her hands. Her twin Colts were snugly strapped to her thighs. Her shining chestnut hair hung down her back in a soft curl, the blue of her eyes rivaled that of the summer sky, and her full, pouty lips caused his heart to skip a beat. He wanted to say something all right. He wanted to tell her to give up her quest for revenge, but he knew she'd only argue with him about it, and in the end she would do exactly as she chose, despite anything he said.

"Come on, Brett. I can tell you're about to explode," she prodded.

Grimacing, he spoke. "Will what I say make any difference to you?"

"Depends on what you say. If you tell me you think stringing barbed wire is a good way to flush out Tylo, then I'll agree with you. If you tell me not to do it ... I'll do it anyway," she answered honestly.

Brett sighed. "Just as I thought."

Cass smiled. "I know what I'm doing, Brett."

"I don't think you do. Tylo made a good point back there, Cass."

"You mean Ramsey?"

"No, his father, although Ramsey echoed the statement. You're so certain that Tylo had something to do with the murders, but what about the other ranchers who use your land to get to the Losee? It might have been one of them who did it. You really haven't narrowed the field at all with this action."

Cass smiled again. "Brett, I thought about that. First of all, my father never planned to put up wire; he only told Tylo to keep his huge herds off our land. The small herds from our other neighbors never ate away enough grass or did enough damage to warrant refusing them access."

"But that's going to change now with the wire."

"No, it won't. I plan to put in several gates around the

place, just none on the Lazy T side. I'm going to tell the small ranchers they can still run through if they want to."

"Tylo will hear about it. He'll know you've singled him out, and he'll take it personally."

"Exactly," she said triumphantly.

Riding into town with the marshal, Cass was surprised to see a huge campaign sign sporting the words "Jaybird Johnson for Sheriff" and the slogan, "A man of the people."

"What's going on here?" she asked.

"The town's holding an election to fill Jackson's place as sheriff," Brett explained.

"But Jaybird Johnson? He's a meddlesome bully," she exclaimed.

Brett shrugged his shoulders. "It's not my problem. I don't live here."

Cass narrowed her eyes as she looked at him. His dark hair curled softly over his collar, the slightest brush of a beard showed on his strong jaw, though she knew he must have shaved that morning. The color of his eyes was barely discernible beneath the shadow of his hat, but she knew their steely silver glint better than her own. He'd been in town only a short time, and yet she'd grown so used to the idea of him being around that she'd forgotten he'd be leaving soon. "Yes, you'll be heading back east, won't you?" she asked.

Brett met her gaze. "Probably," he answered. "It depends on you," he said softly.

Cass flushed a deep crimson when she remembered he was waiting to see whether or not she was pregnant. She realized she should know in a matter of days. "It won't be long," she told him shyly.

Brett studied her hard. "Just let me know," he said.

Cass cast her gaze downward. She wasn't pregnant, was she? She didn't feel any different. The odds were against it. And yet there was the possibility. Swallowing, she looked back up to see Brett still watching her. "You'll be the first to know," she practically whispered.

Sighing, Brett forced himself to look at something other than Cass's beautiful face and form. "Look, there's another sign," he said, changing the subject.

Looking for it, Cass was grateful for the respite. "Conroy? The barber?" She giggled.

"He's not exactly what you'd call forceful," Brett commented, smiling.

"I'd say not. I wonder what makes him think he could do a good job as sheriff."

"I'd guess the guaranteed salary," Brett said with a sardonic twist to his lips.

"You're probably right," she agreed. "And Jaybird wants the job so he can bully people legally."

"That'd be my guess."

"Are they the only candidates?" she asked, looking around for more signs.

"So far, though I've heard the undertaker is thinking about running."

"Old Mr. Smithers? He must be seventy-five," she said, her eyes open wide with surprise.

Brett shrugged. "Some people think being a lawman sounds easy."

"Humph," Cass snorted. "The only man in this whole town who's qualified is you."

Brett raised an eyebrow. "Is that an invitation to run?"

Cass looked at him once more. "I was only thinking out loud," she explained. "But you know, it wouldn't be a bad idea," she added after a moment. "You'd have to quit your job as a marshal, though."

Brett had already been thinking about running for the office. He just hadn't put it into words yet, and now Cass had done it for him. It had occurred to him lately that he was getting tired of all the traveling he'd been doing in the last few years. Maybe he was ready to settle down. "Yes, I'd have to do that," he commented.

"Would you want to?" Cass asked, suddenly apprehensive about his answer.

"I'm not sure. I'll have to think about it." He wondered

what she was thinking. If she was pregnant, he'd want to do the honorable thing and marry her. It would make things a lot easier if he held the job of sheriff. "Would you want me to stay in Twisted Creek?" he asked.

Cass looked down. Was he asking her for some kind of commitment? She couldn't give him any. She wasn't sure how she felt about him. He was stunningly attractive, and she was still in shock that she'd made love to him. It was true that he could set her on fire with a single touch, but did that mean she was in love with him? She didn't think so, and besides, she couldn't let herself love anyone until she finished what she'd started. "You have to make your own decisions, Brett," she finally said.

Brett felt deflated. She hadn't said what he'd hoped she'd say. "You're right. I'll have to think about it a while longer," he said.

"When are the elections?"

"The end of next month."

"You still have time, then, to throw your hat in the ring." He nodded.

"You'd win, you know," she remarked.

"So far, Jaybird is the favorite."

"That pompous ass? You'd beat him with one fist tied behind your back."

"It's not a brawl, Cass." He smiled at her. "But thanks for the vote of confidence."

"You're welcome." Pulling her horse to a stop in front of the general store, she dismounted. "You don't have to come in with me if you don't want to. I know you're against this."

Brett swung down out of the saddle. "No, I think I should stick close to you while you do this crazy thing. Just in case there's trouble."

"Suit yourself." She flipped the reins over the hitching post and stepped up on the sidewalk. The store looked busy today. Several ladies were buying fabric. One or two women were picking over the produce, and one was trying on a pair of shoes. Two old gentlemen smoked their pipes and played checkers on top of an empty pickle barrel, and three young men were ogling a new rifle in the display case. Cass took a deep breath and walked in through the open doors.

"Hello, Cassidy, I'll be with you in just a minute," called the storekeeper, Jasper Martin.

Cass heard his voice but had to look around for a minute to find him sitting on the floor behind a stack of shoe boxes in front of the woman trying to make up her mind. "That's all right, Mr. Martin. I'm in no hurry," she called back.

Brett noticed that the women buying fabric began to whisper when they heard Cass's voice. The three young men also took notice of her, their voices, too, becoming muffled. He took a step closer to her.

Cass looked up at Brett. "Trying to shield me from gossip, Brett?" she asked, a tender smile lighting up her features.

"I just—"

"It's okay. I'm fairly used to it."

"I didn't notice it on the Fourth."

"I wasn't wearing trousers and guns that day."

"That does seem to have an effect on people."

"That it does." She then noticed a catalog behind the counter. "Mr. Martin, may I look at your catalog?" she called to the storekeeper.

"Certainly, Cass. Help yourself," he replied.

Cass bent over and pulled the heavy catalog from behind the counter. Laying it on the countertop, she started turning pages, looking for the barbed wire.

"Look in the farming section," Brett suggested.

"I'm getting there," Cass observed.

Several pages later, she was looking at plows. "You know, if I put part of my land into wheat I might make a good profit."

"You might," Brett agreed.

"Oh, well, I don't have time for that now." Turning a few more pages, she finally found the section on fencing. There she found the barbed wire. "I didn't know there was more than one kind," she remarked.

"What can I do for you, Cassidy?" Jasper Martin asked her, stepping behind the counter.

"I'd like to order some barbed wire, Mr. Martin."

Jasper looked suspiciously at her.

Brett noticed that all conversation in the store stopped completely.

"You having trouble keeping your cows out of a garden or something?" he ventured.

"No, sir. I'm going to fence my entire property. You can put in the order for me, can't you?"

"I can." Martin looked around the store at his other customers. They were all waiting to hear what he was going to say. "Are you sure you want to do this, Cassidy?"

"Yes. I've thought about it for quite a while. It's the only way I'll accomplish what I've set out to do," she answered.

Brett's eyes narrowed at her explanation. She was being vague in her truth-telling. "I've discussed it with her, Mr. Martin. There's no talking her out of it," he said.

One old gentleman left his checker game and crossed the room. "You'd better talk her out of it, Marshal. I know folks around here who'd kill for less."

"Someone already did." Cass's voice cut coldly through the room.

The old man turned to face her directly. "Yes, they did. But from what I've heard, you're no better than them murderers."

"I only made them pay for killing my family."

"Killing is killing. It ain't right for no reason."

" 'An eye for an eye,' " quoted Cass.

"And 'Vengeance is mine, sayeth the Lord,' " the man responded. "You can quote Scripture to me all day and it won't change the facts. You're a killer, Cassidy. Where you go, trouble follows. And this thing with the barbed wire will start trouble, as sure as I'm standing here."

Cass stared into the rheumy eyes of the old man. "I'm not closing my land to everyone. I'm going to talk to my neighbors. They'll understand."

"You're a fool if you believe that," he said as he turned away from her. Walking back to his seat next to the barrel, he sat down, apparently through talking.

Cass sighed and turned to face the storekeeper once more. "Will you help me figure out how much wire I'll need?" she asked.

Martin just nodded and reached for some paper and a pencil.

Brett watched for the next fifteen minutes as Martin and Cass bent their heads over their figures.

"That should about do it, Cassidy," Martin pronounced.

"Great. Do I pay for it now?" she asked. "I can go to the bank."

"Yes. I'll need the money to place the order."

"When will the order go in?"

"I'll send it out in tomorrow's mail," he answered.

"All right. You write it up, and I'll go get the money." Cass turned and started for the door. "You coming?" she said to Brett as she passed.

"I guess so," Brett answered, shaking his head in frustration.

"Are you really sure you have to do this?" Brett asked one more time.

"I'm sure, Brett," she said adamantly, frowning at him over her shoulder.

Brett watched her withdraw the necessary money from the bank, then followed her back to the store. When they got there they saw that a small crowd had formed.

"What's the meaning of this, Cass?" Seth Baker, one of Cass's neighbors asked. Several others joined in with questions.

"Calm down, everyone," Cass told them, raising her hands to get them to quiet down. "I'm putting in gates. All you have to do is use them. You can still gain access the Losee over my land."

"Then what's the point, Cass? You just trying to make things more difficult for us?"

"Not at all. I know it'll be a little more inconvenient for you, but trust me, it's something I have to do."

Someone in the crowd spoke up: "I've seen what barbed wire does to cattle. It cuts the hell out of them."

"If any of your cattle are injured by the wire, I'll reimburse you. You see, you have nothing to worry about."

Baker piped up again. "Like hell we don't. My cows don't know how to open gates, and I ain't always around to do it for 'em. And August is just around the corner. It's already hittin' near ninety every day."

"Yeah," the others chimed in.

"Look. I'm sorry if this has come as a shock to you. I've already said I'll make it as easy as I can for you to get across my land, and I've offered to pay for any of your cattle that might be injured. There's nothing more I can do."

"You can change your mind about the wire," Baker told her to a chorus of angry voices.

"I won't do that. I'm putting up the wire, and you'll all just have to learn to live with my conditions," she said, standing her ground.

A few in the crowd took threatening steps forward, but stopped when they saw the look in Brett's eyes as he stood behind her.

"This ain't the last of this," grumbled Baker as he stomped away.

"Yeah, you'll be hearing from us," growled another rancher before leaving with Baker.

A few minutes later the crowd had dispersed. Sighing openly, Brett turned to face Cass.

"You don't have to say it, Brett. I already know what you're thinking." Stepping through the doors into the now empty store, Cass walked up to the counter. "Have you got the order written, Mr. Martin?" she asked.

The man nodded.

"Then let's get this over with." She tossed the money on the counter.

Chapter 11

*M*mmm, this is delicious," Cass crooned over a piece of pecan pie a while later in the hotel restaurant.

"I'm glad you're enjoying it," said Brett.

"I'm glad you suggested it," she answered, smiling up over a bite of pie. "Are you finished already?"

Brett looked down at his empty plate. "Appears so. I don't think my piece was as large as yours."

"Hah. If anything, it was almost twice as big. If I didn't know better, I'd swear Rosie had a crush on you," she teased.

"Rosie didn't cut the pie. The other waitress did," he answered.

"Maybe," Cass mumbled, her mouth full of pie, "but Rosie's been staring at you ever since we came in."

Brett turned slightly in his seat and looked at Rosie standing behind the counter. She was staring at him, just as Cass said she was. Something about her expression disturbed him. It was almost as if she wanted to speak to him, but was afraid to. "Excuse me a minute, will you, Cass? I want to find out what's bothering her."

"Sure. I'll just sit here and stuff my face." She grinned up at him as he left their table and crossed the room.

"Rosie, is something wrong?" Brett asked as he approached the counter.

"No, Marshal, nothing," Rosie answered a bit too quickly.

"Are you sure? You seem uneasy. You know you can talk to me," he offered.

Rosie glanced down at her hands, which were nervously twisting a damp towel. She stopped them. "No, really. I'm fine," she said.

Brett stood there a moment longer. Rosie's complexion was sallow and her eyes were dark-rimmed, as though she hadn't been sleeping. He decided to try another angle. "Is it a female thing, Rosie? I could send Cass over to talk to you if—"

"No! I don't want her." Rosie lowered her eyes. "I mean, I don't want to talk to anybody about my troubles."

At least she admitted she had trouble, he thought. "Cass is a good person, Rosie. You should give her a chance," he said.

"She killed all those men," she said, glancing apprehensively in Cass's direction.

"Yes. She did what she felt she had to do. Can you honestly say you wouldn't want to do the same under similar circumstances?"

Rosie met his gaze again. "I suppose I'd be lying if I said I never felt the desire to kill anyone."

Brett's brow knitted in curiosity. He wondered who a usually happy person like Rosie would have wanted to kill. Then the answer struck him. "Ramsey?" he said softly.

Rosie's eyes became wide with fear. "I didn't say that. I didn't say nothin' about Ramsey Tylo. You didn't hear me say that," she gasped.

"All right, Rosie. Calm down. You didn't say anything. I'm sorry I suggested it," he said quickly.

"Don't ever say that again, Marshal Ryder. Don't ever tell anyone I said any such thing."

"All right, Rosie," he assured. "I promise. I won't ever mention it again."

Rosie let out a sigh of relief. "I gotta go now. I've got work to do,"' she said, laying the towel on the counter. Picking up the coffee pot, she went to refill her customers' cups.

Brett leaned against the counter and watched her go. It took him a second to realize she was limping slightly. Walking back to where Cass was scraping the last crumbs from her plate, he sat down. "You've known Rosie for a long time, haven't you?" he asked.

"Yes. I've known her most of my life," she answered.

"Does she have a limp?"

"Not that I'm aware of," she answered, swiveling in her seat to look in Rosie's direction. "She *is* limping, Brett. Did you ask her why?"

Brett shook his head. "I didn't notice it until we were through talking."

"Maybe she fell," Cass surmised.

"Maybe," Brett answered.

"Did she tell you why she was staring at you? Did she confess that she's madly in love with you?" she teased.

Brett gave her a half grin. "I told you on the Fourth that I thought there was something wrong with her. I think she's in some kind of serious trouble, and I think it has something to do with Ramsey."

Cass thought for a moment. "He did say they'd spent time together," she offered.

"Did he say anything more than that?"

"No. I was surprised, though," she remarked.

"Why?"

"Well, this may sound a bit snobbish, but Rosie just isn't Ramsey's type."

"And you are?" Brett asked.

"I knew you'd take me wrong. To be. honest, I'm still baffled as to why he wants to spend time with me," she confessed.

"Really, Cass," he said sarcastically, rolling his eyes for emphasis.

Cass frowned at him. "Ramsey never knew I existed when we were growing up. He's only just noticed me since he came back home. And as far as Rosie's concerned"—she paused here, remembering the taunts—"he was cruel to her, Brett."

"Cruel?"

"He teased her unmercifully. And not just the usual kind of teasing children do to one another."

"Like what?"

Cass thought for a moment. "Rosie was the first girl in our school to develop. All the boys noticed, of course, but Ramsey used to chase her home. He'd corner her, then grab her breasts and yell to everyone that she felt just like his old milk cow. It was really horrible," she recalled.

"He never did things like that to you."

"As I said, he never noticed I was alive. Something I was grateful for at the time," she said.

"Really?" he teased.

"Ramsey was the son of the wealthiest man in town. A lot of the girls had secret crushes on him. But not Rosie. I'm sure she hated him."

"Maybe that's what she meant," he said, thinking out loud.

"By what?"

"She said she'd wanted to kill someone."

"And you think she meant Ramsey?"

"Maybe."

"But that was years ago, Brett. We've all grown up."

"Then why is Rosie still so afraid of Ramsey?"

Cass looked down at her empty plate for a moment. Shrugging, she glanced back up. "I don't know."

Two days later Cass woke up to discover she wasn't pregnant. A great sigh of relief escaped her as she dressed. Now she had to tell Brett. But if she told him, would he leave? Biting the inside of her lower lip, she wondered why the thought of him leaving gave her such an empty feeling.

"Missy Cass," Soony called down the hall.

"Yes, Soony, what is it?"

"Your uncle wants you to come quick," he said.

Cass opened her door. "Where is he?"

"Outside, missy."

Cass ran through the house and raced outside, fearing that Darby was ill or injured. "What is it, Uncle Darby?" she asked when she reached him. He was standing by the barn.

Darby looked sadly up at her. "I have to show you," he murmured.

Cass followed her uncle behind the barn. The stoop to his shoulders and his slow gait told her something was terribly wrong. It wasn't until they climbed the hill and looked down to the little valley below that she knew what was troubling him so. Someone had desecrated her family's graves. "No!" she shouted in anger as she ran toward the tiny cemetery.

The gravestones had been ripped from the ground and dragged by horses some distance from the graves. Then the same horses had trampled the mounds, destroying the grass and flowers that had grown there. "The bastards!" she swore, running to where the gravestones were strewn haphazardly across the ground. When she reached them, her anger grew even hotter. Across her mother's stone someone had scrawled the word "slut" with a piece of charcoal apparently taken from the burned-out house.

Falling to her knees in front of the stone, she began to rub out the offensive word. "I'll get them, Mama. I'll get them for doing this. Those bastards are going to pay for this," she promised.

She then found her father's headstone. It was lying face down, the inscription hidden beneath it. Struggling with all her might, she turned it over. There was a message scribbled there, too: "You started this." Letting her head fall back, she screamed to the sky, "And I'll finish it, too!"

Two hours later she replaced the last of the gravestones, that of her little sister, and smoothed over the mounds as best she could. Kneeling on the ground, looking over the grave sites, she burned with a renewed hatred. "Tylo has to be stopped," she said.

Standing up, she brushed the dirt from her trousers and turned back toward the house. It took her only seconds to strap on her guns, then mere minutes to saddle her horse. As she rode out, she could hear her uncle calling after her, but she didn't stop. She was headed to the Lazy T.

As she rode, Brett's words of warning rang in her ears, but she pushed them back, refusing to listen to his logic. She knew Tylo was responsible for last night's destruction, just as she knew he was responsible for murdering her family.

When she rode into Lazy T property she was met by several riders.

"You got business here, gal?" one man asked her.

"I want to talk to Hunt Tylo," she stated flatly.

"Say, ain't you that little gal Ramsey's taken up with?" He turned to his cronies and laughed, continuing before she could confirm or deny his statement. "Yeah, this is Cassidy Wayne, our neighbor, boys. Ooooh, don't we feel honored you've come to call," he said snidely.

His tone informed her she probably wasn't welcome on the Lazy T after telling them their cattle could no longer use her land, but it didn't matter. She wouldn't be welcome after she talked to Tylo, anyway. "So where's Tylo?" she asked.

"He's up at the house. But I don't know if he wants to see you. You better wait here while one of us goes back and asks him. The rest of us will keep you company." He turned to an underling. "Go on up to the house, Squirt. Tell the boss Cassidy Wayne wants to talk to him."

"Aw, Jake, do I have to?" Squirt bellyached.

"Don't give me no lip, boy. Do as you're told."

"Yes, by all means do as you're told, Squirt," Cass taunted.

Squirt glared at her, but he turned and rode toward the house.

"Now what should we do with you while we wait?" the leader asked innocently.

Cass stared at the dirty man. He was thin, with a scraggly beard and bad teeth. "I think we'll just sit here and wait," she told him in a monotone.

"I don't know. Maybe we could think of something else to do?"

Cass pulled one gun with lightning speed and shot a hole through the middle of the letter *a* in the Lazy T sign hanging over the gate. "I think we'll sit here and wait," she repeated.

The men's eyes were wider after her demonstration. They'd all heard about her. They'd heard she was fast. But their male egos had refused to let them believe she hadn't been lucky. Now they shut up their blustering and waited quietly until Squirt returned.

"The boss says let her come," called Squirt, riding hard to rejoin them at the gate.

Cass aimed her gun at them. "After you, gentlemen," she ordered.

Following them to the house, she fought the urge to shoot them out of their saddles. They might have been the ones who had desecrated her mother's gravestone and trampled the graves. They might have written the message letting her know the war had started. But she couldn't shoot them in the back even if they were the ones. And she wasn't sure yet that they'd had anything to do with it. "Damn," she muttered.

"Why do I have the honor of your presence, Cassidy?" asked Hunt Tylo as he sat behind his big desk smoking a cigar. His tone was sarcastic, his expression rude, his eyes filled with evil intent.

"There was some trouble out at my place last night," she told him.

"Really? What kind of trouble?"

Cass glowered at him. She could tell he was well aware of what had happened at her place. "You don't know?" she challenged.

"How would I know, Cassidy? Are you insinuating I had a part in whatever it was?" he drawled.

"I'm more than insinuating, Tylo. I'm saying it to your face. You did it yourself, or you had some of your boys do it. Either way, my family's graves were desecrated during the night."

Hunt flicked the ash from the end of his cigar into a huge copper ashtray and leaned forward. "I don't take kindly to people coming on my land and accusing me of doing things I don't know anything about," he said in a menacing tone.

"You told me there'd be trouble if I fenced my place. You know I ordered the barbed wire. The trouble began last night."

"The whole town knows you ordered the wire, Cassidy. And I never threatened you. I just gave you a friendly warning. There are a lot of folks around here who don't take kindly to the idea of barbed wire. It could have been any one of them who was at your place last night. But it wasn't me."

Cass took a step toward the desk, a menacing scowl darkening her features.

"Are you going to shoot me here in my own study, Cassidy?" he asked mockingly.

"I'd like to, Tylo. I'd like to."

"Talk is cheap, Cassidy. So until you can prove I'm guilty of anything, or you're ready to pull the trigger on one of those Colts, get the hell off my land," he ordered.

Cass scowled and stood her ground. She wanted so badly to rid the world of Hunt Tylo. She knew in her gut he was the man she'd been seeking for so long. "I'll be waiting for your next move, Tylo." She ground the words out between clenched teeth.

Hunt laughed at her. "You do that, Cassidy. And we'll see who loses more sleep, me or you."

Cass turned on her heel and stormed from the room. As she flung open the front door, she ran headlong into Ramsey.

"Cass? What is it? What's wrong?" he asked when he saw her expression.

Cass looked up into his thin face, his pale blue eyes. She shook her head. "Go ask your father," she said, stomping away from him.

"My father? What's my father got to do with anything?" he questioned, alarms going off in his head. He followed her down the porch steps and stood by as she swung up into the saddle.

Cass looked down on him from her vantage point high atop her horse. The sun glinted off Ramsey's blond hair. His complexion had tanned some since he'd arrived home, giving him a healthier look than he'd had when he arrived, but she still found him wholly unappealing. "Just go talk to your father. I'm sure he'll enjoy filling you in."

"But, Cass, you're so angry. You're not angry with me, are you?" He let himself hope.

She couldn't respond. She couldn't give him any encouragement. Right now all she felt was frustration and hatred. She finally spat out a reply: "We'll talk later, Ramsey." Then she glanced up at the house. "Maybe," she added. Tugging on the reins, she turned her horse around. "Good-bye, Ramsey," she said. Spurring her mount, she took one last look over her shoulder as she headed toward town, and Brett. She had to tell him what had happened. As she rode away, she could hear Ramsey bellowing for his father, demanding to know what he'd done.

Shaking her head, she almost felt sorry for him. Almost.

Brett had just come out of the hotel where he'd been told Sharky had never shown up again, when he saw Cass riding into town. Tugging his hat farther down over his eyes, he walked out to meet her. She was just tying her horse when he approached her. "Cass?" he said with a smile.

Cass whirled to face him, her torment showing clearly on her face.

"What's wrong? What's happened? Is it Darby? Soony?" he demanded instantly.

"No. Let's go inside," she said, walking toward the door of the sheriff's office.

Once inside, she slammed herself down into the chair in front of the desk, then restlessly stood back up.

"Cass, what's wrong?" Brett asked again.

"It's Tylo," she stated. "He's started the war."

"What did he do?" Brett's gut clenched tightly as he waited to hear the worst.

"He desecrated my family's graves. He pulled out the headstones and trampled the mounds."

"You saw him do this?"

"Of course not. If I had, he'd be dead."

"If you didn't see who did it, how do you know it was Tylo?"

"I just know."

"You can't accuse a man without proof."

"That's pretty much what he said, but I didn't believe him."

"You confronted him already?" Brett demanded.

"Yes." Cass raised her chin defiantly.

"At the Lazy T?"

"Yes."

"You are crazy," Brett accused. "Do you know you might have been killed? Jesus, Cass, would you think before you go running off like that?" he scolded.

"Well, I wasn't killed, and I'm not going to be, so you can stop your worrying."

Brett sighed an exasperated breath. "What did Tylo say when you accused him?" he finally asked.

"He denied it, of course. He said a lot of people are angry over the barbed wire, and any one of them could have done it."

"He's right," stated Brett.

"Like hell, he's right. He did it, Brett. I know he did. I could tell by the way he looked at me when I accused him of it."

"You *think* he did it. You don't know it for sure. And

until you get some solid evidence against him, there's nothing I can do about it."

"Damn you, Brett. Whose side are you on, anyway," she demanded.

"I'm on yours, only you're too pigheaded to see it."

Cass turned her back on him and stomped to the window. Staring out into the street, she saw nothing. She was remembering. Remembering just enough to keep her tormented, but not enough to solve the mystery. Rubbing her temples, she felt Brett walk up behind her.

"Cass, I know how hard this is for you. But you have to trust me. So far, the men you've killed have deserved it, and you've committed no crimes. But if you go out to the Lazy T without proof of Hunt Tylo's involvement in any of this, and you end up shooting him, I'll have to arrest you. Do you understand?"

She nodded, her back still turned on him.

"I'd fight to the death to protect you, but I don't think the good people of Twisted Creek would wait for the circuit judge to convict you. Have you ever seen a lynch mob, Cass? Have you ever seen a man hanged?" he asked.

She shook her head.

"I'd prefer a bullet to a rope any day."

Cass turned slowly to face him. "I know Hunt Tylo did it," she said softly, letting her eyes stare up into his. "And I know this is only the beginning."

Brett thought for a moment. As he stared down into Cass's blue eyes, his heart contracted with emotion. He wanted to protect her. He wanted to take care of her. Suddenly he knew he would feel this way for the rest of his life. Catching his breath as his heart seemed to stop, he realized he'd fallen hopelessly in love with Cassidy Wayne, the Lady of the Gun.

Cass saw a change in Brett's eyes. Somehow they delved deeper into her own. They caressed hers with a gentle emotion that touched her soul. Reaching up with one hand, she touched him on the shoulder. Rising onto her toes, she leaned forward to kiss him tenderly.

Brett saw stars explode behind his eyes as he closed them to receive Cass's kiss. The merest brush of her lips sent him reeling and caused his passion to rise to a heated pitch. Opening his mouth, he deepened the kiss that had started out gentle, touching her lips with his tongue, then probing deeper when she opened to him.

Cass felt the desire within her flame to life. Brett's taste and smell filled her senses. His touch drove her mad with the urgent need for more. But not now, she thought, not with things the way they were in her life. She pulled away gently.

Brett opened his eyes and gazed down at her curiously.

"I can't. Things are too mixed up right now," she whispered.

He smiled. "That's okay, I understand." He leaned forward and placed his arms around her, pulling her into a protective bear hug.

Cass felt no threats in his embrace. She let her head fall to his chest, listening to his strong heartbeat. He was solid and real. He made her feel safe, and she found herself hoping he would stay in Twisted Creek. Then she remembered why he was staying. She had to tell him she wasn't pregnant. "Brett?"

"Yes?"

"Brett, I'm not . . ." She stopped.

"Not what?"

If she told him, would he pack up and leave? Not until the new sheriff was elected, probably, but shortly thereafter. Taking a deep breath, she knew she had to be fair to him. Leaning away from him a bit, she said, "Brett, I'm not pregnant."

Brett stood stock-still. He knew he should feel relieved, but he didn't. Looking down at her beautiful face, he realized that he'd been hoping she'd tell him otherwise. "Oh," he murmured.

"Aren't you happy about it?" she asked quietly.

"Sure," he answered. Releasing her from his arms, he stepped back a few feet and leaned on the back of the chair. He studied her features—her eyes, her nose, her skin, her

164

mouth. He loved every one. He loved almost everything about her, everything except her need to exact revenge for the murder of her family. But even that couldn't change the fact that he'd fallen in love with her. If she'd been pregnant she would have been tied to him forever. Now he had to find another way to stay close to her. "I've decided to run for sheriff," he said suddenly.

Cass blinked at his rapid change of subject. "You have?"

"Yes. This town needs a good sheriff, and I need a place to settle down," he sounded convincing, even to himself.

"Good. I'm glad," she responded, smiling.

"Are you?"

"Yes. You'll make a great sheriff."

"Is that all?"

Cass lowered her eyes. She knew she had feelings for him. She just couldn't define them yet. Her life was much too complicated. "No. That's not all." She looked up at him once more. "You're my friend, Brett. I don't have many. I'm glad you're staying."

He grinned sardonically. Leave it to me to fall in love with a woman who considers me a *friend,* he thought. Then a little voice inside his head reminded him that she might talk like a friend, but she kissed like a lover. His grin turned into a wide smile. "Yes, I'm your friend, Cass," he told her, then started for the back of the sheriff's office. "Come help me pack," he said.

"You're packing? But you just said you were staying in Twisted Creek." She followed him down the hall to his room.

"I am." He began pulling his things from the armoire and rolling them up to put in his saddlebags.

"Then where are you going?" Cass asked from the doorway.

"To your place," he said over his shoulder.

Cass was stumped. "My place?"

"As you said, I'm your friend. Well, friends stick together in a crisis. You can't watch your place night and day, and that's what's going to have to be done from now on if we're ever going to catch whoever's responsible for the trouble."

"We?"

"We."

Cass grinned and entered the room. Walking up behind him, she threw her arms around his middle. "Thank you," she said as she squeezed hard.

Brett turned in her arms. "You're welcome, but wait to really thank me until after we catch the bad guys, okay?" he said in a seductive tone.

Cass felt him heating up in her arms. "This isn't going to work if you react like this every time I touch you," she said.

"Are you planning on touching me often?"

"I don't know. Sometimes I just can't help myself."

"Like now?"

"Yes. Like now. But the hug is over. You can let me go now." She pushed against his arm.

"I suppose I'll have to." He looked down at the bed.

Cass could read his mind. She pushed her way out of his grasp. "You finish packing. I'll wait outside."

"All right," he gave in. "I'll only be a minute."

Cass left him in the bedroom and headed outside through the office. She sat down on the wooden step of the sidewalk. Smiling to herself, she thought about the teasing side to Brett's personality.

"Penny for your thoughts."

The voice startled her out of her reverie. "Ramsey?" she acknowledged, surprised. Rising immediately, she looked up at him. "What are you doing here?" she blurted.

"What do you mean? Is there some reason I shouldn't be in town?" he asked. He'd had a violent argument with his father, and the anger still burned in his chest.

"No, of course not. I just meant . . . I'm . . . I'm surprised you still want to talk to me after . . ."

Ramsey gazed down at her. "I discussed the situation with my father, as you suggested. He told me about your false accusations. Cass, I told you before that I understand why you feel you must point the finger at someone. I am, of course, saddened that the person you've chosen to accuse is my father, but that shouldn't come between us. I know my father is innocent, and one day you'll know it too. In the meantime I'm attracted to you, and I'd still like to call on you, if you'll let me."

Cass felt that something was terribly wrong with his words. He seemed sincere enough, but she couldn't help but think that if someone had accused a member of her family of murder, she'd be spitting fire and ready to knock his block off. She certainly wouldn't want to spend time with him. She didn't answer.

"Please don't say no, Cass," he asked.

She watched the emotions that crossed his face. She'd led him on by going out with him once, and whether or not her motives were reasonable, she shouldn't have done it. She wasn't attracted to him in the least. Continuing to let him hope would be cruel. "I don't think—"

"Please, Cass?" he tried again. "I have to admit, I have some plans for us," he said hurriedly.

Brett stepped out of the office at that moment, slamming the door behind him. "Ramsey, what do you want?" he demanded. "Are you bothering Cass?"

Ramsey's eyes narrowed in anger. "What goes on between Cass and me is no one's business, least of all yours."

"Is that right, Cass?" Brett asked.

"No . . ." she began.

"Cass?" Ramsey turned to her.

Cass let out an exasperated breath. "Ramsey, I think you've misunderstood—"

"But, Cass—"

"You heard her, Ramsey. Now back off," ordered Brett.

Ramsey glared at the marshal with enough hatred to fill hell. "Who do you think you are, telling me to back off? You've got no claim on Cass." He sneered at Brett, then turned to Cass. "Or does he?"

Cass couldn't admit out loud that there was anything between her and Brett. "Things are very complicated right now. Brett is going to be staying out at my place for a while, just until things settle down a bit," she explained.

Brett frowned at her explanation.

"He's staying in your home?" Ramsey questioned, obviously surprised.

"Yes, just until—"

"And where will he be sleeping?" he demanded. A split second later a powerful fist crashed into Ramsey's face, and the world disappeared.

Chapter 12

"*B*rett! Oh, my God! What have you done?" Cass demanded, instantly kneeling beside Ramsey, who lay flat on his back on the sidewalk.

"Did you hear what that bastard implied?" Brett bellowed. "I ought to punch him again!" He doubled up his fist.

"You'll do no such thing." Leaning over Ramsey's bleeding face, she saw his eyes flutter open. "Good God, Brett, I think you broke his nose," she told him, grimacing at the sight.

Ramsey felt as if he'd just been kicked by a mule. His head felt as if it might explode, and his nose—oh, Lord, his nose throbbed so badly he could barely stand it. Raising his hand to feel it, he was swept by a wave of acute nausea when he found the crushed mass that was once his nose. "Ohhh," he moaned, rolling onto his side to retch.

Cass helped him turn over, then held his head while he vomited. "Brett, the least you could do would be to go inside and get some towels and the washbasin."

"The least I could do is nothing," he returned.

Cass glared at him with such a vengeance that her eyes

snapped with angry fire. "Get me some towels," she demanded. "And do it fast."

Brett turned on his heel and stomped back into the sheriff's office. That bastard had received exactly what he'd deserved. Why couldn't Cass see that and leave him to take care of himself? Grabbing a towel and the washbasin, he went back out and set them roughly on the sidewalk beside her. Water sloshed over the side, wetting Cass's trouser leg and causing her to give him another scathing look.

Ramsey moaned again. Things were becoming clearer now that his stomach was empty. Someone had hit him. He opened his eyes and looked around. He was surprised to see Cass sitting next to him, helping him. Looking up, he saw Brett. It was Brett who had broken his nose. "You son of a bitch," he groaned. "I'll get you for this, Marshal. If it's the last thing I do in this town, I'll get you for this."

Brett looked down on him with disdain. "Don't make threats you can't carry out, Tylo."

"Oh, I can carry this one out. And by the time I'm through with you, you'll wish you'd never been born."

Brett scoffed. "You're too late. I have days like that already." He turned to Cass then. "Are you ready to go?"

"I have to stay here and help Ramsey," she said, dipping the towel in the basin. She couldn't leave him lying in the street despite her own distaste for him.

"Fine. I'll be in the office when you're finished with him," Brett told her, turning his back on both of them. Closing the door behind him once inside, he sat down on the edge of the desk. Crossing his arms over his chest, he fumed. Why was Cass so angry with him? He'd only given Ramsey what he deserved. Shaking his head, he pondered the female mind. "I'll never understand it," he said out loud.

"Ramsey, can you stand up?" Cass asked when Brett was inside.

Ramsey still felt as if he'd been kicked by a mule, but he nodded, the motion sending another torturous spasm of pain shooting through his face. With Cass's help, he pushed himself to his knees. Then, using her for support, he managed to stand.

"Can you walk?" she asked.

Breathing through his mouth, he answered, "I think so."

Cass pulled his arm over her shoulder and started them on their way to the doctor.

Ramsey felt as though the whole world were spinning around him. His legs felt wobbly, making his steps uncertain, and he relied on Cass's strength to pull them along. After what seemed like an eternity, they were climbing the steps to the doctor's office.

"Doc?" Cass called as they entered the tiny waiting room of the town's only doctor.

"Yes?" a voice called from the back of the building. "Is someone here?"

"Doc, it's me, Cassidy Wayne," she called.

The doctor, a tiny, balding man with thick spectacles, came through a curtain-covered doorway. "Cass, are you injured?" he was saying. "Oh, my, it's seems not. But someone is." He hurried to help. "Bring him in here," he directed, leading them through the curtain to an examination room.

Cass helped Ramsey get up on the table, then stepped out of the way. "I think his nose is broken," she offered.

The doctor looked over his spectacles at Ramsey. "I'd say you've made an accurate diagnosis. How many men jumped you?" he asked Ramsey.

Ramsey just glared at him.

"Brett Ryder, the marshal, did it," Cass explained.

"One punch?" the doctor asked.

Cass nodded.

"My, my. He does seem to pack a good one," he said. Turning toward Cass, he stepped closer. "I think you might want to leave while I set his nose, Cassidy. It won't be a pretty sight." He glanced back over his shoulder at Ramsey. "And he might do a little yelling. That can embarrass a young man."

"Oh. All right. I'll wait outside."

"Cass," Ramsey said, his voice thick with pain and anger, "you go on home now. I'll be fine."

Cass stepped around the doctor and went to Ramsey's side. "Are you sure? I'll wait outside if you want me to."

"No. You don't have to wait." He lowered his eyes. "The marshal is waiting for you," he said accusingly.

Cass felt a small stab of guilt at hearing the jealousy in his voice. She'd really started trouble by accepting that one date with Ramsey. And right now, with his face so swollen and his nose broken, she felt truly sorry for him, even though his own stupid remark had caused the punch. "Brett's coming out to the ranch because of what happened last night. He's worried there'll be more trouble and that I won't be able to handle it alone," she told him, feeling compelled to explain.

"My father told me someone desecrated your family cemetery, but you and your uncle weren't harmed. Perhaps the trouble is over," he mumbled through swollen lips.

"I don't think it is. The intruder left me a message, Ramsey. Last night was only the beginning. Having Brett on the place will give me another gun. I can't turn that down."

"I see," he said, frowning angrily through his pain.

Cass shivered at the painful grimace covering Ramsey's face. "You let the doctor do what he has to do. I'll see you later," she told him.

Cass turned toward the doctor. "Okay, Doc, he's all yours." She raised one hand in farewell to Ramsey as she left.

Ramsey watched Cass leave and felt the urgent need to follow her. Glancing up at the doctor approaching him with the wooden sticks he would use to straighten his nose, Ramsey knew it would be a while before he'd be up to courting her again. Filled with intense hatred, he thought about the marshal staying out at the ranch with her. The marshal wanted Cass too, that was obvious, but how did Cass feel about the marshal? It would be too bad for her if she fell in love with the wrong man.

Back at the sheriff's office, Brett paced impatiently, waiting for Cass to return. He'd seen her help Ramsey in the direction of the doctor's office, and was glad he knew what the doc was going to do to him.

Having a broken nose set was wholly unpleasant; he knew that from experience. When he'd had his own broken in a bar fight several years earlier, he'd discovered that having it set was worse than having it broken in the first place. "It couldn't happen to a more deserving person," he said out loud about Ramsey.

Cass stepped up on the sidewalk outside the sheriff's office and yelled, "Let's get going if we're going."

Brett heard her and headed for the door. Swinging it open, he saw she'd left the sidewalk and was mounting her horse.

"I'm not waiting for you," she told him angrily, turning her mount and spurring him to a trot.

Brett hurriedly closed the door and picked up the saddle-bags he'd dropped when he punched Ramsey. He flipped them over the back of the horse, just under the saddle cantle. Mounting quickly, he nudged his horse to follow Cass. "Damned stubborn woman," he said to himself.

Cass barely spoke to Brett during the next few days. When he tried to explain himself, she shunned him. She already knew why he'd punched Ramsey; she just didn't like the fact that he'd taken it upon himself to defend her honor. It wasn't his place.

Uncle Darby, however, had been thrilled to hear that Brett had broken Ramsey's nose, and their friendship seemed to grow even stronger because of that. Each evening they played checkers after dinner. At first Darby offered Brett drinks of whiskey during their games, but Brett always refused. After a few days, the older man stopped offering and slowed his own drinking considerably. Cass noticed this and was at least grateful that Brett's presence seemed to be having a good effect on her uncle.

Soony, too, seemed to have adopted Brett and had begun fixing his favorite dishes, something that irritated Cass, though she was loath to understand just why.

She was standing near the window, having just finished dinner, listening to Darby and Brett set up the checkers when she decided to go for her usual evening walk, something she'd stopped doing lately because of the trouble. "I'll be back in a little while," she announced.

"Ten minutes?" said Brett, which was his way of asking if she was going to the outhouse.

"No. I'm going for a walk."

"I don't think that's a good idea. It's almost dark," Brett told her.

"I don't care," she returned. "I've got to get outside for a while." She rubbed her arms nervously.

Brett could tell she was antsy. "I'll go with you. Can we play checkers later?" he asked Darby.

"Sure, Brett. Don't worry about it at all. We can skip a night. You go take Cass for a walk," he answered.

"I don't need a bodyguard," she protested.

"How about a friend?" Brett asked.

Cass didn't answer. Instead, she opened the door and stepped outside into the early evening air.

Brett walked out behind her, careful to give her enough space as they started toward the barn. He figured she was headed for the cemetery, and decided to wait for her at the top of the hill. She needed the time alone.

Cass crested the hill and gazed down over her valley. It was smaller by far than the Lazy T, but it was more beautiful. The Losee River ran smack through the middle of it, willow, aspen, and some pine marking its path with their foliage. She could see her herd just on the other side of the river, munching on tall grass. There wasn't much to do with the herd during the summer months except watch them fatten up. She'd have to hire a few temporary hands in the fall, but until then she could handle the work. Next year, if her plans for expansion went well, she'd have to hire one or two permanent people.

She'd surprised herself a few days earlier when she realized she liked the idea of expanding her ranch. She'd begun the whole thing as a ruse to coax Tylo into the open, but somewhere along the way she'd become serious about it.

Letting her gaze sweep downward, she looked upon the graves of her family. Starting down the hill, she glanced over her shoulder to see if Brett followed. She was grateful to see he'd thoughtfully stopped at the top. She suddenly felt foolish for being so cross with him the last few days.

"I'll only a be minute," she called to him.

Brett was surprised. It was the first time she'd spoken directly to him in what felt like a very long while, and her tone had softened. The harsh, condemning edge had disappeared from her voice. "I'll be waiting," he replied, his thoughts jumping ahead now that she didn't seem angry with him anymore. His pulse rate increased as he watched the swing of her hips as she continued on down the hill.

Cass knelt beside the graves and talked to her family as though they could answer her. Brett watched this from the hill, and his heart broke for her. She should never have had to go through this, he thought.

After a while, Cass started back up the hill. "Do you want to walk down to the Losee?" she asked.

"It looks pretty far. I don't want to be out too long after dark," he said.

Reaching forward, she took his hand. "Come on. I'll race you. And I'll win," she challenged.

"You want to bet?"

"Certainly. What do you want if I lose?"

"A kiss."

She scrunched up her face. "I should have expected that," she teased. "And what do I get if I win?"

Brett lowered his voice seductively. "Anything you want."

Punching him playfully on the arm, she grinned up at him. "I'm serious. What do I win?"

"A kiss."

"A kiss for winning or losing? Then what's the point?" she asked.

"All right, then. What do you want?" he questioned.

Cass thought about it for a few seconds. "A kiss. *Go!*" she shouted, taking off as fast as she could run.

Brett raced after her. "You cheat!" he yelled after her retreating form. He knew he could catch up with her. This race was really no contest at all. Gaining rapidly, he began to laugh. "Cass, I'm going to win," he told her when he was only a few feet away and closing.

"I don't think so," she said. Just then she took a flying leap, jumping as high and far as she could.

Brett didn't have time to understand what she was doing. It was too late. He'd run headlong into a wash that wasn't visible until he was right on it. Flailing about in the dirt, certain he'd broken vital bones, he heard her laughing as she continued to run. *"You cheat!"* he yelled as loud as he could.

Cass lay in the grass giggling and catching her breath some time later when Brett came limping up to find her. "I won," she stated simply.

"You cheated," Brett said accusingly.

"I never cheat. I simply knew the course. You didn't. That's not my fault."

"Really?" he said sarcastically as he fell to the ground beside her.

"Nope. I'd never accept a challenge to race unless I knew the course. It just makes sense." She began to giggle again. "You should have seen yourself fly into that wash."

"I could have been killed," he said.

"Not likely."

"I could have cracked my head open."

"Hah! Your head's too hard."

Brett closed his eyes. "I still say you cheated."

Cass continued to giggle as they lay there side by side, the soft sounds of the river soothing them.

"When do I have to pay up?" Brett asked her quietly.

"Pay up?" She wouldn't admit she'd been thinking the same thing.

"The kiss?"

"Oh, that. You don't really have to pay up. I guess I did cheat a little."

"Nonsense. I always pay my debts." Rolling over, he poised himself above her. "Cass, open your eyes," he instructed.

Cass's heart leaped at the sound of his words. Opening her eyes, she saw his dark gray ones watching her. "Yes?"

Lowering his head slowly, Brett stared into her eyes. They shimmered like sunlight on the surface of a deep blue lake. When his lips touched hers, she closed them. "Cass, keep your eyes open," he said.

Cass obeyed. She lost herself in his eyes as she savored the sensuous kiss he gave her. Minutes passed slowly, his mouth possessed hers, his tongue darted between her lips, his breath mingled with her own. And then he stopped, lying back on the soft ground next to her once more.

Brett took deep, cleansing breaths as he lay very still. If he kissed her much longer, he'd end up doing much more. And although he could think of nothing he'd rather do, Cass had to want it as badly as he did before he'd go any further. He didn't know what had come over her the first time, but she'd only been able to call him her friend since then. He wanted much more than that.

The warm evening air actually felt cool to Cass's feverish skin. Her temperature had risen several degrees in but a few seconds, and her heart was beating out of control. She didn't know why Brett had stopped kissing her, but she hadn't had enough of him yet. Turning her head to the side, she let her eyes search his body. It was evident that he too wanted more. Rolling toward him, she reached up to touch his face, his whisker stubble feeling rough to her hand. "Brett?" she murmured into his neck as she nuzzled him.

Brett felt a sizzle of excitement course through him as her breath caressed the underside of his jaw. She wanted him, and the knowledge sent a surging rush of blood to his loins. Turning toward her once more, he wound his arm around her back and pulled her to him, molding her curves to the heated length of his body. Parting his lips over hers, he delved deep into the sweet, warm cavern of her mouth.

Cass arched against him, moaning into his kiss, the taste of him sending her over the edge of complete desire. She felt the pressure of his manhood throbbing against her and moved her hips in a rhythmic pattern.

Brett was on fire, burning with a need and a passion that exceeded the first time he'd held her. He was stunned by the level of desire he felt for her. Reaching between them, he began to unbutton her shirt.

Cass raised her hands to assist him, her desire flaming out of control. She needed to feel him next to her naked skin. She needed to feel him inside her once more. She felt the night air touch her flesh when he pulled her shirt open and pushed it off her shoulders. She gasped as he lowered his head and suckled urgently on the hardened bud of her nipple. "Brett, Brett," she moaned.

Teasing Cass's breast with his teeth, he tugged gently, pulling her swollen nipple deep into his mouth, feeling her quiver with emotion—emotion that he too was feeling.

Cass clenched her jaw against the shivers that coursed through her at Brett's touch. Sliding her hands down his chest to his waist, she fumbled as she tired to hurriedly undo his belt. She finally managed to release the buckle and pull the leather strap from its loops. She then unfastened his trousers and pushed them down, urgently needing to touch the heated shaft of his passion.

Brett groaned as Cass's fingers closed over him. He had to hold still, her nipple still pressed against his tongue, as a deep shudder began to course through his body. Rising slightly, he released her breast and pushed her hands from his body. He saw the look of curiosity that crossed her beautiful face and smiled. Unfastening her trousers, he pulled them down over her hips, stopping only to remove her boots before pulling them completely free, baring her long, shapely legs to his sight. He then tugged his own trousers downward, letting Cass see his desire, his need for her projecting upward.

Cass lay dazed by the desire she felt for this man. He was so beautiful, so perfect, so ready to satisfy her. She watched as he finished removing his clothes, then lowered himself to her. The hot tip of his manhood instantly found the moist center of her need and prodded forward, plunging deep within her as she rose up to meet his claiming thrust. Stars began to dance behind her eyes as he moved within her.

"Cass . . . I can't wait . . ." Brett groaned, shocked by the overwhelming battle he was losing with his control. He felt the throbbing spasms of his manhood within the molten confines of her body and shuddered at his release, exploding again and again, spilling his seed to once more nest deeply, safely inside her.

Cass felt as though she were being pierced over and over again by a huge, pulsing bolt of pure lightning. Rising to capture it with her legs, she twisted and turned with the wild storm raging within her. Lights burst in maddening explosions, blinding her to everything but the passion of belonging to Brett, being one with him, riding the maelstrom together. She rose, then descended with him, only to rise again in the molten eruption of their lovemaking. She ceased to feel separate from him, her body becoming part of his, and his a part of hers. The frenzied pounding in her ears became both their hearts beating in perfect unison. Many long minutes passed before she heard their hearts slowing once more.

Brett lay replete over Cass's body, cradling her to him. Her breath fluttered softly against his chest, fanning him with her moist warmth. She was truly an amazing woman, flying with him to an impassioned level of lovemaking he had never known existed until this moment. "Cass," he murmured hoarsely into her hair.

Cass heard her name but could barely remember how to speak. "Hmmm?" she breathed.

"Are you all right?" he asked.

"Mmmm," she replied, smiling. Opening her mouth, she let the tip of her tongue flick over the damp skin of his chest, tasting the saltiness there.

Brett's heart took a startling leap at the unexpected touch of her hot little tongue. "Cass?" Did she want more? he wondered. Surprisingly, his body stirred, nearly ready to make love again. He caressed the smooth curve of her shoulder.

Cass opened her eyes and looked up at the man lying over her. He was so beautiful, so masculine, so desirable, so nice to have around. She closed her eyes again and wondered at her thoughts. She knew she was on dangerous ground thinking about him in this manner. It was nice to have Brett around, and not just for sex, although she doubted she'd ever feel this way with another man, but until she finished what she'd set out to do, she couldn't allow herself the luxury of feeling these emotions for anyone. "I'd say your debt for losing the race is paid in full," she said in a teasing tone.

Brett's heart skipped a single beat at her words. She was going to keep things easy between them. She wasn't yet ready to face the fact that people didn't experience the kind of ecstasy during lovemaking that they did without it meaning much more. He smiled to himself. He was willing to wait. He knew she'd have to face the truth sooner or later. "I'd say the debt is paid," he agreed. "In fact, you owe me change." He grinned at his own wit.

"You think so, do you?" Cass was relieved he hadn't been offended at her lighthearted attitude.

"Yep. I just wonder whether I should go after my change tonight or wait until another time," he commented, trying to sound serious.

"I think you'll have to wait. Right now I'm going to take a swim." Cass tried to sit up. "The water should feel wonderful about now."

Brett pushed himself to his feet. "I agree." Stepping away from her, he walked quickly to the water's edge, being careful where he stepped in the darkness. "I'll race you," he called, then waded quickly out into the river.

Cass giggled. "You win," she announced, standing up. She noticed her body was slightly sore from their lovemaking. Sighing, she let herself enjoy this particular soreness. Walking to the riverbank, she could barely see Brett swimming lazily against the slow current. Wading out to meet him, she lowered herself into the water and closed her eyes as the soft fingers of the river touched her all over. "This feels so good," she murmured.

"I can think of a few things that feel better," he answered suggestively.

"So can I," she replied with a husky laugh. Moving to the water's edge once more, she anchored herself by grabbing the roots of a tree that had grown into the river. Floating, she heard Brett follow her. He too grabbed the roots and floated next to her.

Minutes passed quietly. Brett reveled in the fact that Cass hadn't immediately become defensive after their lovemaking. This quiet, friendly time they were sharing meant she was becoming used to the idea of their being lovers.

Cass sighed deeply. She knew they'd been gone a long time, and that Darby would begin to worry about them if they didn't hurry home. She sat up in the water. "I guess we'd better head back," she said.

"I suppose so," Brett reluctantly agreed. He stood and gave her his hand to help her up. As he led her from the water, he asked, "Any more surprises like the wash on the way home?" he asked.

"None that I'll tell you about," she teased.

"Well, I'm certainly glad to see you two gettin' along again," said Darby as Cass and Brett came into the house laughing.

"Me too," Brett agreed. The look he sent Cass caused her to blush hotly. "Are you ready for that checker game now, Darby?" Brett asked, remembering he'd told the older man they'd play when he got back.

Darby stretched in his chair. "I don't think so. I'm gettin' kind of tired. I think I'll turn in." He stood up and headed for his room. "Good night, you two," he said over his shoulder.

"Good night, Uncle. Sweet dreams," said Cass. Turning to Brett, she crossed her eyes and briefly stuck out her tongue. "What about you?" she then asked, grinning.

Brett grinned back at her. Cass had taken the first watch every night so far because of her insomnia. It had been hard for Brett to sleep on the small daybed with her still awake in the room. "I think I'll stay up and keep you company for a while."

"Okay," she said. "But I'll warn you. I might talk your head off."

Five hours later Cass was finally getting sleepy. Brett had dozed off in the middle of a conversation about cattle, and she'd sat in Darby's chair staring off into space since then. Standing up, she stretched and yawned. It was time to wake Brett for the next watch. As she leaned over him, she thought she heard something outside. "Brett," she whispered urgently, shaking him with one hand. "Wake up."

Brett opened his eyes. "Is it time?" he asked groggily.

"I heard something," she whispered, crossing quickly to where a small candle burned on an end table. Blowing it out, she listened again.

Brett sat bolt upright, suddenly wide awake. "What did you hear?"

"I'm not sure, listen."

Cass walked to the door and peered out. Brett followed her. Together they searched the yard with their eyes. All at once they saw it. A glow from the barn. "Brett?" Cass said as she realized what was happening. Grabbing the doorknob, she jerked it open. "Uncle Darby! Soony!" she yelled to awaken them. Then with Brett by her side, she ran out to face her attackers.

Brett pulled his gun as he ran. He saw Cass draw one of hers. "Stay low, Cass. You don't know if they're still around."

The sound of hoofbeats coming from behind the barn gave credence to his statement. "I'll get the bastards," Cass yelled, heading for the sound.

Brett ran after her. When they rounded the back of the burning structure they saw only the tail end of a black horse running away in the dark. Cass fired off a couple of rounds, but she knew she'd missed. There was no way to hit an invisible moving target. "Damn it," she hissed, holstering her gun.

Darby and Soony ran out then, their nightshirts flying. "Oh, my Lord," shouted Darby.

"Pork Chop! Pork Chop!" Soony screeched, holding his head in his hands.

"Does he mean?" Brett asked.

"Yes, Pork Chop stays in the barn at night. So does Mirabelle, but I'm sure she got out one of the cracks."

Brett put his gun in its holster and ripped off his shirt. Racing to the pump, he doused the shirt with water, then pulled it back on. Putting his head under the pump, he tugged the handle another time and wet his hair. He also splashed water as quickly as he could on his legs.

"What are you going to do?" Cass asked suspiciously.

"I'm going to stop Pork Chop from ending up a fried chicken dinner. You get the horses out of the corral and away from the fire," he told her, running for the barn.

"You can't go in there. That wood's dry. It's going up like a bonfire!" she yelled at his retreating back. "Damn it, Brett. Listen to me!"

It was too late. He'd disappeared inside the inferno.

"Darby, get the horses," she called as she ran to the open door of flame that had engulfed Brett.

Brett could barely see where he was going in the barn, the air was so full of smoke. Pulling the hem of his shirt up over his mouth and nose, he ducked around the burning stalls and beams looking for Pork Chop. The heat was so intense that his shirt was drying fast. His hair already felt as if it was on fire. He knew he'd have to get out soon. Then he saw her perched at the top of a burning ladder. "Damn it, Pork Chop. You couldn't have picked a lower spot?" he said.

Taking a running leap, he jumped higher than the flames on the ladder and climbed quickly to where Pork Chop was sitting. She began to flap wildly when he grabbed her, squawking and pecking his hand. "Cut it out, you stupid bird, or I'll let you cook in here."

Pork Chop didn't cooperate. She fought him as hard as she could as he climbed down partway, then jumped to the ground. Running from the barn as fast as he was able, he gulped in the cool night air and fell to his knees.

"Pork Chop!" Soony wailed, running to take his pet from Brett's hands. "Pork Chop, you're safe." He looked at Brett. "Thank you, Mr. Brett. Thank you. You saved Pork Chop. She'll be very grateful chicken. She'll give you extra eggs in the morning."

Cass fell at Brett's side. "You fool. I can't believe you'd risk your life for a chicken," she yelled at him.

"Pork Chop isn't just a chicken to Soony, Cass," he said, still gulping the fresh air.

The barn roof caved in with an explosive crash, sparks and flames shooting into the night sky, illuminating the yard. Cass jumped at the sound, her anger setting in now that she knew Brett would be safe. Darby had gotten the animals safely out of the corral, but that didn't curtail her rage. Staring at the giant fire destroying her barn, she seethed. "If Tylo thinks he can get away with this, he's crazy," she threatened.

Brett looked her in the eye. "He did get away with it. Or somebody did. We didn't see enough to know who started this fire, Cass."

Cass's eyes blazed hotter than the fire. "That's ridiculous. Somebody has to know about this. Somebody will talk."

"Did anyone talk about the murders of your family? You were the last one to see any of the criminals alive. Could you get even one of them to tell you he'd been hired?"

"No," she mumbled.

"Then whoever did this"—he pointed at the barn—"did get away with it."

Cass sat back in the dirt. She'd been thwarted twice now, first her family's graves, and now the barn. "What's next?" she asked, looking up at Brett.

He shrugged. "I told you it wouldn't be easy."

"I know, but what's next?" she asked again.

"Maybe the house?" he said. "You could change your mind. You could cancel the order for the wire," he suggested.

"And let Tylo think he's won?"

"Maybe you'd be the winner, Cass."

"Tylo would be getting away with murder. I can't let that happen," she said with conviction.

Darby came running over then. He'd tied the animals on the other side of the house. "Thank God it's summer and the barn was empty," he said, panting.

Cass nodded. "I guess there's that to be grateful for," she mumbled.

Brett pushed himself up. "I think I'll head to the pump again. My eyes are burning."

Cass rose to help him. "You go back to bed, Uncle Darby. We'll be inside in just a minute."

"All right, but don't take too long. I'll be worried about you."

Cass nodded. She walked to where Brett had removed his shirt once more and was pumping water awkwardly over his head and upper body. "Let me do that for you," she said, removing his hand from the pump handle.

Brett released his hold and bent over in front of the pump. "That feels good."

"You did a better job when you were in a hurry," she commented.

"I didn't have time to think about it." He straightened and looked at her. "What if it had been the house, Cass? What if Darby or Soony couldn't get out?"

"It wasn't the house."

"It might be next time. What are you going to do then?"

"Kill Tylo."

Brett wiped his face with the damp shirt. "I can't let you do that, Cass," he said.

"I know."

"So what's next?"

"I rebuild," she said. "I've done it before," she reminded him.

"You have enough money to keep doing that?"

"My father left a good chunk of money in the bank when he was killed. It was the money he was going to use to buy a bigger herd. I only used a small part of it to build this house. I've more than made up for that in the interest earned on the balance during the last five years. I did make a dent in it when I ordered the barbed wire, but I've still got plenty. And there's always Uncle Darby's mine," she said in a lighter tone.

"Your uncle's mine?"

"Yes. It's called Darby's Dream, and that's all it's ever really been. Just a dream. Oh, Uncle Darby worked it for years. The claim is at the northernmost tip of our land, just at the base of those mountains," she pointed toward the dark shadows against the horizon in the distance, "and he's even gotten a little gold out of it, but only enough to scrape by."

"A gold mine?"

She nodded. "Uncle Darby's certain that the mother lode is up there, but he's never found it." She sighed. "And his heart's not in it any more. Sometimes I see him staring off toward the mountains and I can tell what he's thinking."

"He wants to go back up there."

"No," she said.

"Why not?"

Cass's eyes saddened. "He was working the mine for us."

Brett looked questioningly at her.

"For our family," she explained. "He wanted to make us all rich, so my father wouldn't have to work so hard ranching. He used to tell us that when he struck it rich he'd send the boys to college and Becky and me to finishing school."

"Becky?"

"My little sister. We used to stay awake some nights, giggling over how wonderful it was going to be when we were rich. After . . . well . . . Uncle Darby changed. He began drinking a lot. There just didn't seem to be any point to mining anymore."

Brett took a step forward and put his arms around her. Every time she talked about her family he was astounded by how much she'd lost. It was a miracle she was sane.

Chapter *13*

*W*hen Cass awoke the next morning she could smell the acrid scent of smoldering wood in the air. "Damn," she breathed. Lying in bed, she thought about what course of action she should take next. Listening to Soony in the kitchen, she remembered Brett's words of the night before. What if fire had been set to the house instead of the barn? What if her uncle or Soony had been injured or killed? Pushing these grim thoughts from her mind, she sat up, swinging her legs over the edge of the bed. "I might as well get up," she said out loud. "I've got a lot to do today."

A few minutes later she entered the living room and saw that everyone was already seated around the table. "Eating without me?" she asked.

Brett turned in his chair and looked at her, his eyes glowing warmly. "Good morning. I told Soony to let you sleep. I figured you needed your rest after last night."

"I'm fine. And I'm starving," she answered him.

"All right. We're having eggs this morning," he said, grinning.

"I said Pork Chop would be grateful," Soony said, beaming.

"You mean?"

"Yep. These are thank-you eggs from Pork Chop," said Brett, shoveling a large spoonful of scrambled eggs from the serving bowl to his plate.

"I don't believe it," murmured Cass, pulling out her chair, her eyes wide with wonder. Sitting down, she filled her plate and then her stomach.

"What are you going to do about the barn?" Darby asked as he sipped from his coffee cup a while later.

"I'll clean up the mess, then build a new one," Cass answered, pushing her now empty plate away from her and reaching for the sugar bowl to sweeten her coffee. "In fact, I think I'll go into town today and order the wood." She looked down at the table. Her expression saddened.

"What is it, Cass?" Brett asked.

"I was just remembering. Right after my family was killed the townspeople helped us build this house," she glanced at her uncle. "Remember, Uncle Darby? Then, a month or two later, they gave us a barn raising, although I have to admit I wasn't much fun to be around back then." She set her cup down and rubbed her eyes with her fingers. "I doubt anyone would give me a barn raising now."

"I don't know, Cass. Sometimes people can surprise you," Brett offered.

Cass let out a short, bitter laugh. "Not in my case." She pushed herself away from the table. "Oh, well," she said with a sigh, "there's no point in worrying about it. I'll hire whatever help I need to put up the barn." She walked to the pegs beside the door and pulled down her gun belts. Buckling them on, and tying their leather straps around her thighs, she looked at Brett. "I'm going to town. Are you going to come with me or stay here?"

"I'm going with you," he answered, rising from the table. "Just give me a minute." He stepped outside and headed for the back of the house.

"Uncle Darby, you and Soony take care while we're gone," she told him as he stood up and stretched.

"I think we'll go with you, if you don't mind," Darby said.

Cass grinned at him. "Of course I don't mind. I'm glad you're coming."

Soony smiled. "I need supplies for the kitchen."

"I'll go hitch up the wagon," she offered, turning toward the door.

"I'll do the dishes," said Soony.

An hour later they were riding into town, Darby and Soony in the wagon, Brett and Cass riding along on horseback.

"Things look pretty quiet here today," observed Cass.

"It's Sunday," remarked Darby. "Folks must still be in church."

Cass's eyes narrowed as she got an idea. "We're going to church," she announced.

"We're what?" asked Darby. "But we haven't gone to church since ... I don't know when."

"We're going this morning," she said firmly.

"What are you up to, Cass?" Brett asked, suspiciously.

"I just feel that I need a little spiritual guidance this morning," she answered.

"Why don't I believe you?" he asked.

Cass shrugged innocently.

Leading the way to the church, she let Darby park the wagon, then dismounted and tied her horse to one of the side rails. She watched as Brett did the same. Moments later she led the way into the church itself, walking up the aisle as far as she could, looking for seats. She heard the murmurs of disapproval as she passed. It was the reaction she expected and, today, wanted. She'd worn her trousers and guns into the church, and she meant business.

Cass sat down in the third pew from the front. Darby and Soony sat next to her on one side, Brett on the other. As she settled herself, she looked at the minister, who was just finishing his sermon. He was watching her, and she could read the displeasure in his eyes at her late arrival. She smiled up at him and winked, causing him to look away.

After she'd lost the minister's attention, she scanned the

front pews, searching for Hunt Tylo's gray head among the other churchgoers. He was sitting in his usual spot, just in front of the pulpit. She was surprised to see Ramsey sitting next to his father. If she remembered correctly, Ramsey had seldom attended church as a young man, She couldn't see his face, and wondered how his nose was doing.

Brett watched Cass's eyes as she sat next to him. He noticed how she searched out Tylo, and anticipated trouble. Nudging her with his elbow, he frowned a warning at her.

Cass smiled innocently at Brett and looked back up at the minister. He'd once again begun to stare crossly at her as he sermonized. She grinned defiantly and waited.

"Let's all rise and sing," Reverend Wallace told the congregation. "Turn in your hymnals to number twenty-seven."

Cass sang loudly, though her voice was less than lovely. She smiled the entire time she sang.

Brett sang along, wondering what she was up to.

The song ended and all sat down. Reverend Wallace gave a closing prayer, then looked directly at Cass. "Before we all leave today, I would like to address the congregation."

Cass raised her chin and met his stare.

"It seems," began Wallace, "that my instructions are being ignored."

Whispers floated through the crowd.

"A while back I had to ask one of you to dress properly when attending my church. That person has disregarded my wishes and shown up today wearing guns. It would seem—"

"Excuse me, Reverend Wallace," Cass interrupted, standing up.

Shocked silence filled the room.

Wallace glared down at her. "Yes, Cassidy?"

"Let's get to the point. I'm the person you are referring to. Everybody knows it, so why try to be subtle?"

"Well . . . Cassidy . . ." stammered the flustered minister.

"I know you don't want me wearing guns into your church, but I want the people of Twisted Creek to be aware of what's going on out at my place." She turned to face the crowd. "Someone did some damage out at my ranch last night." She heard several whispers. "Don't worry," she said rather sarcastically. "As you can see, I'm fine. We're all fine." She gestured with her hand toward Darby, Soony, and Brett. "I know how concerned some of you are about my welfare." She turned her head and looked directly at Hunt Tylo, glancing for just a second at Ramsey's broken face and blackened eyes, then back at his father. "I know who's responsible for the damage, and I wanted to let you all know what's going on, and that I intend to shoot to kill anyone who comes around my place without good cause."

"What about the cattle?" someone asked from the back of the room.

Cass swung her gaze back to the crowd. "I said, without good cause. Anyone tending cattle that have wandered onto my property will be safe." Her eyes scanned the congregation again, then met the minister's. "I won't be back to church until I can come without my guns, and that won't be until this trouble has ended once and for all. Good-bye, Reverend Wallace." She stepped past Brett out into the center aisle. "Let's go," she said, looking back at Darby and Soony, then at Brett. She smiled when they rose to follow her.

Brett admired her back as she led the way out of the church. She hadn't started trouble, as he'd feared she might. She'd just chosen a place where most of the town would be gathered at once to get her point across. She'd done it very well.

"I guess that takes care of that," she announced as she half jumped down the church steps. "Now we'll wait here to see what comments are made as everyone leaves."

In only minutes people began pouring out of the double doors of the church. Several walked to where Darby was sitting on the wagon and expressed their condolences about the trouble. A few even asked if there was anything they could do to help.

Cass waited.

Ramsey exited the church and glared his hatred at Brett. His nose felt as though it was permanently closed, making eating and sleeping almost impossible, and both of his eyes were nearly swollen shut and turning several different and hideous shades of purple, green, and yellow. He vowed for the millionth time since Brett had punched him to make the lawman pay a hundredfold for what he'd done. It galled him now that the man stood so close to Cass. Brett's interference was making it more difficult for him to carry out his plans for her.

"Ramsey, look at you," Cass said with sympathy now that she could get a good look at him.

"I'm fine," he said, stepping closer to her.

"You don't look fine. Does it hurt much?" she asked.

He gave Brett a glowering glance of pure hatred. "Not much." It took the pain away some to think about how he was going to make the marshal suffer. "Not much," he repeated, looking back at Cass. "What happened out at your place, Cass?" he asked.

Glancing around her, she leaned forward and quietly whispered, "Someone burned our barn last night."

"No! Who would do such a thing?"

Cass shrugged. "I'll find out eventually."

"I'm sure you will," he assured her.

"Ramsey, are you ready to go now?" Hunt asked, walking over to join them.

"Yes, Father."

"I heard Darby say your barn was burned, Cassidy. I warned you there might be trouble," Hunt said with no sympathy in his voice.

"Yes, you did," she answered. "Do you think there might be even more?" she asked, false sweetness dripping from her voice.

"Probably."

"Thanks for the warning. Now I'll know to keep watching for you."

Hunt laughed. "You're single-minded. I gotta give you that." He began walking away.

"It's called persistence, Tylo. I always finish what I start," she called after him.

"I've got to go with my father in the buggy, Cass," Ramsey said. "I can't ride a horse yet." He pointed to his nose.

Cass glanced back to Ramsey and nodded.

Ramsey tipped his hat to her, and walked after his father.

"Looks pretty good, if you ask me," said Brett as soon as Ramsey had left. "I should have hit him harder."

"Brett, that's a horrible thing to say," she scolded.

"I'm honest."

"You're despicable," she said.

He only grinned at her intended insult.

"Cass!" Darby called to her excitedly as he approached.

"What is it, Uncle?" she asked, concerned by his agitated state.

"We're having a barn-raising," he said, a giant smile creasing his face.

"We're what?"

"Some of the folks want to give us a barn raising," he repeated.

"They do?" Cass said incredulously.

Brett leaned over to her and whispered in her ear. "It seems you're not so hated as you think."

She turned and gave him a doubting look. "They're doing it for Uncle Darby," she said.

Darby shook his head. "Mrs. Thompson and Mrs. Wettle think it's real sad, what you went through. They said they'll help Soony plan the food. Of course the womenfolk always bring too much food to these things. We'll end up eating leftovers for a month," he said as though he were complaining, but his face was lit up like a Christmas tree.

Cass smiled at her uncle. This was the first time he'd seemed so happy in a long time. "I guess I'd better go order the lumber so we can give the folks a date, eh?"

Darby nodded, dancing from one foot to the other.

Brett was glad the townspeople had decided to help out, even if it was mostly because of Darby. "I'm going to go put my name on the ballot," he said. "I want to live in this town for a long time."

Cass smiled at him, then looked at Soony. "Let's go do our shopping. Uncle, will you be going to the Best Bet?"

she asked, knowing her uncle visited the saloon whenever he came to town.

"No, I'll go with Brett." He turned to look at the marshal. "Is that okay?"

"Sure," Brett said happily.

Cass stood in pleased surprise for a moment. Darby's drinking had slowed so much lately that the bottle she'd purchased the day she met Brett still had two inches of amber liquid in its bottom. "We'll see you in a few minutes, then," she called after them as they left.

Soony took his time with the shopping. He always did. It seemed to give him great pleasure to decide whether he needed one or two pounds of certain things. Cass could never figure out whether or not he really didn't know how much they needed or whether he thought his job became more important if he made it look difficult. She'd told him once to order two pounds of everything and be done with it. He'd rolled his eyes, clucked his tongue, and said one word: "Weevils." Since then she'd let him take his time.

Today, after ordering her lumber, she sat in a corner and chewed on a peppermint stick she'd purchased with a penny. As she sat there thinking, she realized that if it weren't for the cloud of revenge that hung perpetually over her heart, she'd be very happy. The thought struck her like a physical blow. She hadn't thought about happiness, or her right to it, since her family had been killed.

The sound of bootheels on the wooden sidewalk outside caused her to look up from her reverie. It was Brett, coming back after signing up to run for sheriff, and as he entered and spied her in the corner, she realized he was the reason her life had become more pleasant. "Hello," she said softly.

"Hello yourself. You look like the cat who swallowed the canary," he said, his heart taking a sudden lurch at the tone of her voice.

"Do I?" She giggled.

Brett filled with warmth at the sight of Cass's happy smile. He wished she always looked like this, her eyes free of the pall of death forever.

"Where's Uncle Darby?" she asked.

"Did you know Mrs. Wettle is a widow?" Brett asked.

"Yes."

Brett grinned. "She cornered your uncle to discuss the barn raising, but I think she has other things on her mind," he told her, his grin widening.

"But Mrs. Wettle is old enough to be my grandmother!" exclaimed Cass.

"So's your uncle."

Cass snorted her laughter. "Imagine that. Does he seem interested in her?"

"He was standing awfully straight when I left him."

"Good for him," she said.

"That's what I thought," Brett agreed.

"I'm all done now," said Soony, joining them. "Where is Mr. Darby?"

Cass and Brett both started laughing. "He's talking to a friend," Cass informed him after a moment.

Soony nodded, obviously bewildered about why this information was so funny. "Let's go home now," he said.

Cass stood up, popping the last of her peppermint into her mouth. "Home it is," she said.

The ride back to the ranch was merry. Cass teased her uncle unmercifully about Mrs. Wettle, and Darby called Brett a traitor for telling on him.

The evening came with a beautiful sunset. The sky turned to a brilliant orange, then pink, and then in a last defiant show of color, it glowed a deep lavender before giving in to the soft caress of the night. Cass stared at the sky in wonder. Sunset was her favorite time of day.

Brett sat next to her in one of the chairs they'd carried outside to enjoy the sunset and drink their after-dinner coffee. He watched the play of emotions on her face. He saw the contentment there. If only she'd give up her quest for revenge everything could be perfect. Every night could be like this. "Cass?" he said softly.

"Mmmm?" she responded lazily.

"Have you ever thought about what your family would have wanted for you if they'd lived?" he asked carefully.

"Sometimes," she said.

"Well?"

"Mother would have liked to see me get more education. She wanted that for all of us, especially the boys, but for Becky and me, too."

"She must have been a remarkable woman."

Cass turned and gave him a grateful smile. "She was. She had to be. We kids were a handful."

"You were never naughty," he teased.

"Not me," she agreed playfully. "I painted one whole side of our barn pink once," she said. "At least as high up as I could reach."

Brett grinned. "Why on earth would you do such a thing?"

"The boys dared me to. They were always daring me to do one crazy thing or another."

"And your father? What did he want for you?"

"To get married and settle down. To give him twenty grandchildren."

"Twenty?"

"He'd have loved it. He loved kids."

"But you're not married, and you didn't get educated," he said.

Cass stared at the ground. "Things changed. I had something else to do."

"Don't you ever regret it?"

She met his gaze. "What are you getting at?"

"What if you never get the last man, Cass? What then? Will there come a day when you say it's over?"

"I *will* get the last man. That's when it'll be over."

"But—"

"No buts. It'll be over when I get the man with the silver gun." She stood up and walked away. "I'm going to visit my family," she said over her shoulder.

Brett got up and followed her, catching up as they passed the burned barn. "I'll help you get started on cleaning this up in the morning," he said, dropping the subject of her future for the time being.

Cass gave him a sidelong glance. "I don't expect manual labor from you," she said.

"I know, but you need the help, and as long as I'm here I might as well keep myself busy."

"Suit yourself."

Cass knelt beside her mother's grave a short time later. She'd managed to wipe all the charcoal from the headstone, but the flowers and grass were still missing. "I'll make your grave pretty again, Mama," she whispered. Staring at the words on the stone, "Beloved wife and mother," she felt all the tears she'd never cried pressing to get out. She would never let them. She couldn't let herself start.

Seeing Brett on the hill, she gazed at her father's grave. "You'd have liked him, Papa. He's a good man," she said. Letting her head fall forward, she pictured her little sister. "You would have been fifteen this summer, Becky. The age I was when you were murdered." She sighed and glanced once more at Brett, sitting patiently on the hill. "I'll bet you'd have had a crush on him," she said.

She sat for a while longer, remembering and talking; then she said her good-byes and started back up the hill. It was almost completely dark when she reached the top.

"Okay?" Brett asked. He was always surprised to see her come back from the graves dry-eyed.

"Fine," she answered.

The sound of the first shot rang through the air. Brett grabbed Cass and threw her to the ground, covering her body with his own.

"Brett, where did it come from?" she yelled.

Brett raised his head slightly and looked around them. More shots broke the night's silence, and it took him a second to locate their source. It took a few more to discover they weren't the target. "The cattle!" he shouted.

Cass struggled beneath Brett. "Let me up!"

Brett pushed himself up quickly, bringing Cass with him. "They're after the cattle, Cass."

"Let's go," she said, taking off at a dead run toward the Losee.

Brett ran after her, anger welling up in his chest.

"Remember to jump," Cass said as they neared the wash.

Brett flew over it with her this time, nearing the Losee, and ducking under the trees for cover. "Stay down and follow me," he said.

More shots rang out, and Cass could hear the pained bawling of some of her cattle. "The bastards are shooting my cows!" she hissed. "Damn them to hell!"

Crawling on all fours, Brett led the way along the bank of the river toward the sound of the shots. Pulling his gun, he got to a place where he could see the dark shadows of several riders on the opposite bank.

Cass pushed aside some brush and saw the men on horseback. Drawing her gun, she began firing. Her gunshots exploded through the dark. Brett took her cue and pulled the trigger.

"Jesus Christ, I'm hit!" one voice yelped.

"Someone's over in those trees! Hell, I ain't gettin' paid enough to get shot at," another voice said.

Cass continued to shoot until her gun was empty. She then pulled the other.

"Oh, God, I'm bleedin'!" someone else shouted. "Let's get the hell out of here."

"Like hell," another voice ordered. "You all get down and fire back."

"I can't tell where the shots are comin' from," a voice wailed.

"Brett, it's getting too dark to see," Cass whispered.

"Wait until you see the report when they fire. You'll be able to tell where they're at," he told her.

"I don't care what the boss says, I'm gettin' out of here!" someone yelled.

Cass heard hoofbeats retreating in the distance.

"I'm gettin' outta here, too. Hell, I think Charlie's dead!" More hoofbeats retreated.

The zing from a bullet overhead kept Cass and Brett down. Cass pinpointed where it came from and fired again.

"You can stay and get killed if you want to. I'm leavin'!" another voice called.

"Damn you. Damn you all to hell, you cowards."

"We was only hired to shoot some mangy cows. We wasn't hired for no gunfight!" Another rider left.

Cass held her breath. Brett listened intently. Minutes passed before they heard what they thought was the last rider take off.

Cass started to stand up, but Brett pulled her back down. "Me first," he said.

"Don't be ridiculous." She started to stand again, only to feel Brett's strong fingers on her arm.

"Sit your ass down and wait until I say it's safe to get up," he ordered her.

Cass's eyes widened with surprise. "So you can get shot instead of me?" she demanded.

"Exactly." Brett didn't wait to listen to any more of her arguments. Standing slowly, he watched for movement in the dark. After a few minutes, he signaled to Cass to let her know she could move. "Is there any way across this river?" he asked when she stood beside him.

"Yes. There are some large stones farther up river that we used when we were children," she told him.

"Lead the way, but stay low. Someone might still be playing possum over there."

Cass slipped through the trees and brush with Brett right behind her, and soon they were crossing the river. When they reached the other side, Brett took the lead now and then to listen. When they finally reached the site of the shoot-out, they found several of Cass's cows lying dead in the grass. They also found two men. One dead, one moaning from his wounds. The other gunmen had fled.

"Cass, go back to the house and get my horse. We've got to get this man to the doctor. He's gut-shot."

"Ask him who hired him, Brett."

Brett knelt beside the injured man. "Mister, what's your name?"

The man just continued to moan.

Cass fell to her knees next to him. Touching him on the forehead, she leaned over and looked into his eyes. "Who are you? Who hired you to do this?" she demanded.

"Cass, go get my horse," Brett told her again.

"I need to get him to talk, Brett," she answered.

"We will, but we can't ask him anything if he dies on us."

"All right." Cass stood up reluctantly and turned back toward the river. She'd only gone a few feet when Brett called her back.

"What is it?" she said, running the short distance back to where he knelt beside the man.

"Never mind," he said solemnly. "He's dead."

"Damn it," Cass swore. She turned her back on the body and stared up at the newly emerging stars in frustration. "Damn it!" she shouted to the heavens.

"Cass," Brett said softly.

She turned back around.

"Do you recognize either man?"

She walked back to the man who'd just died. Searching his features in the dark, she shook her head. "Not this one I'm sure of it."

"What about the other one?"

She went to his side. A bullet had found the side of his head. She looked at what was left of his face. "No, I've never seen him before, either." Twisting to face Brett once more, she grimaced. "Tylo hired men from out of town to do his dirty work," she said.

"If it was Tylo."

"These sure as hell aren't any of my neighbors, Brett," she fumed. "And my neighbors can't afford to hire guns."

Brett glanced at the bodies. "Maybe you're right," he murmured.

Chapter 14

$\mathcal{A}$ week later Cass stepped out the front door of her house to see the first of the townspeople arriving for the barn raising. She was still astonished that it was happening, but she couldn't have been more pleased, not for herself so much as for her uncle, who'd stopped drinking completely since the preparations began.

"Looks like things are getting started," said Brett behind her.

"Looks like," she answered, glancing over her shoulder at him.

They'd spent a grueling week tearing down what was left of the old barn and dragging away the burned wood. They'd also hit a dead end on trying to identify the members of the raiding party who'd been killed. No one, it seemed, had any idea who the two men were. Hunt Tylo had laughed in their faces when they questioned him about it.

"Soony's been tending the beef all night," Cass remarked, looking to where a whole cow was roasting over an open fire.

"It smells good."

"He told me he uses some kind of secret sauce to season the meat while it cooks," she said.

Brett studied Cass's profile. He was worried about her. She'd worked hard with him on the old barn this past week, she had helped with the preparations for the barn raising, and she'd even called on Mrs. Wettle to let her know that one of the cows killed in the raid would be roasted for the meal, but while she'd done these things she'd seemed a million miles away. And often he'd seen a profound sadness filling her beautiful eyes. Even now, with people arriving and shouting their greetings, she seemed distracted. He longed to get back to where they'd been before the barn had burned. He'd been sure they were close to coming to some kind of terms on how they felt about each other. Now Cass seemed to have distanced herself from him, and during the past week, whenever he'd tried to broach the subject of a relationship, or tried to touch her affectionately, she'd managed to pull away or change the subject. His heart ached with frustration. "Are you all right, Cass?" he asked softly, willing to try again.

"Sure, I'm fine," she answered.

"You've been acting . . . different," he said, placing his hands at the base of her neck.

Shrugging her shoulders, she began to walk away from him. "You're imagining things," she told him.

Brett took one long step and stopped her with a touch on the arm. "I don't think so. Won't you talk to me?"

Cass gazed up into the gray of his eyes. "There's nothing to talk about." She gently pulled her arm away from his fingers. "I'd better go get everyone started," she said, once more walking away from him.

Cass saw the hurt in Brett's eyes before she left him. She felt a pang of guilt over it, but she couldn't yet put what she'd been feeling into words. She was beginning to think she'd never catch Tylo, and this doubt had filled her with a sense of loss. Her sole purpose for existing the last five years had been to exact revenge for the death of her family. If she wasn't able to complete the task, what would she do, just sit on her ranch for the rest of her life and feel that she'd failed them? Brett's entrance into her life didn't change things. She wouldn't let him or anyone else stop her from finishing what she'd started.

Another wagon pulled up and stopped. Cass looked to see who else had arrived to help and was a little surprised to see Rosie among the people climbing down. As she walked away from the wagon, Cass noticed she still limped a little. "Rosie?" she called, walking to meet her.

Rosie looked up nervously at the sound of Cass's voice. "Yes?"

"Thank you for coming today," Cass said, looking closely at the waitress as she neared.

"You're welcome." Rosie lowered her eyes. "I better go help Mrs. Wettle," she said quickly, walking away.

"She's certainly nervous about something," observed Brett as he joined Cass where Rosie had left her.

Cass studied Rosie from behind. "She looks as if she's lost weight, too."

Brett nodded.

"You know, Rosie was always happy when we were growing up," Cass commented. "Except when Ramsey was around, of course."

"Except when Ramsey was around," he repeated.

Cass looked up at him, then back at Rosie. Was Brett right in assuming Ramsey had something to do with Rosie's current state? "I wish she'd talk to me."

"Try."

"She shuns me at every turn."

"Keep trying, Cass. I think Rosie needs a friend right now," he said.

"She's got friends in town. Lot's of them," she said.

"Sometimes it takes a special kind of friend to get to the truth."

She snorted softly. "Special friend?"

"Yes. Someone who won't judge her or make her feel like less of a person if she's done something she's not proud of."

"And you think I'd be that kind of friend?" she asked.

"Who better than you, Cass?"

Cass lowered her eyes remembering the lives she'd taken. "I guess you're right. Who am I to judge anyone, right?"

"That's not what I meant."

Cass looked back up at him, one eyebrow raised in question.

"You understand that sometimes people have to do things they don't want to do. If Rosie's in a situation where she feels helpless, you'd understand that."

Cass shrugged again. "I suppose so." She searched for Rosie in the growing crowd. "I'll try to talk to her again when I get the chance."

"Good. I don't think you'll regret it."

Just then another wagon pulled up to distract them. A young man with brilliant red hair jumped from it as soon as the team came to a stop. He turned and helped Mrs. Thompson to the ground. She proceeded to pinch his cheek affectionately as though he were a child. The young man allowed this, but rolled his eyes at her gesture. They both then turned toward Cass, Mrs. Thompson pulling the man by the arm.

"Cass," she called, "I want you to meet my nephew, Buster," she said before they'd even stopped walking.

Cass smiled and held out her hand. "It's nice to meet you, Buster. This is Marshal Brett Ryder," she offered, turning toward Brett.

Buster took Cass's hand, then the marshal's. "It's good to meet you both. My aunt here's been tellin' me all about you. Sure sorry to hear about your troubles. I'd like to help with the barn, if I could. And if there's anything else needs doing, I'd be happy to pitch in."

Brett and Cass both grinned at Buster's friendly attitude. His smile was infectious, his manner charming.

"Thank you, Buster. We'd appreciate any help with the barn, but we don't expect you do more," said Cass.

Buster grinned widely, his sparkling blue eyes squinting merrily. "Oh, I don't mind helpin' out."

"That's the truth," interjected Mrs. Thompson. "Buster

just arrived yesterday for a visit, and already my windows are all washed, my garden's been weeded, and he started painting the outside of the house. The boy just can't sit still long enough to suit me."

Case laughed. "Are you here for a long visit, Buster?" she asked.

"Well, you know, I've been thinking about stayin' awhile. But I might drive Aunt Selma here crazy if I do." He squeezed his aunt affectionately.

The older woman beamed up at him with pride.

Buster noticed another wagon coming to a stop in the yard. "Looks like those folks need some help unloadin'. Guess I'll go make myself useful. It was a real pleasure to meet you, Cass. Marshal." He tipped his hat and turned toward the new arrivals.

"Whew, that young man's got more energy than I've seen in a while," commented Brett, smiling at Buster's retreating back.

Mrs. Thompson nodded. "He surely has. He's my sister's son, and she's the same way. I don't know where they get their energy. It makes me tired just watching them." She looked after Buster and smiled softly. "It would be nice to have him settle here, though. Mr. Thompson and I were never blessed with children of our own," she added wistfully.

Brett nodded in agreement, then glanced at Cass to see if she'd noticed Mrs. Thompson's sadness at never having had children.

Cass knew what Brett's look meant and glanced away, ignoring him. "I think I'll go see if Soony needs any help. See you later," she said noncommittally to both Mrs. Thompson and Brett. Raising her hand in a light farewell, she headed for the house.

The day passed quickly after that. Cass helped the men with the construction as much as they would let her, and the women as much as she could, her lack of cooking skills keeping her on the sidelines. She ended up being more of a waitress than anything else, serving cool drinks to the men while they worked.

As the sun began to set, the roof was raised and a cheer went up from the crowd. It was time to party. Two guitars, a fiddle, and a squeeze-box magically appeared from under wagon seats, and everyone made ready for some foot-stomping music.

"May I have the first dance?" asked Brett.

Cass looked up, surprised. She'd been helping clear away the enormous dinner mess and was up to her elbows in grease. "I, ah . . ." she stammered. "I haven't danced since I was a child."

"Then you'd better make up for lost time," he told her, staring playfully down into her eyes.

"Go on, Cassidy," said Mrs. Thompson from the other side of the table. "Let us old married ladies take care of this mess. You go on and have some fun now before some other girl comes along and tries to snatch up this handsome young man."

Cass looked wide-eyed with surprise at the older woman. "Yes, ma'am," she said. After she'd wiped the grease from her arms and hands with a wet towel, she let Brett lead her toward the new barn, where the dancing had begun.

Brett took Cass into his arms and began to move with the music. He gazed down into the blue of her eyes and felt his heart pounding fiercely within his chest. "Cass, you're the most beautiful woman here," he whispered.

Cass flushed at his words. "I doubt that," she demurred.

"You are," he assured her. "And I'm the lucky man you're dancing with."

"I don't see too many others standing in line, Brett," she said.

"That's because they know they don't stand a chance with you as long as I'm around," he teased warmly.

"Is that so?"

"That's so." He whirled her around in a dizzying circle and felt her begin to laugh. His own laughter mingled with hers as the music ended.

"I need a drink," Cass said breathlessly.

"I'll get you something," Brett offered. "Wait here for me and we'll dance the next one."

"All right," she answered, smiling. As she watched him head toward the tables near the house, she remembered what it felt like to make love to him, and her pulse took a sudden wild leap.

"Cass? May I have the next dance?"

Cass jumped at the voice behind her. "Ramsey? What are you doing here?" she blurted.

Ramsey frowned. "Cass, I was hoping you'd be happy to see me," he pouted.

"I'm sorry," she said. "It's just that . . . Well, you weren't here all day. I didn't expect you to show up now."

"I know, and I'm sorry. I should have come and helped with the barn, but I still find myself a little incapacitated."

Cass looked at his nose. "The swelling around your eyes is about gone, and you're not quite so black-and-blue," she commented. The thinness of his face seemed to exaggerate the bruises left behind by Brett's punch, but she didn't have the heart to be cruel to him. She still felt a little guilty for having let him think she was interested in him.

Ramsey nodded. "I still can't breathe through my nose, though. The doc says it'll be at least another week for that."

He looked so pitiful that she couldn't help but feel sorry for him.

"Cass, please dance with me?"

Cass looked quickly around. Brett hadn't started back with the drinks yet, and the next song had begun. "I guess it wouldn't hurt," she murmured.

"What's that?"

"Nothing," she said. "All right, I'll dance this dance with you."

Ramsey beamed a huge smile, then flinched. "It still hurts to move my face too much," he quickly explained when he saw her curiosity. Taking her in his arms, he began to lead her gracefully around the wooden floor of the barn. She followed him easily, the music flowing through her as she moved, and his heart filled with excitement at her nearness. Pulling her closer to him, he relished the feel of her breasts against him.

"Ramsey, please," she urged, stepping back from him slightly. The feel of him so near reminded her of his advances in the buggy and caused a shiver of revulsion to course through her.

"I'm sorry," he said sheepishly. "But you can't blame me. You're so beautiful."

"Thank you," she acknowledged his compliment stiffly. Just then she saw Brett at the edge of the dance floor staring blackly at her. She averted her gaze quickly, not wanting to duel with him now. As she glanced elsewhere, she noticed Rosie sitting on a bench in a shadowed corner. She was staring directly at Ramsey.

"Do you really think I'm beautiful?" she asked.

"Of course. Do you think I'd pay you false compliments?" he asked, feigning hurt.

"I don't know. You didn't know I was alive when we were children."

"You've grown up since then."

She glanced back at Rosie. "We've all grown up, haven't we?"

"Yes, and you've become a very exciting woman."

"Thank you again. What do you think of Rosie?" she asked innocently. "You told me you and she have spent time together. What do you think of her?"

Ramsey studied her for a moment, his jaw tightening. "Why? Has Rosie been talking about me?"

"Not at all. She'll barely speak to me about anything. We're certainly not close enough to discuss men."

"Then why would you ask me about her?"

"I was just remembering how you used to tease her. She was truly afraid of you. I would have never guessed you'd end up friends."

"Yes ... well ... she's a nice enough person," he finally said. "But enough about her. Right now I'd like to get a drink. Care to join me?"

"That won't be necessary, Tylo," Brett's voice broke in. "I have Cass's drink right here." He handed her a glass of punch, then placed his hand possessively at her waist.

Ramsey glared at Brett. He was going to destroy this man. "Very well," he murmured. "I'll get myself a drink." He stared down at Cass. "I'll be back to dance with you again," he informed her.

"She'll be busy," answered Brett.

"I'll let the lady decide," challenged Ramsey.

"Brett, Ramsey, that will be enough," Cass cut in. This verbal parrying over her was tiring, especially when it was so unnecessary. Brett knew the only reason she'd paid attention to Ramsey was to get information about his father. "If you'll both excuse me, I have something to take care of," she announced abruptly. Turning her back on the two men, she left the barn and headed toward the house. Once inside, she went to the kitchen where Soony was preparing a fresh pot of coffee. She set her glass of punch on the counter, and thought about Brett and Ramsey, probably still butting heads. There was no satisfaction in having two men fighting over her so ridiculously.

"You look tired, Missy," Soony observed.

"I am tired, Soony," she sighed. "But I don't think I could sleep. I'm going to take a walk. If anyone comes looking for me, tell them I'm lying down."

"Very good," he told her.

Cass left the house and stayed in the shadows, skirting the party and heading toward the Losee. On her way she noticed her uncle and Mrs. Wettle laughing together at a small table set outside. She smiled at the sight.

She looked for Brett's tall form and saw him standing in the open doorway of the barn. He was watching the house—probably looking for her. She searched the faces of the others, looking for Ramsey. Not finding him, she wondered if he'd left. "Not likely," she said out loud.

As she wandered down to the river, she felt herself begin to unwind. The heat of the day had softened, cooling the night with a light breeze. She could hear the leaves rustling overhead, and the trickling, burbling water soothed her frazzled nerves. Sitting down in the tall, soft grass beside the river, she let herself fall back, cradled by the earth, and gazed up at the stars. Maybe I should sleep out here tonight, she thought, This has to be the most peaceful spot on the earth. Closing her eyes, she let her mind wander back to the days before the massacre of her family, back to a time when she'd spent every day laughing with her brothers and sister. She was soon breathing deeply and evenly, dreaming of happy times.

Brett watched the house and waited. Ramsey had disappeared, and that made him nervous. What if he was with Cass? What if he harmed her in some way? Finally, when he'd worried himself into a frenzy, he went to the house. "Soony, where's Cass?" he asked, entering the kitchen.

"She's sleeping," he answered.

"Sleeping?" Brett asked, disbelieving. "Cass wouldn't go to bed before the party was over," he said.

Soony shrugged. "She said to tell anyone who asked that she'd be sleeping," he repeated.

Brett left the kitchen and stood in the empty living room. Glancing down the hallway, he knew there was only one way to find out. He'd never been in Cass's room, but he needed to find her. If she was in there, and was angry with him for intruding, he'd deal with her anger. And if Ramsey was in there with her ... His fists doubled up at the thought of punching the blond man again. Turning the doorknob, he pushed open the door. "Cass, are you in here?"

Cass had left a lamp burning low on her nightstand. The room was empty. "Where are you?" he whispered. After backing out of the room and down the hallway, he turned and charged through the living room, then headed outside. His heart pounded in his chest as he thought of all sorts of horrible things that could be happening to her at that very moment.

Cass lay sleeping in the grass near the Losee. Her dreams were pleasant, fond memories of childhood pranks and loving afternoons. She could see herself running over their land with her brothers. She could see Becky trying to keep up and failing, and the boys finally picking her up and bringing her along. She could see her parents holding hands, following their children on a sun-soaked afternoon.

Then the sun was suddenly blotted out by an ominous black cloud. "No, not again," Cass murmured in her sleep.

The clouds kept coming. Then she heard the hoofbeats of the horses—dark horses that carried even darker figures. She could hear her mother cry out in anguish as she watched her husband murdered. She could see her brothers, brave and strong, running toward the house to save Becky. She watched as they were riddled with bullets, their beautiful bodies falling awkwardly to the ground. She heard Becky crying in the house, the flames bursting through the windows. Then she saw her mother, her beautiful mother, lying over her husband's body. She saw the men, two of them, standing over her. One seized her mother's arm and pulled her up while she fought and cursed him. Then she heard the bullet, one bullet for her mother.

Cass was gasping for air. She usually woke up here, but this time as she fought to leave this dream place she found she couldn't. Instead, she heard the men. "This one's for the old man," one of them said, his voice grating in her head like the grinding of a millstone. "This one's for the old man . . . for the old man . . . for the old man. . . ."

Cass's eyes flew open as she screamed for him to shut up. *"Nooo!"*

Brett heard Cass scream, and his heart stopped beating. He hadn't found her anywhere at the party and had started looking for her out in the dark. Running toward the sound, he was ready to murder whoever was hurting her. He'd do it with his bare hands. "Cass, where are you!" he shouted.

Cass wasn't sure she was awake yet. Did someone call her? Was her dream another new piece to the puzzle?

"Cass, try to answer me!" Brett called again, running in the direction of her voice.

Cass realized the sound was real. Someone was looking

for her. Sitting up and wiping the perspiration from her neck, she called back, "I'm over here."

Brett nearly choked with relief. He'd managed to get very close to her, and within a few seconds he'd reached her. Kneeling beside her, he reached out to make sure she was all right. "Are you hurt?" He felt her forehead and cheeks and found them damp. "Have you been running from someone?" he demanded. "Tell me who it was and I'll kill him. Was it Ramsey?"

"It wasn't anyone." She sighed. "I wasn't running. I was sleeping . . . and dreaming."

Brett looked at her, confused. "Dreaming?"

"A nightmare. I don't have them as often as I used to. They're always the same."

"About your family?" he asked softly.

She nodded. "This time I remembered more. I remembered something one of them said."

"Will it help you identify the last man?"

She shook her head. "It doesn't make any sense. He said, 'This one's for the old man.' I don't know what he meant. What old man, Brett?" Her frustration put an edge in her voice.

Brett touched her gently on the shoulder. "It probably doesn't matter, Cass. It's just another small clue. Someday you'll remember something that will tie all of the details together. Then everything will make sense."

"I hope so. I'm beginning to think I might never catch Tylo," she confessed.

"I know," he murmured.

Pulling her knees up under her chin, she sat very still. "What will I do if I can't—"

"You'll get on with your life. You'll get married and start having those twenty kids."

She let out a sardonic laugh. "And when those twenty kids ask me what I was like when I was younger, I get to tell them I killed five men . . . so far."

"You don't have to tell them."

"If I don't, somebody else sure will."

"I suppose you're right. It's kind of hard to live down being a legend."

"Lady of the Gun?" She grimaced.

"Exactly."

"I can just hear it now. 'Little Suzy, what did your mama do before she got married?' 'Oh, my mama was a killer. She hunted men down and shot them,'" she said sarcastically. "Or how about this one? 'My mama can beat up your mama.'"

"Cass, don't do this to yourself. You did what you thought you had to do. Your children will understand."

She looked up at his handsome face, and her heart twisted at the sight of him trying to console her. Sighing heavily, she spoke, "I guess I am what I am, and there's nothing I can do about it now. Everyone has to live with the past. Besides, I'm not through yet. One more man still has to pay."

Brett stared down into her eyes. "Unless you stop."

"I can't," she whispered.

"Just for tonight?"

Something inside her rebelled against giving up for even a second, but his expression was so plaintive, so eager for her to give an inch. "All right, for tonight it's forgotten."

Brett lowered his head and brushed his lips tenderly across hers. His heart was so full of emotion. "Cass, love me," he whispered over her lips.

"Brett . . ." She tried to pull away.

"Don't fight me, Cass," he begged. "Don't let anything come between us right now."

Cass remembered their first night of passion. It had been hot and fiery, full of blazing passion, an adventure in desire. Their second time together had been just as hot, but even more urgent. Tonight was different. Tonight he was gentle, tender, loving. Letting him lay her down on the soft grass, she relaxed as he bent over her.

Brett covered Cass with his body, letting the sweet warmth from her body mingle with his. He kissed her again and again, touching her face, her neck, her hair. He wanted to love her gently. To take away the hurtful memories. To replace them with something beautiful. "Cass?" he whispered her name. When she nodded, he sat up and began to remove his clothes.

Cass reached up and unbuttoned her shirt. Her trousers, boots and undergarments all came off in order. She then watched as Brett lowered himself over her once more. He entered her slowly, fully. She felt as though her very soul was being filled, and it was wonderful. It was as though something within her that had never quite formed was now becoming complete. She reached up and pulled his face to hers for another kiss. She kissed him as though she were dying of thirst and his lips possessed the sweet springwater from an early morning rain. Meeting his thrusts with her own urgent writhings, she soon felt herself rising to that explosive peak he'd taught her about the first time. "Brett," she gasped his name. "Brett . . ."

Brett felt her tightening around him. He thrust again and again until he knew he'd given her what she needed. As she shuddered and cried his name, he filled her with his seed, this time praying they'd created a new life.

Afterward Cass lay nude in his arms, contented to stay there, listening to his heartbeat and the night breeze. How could I ever feel any safer than this, she wondered, snuggling closer to him.

Brett felt her stirring against him and pulled her closer to his chest. He loved her so dearly that he wanted never to let go of her. He wanted to build a fortress to keep her in, and to hire a thousand men to protect her. But no, he would never try to lock her up or stifle her. She was a wild thing, fragile in her strength. If he tried to hold her too tight he'd lose her. Sighing against her hair, he breathed almost silently, "I love you."

Cass thought she heard him say something. "What?" she whispered.

"Nothing. I was just thinking out loud," he whispered back.

After a few seconds she tilted her head up to look at him. "Do you think anyone misses us at the party?" she asked.

"I'd completely forgotten about the party," he said.

"Me too," she breathed, then giggled.

"But you've got Soony telling anyone who comes looking that you're sleeping, so I don't think anyone will worry."

"That's true." She cuddled even closer. "You smell good," she said.

"I'm glad you think so," he replied, smiling.

A few seconds passed. "Well?"

"Well what?" he asked.

"Do you like how I smell?"

"I like everything about you," he growled.

"Everything?"

He thought for a moment. "No. I lied."

She pushed herself up. "What don't you like about me?"

"Your singing," he said. "It's absolutely awful."

She began to laugh. "It is, isn't it? I never could carry a tune."

"I could tell in church. The minister probably wouldn't care whether or not you wore your guns into the church if you promised not to sing," he teased.

"Take that back!" she ordered.

"I will not. The poor man is probably worried he'll lose his hearing if he has to listen to you any more."

"Oh!" She reached out and pinched his arm. "Take that, you beast."

Brett laughed at her attack. It was hard to picture this beautiful, teasing creature as a gunfighter. Here, naked in the moonlight, she looked more like a wood nymph giggling under the stars. The chestnut curls that lay over her shoulders, half concealing her breast, glistened in the soft light of the night sky. Her eyes twinkled with mischief, and the lips he so loved to kiss were parted with laughter. Raising one finger, he poked her in the side, testing whether or not she was ticklish, grinning when she squealed. "I've got you now," he threatened wickedly.

"No, Brett. No fair tickling," she warned, trying to scoot away from him.

"You have no chance of escape," he said like an evil villain. Grabbing her around the waist, he wiggled his fingers at her rib cage, sending her into a wild fit of giggles.

"Brett . . . you stop . . . this . . . this instant!" she shrieked between gasping laughter. "I . . . mean . . . it!"

Brett continued to tickle her until she lay in a helpless heap of uncontrollable giggles. When he stopped, he pulled her on top of him. "Gee, I guess you're ticklish," he said calmly.

"I hate you," she said, still gasping for air.

Brett laughed at the lack of conviction in her voice. "You wound me, madam."

"I will wound you," she said, and instantly grabbed a bit of his chest between her teeth.

"Cass, you wouldn't," he said, already knowing it was too late.

Cass bit down on his flesh with just enough pressure to leave a mark.

"Ouch! That's childish," he accused.

"And tickling me for an hour is mature?"

Brett rubbed the spot where she'd bitten him. "Exaggeration is also childish. I only tickled you for a minute."

"When I'm being tickled, a minute feels like an hour."

"I'll remember that next time."

"You're planning a next time?"

"Yes, and next time I'll tickle you for two minutes."

"No . . ."

"Yes, I will. If I'm going to be wounded for doing it, I'm going to make sure it's worth my while."

"Brett Ryder, I warn you, I always give back more than I get."

"I've noticed," he said, his voice once more a sexy growl.

"Mmmm," she purred.

Chapter 15

*W*alking back toward the barn a while later, Cass could see most of the wagons had gone. Only a few stragglers were still standing around exchanging the last stories of the evening. "Looks like it's about over," Cass said, glancing up at Brett as he walked beside her.

"Looks like. And look at your new barn. Pretty nice, if you ask me."

Cass did look at the barn. It was bigger than the one that had burned, and its new wood glistened in the moonlight. "Now all I have to do is paint it."

"How about pink?" he said, reminding her of her childhood prank.

"Not a bad idea," she agreed, grinning.

When they'd just about reached the new structure, Cass turned her head at a sound. "What was that, Brett?" She slowed her walk.

Brett listened. "I don't hear anything."

"Wait a second." She put her hand on his arm and stopped walking. "There. Hear it?"

Brett strained to hear. "I'm not sure. It sounds like a cat meowing. It might be Mirabelle."

"No. Believe me, if Mirabelle were meowing you'd know it. She makes her desires very well known. No, this is . . ." She waited again. "Brett, someone's crying." She started toward the back of the barn. "This way."

Seconds later Cass saw a figure in the dark. Someone was curled up, leaning against the barn. "Who's there?" she said as she approached. Hearing quick sniffling sounds, she knew that the person was trying to quit crying before being discovered. "Who is it?" she asked as she hurried forward. "Rosie?" she ventured, kneeling. "Is that you?"

"Rosie?" Brett echoed, lowering himself to sit beside her.

"I'm fine," Rosie said, wiping her eyes with her sleeve.

"Why are you out here crying? Did someone hurt you?" Brett demanded.

"No. No one hurt me. I'm fine," she said.

"Why are you crying?" asked Cass.

Rosie didn't answer right away. She looked nervously from one face to the other. "I fell," she finally answered.

"You fell?" Brett said in a disbelieving tone.

"Yes. I was walking in the dark and I tripped," she embellished.

"You fell, or you were pushed?" Brett inquired.

"Nobody pushed me. I told you I fell, and I did," she said.

"Are you sure, Rosie?" Cass asked.

Rosie nodded, wiping her eyes again. "I'm clumsy."

"Did Ramsey hurt you, Rosie?" Brett bluntly asked.

"No! I would never say anything bad about Ramsey," she protested, her eyes growing wide in the moonlight.

"Even if he did something bad?" Cass urged gently.

"He didn't. I fell," she said defiantly.

Brett sighed and rubbed his eyes with one hand. "How can we help you if you aren't willing to help yourself?"

Rosie looked down at her hands folded around her knees. "I fell," she whispered.

"All right, you fell," said Cass. "Let's go to the house and see what damage your 'fall' caused."

Rosie let herself be helped up, groaning a little when she put her weight on her right foot.

"Your foot?" Cass asked.

"No, my hip," Rosie answered. "I landed on my hip."

"I'll have a look at it in the house," said Cass. "If it looks serious we'll have Doc examine you in town."

Cass and Brett helped Rosie into the house and to Cass's room. "Leave us alone now, Brett," Cass told him. "I'll let you know," she whispered as he left the room.

Turning to face Rosie, she was astonished at how bad the girl looked. The right side of her face was bruised and swollen, and her eyes were sunken, her skin sallow. "Rosie, what's happened to you?" she asked, a concerned frown creasing her brow.

"I fell," said Rosie, her eyes not meeting Cass's.

"I mean, what's happened to bring you to this?"

Rosie raised her eyes, and a tiny spark of defiance flared for second before it vanished. "I don't know what you mean," she answered.

"Someone hit you, Rosie. He hit you hard enough to knock you down." She stepped closer and brushed a fingertip gently across the bruised cheek, seeing Rosie flinch from even such tender contact. "You don't deserve to be treated this way, Rosie. You deserve so much better than this."

Rosie looked into Cass's eyes. "Why are you being so nice to me?"

"You and I grew up in the same town. We went to the same school. You know me. We used to play together. We were friends. But even if I didn't know you, I'd feel the same way. No woman, no person, deserves to be treated the way someone is treating you."

"But you killed all those men," Rosie said accusingly.

Cass sighed. "The men I killed deserved what they got. They were the men who murdered my family. I've never harmed anyone who was innocent, Rosie. And I would never harm you."

Rosie looked sideways at her. "Are you telling the truth?"

Cass nodded. "I want to help you, Rosie."

"I . . . He . . ."

Cass held her breath waiting, hoping Rosie would say who'd hit her.

"No, I can't," she blurted. "He'd kill me for sure if I told on him."

"But, Rosie—" Cass pleaded.

"No!" Rosie interrupted. "I can't. You don't understand. You're not afraid of anything. He won't hurt you." She began to shake.

"Calm down, Rosie. It's all right. I won't ask you again tonight." She put her arm around Rosie's shoulders. "It's all right," she repeated.

Brett knocked. "Can I come in?" he called through the door.

"Not yet. We'll be out in a minute," Cass replied. She then addressed Rosie. "You'd better lift your skirt so I can look at your hip. Then you can wipe off your face."

Rosie nodded. Turning toward the bed, she leaned on the footboard and began to lift her skirt.

Cass was horrified at the sight of Rosie's legs. They were covered with bruises in every stage of healing, some looking several weeks old, others brand new. But it was her hip that caused Cass to gasp. A huge purple bruise the size of a frying pan was forming over the hip joint. "Oh, my God, Rosie. You'd better let Doc look at this," she advised.

"Do you think so?" Rosie whimpered. "I don't think anything's broken."

"He might suggest a poultice or some medicine for the pain," Cass told her. "Anyway, I'll have Brett hitch up the wagon so we can give you a ride back to town."

"What about the people I came with?"

"I noticed their wagon was gone when we came in the house."

"They left without me?"

"I'm sure they thought you'd gone with someone else. But I'll see to it you make it safely back to town."

Rosie straightened, dropping her skirt. "Thank you," she murmured.

"You're welcome," Cass replied. "Wash your face. I'll be waiting in the living room for you when you're finished."

Rosie nodded.

Cass met Brett in the hallway as she left her room.

"Did she tell you what happened to her?" he questioned hurriedly.

"No. She wouldn't tell me. But someone has beaten her up pretty badly."

"Damn it," hissed Brett.

"I think she wanted to tell me about it, but she's too afraid. She thinks he'll kill her if she tells."

"I tend to agree with her."

"Brett, we've got to do something. You should see her legs. She's getting beaten regularly," she said, her voice full of pity.

"What can we do? I can't arrest the bastard if she won't tell me who he is."

"I know." Cass led the way back into the living room. Sitting down in her uncle's favorite chair, she rested her chin on her hands, leaning forward, her elbows on her knees. "I told her we'd give her a ride into town. Will you please hitch up the wagon?"

"Of course," he said. "Do you think if you tried again . . . ?"

Cass shook her head. "She began shaking when I tried to get her to talk."

Sighing, Brett left the house to take care of the wagon. His gut feeling told him the man was Ramsey, but like Cass in her quest, he had no proof.

Two hours later the doctor finished his examination of Rosie and walked out to question Cass and Brett. "Who did this to her?"

"We don't know. We tried to get her to tell us, but she wouldn't," said Cass.

The doc shook his head in disgust. "Well, whoever he is, he should be horsewhipped."

"I agree, Doctor. If you can get her to tell you who it was, I'll be happy to oblige."

"I'm afraid she's not going to tell anyone anything for a while. I gave her something to help her to sleep. She needs to rest."

"We thought so too," said Cass. "Is there anything else we can do?"

"No. Just leave her here. I'll see she gets home in the morning." He turned to go back to the examination room. "It's too bad she won't tell us who did this to her."

Cass nodded and started to leave with Brett. "Thanks, Doc," she said.

Brett had just stepped outside when Cass heard the doctor call her back. "Wait for me, Brett," she said. "The doctor wants something else."

Brett nodded and took another step out onto the sidewalk. "I'll wait for you in the wagon."

Cass closed the door behind him and turned to face the doctor. "Yes? What is it?" she asked.

"Well, Cassidy, I question the wisdom of what I'm about to do .. but, well, you being Rosie's friend ..."

"Yes, Doc?" Cass asked.

"I really wish you'd try to find out who beat her."

"We've tried. She won't tell."

The doctor rubbed his chin. "You've got to try again," he finally said.

"Why? What aren't you telling me about Rosie?"

"Cassidy, I have to trust your discretion in this." He glanced back to the curtain that hid the door to the examination room where Rosie slept. "I think Rosie's pregnant. I'm not positive. Rosie may not even realize it yet. If she is, she's just in the beginning weeks, but you can understand how dangerous this situation is for her. Another beating and she might lose this child."

Cass stared in wide-eyed surprise at the curtain. Rosie was pregnant? She looked back to meet the doctor's eyes. "I'll do what I can, Doc," she promised.

"And you'll use discretion? Rosie's unmarried...." He left the implication dangling.

"I wouldn't hurt Rosie for the world, Doc. She's my friend," Cass said, and she knew in her heart it was true.

"Thank you, Cassidy. Now I'd better go check on my patient."

Cass nodded and left the office.

"What else did the doc want?" Brett questioned as she climbed up into the wagon beside him.

Cass stared up at Brett. "I have something to tell you, but you have to promise me you'll tell no one else."

Brett gazed down into her serious blue eyes. "You know you can trust me, Cass."

"I know." She let her gaze drop for a moment as she thought about what the doctor had told her. "Rosie might be pregnant," she said softly. "The doctor thinks she may not even realize it herself yet."

"And the father?" Brett said.

"I don't know. If it's the same man who's been beating her, she may not want him to know she's expecting."

"He'll find out sooner or later."

"Everyone will find out sooner or later. Poor Rosie," she whispered.

"What if it's Ramsey?" he commented a few minutes later.

Cass thought about it. "What makes you think it's Ramsey?"

"The way Rosie acts around him. Think about it, Cass."

Cass nodded. "I know. I have been thinking about it. Surely a man who's sleeping with a woman would want to spend time with her," she said, her naïveté showing through, "but I've never seen them together."

"If a man is proud of the woman he's sleeping with, he'll want to spend time with her. But if he thinks of her as a whore, or as someone who's beneath him, he'll avoid being seen with her," Brett explained.

"Rosie's not a whore."

"Of course not, but you told me once that Rosie's not Ramsey's type. Maybe he thinks she's good for only one thing."

"Rosie would refuse him."

"If she had a choice."

"You're not suggesting . . ."

"People get themselves into very complicated situations, Cass."

She opened her mouth to question him.

Brett held up a hand to stop her. "I can't accuse Ramsey of anything yet. I'm just trying to cover all bases. You yourself told me about Ramsey's cruelty to Rosie when they were children. . . ." He left his statement open-ended.

"I understand," Cass said quietly. She couldn't help but remember the way Ramsey had acted with her in the buggy on the Fourth of July. He hadn't raped her, certainly, but he had gotten carried away, and she had felt threatened. Still, rape was a serious charge. "Maybe Rosie has a boyfriend, someone she's been seeing for years. He'd be the prime suspect."

"I intend to ask a few questions around town tomorrow for just that reason. I want to narrow down the suspects."

"And if it turns out to be Ramsey?"

"I'll arrest him, and he'll stand trial."

Cass let her gaze fall. "And the whole town would know what happened to Rosie. She'd want to die from the humiliation."

"What would you have me do?" Brett asked.

Cass knew what she'd do if it were her choice, but she and Brett didn't see things from the same angle. Sighing, she met his silver gaze once more. "I suppose you have to do what you think is best," she replied.

Brett clenched his jaw. He knew exactly what Cass was thinking. He knew that her solution to Rosie's trouble would be to challenge Ramsey, or whoever the culprit turned out to be, to a gunfight. He studied her beautiful face, the sky-blue eyes, the full, pouty lips, the sun-kissed complexion. He loved her so, but would she always think this way? Would her beliefs about justice ever swing his way? "Let's get home now," Brett said, dropping the subject, futility nagging his soul.

Cass read Brett's thoughts as though they were printed across his forehead. He just didn't understand how a woman would feel in Rosie's place. He didn't understand what it was like to be ostracized by the people you grew up with. She did. She wasn't humiliated the way Rosie would be. She was still able to hold her head high, feeling justified in her actions against the murderers, but she knew what it was like to feel like an outcast. Sometimes Brett's kind of justice was the wrong kind. Sometimes her way was the only way. "All right," she finally said, tearing her gaze from Brett's. "Let's go home."

Brett turned the wagon and snapped the reins, starting the horses on their way back to the Wayne ranch.

The sun was a blazing ball of merciless fire early the next morning. Cass glared at Brett over her coffee, but neither spoke a word about Rosie's condition.

"I think I'll go into town today," Cass finally said. "I need to check on some things."

"I'll go with you," said Brett. "I have things to do also. I mentioned it last night, remember? There are a few people I need to talk to."

"Oh, yes," Cass remarked. "Well, I'll be outside when you're ready."

"I'm ready now." Brett stood up from the breakfast table. "That was delicious, Soony. Thank you."

"You're very welcome, Mr. Brett."

"Is there anything you need in town?" Cass asked.

"No."

"Uncle?" Cass asked.

"No, thank you," he replied, yawning. "I don't need a thing. I'm going to just sit here and drink my coffee and wake up."

"All right. Then we'll see you when we get back." Cass turned to follow Brett from the house.

"You're angry with me," he said as soon as they were outside.

Cass looked sideways at him. He couldn't help the way

he felt about things any more than she could, and his sad little boy expression made her smile. "I guess not. I can't seem to stay mad at you for very long."

"Good. Then may I have a good-morning kiss?" he asked leaning toward her.

"No!" she hissed. "Uncle Darby might see us."

"He won't. He's drinking his coffee, remember? Besides, so what if he sees us? Come on. One little kiss?"

By now they were entering the new barn where they'd tossed their saddles the night before. "No."

"But why? It's cool here in the barn. And kind of romantic."

"You think a barn is romantic?" Cass giggled. "You're hopeless."

"You thought a rocky patch of ground was romantic," he said, grinning boyishly.

"You!" She reached out to punch him on the arm.

Brett caught her as she lunged and pulled her to him. "I knew I'd get my kiss," he growled, lowering his lips to hers.

Cass didn't even try to struggle in his arms. She instantly melted against him. "It was my idea all along," she whispered into his kiss.

"You're such a liar," he breathed, relishing this gentle, teasing moment together.

Cass parted her lips for a deeper kiss.

Brett felt himself responding to her kiss in a way that could cause them to forget about going into town. "Cass," he whispered, "we'd better get going."

"What?" Cass was caught up by the wave of desire that rushed through her at Brett's touch.

"I said we'd better get going."

Cass sighed. "Yes, you're right." She straightened, releasing herself from his arms.

"Don't look so sad. We can continue this tonight," he promised. "That is, if I ask you for a good-night kiss," he renewed the teasing.

"If I deign to give you one," Cass responded haughtily. She picked up her saddle and walked outside to her horse.

Brett followed suit. "Does Rosie have any family in town?" he asked on a more serious note.

"She lived with her grandmother when she was growing up. I think her parents died in an epidemic back east somewhere."

"Is her grandmother still alive?"

"I don't know. But if she's not, you can talk to the other waitresses at the hotel. I'm sure one of them would know if Rosie was seeing anyone."

"Planned to," Brett said.

Mounted and riding toward town a short while later, they were surprised to see a rider coming toward them fast.

"Do you know who it is?" asked Brett.

"I can't tell from here."

Brett rested his hand on the butt of his gun as the rider approached.

"It's Buster," Cass said, surprised, as Mrs. Thompson's nephew brought his horse to a skidding stop in front of them. His hat hung loose behind him, his clothes were dusty, and sweat dripped from his skin.

"Buster, what's wrong?" Brett questioned, his nerves instantly on edge.

Buster was gasping for air, out of breath from his wild ride. "I decided to stay on in Twisted Creek," he breathed. "So I need to get a job. A man in town told me to go out to the Lazy T. Said it'd most likely be the best place to start askin' for work." He stopped once more to breathe.

"Yes, Buster?" Brett asked, alarms going off in his head at the mention of the Lazy T.

Buster breathed deeply. "Well, sir, I got lost straightaway. It sure is easy to get turned around out here. It took me a while to get my bearings. Then I figured out where I was, or at least I thought I did, and I headed back to town to start over. That's when I found it."

"Found what?" Brett asked.

"The body. I found a dead body out there. I rode back to town quick as I could. I forgot you were stayin' out at

Miss Wayne's place. When I remembered, I headed straight out to find you."

"Where's the body?" Brett asked with narrowed eyes.

Buster turned in his saddle and pointed. "It's out thataway."

"The Lazy T," breathed Cass.

Brett glanced at her. "Maybe."

Cass responded, "Probably."

"Take me to it," he directed Buster.

"Yes, sir, Marshal."

"Cass, you go on into town. I'll be back as soon as I can."

"Like hell," she fumed. "I'm going with you, and you should know by now you can't stop me."

Brett sighed and shook his head in frustration. Nudging his horse in the direction Buster had pointed, he looked at the young man and said, "Don't ever get mixed up with a stubborn woman."

Cass rolled her eyes and smiled at Buster, causing him to blush.

"The body ain't pretty, miss," he stammered.

"I've seen dead men before," Cass assured him.

"I think this one's been out there awhile."

"I'll manage."

"Don't try to discourage her, Buster," Brett called over his shoulder. "She'll take it as a challenge."

Brett rode on ahead until Buster needed to guide the way. The body was in a deep wash. Brett looked down on it from up above. "Whoever did this wasn't concerned about concealing the body. I guess they figured no one would find it way out here," he speculated.

"We're on Lazy T land," Cass informed him.

"I guess I wasn't so lost as I thought," said Buster.

Brett led the way down the side of the wash and rode to the body. Pulling his kerchief over his mouth and nose to filter the stench of death, he motioned for Cass and Buster to do the same. Then, dismounting, he walked closer. The man had been shot in the head, leaving not much of his face to identify him, but his clothes looked familiar. Prodding the body with the toe of his boot, Brett lifted the edge of the man's coat. A deck of cards fell out of the inside pocket and scattered beside the body. "Sharky?" Brett breathed in horror. "Sharky Draper?"

"You know him?" asked Cass.

"I know him," he replied, clenching his fists in anger.

"I didn't have nothin' to do with it, Marshal. Honest. I just found him," Buster sputtered.

"I know you didn't kill him, Buster," Brett assured him through clenched teeth. He suspected he knew who did this. There was just no way to prove it. "We'll have to send a wagon out here for him. Would you guide the undertaker out here later today?" he asked Buster.

"Sure thing, sir," Buster agreed.

"Good." Swinging back up into his saddle, Brett sat very still on his horse and stared at the body. He had a gut feeling he even knew exactly when Sharky'd been murdered—that night he'd heard the shot on the Lazy T. It had sounded closer, but on a clear night sound could travel for miles. "I'm going to talk to Tylo," he announced.

"I'm go—"

"I know," Brett interrupted. "You're going with me. See, Buster? What did I tell you?"

Buster grinned nervously. "Should I go get the undertaker now, sir?"

Brett nodded and examined Buster from head to toe with one sweeping glance. "I'll see you later in town, all right?"

"Sure thing, sir." With that, Buster turned his horse and hightailed it toward town.

"Let's go," Brett told Cass.

Riding up behind the Tylo house, they were met by six men, guns drawn. "I'm Marshal Brett Ryder, and I've come to ask Tylo a few questions."

"About what?" a belligerent cowboy demanded.

"It's none of your damned business."

"I'm makin' it my business," the cowboy blustered.

"Then I'm making you my business," Brett said, his voice a threatening rasp. "We're going on to the house. If any of you try anything I'm going to shoot you right between the front teeth."

"You talk big, Marshal," the man answered. "But there's six of us."

One of the men began to whisper to one of the others, distracting the man who was doing the talking. "What is it, Lloyd?" he demanded, leaning over to listen. When he sat up straight, his eyes were fixed on Cass. "Cassidy Wayne, is it?"

"That's right," Brett told him.

"That makes a difference. I'm sure Ramsey would want to talk to you."

Brett sent Cass an irritated look.

Nudging her horse forward until she was abreast of him, she leaned closer. "What does that matter, as long as we get to talk to Tylo?" she asked.

"Ramsey's the one I want to talk to," Brett informed her.

"Ramsey? I thought you came here to talk to Hunt."

Brett shook his head, then spurred his horse a bit. Riding to the house, he could feel Cass's eyes on him.

After dismounting, they were led into the house. Ramsey met them in the study. "Cass, what brings you here with the marshal?" he asked.

"She was with me when we were led to Sharky's body," Brett informed him.

Ramsey blinked twice. "Sharky?"

"You know Sharky. The old man who beat you so badly at poker your first day back in Twisted Creek," Brett explained, all the while watching Ramsey's eyes.

"Oh, yes, now I recall. I did play a hand or two that day. But I don't remember the man who beat me."

"Sharky seemed surprised you didn't remember him. He said he'd seen you around since he started coming through town twenty years ago."

"I certainly can't be expected to remember every old poker player who comes through town."

"No. But I think you'd remember this one. He beat you with a royal flush. You seemed quite upset by it."

"I always get a little upset when I lose a hand of poker. Doesn't everyone?" He looked to Cass for confirmation.

Cass was listening to the conversation with interest. Brett hadn't actually accused Ramsey of Sharky's murder, but he was establishing motive.

"You seemed more than a little upset to me, Ramsey," Brett continued.

Ramsey's eyes narrowed. "Well, I certainly didn't kill him over it," he argued.

"Maybe. Maybe not. It does seem to be a very strong coincidence that he was murdered on Lazy T land, though, don't you think?"

"He could have been killed by anyone, anywhere, and dumped here," Ramsey said.

"Nope. There was too much blood around the body. He was killed on your land, all right."

Ramsey stood a little straighter. "I'm sorry some old man was killed on the Lazy T, but you can't implicate me. I had nothing to do with it."

"I may have nothing to go on yet, but I'm going to be watching you like a hawk, Ramsey. You make one move I don't like, and I'll take you down. If you so much as spit on the sidewalk, I'll arrest you."

"You can't do that," Ramsey protested.

"I can do just about anything I damn well please. I'm a federal marshal, remember?"

"What's going on here?" Hunt's voice boomed as he entered the room. "The boys told me you were in here harassing Ramsey. What's the meaning of this?"

"A body was found on your land today, Mr. Tylo. The body of a man Ramsey had played poker with, and lost to."

"So?"

"So that makes him a possible suspect in the murder."

"A man gets accused of murder because he lost a hand of poker? Please, Marshal. Surely you can do better than that. If I killed every man I'd ever lost a hand of poker to there'd be practically no men left alive in Twisted Creek."

Brett scowled at Hunt. "Ramsey hasn't been accused . . . yet," he said.

"You don't think I did this, do you, Cass?" Ramsey asked.

"I don't know, Ramsey."

"Cass, please. You can't think I'm capable of murder?"

"I really don't know you, Ramsey."

"I'll prove to you the kind of man I am. You'll see how wrong you've been to listen to the marshal's jealous lies. That's what they are, you know—lies to make me look bad in your eyes. He's in love with you. He'd do anything to discredit me. Maybe he killed Sharky so he could accuse me of it," he said, his words spilling in a jumble from his lips.

Cass closed her eyes for a moment so she wouldn't have to see his face. "Please, Ramsey. No more." She turned and walked from the room. She had to get away from him, from this house.

Later, after Brett and Cass had ridden off, Hunt looked disgustedly at his son. "So you thought you could get Cassidy to fall in love with you," he taunted. "You were so sure she'd be sweating in your bed by now. Well, look what's happened, boy. She can't stand the sight of you."

Ramsey sat in one of the huge chairs that faced his father's desk and stared miserably at the floor.

"She's probably screwing that marshal on a regular basis. And what are you doing about it? Nothing!" Hunt shouted. "You're not doing a goddamned thing! I told you that bitch was trouble. But did you listen to me? Do you ever listen to me? If you'd done what I told you to do in the first place we wouldn't be having problems with her now. It would have all ended years ago."

"But you agreed," whined Ramsey.

"Yes, damn it. You're my boy, and I gave in to you. You wanted her, so I gave you a shot at her." Hunt slammed his hands on the desk. "But you didn't come through! Don't you get it, boy? She doesn't want you. She's never going to want you. She's in love with that goddamned marshal!"

"But I know I can—"

"Damn it! Listen to me! Cassidy Wayne's time has run out!"

Chapter 16

*W*hen Cass and Brett got to town, they went straight to the hotel to find out where Rosie lived and to discover whether or not she'd been keeping company with anyone. Two other women who worked there said that Rosie lived alone and that as far as they knew, she had no one special in her life. But recently, they said, she'd been very secretive about who she was spending her free time with.

Cass decided she'd like a chance to talk to Rosie alone, so Brett went to the undertaker's to see if he'd gotten back with Sharky's body. He also had some paperwork to catch up on at the sheriff's office, and he wanted to put up some campaign posters. The election was nearing fast.

"Are you sure you're feeling all right?" Cass asked for the tenth time since arriving at Rosie's little house.

"I'm fine, Cass. I really appreciate you coming all the way into town to check on me. I've been alone since Grandma died last summer."

"I'm sorry," murmured Cass.

"It's okay, really. She was eighty-two, and lived a good

life." Her eyes saddened then. "What would she think of me if she knew?"

"She'd understand. She loved you unconditionally."

"I guess so. I just feel as if I've let her memory down," she whispered.

Cass frowned. "Don't ever feel that way. And don't worry about what anyone else thinks, either. You don't owe anyone an explanation for your actions. You don't owe anyone but yourself." She hesitated for a moment, pondering her next words. "But you do owe yourself something better than you're getting, Rosie," she said softly.

Rosie lowered her eyes.

"I'm not going to ask you again who's been beating you, but I will tell you he's no good for you. Don't let him hurt you any more than he already has. If you won't think about yourself, think about the baby."

"I will ... It's just that ... Oh, Cass, I can't explain," she stammered.

Cass put her hand affectionately on Rosie's arm. "I know. You don't have to explain. Relationships are confusing," she said, thinking about her own relationship with Brett. Ramsey had blurted that Brett loved her, but she'd never heard those words from Brett himself. He was attracted to her, and she to him, she admitted. And making love to him was ... well, more wonderful than she'd ever imagined anything could be. But did that mean he was in love with her? Wouldn't he tell her if he was? And how did she feel about him? Sighing, she stood up. "I guess I should be going now so you can get some rest."

"I am awfully tired. Are you sure my boss understands that I'm ill?" she asked, worried about losing her job.

"I'm sure. Brett told him you fell and hurt yourself out at my place last night and that you'd need a few days off to recover." She grinned. "Not too many people argue with Brett," she said.

Rosie let out a sigh of relief. "I'll have to thank him next time I see him."

"Just get well." She turned toward the door. "And don't let yourself be a victim again, okay?"

"I'll try," Rosie murmured.

"All right. I'll check on you again soon. And if there's anything you need, you just get word out to me at the ranch. I can be here pretty quickly if I have to be."

Rosie smiled. "Thanks again, Cass."

Cass shrugged. "What are friends for?"

Leaving Rosie's house, Cass intended to head straight to the sheriff's office, but a little boy in a torn flannel shirt ran up to her and tugged on her arm.

Cass looked down at him. "Yes?"

"Are you Cassidy Wayne?" he asked with a lisp.

Cass grinned down at the waif. He couldn't have been more than six or seven years old. "Who wants to know?" she asked.

"A man in the alley behind the hotel," he answered.

Cass's eyes narrowed. "A man? Who?"

"I don't know. He just gave me a whole dollar to come tell you he wanted to talk to you."

Cass's heartbeat slowed as a deadly calm came over her. Bobby Fleet hadn't shown up yet. Maybe he was waiting behind the hotel for her. "What did the man look like?" she asked.

The little boy blinked several times. He apparently hadn't thought he'd have to answer any questions. "His nose is broke," he offered after several seconds of trying to remember something about the man who'd hired him.

Cass let out a disgusted breath. "Ramsey," she said to the boy.

The little boy raised his shoulders and grinned lopsidedly. "He didn't tell me his name. He just said I should wait till you came out of this house and then tell you to go meet him behind the hotel." He took a deep breath.

"Okay, you earned your dollar. You can go now," she said.

"Are you gonna go? I don't want him thinkin' I didn't do what he told me."

"Yes. I'm going to go," she told him.

"Good!" he burst out, then took off at a dead run for the store.

There's a tummyache in the making, she mused as she watched him go. Untying her horse, she led him to the hotel. Tethering him out front, she started for the alley, wondering what Ramsey wanted and why he had chosen such a strange location to talk.

"Cass?" Ramsey whispered when she passed him.

"Ramsey? What are you doing out here?" She turned to see him sitting on a wooden bench against the back wall of the hotel.

"I wanted to talk to you alone. This is the only place I could think of where the marshal might not interrupt us."

Cass nodded slightly. "All right," she said, sitting down next to him on the bench. "What do you want?"

Ramsey gazed at her. "You're so beautiful, Cass," he told her.

"Thank you." She waited.

"I have so many plans for us, Cass."

She looked at him in surprise. "Ramsey, I don't think—"

"No, Cass, don't stop me. My father wants us to be together." That wasn't exactly true. His father had agreed to give him one more chance with Cass after he'd whined and argued for the better part of an hour. But this was his last chance, and Ramsey knew he couldn't mess it up.

"Your father? What does your father have to do with anything?"

"I just didn't expect to fall in love with you," he continued, ignoring her question.

"Ramsey, please . . ."

"I didn't kill Sharky, Cass. You have to believe that."

Cass noticed that his eyes looked a little glazed. "Ramsey are you feeling all right?" she asked.

Ramsey reached forward and took her hands in his. "You

do believe in me, don't you? You don't think I killed Sharky, do you?"

Cass tried to gently free her hands, but he gripped them tightly. "Of course I believe you, Ramsey," she lied. There was something frightening in his eyes. Something she hadn't seen there before.

Ramsey sighed. "I knew you wouldn't believe what that bastard was saying about me," he said.

"Who?"

"The marshal. The marshal wants you for himself, but I have plans for us, Cass. We're going to be married. Your ranch will become a part of the Lazy T. It'll all work out perfectly."

"What?" Cass gasped incredulously. He'd lost his mind. If only she could get one of her hands free she'd feel much safer.

"We're going to be so happy, Cass," he rambled. "I love you so much. You're beautiful and exciting. When father wrote me you'd murdered all those men I didn't believe him, but now I know it's true."

"I didn't murder anyone, Ramsey. I killed the men who murdered my family."

"I know, and we'll forget all that once we're married."

Cass could take no more. "I'm not going to marry you, Ramsey," she said.

"Of course you are."

"No, I'm not!"

"But I love you. That damned marshal put ideas in your head, didn't he?"

"No. It has nothing to do with Brett."

"I don't believe you. He's done something to you." His eyes narrowed suspiciously. "I can make you forget him," he said, leaning toward her.

"Ramsey, stop this," she protested as he tried to kiss her.

Ramsey clamped both of her hands in one of his own. With the other, he grasped her jaw, holding her head still. "I'm going to make you forget all men but me."

Cass fought to turn her head, but he was too strong. She

nearly gagged when his mouth descended on hers in a crushing kiss, and she clenched her teeth against his attempt to put his tongue in her mouth.

"You'll change once we're married," he hissed, glaring down at her. "I'll not have a wife who refuses my touch."

"No!" Cass struggled. She flinched when he squeezed down harder on her wrists.

"This would be so much easier if you wouldn't fight me, Cass," he said.

Cass's eyes widened as she suddenly realized how easy it would be to free herself. "Maybe you're right, Ramsey," she said, ending her struggling.

Ramsey looked down at her suspiciously. "I am right," he continued to argue.

"I know you are. It just took me a minute to realize it."

He leaned toward her for another kiss.

This time Cass didn't fight his attempt to open her mouth. She accepted him almost eagerly, waiting for her opportunity.

Ramsey was startled by her apparent passion. "Cass, are you teasing me?" he asked.

"I would never do that, Ramsey," she purred.

He couldn't believe his good fortune. He'd been certain it would take longer to make her see the light. He bent to kiss her again.

Cass allowed his kiss, though she wanted to vomit directly into his mouth. "Please, Ramsey?" she asked, wiggling to free her hands from his grasp.

"Not yet," he said, still not sure she wasn't trying to trick him. With his free hand, he cupped her breast, hearing her shocked intake of air when he did. He waited for her to pull away.

Cass nearly shook with anger, but she stayed close to him. She even pressed her breast deeper into his hand, groaning with disgust at his touch.

Ramsey heard her moan and knew he'd won. Releasing her hands, he leaned forward to enjoy her passion.

The second her hands were free, Cass jerked away from

him and leaped up from the bench, pulling her guns. "You stupid sick bastard!" she cursed. "I should plug you full of lead for that!"

Ramsey stared surprised down the barrels of her twin Colts. "But, Cass—"

"Don't even try to say anything. Don't ever say anything to me again."

"But, Cass, I love you."

"Hah! You don't know what the hell love it. I'm not sure I know what it is, but I can guarantee it isn't this!" she exclaimed.

Ramsey's surprise turned to anger. "Put down the guns, Cass," he said. "We need to talk."

"I'm through talking to you, Ramsey."

"You don't understand how important it is for us to marry, Cass."

I would never marry you. Not even if you were the last man on earth," she said vehemently.

"Because of the marshal."

"No, Ramsey. Listen to me—"

"What did he do to you, Cass?"

"Brett hasn't done anything to me."

"He's been staying out at your place. It's been real convenient for him, hasn't it?" His eyes became evil slits in his face.

"Ramsey, you don't know what you're saying."

"I know exactly what I'm saying. Did you make it easy for him, Cass? Or did you string him along for a while before you screwed him?" he demanded.

"You bastard," she hissed. "I'm leaving now, Ramsey. Don't try to follow me, and don't ever speak to me again." Her voice was an even tone, threatening in it's timbre. She began to back away from him toward the front of the hotel.

"Slut!" he screamed as she left. "You filthy slut! You're going to pay for this!"

Cass kept walking backwards until she was once again on the sidewalk and could see other people on the street around her. Letting out her breath slowly, she realized she'd begun shaking, and holstered her guns. Lowering herself to sit on the bottom step of the porch, she let her head fall forward for a moment. She needed to compose herself before seeing Brett again. If he ever found out what Ramsey had just done to her, he'd kill him. And though she'd wanted to kill him herself, she didn't want Brett to spend the rest of his life in jail, or end up dangling from a hangman's noose, because of a demented fool like Ramsey.

It took her a full twenty minutes to calm down enough to go looking for Brett. When she found him, he'd just put up a campaign poster in the store window.

"What do you think?" he asked her, grinning.

She began to laugh, glad she had something to take her mind off Ramsey. "Is that supposed to be you?" she asked, looking at the ridiculous caricature that graced the sign.

"It's not that bad, is it? It's the best I could do."

She laughed again. "You drew that yourself?"

He nodded.

"I thought maybe you'd had one of the grade school kids do it for you."

"Very funny," he told her. "I suppose you think you could do better?"

"I couldn't do worse," she gibed.

Just then Jasper Martin, the storekeeper, stepped outside and looked at the sign. "Hey, I like your sign," he said, a huge smile splitting his face. "It shows you don't take yourself too seriously."

"That's what I thought," said Brett.

Cass snickered.

"You've got my vote," Jasper said, then walked back into the store.

"Because of that sign?" asked Cass incredulously when Jasper could no longer hear her.

Brett laughed. "I didn't know that campaigning was going to be so easy. I figured people would be interested in my record, what I could do for the town as sheriff, and here all I have to do is put up silly-looking pictures of myself."

Cass laughed with him. "I'm sure there are a few citizens

of Twisted Creek who are interested in what you have to offer."

"Are you interested in what I have to offer?" he asked, his voice full of innuendo.

"That depends on what exactly you're offering," she teased.

"I'd love to tell you or, better yet, show you," he said, his voice rumbling deep within his chest.

Ramsey watched this laughing exchange from the alley opening, and glowered. "You'll pay for this, Marshal. And, Cass, you will be my wife," he snarled.

Jasper stepped back out onto the sidewalk. "Cass, I almost forgot to tell you. I got word from the railhead. Your wire arrived early. It'll be here sometime tomorrow morning."

"Great," she said.

Brett grimaced. "Are you still going through with this?"

"Yes. I'm still going through with this," she mimicked. She then looked at Jasper. "Thanks, I'll be here tomorrow to pick it up."

Ramsey had moved closer by sneaking along the opposite side of the street. His jaw clenched in rage when he heard about the wire. Turning back the other way, he headed for his horse. His father had to be told right away.

"King me!" squealed Cass as she jumped another of Brett's checkers.

"I believe you cheat," said Brett.

"I never cheat. I don't have to. I'm simply brilliant at playing checkers."

"Darby, didn't you tell me Cass would never play checkers with you?" Brett asked over his shoulder.

"That's what I said," Darby answered from his seat across the room.

"I think I've been hustled," Brett complained.

"Shut up and king me." Cass giggled.

Brett did as he was told. "All right, you nag. Now it's my move."

"Nag! Did you hear what he called me, Uncle Darby? I think you should throw him out of the house at once."

"Whatever you say, Cass," Darby answered, not moving from his chair. "Although I have to admit you do nag a bit."

"It's a conspiracy," she huffed. "I think——"

The explosion of a lantern being thrown through the front window abruptly ended Cass's sentence.

"Fire!" shouted Darby. "Soony, bring water!"

Brett jumped up and ripped the burning curtains from the window and began to beat out the flames. Cass grabbed a quilt from the daybed and swiped it over the floor where the flames danced on the wood.

"What happened?" shouted Soony, throwing a dishpan full of water over the flames.

Brett didn't have time to answer. Shots began flying through the windows. "Everyone get down!" he shouted.

Darby and Soony fell to the floor. Cass dived for her guns, grabbing them quickly and sliding to the floor with them. Brett got down on his knees and crawled to where his holster hung over the headboard of the daybed.

Bullets ripped through the air over their heads. They could hear shouts outside, and saw more flames.

"They're burning my new barn!" yelled Cass. Rising, she poked one of her guns through the window and began firing.

"Stay down, Cass!" Brett shouted. "Stay down!" He crawled to another window and broke out the shards of glass still clinging to the frame. "Who are you and what do you want?" he yelled through the broken window.

His answer was laughter from outside and more shots blasting through the windows.

"Damn you to hell!" shouted Cass, firing more shots of her own. She could see several riders passing the house when they got in front of the flames from the barn, and she aimed and fired again. A man fell from one of the horses to the sound of an anguished cry.

"I got one of the bastards," she said through her teeth.

Brett fired into the night. "Cass, they're coming with torches," he yelled.

Cass looked out in the direction Brett was staring. Three, maybe four, men were riding hard for the house carrying blazing torches. "They mean to burn us out," Cass breathed.

"They'll not get us," said Darby as he scooted next to Cass. "I've still got my rifle." He raised the weapon and stuck the barrel out of the window.

Cass gave her uncle a smile of encouragement. He'd managed to get the rifle from over the fireplace without getting himself shot. Aiming once again, she fired at the men riding toward them. Brett and Darby did the same. One of the men fell, then another, but two got close enough to throw their torches on the roof of the house.

"The roof's dry. If it catches, the house will go up like a tinderbox," Cass yelled above the noise. Then another torch crashed through a window in the back of the house.

"I'll go take care of it," shouted Brett.

Cass continued to fire, hoping against hope the roof wouldn't begin to burn.

"Missy, Cass!" shouted Soony. "The roof. It's on fire!"

Cass's heart sank at Soony's words. If the roof went, they were lost. Smoke started filling the room. "Damn you to hell, Tylo," she cursed. "You're going to win after all, you bastard!" She turned back to the window and fired several more rounds into the darkness.

Darby fired his rifle again and again.

Brett came back down the hall. "It's no use, Cass. The house is a loss," he said, choking on the smoke billowing around them, thick and black. "We've got to get out."

"And go where? That's what they want. They'll shoot us as soon as we go outside."

"There's an awful lot of smoke. Maybe we can use it to our advantage. I'll kick open the door and all of the windows. They won't know which way we're coming out. We'll leave through Darby's bedroom window. That's the darkest side of the house."

"We don't know how many of them are left. They might have men all around us."

"They might, but this is our only chance."

Cass looked at her uncle, then at Soony. They were looking at her with trust. "All right, we'll try it. I sure don't want to die in this fire."

Brett went to the window by the table. Picking up a chair, he threw it through the broken panes, destroying what was left of the frame. Shots ran out as the chair crashed into the night. He then went to every other window in the house in a haphazard order, including Darby's. When he was done, he came back. "Now for the door," he said. Standing up, he turned the knob and kicked with all his might. The door swung wildly open, breaking the hinges off the frame.

"They're coming out!" someone shouted.

More shots followed the words.

"Come on. It's now or never," Brett said, choking on the smoke.

Cass took her uncle's arm and tugged on him to follow her. Soony went with Brett. The smoke was so thick now they could barely see, and breathing was nearly impossible. Cass's eyes burned, and she coughed on each breath.

Brett darted in front of her, next to the window. "I'll go first. If they see me I'll draw their fire. I'll try to cover for you," he said.

Cass nodded. "All right." She coughed again.

Brett stood up to climb through the window. At the last second he crouched back down.

"What's wrong? Don't you think you can make it?" Cass asked.

Brett took her face in his hands. "No. I don't think I can make it, but this is our only chance. I just had to tell you something."

Cass looked expectantly into his gray eyes.

"I love you, Cass," he whispered, then pressed his lips to hers.

Before she could respond, he stood up and jumped through the window. The gunfire continued around the house, and her heart stopped beating. Holding her breath, she peered over the sill, sure she'd see his beautiful body dead in the dirt. Instead, he signaled from the shadows on the other side of the yard.

"He made it! come on, Uncle, Soony. Let's go."

Darby pushed Soony out ahead of him. When he tried to make Cass go next, she refused. "Get going, Uncle," she ordered him. "I'm right behind you."

Darby climbed over the sill and out onto the ground. Cass jumped out after him. Running together across the yard, they heard hoofbeats coming toward them.

"Cass, get down!" shouted Brett. He could see the rider, but he couldn't get a good shot past Cass and Darby.

"They're over here!" the man shouted. "They're getting out the back!" He started firing.

Cass heard Brett, but turned toward the rider. "You bastard!" She shouted, aiming one of her Colts at him.

Brett shouted again, "Cass, get down!"

The man fired again, his bullet catching Darby in the leg, sending him to the ground.

Cass fired a single shot. The bullet passed through the air like a spear from hell, finding its mark between the rider's eyes. "Meet your Maker!" she shouted.

"Cass, help me," Darby moaned from where he'd fallen.

Cass whirled around. "I'll get you out of here, Uncle," she hissed. Grabbing him under the arms, she began to drag him toward the shadows.

Brett hurried out to help them. He lifted Darby like a baby and ran for the dark again. "Come on, Cass. We've got to keep running. It won't be long before the rest of them come around the house to find out what the shooting was."

Cass ran as fast as she could. Her lungs were filled with smoke and she had trouble catching her breath as she ran. She didn't know how Brett could carry Darby and run, too.

In a little while they caught up with Soony, who waited under a tree. "Mr. Darby, you're shot," he cried. "Please be okay."

"I'm fine," said Darby, his voice a faint whisper.

"We've got to keep going," said Brett.

"Get to the wash," said Cass. "We can hide until they've gone."

Brett nodded his agreement and followed her.

Cass knew the land as well in the dark as in broad daylight. In minutes she led them down into the deep section of the wash where she'd tricked Brett during their race. "We can stop here," she breathed. "Let me look at your wound, Uncle," she said.

"He fainted," Brett said.

"He's not . . ." Cass's eyes grew wide with terror.

"No, he's not dead," Brett hurried to assure her.

Sighing, Cass touched Darby's forehead. "Let me look at him."

Laying Darby on the ground, Brett knelt beside him to help Cass see how badly he was injured.

Cass found the hole in her uncle's trousers where the bullet had entered. Forcing her fingers inside it, she ripped the material apart. The moonlight overhead showed the bullet had entered high on his thigh, and though a lack of forceful bleeding indicated it had missed the artery, a steady stream of dark red oozed from the wound. "We've got to get him to the doctor," she said.

"As soon as we're sure those men have left," Brett told her.

"Ohhhh," wailed Soony all of a sudden.

"What is it? Are you injured?" Cass asked him frantically.

"Pork Chop!" he cried.

Cass sighed. "I'm so sorry, Soony. We couldn't save her this time."

Soony dropped is head and wept for his lost pet.

"I'll go see if it's safe to leave yet," Brett whispered.

Cass looked up at him. "Be careful," she said.

"I will." He climbed up the side of the wash and belly-crawled through the grass back toward the house.

Cass watched him go, her heart hammering in her chest. She then turned back to tend her uncle's wound. She had to try to stop the flow of blood. Scratching some damp dirt from the bottom of the wash, she wrapped it in some grass.

This she placed over the wound. Tearing a section from the hem of her shirt, she tied it tightly around his leg, holding the grass in place. "That'll have to do for now," she whispered.

Brett crawled as close to the house as he dared. He could see several men on horseback riding back and forth around the flaming structure and out into the adjoining fields. They were looking for them. They'd figured out that their prey had escaped. Crawling back to where Cass, Darby, and Soony waited, he slid down into the wash.

"Brett, is that you?"

"Yes," he answered. Lying back against the bank of the wash, he finally tried to catch his breath.

"Can we leave yet?" Cass asked.

"Not for a while. They know we made it out. They're looking for us."

Cass sank back against the bank next to him, anger filling her soul.

Chapter 17

$\mathcal{T}$ he sun was just beginning to lighten the sky when Brett came back from his last check of the house. "They're finally gone, Cass," he whispered.

Cass sat up and rubbed some of the stiffness from her arms, straightening her legs in front of her. "We've got to get Uncle Darby into town to the doctor," she said. "He woke up for a minute while you were gone, but he passed out again almost immediately. He's lost a lot of blood, Brett." Her brow was furrowed with worry.

"He'll be fine, Cass. I'm going to check on what's left of the house to see if there's anything we can use to transport him. You wait here in case the raiders come back."

"I want to go with you," she said, grasping his arm with her fingers.

Brett glanced past her to where Darby lay unconscious. Soony sat next to him, watching his breathing. "I suppose you can come. Soony will keep an eye on your uncle. Just stay low and do as I say," he said, staring down into her blue eyes, his heart beating rapidly at the trust he saw there. She hadn't mentioned what he'd told her the night before, and she hadn't confessed that she loved him too. Apparently she didn't. But he could see emotions in her eyes that gave him hope. "Let's go."

Cass nodded and followed him up and out of the wash, crawling along on her hands and knees through the tall grass. A while later she saw what was left of her house.

"Brett, no," she moaned when she saw the burned-out rubble that had been her home. The only parts left standing were the fireplace and the back corner of what had been Darby's room.

Brett heard the despair in her voice. "I'm sorry, Cass," he breathed next to her.

Cass glanced up at him. Leaning forward a little, she kissed him gently on the jaw. "Thank you for caring," she said. "It's just so hard to see this again. It's just like the last time."

"No. This time your loved ones got out," he said.

Sighing, she said, "You're right. It's just a building, I've still got what's truly important," she smiled up at him. "Thanks to you."

Brett lifted one corner of his mouth. He didn't feel much like a hero. He wished he could have done more. "Let's go see if there's anything salvageable."

Cass nodded and stood up cautiously when Brett did. There was no one around; even the bodies of the men they'd shot were gone. The place was silent except for the sizzle of the fire still smoldering in the timbers of the house and barn.

Searching through the blackened wood and ashes in what was left of Darby's room, they found several blankets. "We can make a travois out of these," Brett suggested.

"Good idea," Cass agreed. She studied the room. Everything Darby owned had been destroyed. Walking through the rubble, she reached what was left of her room. "Gone," she sighed. "It's all gone." Turning to look up at Brett as he wandered around behind her carrying the blankets, she knew he could see the anger and hatred in her eyes. "I'm going to get him, Brett."

"Cass . . ."

"Don't try to talk me out of this, and don't try to convince me Tylo wasn't behind this. No one else would do a thing like this," she fumed.

"We have to get Darby to the doctor, Cass," he said urgently.

"We will. But I'm going to talk to Tylo about this."

"You'll be killed, damn it! Don't you know that?" he demanded. "I can't let you do it."

"You can't stop me, Brett. I have to do this."

"No, you don't. There were enough men here last night that one of them will talk. I'll get a posse together."

"Sheriff Jackson used a posse when my family was destroyed. They lost the murderers' trail. A trail I picked up months later. A trail that didn't go cold until a few months ago when I hit a dead end. You know, it didn't occur to me until I returned to Twisted Creek that there might be a good reason I could find no clues to where the fifth man had gone. There were no ~~clues~~ on the trail because he never left town. Don't you see, Brett? It's Tylo. I know it."

"I won't let you go, Cass. I'm not going to stand back and watch you ride out to start trouble and maybe get yourself killed."

"Then come with me. We'd stand a better chance together."

Brett heaved a great sigh. "I know how badly you want this, Cass, but I won't allow it."

Cass clenched her jaw tightly. She'd made up her mind she was going to the Lazy T, and it didn't matter what Brett said or did to stop her. She was going. She would not stand around arguing about it anymore. "Fine," she mumbled. "Let's get these blankets back to Uncle Darby."

Just then a noise in some nearby brush startled them both. Brett dropped the blankets and drew his gun. Cass readied herself, hands poised over her twin Colts. If one of the bastards who'd burned her house was out there he was going to die.

The grass parted in a flurry of yellow fur and white feathers.

"Mirabelle!" Cass exclaimed.

"And Pork Chop," said Brett laughing. "How did they survive?"

Cass grinned. "I don't know, but I can't wait to tell Soony." Mirabelle screeched as Pork Chop pecked her on the head. "Oh, no, here they go," she warned.

Mirabelle took off at a dead run, the chicken chasing her, landing on her back, and pecking her mischievously. "Pork Chop, you stop that!" yelled Cass. "I'll turn you into chicken soup if you don't stop!"

Pork Chop ignored her threats and kept tormenting the cat, attacking with an even greater fervor.

Brett started to chuckle. "Those two are something else."

"I just wish Mirabelle would learn that she's the one who's supposed to be doing the chasing. If she ever once turned around and gave that rotten chicken a good hard whack, the trouble would stop," Cass said.

Brett continued to chuckle. "Let them sort out their differences on their own. We've got to get back to Darby." Holstering his gun, he picked up the blankets. "We need to find some branches for the travois."

Cass glanced at the two ridiculous pets once more, then back at Brett. "There are some strong young trees down by the Losee. We can use those."

"All right."

Three long, arduous hours later, Cass, Soony, and Brett dragged Darby into town.

"What happened?" Bill Conroy asked, running to meet them.

Several others also ran up to them, taking the travois from the bedraggled trio.

"We've got to get my uncle to the doc's place," said Cass. "He's been shot."

"You look like you've been through hell and back," Bill told them.

"We have," replied Cass.

"Raiders hit Cass's place again last night. Burned her out and tried to kill all of us," explained Brett.

"Holy cow," Bill breathed.

Another man let out a long, low whistle. "Do you know who it was?" he asked.

"I do," said Cass.

Brett scowled at her. "Cass thinks she knows, but we're not certain. We'd like to wait until we're sure before we go pointing any fingers."

"I understand," Bill responded.

The crowd was getting larger as they traveled toward the doctor's office. Jaybird Johnson came out of the bar. "What's going on here?" he asked.

"Some men tried to kill Cass, Darby, Soony, and the marshal," answered a voice in the group. "See, Darby's been shot."

"They was burned out," another added.

Jaybird puffed up in front of the crowd. "Do you all see why this town needs a strong sheriff?" he blustered. "If you elect me sheriff this sort of thing will stop," he promised.

"And just what will you do to stop it?" asked Brett.

"Why . . . I'll make stricter laws. I'll see to it criminals are caught and hanged," he said loudly to the townspeople.

"That's interesting," said Brett. "Seems to me I read somewhere that the laws are made by the government. It's the sheriff's job to enforce those laws."

"Well . . . I . . ." Jaybird stammered.

"And it isn't up to the sheriff to decide who's guilty or innocent. It's up to the circuit judge or the jury that's selected to try a case. Sounds like you're planning on giving yourself all kinds of authority you aren't entitled to, Jaybird," Brett said loud enough for the crowd to hear.

"I never said I would do that," argued Jaybird. "I only said this town needs a strong sheriff so what happened out at Cassidy's place last night won't happen again."

"I agree this town needs a strong sheriff, but it also needs one who knows the law and respects the citizens he works for. Now, if you'll excuse us from your speechmaking, we've got a man here who needs to see the doctor," Brett informed him.

"Yeah, Jaybird. We don't need to hear you talk. We hear enough of you as it is," someone said from the back of the crowd.

"Whoever said that is in for it," said Jaybird.

Brett walked past him and led the way to the doctor's office. The townspeople carried Darby through the doc's door and into the examination room.

"What happened?" asked the surprised doctor.

"He was shot in the leg last night, Doc. We got him here as soon as we could, but he's lost a lot of blood," said Brett.

"Shot, you say?" The doctor began washing his hands at a basin in the corner.

"Yes," answered Cass. "Can you help him, Doc?"

"I'll know after I examine him, Cass. You go out into the waiting room and I'll let you know how he's doing as soon as I can."

"But I want to stay with him," she said, her eyes pleading. The doctor looked questioningly past her to Brett.

"Come on, Cass. The doctor needs peace and quiet to examine your uncle. It's best if we wait outside," he said. Placing his hands on her shoulders from behind, he turned her toward the door.

"Let me know . . ." said Cass.

"As soon as I'm through, I promise."

Cass let Brett lead her into the waiting room. She saw that Soony had found himself a chair and was sitting patiently with his hands crossed in his lap. "I wish I could be more like him," Cass said quietly to Brett.

"Then you wouldn't be you. And I'm kind of partial to you just the way you are," he said softly.

Cass remembered what he'd told her the night before. Did he really mean it? She looked up into his eyes. He meant it. Letting her gaze drop again, she studied the floor. He was so handsome and so good. But the idea of letting herself love someone was frightening. "What's taking so long?" she fretted.

Brett let his hopes drop a bit. She was avoiding talking about it. He knew this wasn't the perfect time, but some sign that she felt something for him would have been encouraging. He then remembered the way she'd made love to him, the fact that she'd given him her virginity. These had to count for something. He'd wait. "I'm sure the doctor will be out to talk to you as soon as he can, Cass," he said.

Sighing, she nodded. "All right, let's sit down."

"Good idea." Brett pulled two of the chairs in the waiting area together. Several of the townspeople had come into the doctor's office and were waiting too.

Just then the door burst open and Mrs. Wettle entered the room in a flurry. "Where is he?" she asked. "Oh, dear, where's Darby?"

Cass blinked at the woman's disheveled appearance. The bun that usually sat so neatly at the base of her skull was drooping, strands escaping everywhere as though she'd run every step from her house at the edge of town. She hadn't bothered to wipe her hands or remove her apron, both of which were covered with flour. And the top two buttons of her shirtwaist were gaping open. "Mrs. Wettle?"

"Oh, dear, Cassidy, is your uncle all right? I heard he'd been shot. Oh, dear," she wailed.

"I think he's going to be fine, Mrs. Wettle. He's in with Doc now. Here, sit down," Cass said, urging the woman to sit next to her.

"I couldn't possibly," she said, rubbing her hands together and managing to lose a good bit of flour in doing so. "Oh, dear," she moaned when she saw the white powder on the floor, "look what I've done."

"It's all right, Mrs. Wettle. Just have a seat," urged Brett.

"Oh, dear, maybe I should," she said, lowering her ample frame into the chair next to Cass. "I'm quite out of breath, but when I heard Darby had been shot . . . well, I rushed right over here. You say he'll be all right? How did he get wounded?"

"Our ranch was raided last night. Everything was burned, and Darby was shot as we escaped from the house," Cass explained.

Mrs. Wettle began to fan herself with her apron. "Oh, dear. You all could have been killed."

"That was someone's plan," remarked Brett.

Mrs. Wettle rocked back and forth as she worried and fanned herself. "Who would do such a dreadful thing? Poor Darby. How seriously is he injured?"

Cass glanced up at Brett and knew what he was thinking. "We don't know who attacked my ranch, and Darby was shot in the leg."

"Oh, dear," she breathed and rocked.

The doctor emerged from behind the curtain. "Cass, your uncle will be fine. I removed the bullet without complication. He did lose quite a bit of blood, though, so he'll need a lot of bed rest while he recuperates."

Cass breathed a sigh of relief. "I won't let him out of bed for a second," she said, then frowned, her face becoming a mask of sadness.

"What is it, Cass?" Brett asked.

"I don't have any place for him to recuperate. I don't even own a bed anymore, let alone a house," she said sadly.

"Darby will recover in my home," announced Mrs. Wettle.

"But—" Cass attempted to speak.

"Hush. I'll hear no argument. You may also stay with me. I'm all alone in that big house since Mr. Wettle passed on some five years ago. Mr. Soony is also welcome."

"But I really can't," Cass told her.

"Tut-tut-tut," Mrs. Wettle clucked. "You have nowhere else to stay, and I have the room. You just have to move your things in. . . . Oh, dear, you have no things. Well, you just come make yourself at home. I'll see to it Darby is nursed properly."

Brett bit the inside of his lower lip to keep from laughing. Mrs. Wettle was as persistent as the tide.

"I'm going to rebuild as soon as possible, Mrs. Wettle," Cass said. "And it's not that I'm not grateful for the offer. It's just that I want to stay out at the ranch."

The woman shook her head. "Well, do what you must,

but your uncle will be recovering in my home. Is that understood?"

Cass nodded, unwilling to argue with this formidable woman. She turned to look at Soony. She wondered if he'd been paying attention to the conversation. He wore a questioning expression. "Can Pork Chop go too?" he asked.

Mrs. Wettle smiled. "Of course your pet is welcome also," she said.

Soony grinned at Cass. "I'll go to Mrs. Wettle's," he said. "Mr. Darby needs me."

Cass smiled. "It looks as if you'll have two houseguests for a while—three, if you count Pork Chop," she said. "And I'll be in and out regularly to check on my uncle."

"Of course, I wouldn't have it any other way," Mrs. Wettle said in a "this matter is settled" tone.

"How soon can Uncle Darby be moved?" Cass asked the doctor.

"Not until tomorrow, Cass. I want to watch him tonight. That bullet went pretty deep."

She nodded. "All right. Is he awake now?"

"No, but he should be before too long. Why don't you go have some breakfast and get cleaned up? By the time you get back he might have opened his eyes again," he suggested.

"That's a wonderful idea," Brett interjected. "Come with me," he said to Cass.

"I'm going to wait right here," announced Mrs. Wettle as though she'd been asked to go.

The doctor chuckled to himself, then turned to face the other people who'd been waiting for news about Darby. "You all heard what I said about your friend. Darby will be fine, so you can go on about your business."

"You sure, Doc?" Bill Conroy asked.

"I'm sure, Bill. Go open the barbershop. You probably have customers waiting."

"All right," Conroy said, nodding his head as he went. Just before he went out the door, he stopped. "Marshal Ryder?"

"Yes, Bill?"

"I won't be running for sheriff after all," he said.

"You've changed your mind?" Brett asked.

He nodded again. "I don't think I'm the best man for the job," he stated quietly and walked out the door.

Brett looked at Cass and shrugged. "Imagine that?" he said, smiling.

Several minutes later the room had just about cleared. Cass yawned widely. "I need some coffee," she said.

"You need a bath," Brett whispered to her.

Cass huffed at him. "How dare you, sir?"

"Look at me, Cass. I'm a filthy mess. You're almost as bad."

Cass looked closely at Brett then down at her own clothes. "I guess you're right."

"Follow me," he said, leading the way to the door.

"We'll be back in a little while," Cass said over her shoulder to the doctor. "And thank you, Mrs. Wettle. We'll see you later."

Brett had the wonderful idea of bathing in the sheriff's office. He pulled out the big metal tub and started the fire to heat the water.

"I don't even care if the water's hot," said Cass.

"You will," he said, smiling.

She looked down at her clothes again. They were ruined. Her trousers were caked with mud and soot. Her shirt looked even worse because she'd torn the bottom off to make the bandage for Darby. "What am I going to put on?" she asked.

"Some of the sheriff's things are still in the dresser drawers," offered Brett.

"Funny," said Cass.

"I'll go buy us some new clothes while you bathe. Will that suit you?"

"Perfectly. Just put my things on my tab at the store."

Brett frowned at her. "I can still afford to buy a few articles of clothing."

"Fine," she said, grinning at him.

Twenty minutes later she was sitting in a tub of warm water. "Nothing has ever felt so good in all my life," she said loud enough for Brett to hear her in the outer office.

"Nothing?" The word was full of meaning.

"When are you going to the store?" she groused good-naturedly.

"Right now," he said.

"Don't you need to know my sizes?"

"Believe me, I already do," he teased.

"You're incorrigible!" she yelled.

He just laughed at her and left the office.

Cass sank down into the water and sighed with relief. He was right: there were several things that felt better than the bath. She blushed, thinking about them.

A little less than an hour later Cass was pulling on new boots in the outer office. "I'm finished dressing, Brett. And I have to say you did pretty well. The shirt's a little big, but other than that everything fits very well."

"Good. I told Jasper they were for you. He already knew your sizes, so I didn't have to guess," he called from the tub, where he soaked.

Cass looked around while she waited. Her stomach growled almost painfully as she perused the wanted posters on the wall. "Brett," she called.

"Yes?"

"How about if I go to the hotel and get breakfast and bring it back here?" she said.

"Sounds good to me. I can soak a little longer."

"Great, I'll be back as soon as I can."

"See you later," he called.

Cass left the office and headed toward the hotel, thoughts of fried eggs, bacon, sourdough toast, and sweet black coffee making her mouth water. As she started to cross the street, Ramsey stepped out from between two buildings right in front of her.

"Cass, I need to talk to you," he said.

She looked at him in disgust. "I have nothing to say to you, Ramsey." Her voice was full of anger.

"Please, Cass. I want to apologize."

"I don't care," she told him bluntly.

"But, Cass, I'm so ashamed of my behavior yesterday."

Was it only yesterday? she wondered. With everything that had happened since then, it seemed like a long time ago. "You should be ashamed," she said.

"I know. I behaved atrociously. I've never acted like that before in my life, Cass. I can only say it's because I've never felt this way about anyone before," he said, bowing his head. "I'm so sorry," he mumbled.

Cass stared at his humbled posture. "That's no excuse," she told him.

"You're right, Cass. I know I have no right to expect your full forgiveness, but I was hoping you'd see it in your heart to at least give me a chance to make it up to you."

"You don't have to do that. Just leave me alone, Ramsey," she said with vehemence.

He lifted his eyes to hers then. "Please, Cass. I won't ask for your love. Just let me be a friend."

Cass was astonished to see tears brimming his blue eyes. Was he really that sorry he'd behaved like such an ass? "Well . . ." She wavered slightly.

"You will!" he gushed. "I can see you'll give me another chance."

"I don't know, Ramsey," she said. His behavior was too erratic. She didn't trust him, would never trust him again.

Stepping forward, he gently reached out to take one of her hands. "No threats. No pressure. Just friendship for a while," he said.

Cass cringed and pulled back when he tried to touch her hand, the memory of his horrid behavior still fresh in her mind. She saw the hurt in his eyes at her action.

"Please, Cass," he whispered.

His remorse did seem genuine, but she couldn't bring herself to touch him. Standing very still, she sized him up. He'd turned out to be such a pathetic creature. "I suppose," she finally said. Then a thought struck her. "Where were you last night?" she asked.

Ramsey glanced up into her eyes. "I heard about what happened out at your place. Are you asking me if I was a part of it?"

"I'm just asking you where you were, Ramsey."

"I was in town, Cass," he said solemnly. "There are people who will tell you I was here. I'll go get them for you. I want you to trust me."

"That won't be necessary. If you say you were here I believe you."

"I botched things up pretty badly yesterday for you to actually think I could be capable of raiding your place. I'm so sorry, Cass."

Cass sighed. "I had to ask," she said.

"I understand, I guess." He looked past her. "Where are you going now?" he asked.

"I'm on my way to get breakfast."

"May I go with you? I wouldn't want you to have to eat alone."

"I'm getting the food and bringing it back to the sheriff's office to eat with Brett," she explained.

Ramsey's mouth drooped at one corner. "That's how it is, eh?"

She didn't want to explain the dynamics of their relationship to Ramsey, or to anyone. "We're friends," she stated simply.

His gaze fell. "I see," he said. "Well, I wouldn't want to keep you. Thank you for listening to me, Cass."

"You're welcome."

He turned away from her and began to walk away. At the last minute he turned back around and flashed one of his old, charming smiles at her. "Besides, you're not married to the marshal. You just might love me yet," he said with a twinkle in his eye.

Cass opened her mouth to protest, but he'd already turned away from her again. "You're one strange man, Ramsey," she whispered, a shiver of revulsion skittering through her at his crazy mood swings.

Starting toward the hotel again, she was almost there

when she saw Rosie coming toward her. "What are you doing out here?" she asked her. "You should still be home in bed."

"I heard some people talking outside as they passed my window. They said your place was burned and someone was shot. I had to find out who. I was on my way to the doctor's office when I saw you talking to Ramsey," she said hurriedly.

"Yes. He wanted to apologize for ... for something. And it was Uncle Darby who was shot, but the doc say's he'll be fine." Cass noticed Rosie's color was high. You're not well. I'm taking you home."

"I'm fine, really," Rosie answered, wringing her hands and breathing in short gasps.

"You're not fine. Come with me." She led Rosie back to her house. Once inside, she made the girl sit in a comfortable chair. "You've got to calm down. You've worked yourself into a state," she said.

Rosie continued wringing her hands. She looked up at Cass and bit her lip. "Cass, you're my friend. When I thought you might have been shot ... it nearly scared me to death," she said.

"Rosie, thank you. You're my friend too. But as you can see, I'm fine."

Rosie took several more panting breaths. "And just now, when I saw you talking to Ramsey ..."

"Yes?"

"It's just that Ramsey can be so awful. I'd hate to see him hurt you."

"He won't hurt me, Rosie. He was a little ... well, more than a little threatening yesterday, but he apologized today. That's what he was doing just now, apologizing."

"He threatened you?" Rosie's eyes grew as big as saucers.

"I guess it was silly. He thinks he's in love with me and was insisting I marry him. When I refused, he became a little too aggressive."

Tears began to slip from Rosie's eyes. "I'm so sorry, Cass," she whispered.

"Rosie? What's wrong?"

"I should have told you sooner."

"What?"

"It's Ramsey. He's the one who's been beating me."

"Ramsey?" Cass repeated. So Brett was right.

"Yes," Rosie sniffled.

Cass looked down at Rosie's stomach.

Rosie noticed where she was looking and nodded. "Yes, he's the father."

"Oh, Rosie," Cass whispered.

"It isn't what you think, Cass. I don't love him. I hate him."

"Then how could you . . ."

"He raped me. And it wasn't the first time."

Chapter 18

C ass looked at Rosie in horror. "He raped you? Why didn't you tell Brett?"

Tears rolled down Rosie's cheeks unheeded. "Ramsey said he'd kill me if I told anyone. But now I'm pregnant. What am I going to do?"

Cass's anger grew hot in her chest. "We're going to report Ramsey's crimes to Brett. He'll arrest the bastard."

"No!" Rosie wailed. "I'm afraid of Ramsey. You have no idea what he's capable of. I wouldn't have told you this much if I didn't think he might do the same to you. I just couldn't bear the thought that he might hurt you."

Cass shook her head. "Dear Rosie, don't worry about me. I can take care of myself," she said, patting Rosie affectionately on the knee. "And once Brett arrests Ramsey he won't be able to get to you."

"His father will get him out of jail. He covered for him before, years ago."

Cass lowered her eyelids slightly. "When?"

"The first time he raped me."

"I thought you meant he'd raped you more than once since his return to Twisted Creek," she said.

"No," Rosie said. "The first time was the day your family was killed." Her head fell forward in sorrowful racking sobs.

"You must be mistaken, Rosie," Cass said quietly. "Ramsey had been gone a week already when my family was murdered. He'd left for college, don't you remember?"

"No, he didn't go, Cass. At least not then. The day your family was killed he came knocking on my window. He was so nice when he wanted to be. He told me he was sorry he'd been mean to me all the years we were growing up. He said it was because he'd always had a crush on me but didn't know how to approach me." She looked up into Cass's eyes, her own puffy from crying. "I wanted to believe him, Cass. I always thought he was handsome," she sobbed. "Even when he was so mean to me. But when I went with him, he took me just outside of town and he . . . he . . . It was so horrible the first time, Cass. It hurt so much."

Cass knelt in front of Rosie and pulled her into her arms. "Oh, Rosie, you've been through so much," she said consolingly. "Why didn't you report it then?"

"I did, but Sheriff Jackson was so busy getting the posse together to go after your family's murderers that he barely listened to me. Then, afterward, he didn't believe me. He believed, like everyone else, that Ramsey had already left town." She leaned back and stared hard at Cass. "It was Ramsey, Cass. He was still in town that day. I even went to Hunt, hoping he would help me, hoping he'd let everyone know Ramsey hadn't left for college yet. He just laughed at me and called me a slut. He told me his son wouldn't have touched the likes of me without an invitation."

Cass remembered that Ramsey had called her a slut the day before—his father's word. "It's time this stopped, Rosie. We're going to put an end to Ramsey's crimes once and for all. I'll tell Brett what Ramsey has done to you. I promise he'll take care of it, and he and I together will make sure Ramsey never touches you again."

Rosie stared hopefully into Cass's eyes. "I can't even remember what it feels like to not be afraid," she said, her voice still full of tears.

Cass took her arms from around Rosie's back and patted her knees for a moment. Standing, she turned toward the door. "You stay here and don't open the door to anyone, understand?"

Rosie nodded.

"Good. I'll be back with Brett," she said. Crossing to the door, she looked back at Rosie's pitiful face. Rage roiled inside her at what Ramsey had done to Rosie's life. Leaving the tiny house, she headed straight for the sheriff's office. She couldn't wait to tell Brett about Rosie. And to think Ramsey had raped her all those years ago. Her anger made her footsteps heavy in the dirt street. And if Ramsey was still in town when her family was murdered, he'd probably known all along that his father was involved. "You acted so innocent," she fumed out loud through clenched teeth.

Brett was waiting patiently for his breakfast when Cass came crashing through the door. The look on her face drove any thought of food from his mind. "What's wrong, Cass?" he asked, standing up and moving around the desk toward her.

"It's Rosie, Brett. Ramsey raped her."

Brett stared at Cass as what she'd said registered. "That son of a bitch," he cursed.

"And he's been beating her, threatening to kill her if she told anyone."

Brett clenched his fists. "I'll ride out to the Lazy T today, right after I get Rosie to sign a report. I'll arrest that bastard."

"And that's not all, Brett," Cass said, touching him on the arm. "She told me something about the day my family was murdered."

"Does she know who did it?"

"No. But Ramsey was still in town then."

"I thought you said he'd been gone about a week by then."

"I thought he had. Everyone thought he'd gone back east to college. But according to Rosie, he paid her a visit on the day my family was murdered. He lured her out of town and raped her for the first time."

"She was just a kid," he said.

Cass nodded. "And when she told the sheriff what had happened he wouldn't believe her. Brett, Rosie's been living with this for five years. Now he's back and treating her even worse than before. He's the father of her baby," she said sadly.

"Let's go talk to her. I'll bring the paperwork with me to her house. As soon as she signs it, I'll go find Ramsey."

"He's in town," she said.

"How do you know?"

"I saw him. He spoke to me."

"Fine. He'll be that much easier to get to."

They left the office and went straight to Rosie's place. She answered the door with tears still dripping from her eyes. "I'm afraid, Marshal," she admitted. "I don't know if I can do this."

"You have to, don't you see that, Rosie?" asked Cass. "It's the only way you'll ever be free of him. He knows he can victimize you, so he'll keep doing it."

Rosie turned around and went back to the chair she'd been sitting in earlier. "My life is such a mess. Even if you do stop Ramsey from hurting me, what am I going to do? I'm pregnant and I'm not married."

Cass touched Rosie on the shoulder. "People will understand when they know what happened."

"No! You can't tell anyone. I'd die of humiliation." She paused for a second. "Maybe that's what should happen. I'd be better off dead."

"Rosie, don't ever say anything like that," Cass pleaded. "I've lost so many people in my life. Don't make me think I might lose you now that we've become friends again after all this time."

Rosie let her gaze drop. "I'm sorry. I just feel so helpless."

"You won't be helpless if you make a report and sign it. You'll be the one with the power, Rosie. You have the power to put this man behind bars for a long time for what he did to you," Brett told her.

Rosie hesitated for a few seconds while she thought about it. "It would be nice to feel safe again," she said softly. "I guess I could stand everything else if I knew he wouldn't bother me again. All right. What do I have to do?"

Brett explained the procedure to her, then started writing down what she told him. As Cass listened to the horrible story again, she wondered why she had not realized how dangerous Ramsey could be.

A few minutes later she felt her stomach growl again. She'd completely forgotten about food while talking to Rosie, but her appetite had come back with a vengeance. "Brett?" she said. "I'm going over to the hotel to get us something to eat."

Brett looked away from Rosie to Cass. "Sounds good."

"Breakfast or lunch?"

"How about a thick roast beef sandwich?"

"Mmmm. I'll get two. Rosie would you like something?"

Rosie sniffed. "No, thank you, Cass. I haven't been very hungry lately."

"You've got to keep up your strength. You're eating for two."

Rosie thought for a minute. "If they have some soup, I suppose I could eat a little," she said.

"Soup it is," Cass answered, heading for the door. "I'll be right back."

On her way to the hotel and food once more, her bootheels dug deep into the dirt in the street as she hurried.

"Cassidy Wayne?"

Cass stopped abruptly, hearing the threatening tone of the voice behind her. Turning slowly, she looked at the man who had spoken. "Who wants to know?"

"The name's Bobby Fleet. I understand you killed my little brother."

Cass's blood ran cold. "I didn't want to. He forced my hand in a fair fight."

"It doesn't matter. Henry was just a kid, and now he's

dead. You killed him. Now I'm gonna kill you. That's how it works, Miss Wayne."

"It doesn't have to. Like I said, I didn't want to kill him. He left me no choice. You and I still have choices. We don't have to do this."

"Henry challenged you because he heard you were fast. He wanted to make a bigger name for himself. I'm going to kill you because he was my brother. You see, it doesn't matter what the reasons are, everything evens out in the end."

Cass sized up this gunfighter while he talked. He was quite a bit older than Henry had been, and he was reportedly a lot faster. She watched his eyes, hard eyes that never left hers. He didn't blink incessantly as Henry had. He wasn't nervous. His arms hung loose at his sides, his right hand poised over his gun. Her heart slowed until it scarcely beat within her chest, the calm coming over her. She was going to have to kill him.

"You ready to die, Miss Wayne?" he asked.

"Are you?" she returned.

"I ain't the one gonna meet the Lord today. You are."

"I doubt it's the Lord you'll be meeting," she answered, "but you can say hello to the devil for me."

"You're funny, Miss Wayne. Real funny. I wonder if you'll think it's funny when my bullet splits your heart in two."

"That's not going to happen, Bobby I'm as fast as you've heard, maybe faster. I didn't want to kill your brother, and I don't want to kill you, but I will if you force me." She watched the way he stood, relaxed, sure of himself. She noticed the slight smile that turned up the corners of his mouth.

"You know, you're real pretty. It's gonna almost be a shame to kill you," he said. "I can think of a lot of things I'd rather do to you than shoot you."

Cass knew he was trying to rattle her. It was a ploy one gunfighter would use against another in an attempt to make his opponent lose his concentration. "I doubt you'd be capable of doing anything that would impress me much," she returned, playing his game.

"You might be surprised. I know you're gonna be surprised when my bullet kills you."

"Likewise."

He took a step to the side, slowly trying to get the sun where he wanted it.

Cass simply backed up, refusing to give him the advantage. She noticed that he was squinting a bit. Good, keep the sun in your eyes, she thought. "Did you teach Henry to shoot?" she asked.

"Why?"

"I just want to know what I'm up against. If you taught Henry and I beat him, I can no doubt beat you. It makes sense," she tried a little rattling of her own.

Bobby chuckled. "Trying to ruffle my feathers?" he asked.

"A little, maybe. We both know what we're doing," she offered, seeing him sidestep again.

"That we do, Miss Wayne. That we do," he said calmly, as though he had all the time in the world to spend standing in the street.

Cass realized this man was different. He wasn't in a hurry. And he wasn't afraid. He just might beat me, she thought in surprise. In all other gunfights, she had known the danger of dying was present. There was always the possibility she'd underestimated her opponent. There was the possibility of a lucky shot from a man who normally couldn't have beaten her on his best day. But this time was different. She could feel it in her bones. She'd have to be at her very best to win this duel. Raising her jaw slightly, she readied herself to draw.

Bobby instinctively adjusted his stance. He could see the time was drawing near.

Cass felt his every move, his every breath. Facing down a gunman was like becoming a part of his soul for a brief period. She realized it was a little like making love, only instead of creating life, you created death.

She thought about making love to Brett. If she died here

today he would never know she loved him. Yes, she realized, she loved him with all her heart. It was so blazingly clear. Why hadn't she seen it until now, when she was staring death in the face?

Then something caught her eye. Several people had seen what was happening and stepped into the street to watch. Ramsey was standing behind Bobby Fleet. Then he reached up to lower the brim of his hat to shade his eyes, something flashed in the sunlight. Cass blinked. There was another flash as Ramsey moved his hand again.

Suddenly it was a morning five years earlier. She was lying on her stomach in the tall grass not far from her home. Becky was screaming as she died inside the burning house. Her brothers lay dead in the dirt. Her mother was crying over her dead husband's body. One of the murderers pulled her away from her husband and shot her. "This one's for the old man," he said, laughing. Then Cass saw the dark figure on horseback sitting not far from the mayhem. He started to come into focus. He was laughing and waving his gun—his silver gun. "Come on, boys, we're through here. I'll take care of Cassidy myself later," he shouted waving to the murderers again. Only it wasn't a silver gun that flashed so brilliantly in the sunlight. It was a heavy silver chain. Ramsey's silver bracelet. It was Ramsey! *Ramsey!* her heart screamed. It had been Ramsey all along!

She was back on the street facing down a gunfighter, but she could see Ramsey behind him. Ramsey the murderer!

Cass had looked away from the gunman for only a second, but that one second was all Bobby needed. She knew it too late. His arm had jerked downward before she could clear leather. Dropping as she drew, Cass pulled her guns, aimed, and fired. The explosions of gunfire ripped apart the stillness of the late morning. Cass felt the impact of the bullet as it slammed into her chest just below her right shoulder.

Brett heard the gunfire and raced out of Rosie's house to see what was going on. The scene that met his eyes nearly killed him. Cass lay bleeding in the street, and a man lay not far from her. Several people were running closer. "Cass!" he shouted in anguish as he rushed to her side. Kneeling in the dirt, he felt for her pulse. It was weak. "What did you do?" he cried. Picking her up, he ran for the doctor's office.

"Doc!" he yelled as he charged inside. The waiting room was empty. "Doc!" he yelled again.

"What is it?" the doctor asked, coming out from behind the curtain carrying a sandwich.

"Cass has been shot, Doc."

The doctor dropped his sandwich on the floor and ran to hold the curtain back. "Bring her in here," he said.

Brett rushed past him, carrying Cass into the examination room.

"Put her here," the doctor indicated an exam table.

Brett gently laid Cass on the table. "Do something, Doc. Don't let her die."

The doctor pulled Cass's shirt away from her body. Inserting scissors in the hole the bullet had made in the fabric, he started cutting. The shirt was soon lying open over her chest. "It looks pretty bad," he commented.

Brett swallowed hard. His heart was slamming against his chest in terror that she'd die. "What can I do?" he pleaded.

"Just let me do what I have to do," the doctor answered. "Please wait outside."

Brett glowered at the doctor. "You couldn't get me to leave by threatening me with a bear rifle," he said.

The doctor sighed. "Suit yourself." He proceeded to probe the wound. "The bullet didn't go through, but I can't feel it. That means it probably ricocheted around inside her a bit. I'll have to go in after it."

Brett watched as the doctor began to cut. His heart ached a little more with each incision, and he wished it could have been him on the table in her place.

"It nicked her lung," the doctor said after a moment.

"Doc?" Brett said anxiously.

"I think she'll be all right, Marshal," the doctor replied. He continued to search for the bullet.

Several people peered into the room through the curtain. "How's she doin', Doc?" one of them asked.

"Wait outside, please," the doctor told them. "I'll talk to you later."

"Somebody sent for Soony. We figured he'd want to know what's happened," someone else said.

"Fine. Fine," said the doctor, feeling around inside Cass's chest with his fingers.

"And we sent that dead gunslinger to the undertaker's. Cass nailed him right between the eyes. That girl can sure shoot."

Brett glanced briefly at the faces of the people trying to see how Cass was doing. He could see Rosie crying between two of them. Leaving Cass's side for only a moment, he went over to her. "Rosie, you go on home. I'll let you know how she's doing as soon as I can," he told her.

Rosie nodded and turned to leave. Brett noticed an expression of fear fill her face as she stepped out onto the sidewalk. Then he saw Ramsey on the opposite side of the street. If that bastard says one word to Rosie, I'll kill him, he thought. He walked outside and watched her make her way home. Ramsey watched her too, but he didn't approach her. Brett glared at the man. "It won't be long until I lock you up," he whispered to himself.

Back at Cass's side a few seconds later, he jumped when the doctor began shouting. Brett questioned, "What is it, Doc?"

"I found the bullet! I found it!" the doctor exclaimed.

"Take it out," Brett urged.

"It'll take me a little while. It's lodged inside her right shoulder blade. I have to be careful digging it out."

It took the doctor several minutes to remove the bullet, then another half hour to close up the wound. As he bandaged her, he looked up at Brett. "Now we pray," he said softly.

"Pray?"

"I did what I could. The Lord has to do the rest."

"But she'll be all right, won't she, Doc?" Brett urged.

The doctor shrugged. "She lost a lot of blood, and though no arteries were severed, the bullet did nick the lung. She could get an infection. She could get pneumonia. She won't be out of the woods for a while, Marshal."

Brett looked down at Cass's beautiful face, so pale right now, and felt tears welling up in his eyes. "I love her, Doc," he said softly.

"I know you do," the doctor answered.

Soony burst in through the curtain. "Missy Cass!" he exclaimed. "She's shot?"

Brett nodded. "But she'll be fine, Soony."

Soony crossed to where Cass lay unconscious. "She looks so white," he said, taking her hand. "Missy Cass, get well please," he said quietly to her.

Brett looked around the examination room and frowned. He'd completely forgotten about Darby. "Where's her uncle?"

"Darby is at Mrs. Wettle's home," answered the doctor.

"I thought you said you wanted him to stay here overnight so you could watch him," said Brett.

"I did. But he woke up and had ideas of his own. I couldn't fight both him and Mrs. Wettle," the doctor explained. "I told him I wouldn't be responsible for what happened if he left. Mrs. Wettle said she would be."

Soony looked up from Cass. "Mr. Darby says he likes it fine at Mrs. Wettle's house. He's sleeping in her bed." He let his gaze fall back to Cass.

Brett and the doctor exchanged glances. Soony obviously didn't realize how his words sounded.

"Mr. Darby will worry about Missy Cass," Soony murmured.

"Oh, no," Brett sighed. "I promised to let Rosie know how Cass is doing." He gazed at Cass's pallor. "I'm afraid to leave her for even a little while, Doc," he said.

"She'll sleep for hours, Marshal. Maybe days. She'll never know you left."

"But will she still be here when I come back?" he breathed.

The doctor hesitated. "The good Lord willing."

Brett said a silent prayer. "All right. I'll be back as soon as I can."

Brett left the office and went to Rosie's house. Finding the door unlocked worried him. Had Rosie forgotten to lock it? Knocking gently, he pushed it open. He could hear Rosie crying inside. "It's all right, Rosie. Cass is alive. She's going to be fine," he called, willing his words to be true. Entering the kitchen, he found Rosie bent over the sink crying. "Rosie, did you hear me? She's alive." He touched her on the back. When she turned to face him, he cursed with rage, "I'll kill that bastard!"

Rosie's nose was bleeding and one eye was swelling shut. "Ramsey came in right after I got back from the doctor's office," she sobbed.

"I'm going after him, Rosie."

"He'll kill you. He hates you for stealing Cass away from him."

"Cass was never his," he hissed.

"He thought she was, or that she could be. Your arrival in town changed all that. He kept saying something about his father being angry he'd botched things up so badly. He's crazy, Marshal."

"Crazy people belong in institutions. I'll do what I can to see to it he spends some time in one, the state prison. Did he say where he was going when he left here?"

"He said he was going home, but don't go out there, Marshal," she pleaded.

"Don't worry about me, Rosie. I'm going out to the Lazy T, and I'll be fine. I have to be. Cass needs me."

Rosie nodded.

Brett left Rosie locked in her house and headed for the sheriff's office. He was going to take an extra rifle with him when he went to the Lazy T. Crossing the street, he passed Mrs. Thompson's energetic nephew, Buster.

"Howdy, Marshal," said Buster. "How's Miss Wayne doing?"

Brett stopped and looked at the red-haired young man. "She's going to be fine."

"I'm right glad to hear that. She seems like a nice person. Sure can shoot, too," he said with some awe.

"Yes, she's special." Brett looked at the young man. "Are you still searching for a job, Buster?"

"Yes, sir."

"Are you set on punching cows?"

Buster shrugged. "It's all I know how to do."

"Ever thought about being a lawman?"

"Who, me? You're joking with me, aren't you, Marshal?"

"No, Buster. I've never been more serious. I'm running for sheriff in this town. If I win, I'll need a deputy. I think you'd be perfect for the job."

"Gosh, Marshal, I guess I'd love that," said Buster, a giant grin stretching across his freckled face.

"Good. Would you be willing to do something for me now?"

"Sure thing."

"I have to go somewhere for a while. I'll probably be gone several hours. There's a lady in that house over there"—he pointed to Rosie's house—"who needs some protection. Would you go sit with her until I get back?"

"You just want me to sit with her?"

"I hope that's all you'll have to do. If Ramsey Tylo tries to get in to see her ... shoot him," he said.

"Shoot him?" asked Buster, his eyes wide.

"Shoot him."

"Dead, sir?"

"Can you do it, Buster? I need to know."

"You betcha."

Brett grinned. "I knew I could count on you, Buster. I'll see you later." He turned and headed for the office once more.

Riding onto Lazy T land a while later, Brett was surprised not to be met by armed riders. He rode right up to the house and dismounted. Knocking on the door, he waited only seconds before Hunt Tylo himself swung the door wide.

"I've come for Ramsey, Mr. Tylo," he announced, entering the house.

"What for?" Hunt asked belligerently.

"Rape and assault," Brett said as he walked deeper into the house.

"Hah! My boy never had to rape any woman. Who's telling such lies? That dirty little waitress, Rosie, right?"

"It doesn't matter who's doing the accusing, Mr. Tylo. The crime's the same no matter who the victim is."

"There is no victim. And you can't just barge into a man's home and start snooping around," his voice boomed as he followed Brett through the house.

"Yes, I can. Ramsey made it very easy for me. I was about to draw up a warrant and get it to the circuit judge to sign, but now I don't have to. Ramsey beat up Rosie again today. I'm in pursuit of a criminal, Mr. Tylo. I'm going to arrest your son and put him behind bars." He continued to search through the many rooms of the house.

"Like hell you are."

"I hope it's like hell for him, Tylo. Now, where is he?"

"He's not here. And you can look all you want for him. You won't find him."

"You've hidden him."

"He's my son."

"Are you willing to let him get away with rape and assault just because he's your son?" he asked, searching through bedrooms.

"I still say he didn't do anything wrong. That little slut's been after him for years," Hunt said, following the marshal through the house.

Brett wanted to smash Tylo's face in with the butt of his rifle, but he controlled the impulse. He stopped searching and turned to stare at Hunt. "Her name is Rosie," he said through clenched teeth. "If I ever hear you call her anything that filthy again I'll knock you on your ass, Tylo. Do you understand?"

Hunt glared at Brett. "I'm entitled to my opinion," he stated defiantly.

"Not around me, you're not," said Brett.

"You're asking for more trouble here than you can handle, Marshal," Tylo said.

"I don't take kindly to threats."

"I don't threaten. I promise."

"And I get justice. Remember that, Tylo." He turned and headed back toward the front door. He hadn't found Ramsey in the house, and the Lazy T was a big place. He could be hiding anywhere. "You tell your son I'm looking for him, Tylo. You tell him the next time I see him I'll arrest him." He stomped down the porch steps and swung up into the saddle.

Hunt walked out onto the porch. "And you hear me, Marshal. If you ever trespass on the Lazy T again without a warrant I'll shoot you on sight."

"I guess we know where we stand, don't we, Tylo?" Brett ground out.

"I guess we do."

Brett tugged the reins, directing his mount away from the house. He spurred the animal to a gallop, frustrated he'd been unable to find Ramsey. "I'll get you next time, Ramsey," he hissed into the wind. "But right now Cass needs me."

After Brett was out of sight, Ramsey sauntered out of the house and stood by his father. "I guess I'll have to kill him," he said, staring in the direction Brett had ridden.

"Seems so," answered Hunt. "Do you think you can handle murdering the marshal better than you handled Cassidy?" he questioned.

"Cassidy is a different kind of problem," Ramsey answered. "Besides, Cass may die from that gunslinger's bullet yet."

"I hope you're right. If not ... you've had your last chance with her, boy. I want Cassidy dead."

"Don't worry. I'll take care of everything."

Chapter 19

*B*rett rode like the wind to get back to town. He cursed the whole way that he'd come up empty-handed in his search for Ramsey. "At least he knows his days are numbered," he breathed.

Before going to the doctor's office, he stopped at Rosie's house to make sure she was all right. He jumped from his horse and took the porch steps two at a time. "Buster!" he called, knocking on the door.

Buster opened the door and met the marshal with a grin. "Yes, sir?"

Brett couldn't help but return Buster's smile. It was infectious. "I wanted to let you know I'm back. I need to be with Cass, but I don't think Rosie should be left alone. Can you stay on here for a while?"

"Sure thing, Marshal. Rosie's real nice."

Brett smiled again. "Thanks. I'll stop by once in a while to see how you're doing. And I'll send Soony to run errands for you, to get you food and things."

"Will I be here long, sir?" Buster asked.

Brett thought for a moment. "Maybe a few days."

"All right. I guess I'll see you later, then, Marshal." Buster backed away from the door and began closing it.

"Remember what I said about Ramsey," Brett reminded him.

"Dead, sir," Buster said.

Brett smiled and walked away, knowing Rosie was in good hands.

Cass was sleeping peacefully when he entered the doctor's exam room minutes later. "How's she doing, Doc," he asked as he went to her side, taking her left hand in his.

"The same. I told you it might take some time to see a change in her. And then it might not be for the better."

"She's going to be fine," Brett said. "She's got to give me twenty children."

The doctor's eyebrows went up. "Whatever you say, Marshal. But do you mind if she recovers first?"

Brett looked up at the doctor and smiled. "Not at all."

"I'll be back in my apartment. Call me if she wakes up," the doctor said.

Brett nodded and watched him go. He then turned his attention to Cass. She was so beautiful, even pale and weak, her dark chestnut hair framing her face with soft curls. Looking at her features, he saw her lashes sending long shadows over her cheekbones. He let his gaze follow their path, slipping downward to her mouth, her lips pallid with just a touch of blue at the corners. How he longed to see those lips pink and curled up into a teasing smile again. "You've got to pull through this, Cass. I love you," he whispered.

Cass hovered somewhere in the dark. She hurt so badly that she didn't want to leave this place of unreality. She didn't want to see the gunman again. She didn't want to see Ramsey's face. He'd killed her family. All these years she'd thought about the silver gun. She'd asked questions trying to find the mystery man, and all along it had been Ramsey. The scene began to play again in her mind. The fire in the house, the gunshots, the screams. She tried to cry out, but could only lie and watch. No, she thought. I don't want to see this again. She let herself fall farther into the darkness.

Brett thought he saw her eyelashes flutter just a bit. "Doc," he called.

"What is it?" the doctor asked, entering the room.

"Her eyelids moved."

"She's dreaming. Or trying to wake up," he said. He checked her pulse and left the room again.

Brett once more watched her sleep. "Cass, come back to me," he whispered.

For hours he stood and watched her. Then, getting a chair from the waiting room, he sat for several more hours. It was growing dark when he heard someone at the door. Standing up, he went to see who it was. Peering out through the window, he saw Soony.

"Mr. Brett, Mrs. Wettle sent dinner," he said, holding up a tray and a glass of milk.

Brett realized he hadn't eaten all day and hurriedly opened the door. "Thank you, Soony. And thank Mrs. Wettle for me when you go back." He sniffed the cloth-covered tray.

"Stew," Soony informed him. "She says it'll stick to your ribs. I say it'll stick to everything."

Brett chuckled. "You don't think too highly of Mrs. Wettle's cooking?"

Soony looked down. "She puts flour in everything, even eggs."

"Eggs?"

"She fixed Mr. Darby some eggs with flour in them. She says flour gives them body. I don't understand," he said, shaking his head.

Brett grinned. "I'm sure she's not as good a cook as you are, Soony, but I'll do my best to eat this. I wouldn't want to hurt her feelings."

Soony nodded. "Yes. We must be nice," he said. "She means well."

Brett took the tray and milk from Soony and carried them back with him into the exam room.

"How is Missy Cass?" Soony asked, following him inside. "Mr. Darby is very worried."

"The same. She's sleeping. Once in a while her eyelids move, but she hasn't awakened yet."

"She's dreaming," said Soony.

"That's what the doc says."

"He's right," confirmed Soony as though he were an expert.

Brett devoured Mrs. Wettle's stew with fervor. He was so hungry he didn't stop to analyze it. It was food. And it did feel as if it would stick to his ribs. He washed it down with the milk. "How is Darby doing?" he asked when his stomach was full.

"Mr. Darby says he's fine. Mrs. Wettle says he's stubborn. She says he must stay in her bed for a week," Soony informed him.

Brett started to chuckle when Soony mentioned the sleeping arrangements at Mrs. Wettle's home.

"Did I say something wrong, Mr. Brett?" Soony asked.

"No, don't change a thing," Brett told him. Though Soony had a remarkable grasp of the English language, his occasional misunderstandings of certain things were quite entertaining.

Soony nodded. "I'll go now. I told Mrs. Wettle I'd do the dishes."

Brett smiled at Soony. "All right. Tell Darby I'll stop by in the morning to see how he's doing."

"Yes, Mr. Brett."

"And would you do me a favor? Would you go to Rosie's house tomorrow to see if she and Buster need anything from the store?"

"Buster?"

"Mrs. Thompson's nephew. You probably met him at the barn raising. He's keeping an eye on Rosie for me." He noticed the bewildered expression on Soony's face. The man didn't know all that was going on. "Rosie has been threatened," he explained.

Soony nodded. "I'll be glad to go to Rosie's tomorrow."

"Thank you," Brett said, handing him the empty tray and glass.

After Soony had left, Brett returned to his vigil, watching over Cass. Several hours later he dozed off with his head resting on the edge of the table where she lay.

Cass was running. Running from the men who had killed her family. Running toward something. She couldn't catch her breath, and she felt as though her chest was about to explode. She tried calling out for help, but she couldn't remember who was left alive to help her. She saw her mother and father, but they were both dead. She saw her brothers and sister. They were dead too. Then she saw Brett. She opened her mouth to scream for him to help her, but she could make no sound. She was drowning in thick water. It sucked her downward, choking her, pressing on her chest so she couldn't breathe at all. Then the flames began to lick at her flesh. She was on fire. The heat seared her painfully. She tried to call for Brett again, but again she could make no sound. Ramsey's face floated before her, smiling. He dangled a silver chain in front of her. "It was me, Cass," he taunted. "It was me." He began to laugh at her. She struggled against the sound, but it wouldn't stop. No matter what she did, her torment wouldn't end.

Brett felt Cass move and was suddenly awake. "Cass?" he said, his voice raspy with sleep. "Cass, are you awake?"

He looked at her face. She was still unconscious, dreaming dreams that caused her to writhe. Touching her forehead, he was filled with dread. She was burning up. "Doc!" he called. "Doc, get in here!"

Seconds later the doctor ran into the room in his nightshirt. Feeling Cass's forehead and arms, he shook his head. "I warned you fever might set in."

"What can we do?"

"Keep her as cool as possible and let her ride it out. Let's hope she's strong enough to live through it."

The doctor helped Brett remove Cass's clothes, then gave him a basin of cool water and a sponge. "Just keep her cool, Marshal. That's all you can do."

Brett began to sponge her off, starting at her head and working his way down her body. Once in a while he'd hear her moan and see her eyelashes flutter, but she never woke up. The night turned into one long stretch of continuous work. "Come on, Cass. Fight. Fight for me. You've got to come back to me," he pleaded.

Cass once more suffered through the fire. Her fingers burned. Her toes burned. The ends of her hair burned. And through it all she heard Ramsey's laughter. At one point she was certain she saw Satan smiling down on her, but his face turned into Ramsey's and she knew she wasn't dead yet. She shivered as something cold touched her.

Brett watched the sun come up through the windows of the office. He'd spent nearly the entire night sponging Cass off, but she was still almost too hot to touch. His eyes were red-rimmed, and his muscles ached.

"You look a sight," said the doctor when he came in carrying two cups of steaming black coffee.

"I need this," Brett whispered over the cup the doctor handed him.

The doctor felt Cass's forehead, then checked her pulse. "She seems about the same."

Brett nodded. "I'm going to keep trying to cool her off. She'll make it, Doc. I know she will."

The doctor nodded and walked back to his apartment.

About an hour later Mrs. Wettle brought another tray of food for Brett. "I can't stand the thought of a man being hungry," she said, setting the tray on a small table in the examination room. "How's she doing? Darby wants me to give him details."

"She's got a fever. I'm working to get it down."

Mrs. Wettle nodded her head approvingly. "She's a lucky girl to have you," she said.

"Darby's lucky to have you," Brett returned.

"Yes, he is," she agreed. "I'd best be getting back to him. Soony will stop by for the tray a little later."

"All right. And tell Darby I said hello."

"Of course," she said, and left.

Several other people stopped by to ask about Cass's condition. He told them all the same thing: she was going to be fine. Soony came and went, and said he'd let Rosie and Buster know what was going on.

Brett continued sponging Cass off during the rest of the day. His shoulders ached from the constant repetitive movement, but he wouldn't stop except to eat or make a trip to the outhouse. "Cass, when you wake up, you're going to listen to me. You're going to stop this quest for revenge. I couldn't go through this again," he said quietly, his heart aching with worry for her. "I love you, Cass," he told her again. "I love you, and I won't lose you. Do you hear me?"

Cass thought she heard someone calling her from very far away. She tried to move toward the sound of the voice, but it was no use. Every time she attempted to surface above the darkness that held her, she saw Ramsey. Ramsey, who'd killed her family. Ramsey, who'd said he would "take care of her" himself. He meant to kill her. Why did he want to marry her? Because he wanted her land to become part of the Lazy T. Had she been right? Had her family been murdered simply for easy access to the Losee? She'd thought it all along, but to know it was true sent her spiraling backwards again. The evil necessary to do such a thing was beyond her ken. She shuddered and fell once more.

Brett watched the sun set and rise again. He'd dozed fitfully during the night and could barely keep his eyes open in the morning.

"You'd better get some rest, Marshal, or you'll be my next patient," the doctor told him.

"I can't rest until her fever's broken."

"Then I suggest you get to resting. She feels cooler," he said smiling. "You've done it, Marshal. I think she's out of the woods."

"What?" Brett jumped up to touch her. "How could I have missed it?"

"You're exhausted. Go get some sleep."

"But I want to be here when she wakes up."

"She might sleep for hours yet. And excuse me for saying so, Marshal, but you need a bath."

Brett started to laugh. "I suppose I do."

"You don't want to offend her the minute she wakes up, do you?" The doctor smiled at him.

"No. I'll go to the sheriff's office and take a bath." He touched his whiskers. "And shave," he added. "But I'll hurry."

As Brett left the doctor's office, his heart felt lighter than it had in several days. He still had Ramsey to deal with, but Cass was going to be all right. He just had to clean up, and stop and check on Rosie and Buster, and then he'd be back beside Cass.

Ramsey scowled as he watched the marshal enter the sheriff's office "You'll be next, Marshal. But first I have to take care of Cass." Sneaking around behind several buildings, he made his way toward the doctor's office.

Cass felt something cool on her forehead. Someone was touching her. Opening her eyes, she looked up and saw the doctor. "Hello, Doc," she whispered weakly.

"Cass?" The doctor glanced down at her face. "Don't try to talk. You've been through quite an ordeal, but you're going to be fine."

"Brett?" she asked.

"I made him go take a bath. He hasn't left your side since you were shot."

She tried to smile, but it was too much effort. She smiled inside. Sleep tugged at her mind again.

"You go ahead and sleep. The marshal will be back soon, and I'm sure he'll tire you out with his attention."

Cass drifted off. She wanted to see Brett. She had to tell him she loved him. And she had to tell him about Ramsey. She had to tell him. . . .

Ramsey peered through a small window in the back of the doctor's office. He seemed to be looking into an apartment of some kind. He saw some movement and ducked back against the building. After waiting a few seconds he looked again. This time he saw the doctor sit down at a small table and begin to read the newspaper. "Perfect," he breathed. Making his way to the front of the building, he slipped inside unnoticed and walked silently toward the examination room.

Cass was dreaming again. She was with Brett, and he was loving her. She smiled up into his beautiful gray eyes as she told him she loved him.

Brett soaked in a cold tub. He hadn't wanted to take the time to warm the water, and now he was paying for it. "Brrr," he shivered. Although the sun outside was beating down with a fury, sitting in cold well water was freezing him through and through. Then he thought about Cass again. Her smile, her laughter, the way she kissed him. The way she did certain other things that raised his blood pressure. He smiled to himself and rinsed the soap from his back. Reaching for his razor, he began to remove several days' growth of beard.

Ramsey moved stealthily into the exam room. His heart filled with evil glee when he saw Cass lying helpless on the examination table with her eyes closed. How could he have gotten any luckier? She was sleeping. She'd never even know what was happening until it was too late. Looking around, he searched for a way to kill her quietly.

Brett finished drying off and reached for his clothes, grateful he'd thought to buy a few extra things for himself the day he'd shopped after the fire. Pulling on his undergarments, then his shirt and trousers, he couldn't help but grin with happiness. Cass was going to be all right. She'd lived through getting shot, and she had survived the fever. She's going to be all right! his mind shouted with joy. He tugged on his boots, then strapped his gun belt around his hips. Grabbing his hat, he headed for Rosie's house. "One stop to make, then I'll be back with you, Cass," he whispered to himself.

Ramsey spotted a pillow under a shelf along the wall. Crossing silently, he pulled it from its place and returned to Cass's side. Raising the pillow above her face, he sneered, "You won't cause us any more trouble, Cass."

Cass was floating in a dream state. Her mind wandered from Brett to the past. She now knew everything. She remembered everything. All the horrible things she'd forgotten, she could now look at, and she knew she'd be able to finish what she'd started. She could see herself killing Ramsey and Hunt. She could feel herself pulling back on the triggers of her guns, could see her enemies dying before her. She was so close to the end of her quest. When it was over, she could concentrate on Brett. She could get on with her life. She'd hang up her guns for good. There would be no more Lady of the Gun.

Something ended her reverie. A voice close by. She struggled back up through the layers of consciousness. Had Brett come back? She had to see him. She had to tell him about Ramsey.

Ramsey studied her face as he hovered over her. Lowering the pillow to his side, he hesitated for a moment. "It's too bad you wouldn't cooperate, Cass. I wanted you, you know. I wanted to make love to you. I wanted to touch you everywhere. I wanted to feel myself inside you. But you wouldn't let me." He frowned down at her. "And now I have to kill you. It's such a waste, Cass. We could have been so good together."

Cass was sure she heard a voice close by. It was a man's voice, but it wasn't Brett's. Was it the doctor's? She made her way upward through the darkness. She could almost touch the top now. She tried to open her eyes.

Brett banged on Rosie's door. "Buster?" he called.

Buster opened the door. "Howdy, Marshal. How's Miss Cass?"

"The fever broke, and the Doc says she should be fine," he answered, grinning. "I went and had a bath and changed clothes. I'm on my way back to her now, but I wanted to stop and see how you and Rosie are doing."

Buster stepped outside and closed the door behind him. He leaned closer to the marshal and whispered, "You know, sir, Rosie's really pretty."

"Yes, Buster, she is," Brett answered.

"Well, sir, do you think it'd be all right if I asked to keep company with her?" he asked.

Brett thought for a minute. "I think that's a fine idea, but it's up to Rosie. She has some things going on in her life right now that she may feel she needs to work through before she'd be ready to start a relationship with anyone."

Buster glanced both ways and leaned even closer. "You mean the baby?"

"She told you about it?" Brett asked, surprised.

"Yes, sir. And you know, she acted like I should think she was a bad person for it. Can you imagine that?"

Brett smiled warmly at his new friend. "No, Buster, I can't."

"Anyway, sir, I just thought I should check with you before I go makin' plans."

"Plans?"

"In case things work out with me and Rosie. Can a deputy be married?"

"This is happening pretty fast, isn't it?" he asked.

"I figure when a man finds a good thing he shouldn't let it go," Buster answered with a wisdom beyond his years.

Brett thought about Cass. "When you're right, Buster, you're very right." He reached out to shake his hand. "I'll be with Cass for a while. You stay here, and I'll come back over when I can."

"Yes, sir," Buster replied, shaking the marshal's hand.

"One more thing, Buster."

"Yes, sir?"

"My name's Brett."

"Yes, sir, Brett," Buster answered, smiling.

Cass opened her eyes slowly and saw the outline of a man standing over her. "Brett?" she whispered.

"No, Cass. It's not Brett. It's me, Ramsey."

Cass's eyes widened in terror. She knew she was nearly helpless. Where was Brett? Where was the doctor? Then she remembered that Ramsey didn't know she was aware of his misdeeds. "Hello, Ramsey," she breathed weakly. "It's nice to see you," she lied.

"It's nice to see you again, Cass," he whispered. "You don't look so well."

"I don't feel so well."

"The other guy is worse. You laid him out like a slab of beef."

"I wish I hadn't been forced to shoot him. He made me do it," she murmured.

"I understand that, Cass, because, you see, I also have to do something I don't want to," he replied softly.

Something in his voice frightened her. "What's that, Ramsey?" she asked.

"I have to kill you," he answered.

Cass's heart leaped in fear. "Why, Ramsey? I said I'd give you another chance. We can start over."

Ramsey shook his head. "I'm afraid not. You getting shot made me realize it would be best for all of us if you simply died. Trying to get you to marry me was proving to be too much work." He raised the pillow again.

Cass saw the pillow and knew instantly what he intended to do. "You'll never get away with this, Ramsey. Someone will find out what you've done. You'll hang."

"Do you really think I'm intimidated by those threats, Cass?" He raised the pillow higher.

Cass brought her left hand up to fight off his attack. "I won't let you," she said, breathing hard from her simple exertion.

Ramsey chuckled softly. "A fighter until the end. I have to give you credit for that." He slammed the pillow down over her face.

Cass tried to scream, but the pillow muffled the sound. She tried to fight with her left hand, but she was too weak. I'm going to die at Ramsey's hands, just like my family, she thought pitifully.

"What's the meaning of this?" Mrs. Wettle demanded as she burst into the room. "—*Doctor!*" she screamed. "*Doctor!*"

Ramsey looked up in surprise as the shocked woman began screaming. Releasing the pillow, he ran away from the table and out of the room, shoving Mrs. Wettle into the wall. "Get out of my way!" he growled as he ran. Once outside, he raced to the back of the building and down the alley toward where he'd left his horse. "Damn that interfering bitch!" he hissed. "Now it'll be all the harder to kill that slut Cassidy!"

Brett heard a scream and took off at a dead run toward the sound. His heart beat wildly in fear as he neared the doctor's office. Had something happened to Cass? Shoving his way through the small crowd that had gathered, he found Mrs. Wettle huffing and puffing in the exam room while the doctor hovered over Cass. "What is it, Doc? She isn't . . ."

The doctor turned to face him. "She'll be fine. But it was close. Someone tried to kill her. Thank God Mrs. Wettle arrived when she did. Someone was trying to suffocate her."

"Someone tried to kill Cass?" He stepped past the doctor and looked down at the woman he loved. "Cass? Are you all right? Please, darling, open your eyes."

Cass heard Brett's voice and opened her eyes slightly. The struggle with Ramsey had sapped what little strength she had left. Trying to smile up at him, she tilted the corners of her mouth only a little. Wiggling the fingers of her left hand, she indicated she wanted him to take it in his, and closed her eyes again when his strong fingers closed over hers.

Brett looked across the room to Mrs. Wettle. "Who was it?"

Mrs. Wettle was fanning herself and taking deep breaths. "It all happened so fast, but it looked like it might have been that Tylo boy. Ramsey, is it?"

"Ramsey!" Brett said through his teeth. "I'll kill that son of a bitch," he hissed.

"Oh, dear," puffed Mrs. Wettle.

"I'm sorry, ma'am," said Brett.

"That's quite all right, Marshal. I would call him worse myself if I weren't a lady."

Chapter 20

*B*rett wouldn't leave Cass's side for the next two days. He knew he'd catch up to Ramsey sooner or later, and Cass's safety was uppermost in his mind now. If Ramsey tried to kill her once, he might try again.

Cass slept most of the time. Her wound had begun healing, but her strength had been sapped. There were a lot of things she needed to tell Brett, but she wanted to feel stronger before she did. On the morning of the third day after Ramsey's attack she awoke with a new feeling of strength in her limbs. "Doc, may I sit up?" she asked.

"Feeling that much better, are we?" the doctor said.

"I think so."

Brett had made a brief trip to the outhouse and was just walking back into the room when the doctor lifted her to a sitting position. "Doc, should she be doing that?" he asked, concerned.

"She thinks so. And the customer is usually right," he teased.

"I feel much better, Brett," she said almost shyly. He was so handsome standing there with his hands on his hips, concerned about her welfare.

Brett felt his heart do a flip at the sight of her smile. He'd waited for days to see some sign that she was getting stronger, and here it was. A beautiful shy smile. Swallowing, he walked to her side. "You look better."

"Do I? I'm sure I look horrible. I haven't brushed my hair in days."

"It looks fine to me."

Cass blushed. She had little on under the blanket, and the thought suddenly embarrassed her. "Doc, when can I get dressed?"

The doctor had been preparing to change her bandage. He glanced over his shoulder at her. "Any time you feel up to it."

"Today?"

"If you say so. Just don't wear anything too elaborate. All those female corsets and chemises and such could make it difficult for me to check your wound."

Brett chuckled. "You don't have to worry about those things with Cass, remember?"

The doctor blinked, then remembered that Cass rarely wore feminine clothing. "Oh, yes, well, in that case . . ." He walked toward the exam table. "Any time you're ready would be fine." He reached for the top of Cass's blanket. "Let's get this bandage changed," he said.

Cass grabbed the blanket with her left hand. "Ah . . . could we do this in a minute?" she asked.

"But why?"

Cass looked at Brett. "Would you mind waiting outside for a while?" she asked.

Brett frowned a bit. "Cass, I've been here for everything. I sponged you myself for nearly two days."

"I know, but that was different. I was unconscious. I'm not anymore, and I'd like some privacy." She blushed when she spoke.

Brett grinned at her. "All right, but I think you're being silly," he said.

"She's being female," offered the doctor.

"Oh, hush," she said.

Cass watched Brett leave the room, then allowed the doctor to clean and re-bandage her wound. "How's it healing, Doc?" she asked.

"Seems to be doing well. You won't be able to move that arm for a while yet, and you'll have a scar, but I think you should heal up good as new in several weeks."

"Good," she said. "Can I get up and walk around?"

"Don't see why not if you feel up to it."

"Can I go to the outhouse instead of using that horrid bedpan?" she asked.

"I suppose."

Cass smiled. She was getting all the right answers. "What about riding? Would it hurt me any to ride?"

"Why on earth would you want to climb on a horse now?" he asked.

"I'm not saying I'm going to. I just want to know if I could," she answered.

The doctor finished tying her bandage and began to organize his supplies. "I wouldn't advise it, but it wouldn't kill you, if that's what you're asking."

"I'm not asking anything in particular. I was just making conversation."

The doctor sighed. "All right, Cass. I'm finished here for now. May I call the marshal back?"

Cass pulled the blanket up to her neck again. "Yes, call him in."

Brett was smiling when he entered the room. "Doc told me you were talking a mile a minute while he bandaged you."

"He did?"

"Yep. What were you saying?"

Cass thought for a moment about what she was going to say. "I have several things to tell you, Brett," she said quietly. "But I'd really like to be dressed before I start."

Brett sighed. He could sense that what she had to say was important. "All right. I'll get you some clean clothes. Then will you tell me what's on your mind?"

"I promise."

An hour later Rosie was helping Cass pull on her trousers.

"I don't understand why you won't let me help you into a dress. These things are so . . ."

"Ugly?" Cass supplied.

"No. I wasn't going to say ugly," Rosie insisted.

"Trousers serve my purpose, Rosie. Someday I'll wear nothing but pretty dresses, but for now I need the freedom that trousers give me."

"But you don't need to do anything right now except recover," Rosie said.

Cass didn't answer. She did have something to do. "Do you know where Brett and the doc put my guns?" she asked as nonchalantly as she could.

Rosie looked around the room. "I don't know. Maybe here?" she said, crossing to an armoire that stood against the far wall. Pulling it open, she peered inside. "I should be a detective," she said. "Here they are, hanging safely on a hook, but you don't need them now."

"No. Are my boots in there too?"

"Yes."

"Good. Just in case I need to go to the outhouse," she added.

Rosie nodded. "You're all dressed. Should I go get the men?"

"No, let me walk out to see them." Cass started for the curtain. Halfway across the room she started feeling a little weak and swayed a bit.

Rosie rushed to her side. "You're overdoing it, you know. Just because you're feeling some better today doesn't mean you're ready to rush out and conquer the world."

Rosie's choice of words amused Cass. She wasn't going to conquer the world, just two men. Two very evil men.

Brett looked up at Cass and Rosie as they came through the curtain. "You're dressed," he observed.

Cass nodded.

"I liked you better in a blanket."

"Brett!" she scolded.

Buster laughed. "I know I'd like to see someone in a blanket," he remarked.

Rosie turned three shades of scarlet and couldn't speak.

Brett burst out laughing.

"You two are horrible," said Cass. "Rosie and I should just leave," she threatened.

"No, you don't," said Brett, standing and putting his arm gently around her shoulders. "You're going to come over here and sit down next to me. You owe me some conversation, remember?"

"I remember." She looked expectantly at Rosie.

"Come on, Buster. We have to go now," she said, getting the message.

Once alone, Cass didn't know where to start. Sitting down, she gathered her thoughts. She wanted Brett to know how she felt, to pour out her heart to him, to let him know she wanted to spend the rest of her life with him. But she also had to tell him about Ramsey. She wanted to explain why she had to finish what she'd started.

"Brett," she began.

Brett had taken the chair next to hers, and reached for her hand. "Yes?"

Cass relished the feeling of his strong fingers caressing hers. His touch was sending little spasms of delight skittering up her arm. It was very distracting. "I want to tell you something."

"Yes?" he growled, leaning closer to her.

She shivered as her heart skipped several beats. "Actually I have several things to tell you."

Brett bent forward and nuzzled her neck, nipping at the tender skin there with his lips. "Go ahead," he breathed.

"You're not making this any easier," she said, her voice coming out on a husky sigh.

"I'm not?" he asked innocently.

"Brett . . . I . . . I love you," she whispered.

Brett's heart nearly exploded when he heard her words. "I love you so much, Cass," he said, wrapping his arms gently around her so as not to hurt her. "I was afraid I'd never get to hear you say those words to me. When I saw you'd been shot I nearly died. Then when you developed a fever . . ." He let his voice trail off at the memory.

Cass pulled back from him a little. "You didn't let me finish," she said.

Brett gazed into her beautiful eyes. "What else did you want to say?"

"I love you, but there's something I have to do before we can be together."

Brett began to feel suspicious. "And what would that be?"

"I have to go after Ramsey."

Brett hit his thighs with the heels of his hands. "I knew you were going to say something ridiculous like that," he fumed. "I know Ramsey tried to kill you, Cass. I curse myself for leaving you and making his attempt possible, but believe me, I'm the one who's going to make him pay for that act, not you. I've only been waiting for you to get well enough for me to feel comfortable leaving your side."

"I'm not going to kill Ramsey for trying to kill me, Brett. I'm going to kill him for murdering my family."

Brett stared hard into her eyes. "Ramsey?"

"I remembered, Brett. I remembered when I saw the sun on his silver bracelet. Don't you see? My memory played a trick on me. I thought I'd seen the reflection of the sun on a silver gun, but it was Ramsey's bracelet all along. He did it, Brett. He helped murder my family. Now I'm going to kill him for it."

Brett listened to her and his heart hardened. "I won't let you do it, Cass."

"But you heard me. Ramsey and his father are the last of the murderers. I have to finish this."

"I agree it has to be finished. But not by you. I watched you lie on that table in the other room and nearly die. I won't go through that again. I'll be the one to go after Ramsey."

"It's not your fight, Brett. I started this, and I have to finish it."

Brett stood up and faced her. "No, Cass! I won't let you do it," he told her.

"You can't stop me."

"I won't let you out of my sight."

"For the rest of my life? That's what it would take."

Brett rubbed his hands over his face in frustration. "When are you planning to do this?"

"As soon as I'm strong enough."

"That won't be soon enough. I'm going to get some men together and go out to the Lazy T tomorrow. We'll bring Ramsey in. He'll be charged with the crimes, and he'll stand trial."

"What if he's not at the Lazy T?"

"We'll hunt him down. Wherever he is, I'll find him and bring him to justice."

"That's not good enough."

"Why? Because you feel that you have to be the one to do it?"

"I have to see him dead."

"You're planning his murder."

"I'll let him draw first."

"Damn it, Cass! You're splitting hairs. If you plan to kill someone, no matter how, it's murder."

"So arrest me."

Brett fell back into the chair beside her. "I know you think you have to do this. I understand your reasons. But I'm going after Ramsey first thing in the morning. I won't give you the opportunity to kill him. I won't take that chance with your life."

Cass clenched her jaw tightly. Looking at Brett, she knew what she had to do. "All right," she said. "I suppose you can't help how you feel."

"I feel like a man in love with the most stubborn woman in the world," he answered.

Cass shrugged, then groaned when the absentminded gesture caused her so much pain.

Brett put his hand gently on her left shoulder. "I love you, Cass," he whispered, leaning toward her.

She looked up at him. "I love you, too," she murmured. Seeing the devotion in his deep gray eyes caused her a moment of guilt, but only a moment. Then she pushed it away. If she died doing what she had to do, she'd accept her fate.

Cass listened to the sound of Brett's soft snoring not far from her. She'd managed to talk the doctor into letting her leave the office, but only by promising not to do too much. Now she lay in the sheriff's comfortable bed while Brett slept on a cot in one of the cells of the jail. It had been difficult waiting for him to fall asleep, but she'd been listening to him snore for the better part of half an hour, and she felt fairly sure he was sleeping soundly enough for her to leave. Pushing back the covers, she grimaced as she sat up.

Her shoulder was still throbbing and her right arm was useless, but she was sure she could get dressed and go outside. Saddling a horse was going to be difficult, but she didn't have a choice.

The night air was warm as she exited the building some twenty minutes later. Leaning against the clapboard siding, she rested for a minute. Moving around so much had taken away a lot of her strength, but she was determined to finish what she'd started. Tonight might be her last chance.

Brett had gotten himself a new horse, a big roan with a long, shaggy mane, and had left him in a small corral in back of the jail. Pulling his saddle off the fence, she grunted as she dragged it to where the animal stood beside the trough. "Make this easy on me and stand still, okay?" she whispered. The horse looked at her with large brown eyes and whinnied. "Shhh, we don't want to wake up Brett," she warned quietly.

By the time she'd managed to saddle the big animal and then pull herself up onto his back, she could barely stand the ache in her shoulder. She reached up to touch the bandage. "Damn it," she breathed when her fingers came away bloody. She'd broken open the wound again, but she couldn't worry about that now. Nudging the horse with her heels, she started out for the Lazy T.

The ride seemed longer than she remembered, and she realized she was getting light-headed when she rode onto Lazy T land by way of a ridge that separated her property from the Tylos'. She shook her head to clear it. Only a little while longer, she told herself. Just two more men and I'm through.

When she could see the house, she dismounted, tethered the horse, and proceeded on foot, running from one rock or shrub to the next, trying to stay out of sight. Her arrival had to be a surprise. She could see lights burning in the house and frowned at her bad luck. Apparently someone was still awake.

Creeping around the house, she peered into several windows. When she reached the study windows her heart began to beat furiously. There, seated with his father, was Ramsey. Both men were smoking cigars and holding glasses of what looked like brandy. They were laughing and enjoying themselves, completely relaxed in the knowledge that they'd gotten away with murder. "At least you think you have," she murmured.

Sneaking to the back of the house, she tried to open the door to the kitchen, but found it locked. Cursing as she went, she made her way back toward the front of the house. She'd go in through a window if she had to. She stumbled once as she neared the front porch, but was able to keep from falling by grabbing the edge of an empty window box. Standing still for a moment, she took several deep breaths, praying she would last long enough to do what she'd come to do.

Looking down at her shirt, she could see that blood had soaked through the fabric and was creating an ever-widening stain of dark red. Her knees started to buckle again, but she forced herself to keep going.

The front door was unlocked, and she said a prayer of thanks. She wasn't sure she could have pulled herself through a window. She entered the house and tiptoed silently down the hall toward the study. In just minutes it'll be over, she thought. One way or another.

Brett turned in his sleep and nearly fell off the tiny jailhouse cot he'd been bunking on. "Damn," he cursed. Sitting up, he stretched his neck and thought about the soft beds in the hotel. But in the hotel there'd be a closed door between him and Cass, and he wanted to be able to hear her breathe. He listened. The hair on the back of his neck stood up as a wave of apprehension swept over him. It was too quiet. Getting up, he raced across the short distance to the sheriff's bedroom. The bed was empty. "Cass?" he called into the silence. His heart started pounding with dread. "Cass?" he called again. Going to the back door, he stepped outside. Maybe she'd just made a trip to the outhouse. "Cass?" he yelled once more. Then he noticed the empty corral. "No!" he moaned, knowing instantly what she'd done.

Hurrying back into the office, he pulled on his clothes in seconds. He was still strapping his gun belt on as he ran down the street toward the livery.

"Wake up!" he yelled, banging on the smithy's door. "Wake up in there. I need a horse now!"

The smithy walked with bleary eyes to the door. "Who is it?"

"It's Marshal Ryder. I need a horse."

"I just sold you a horse," the man said, yawning.

"I need another one, damn it. Now open this door!"

The smithy finally opened the door. "What are you so fired up about in the middle of the night, Marshal? Somebody get killed?"

"I hope to God not," he said, rushing in and grabbing a saddle off the rack.

"That's my saddle, Marshal. Hey, and that's my horse. He ain't for sale."

"I'm borrowing him for the rest of the night."

"Well, I don't know . . ." the smithy said rubbing his ample stomach.

Brett turned to the man and glared down at him. "Go back to bed!" he ordered.

The smithy blinked several times in surprise. "I . . . I . . . all right, Marshal," he finally said, and wandered back to his living quarters.

Ten minutes later Brett was riding toward the Lazy T like a man whose hair was on fire. "Please be alive, Cass," he said. "Please be alive." His words became a chant in his head as he rode.

Cass stepped into the study. "Good evening, gentlemen, and I use the term loosely."

"Cass?" Ramsey spoke, startled.

"Yes, Ramsey, it's me. Are you surprised to see me? You didn't think I'd come for you, did you? You thought you'd have to come to me again." She wavered on her feet slightly.

"What are you doing here in my home uninvited, Cassidy?" demanded Hunt.

Cass glanced his way. "My being invited isn't an issue, Mr. Tylo. Your men have never been invited to my place, but that didn't stop them, did it?"

"I don't know what you're talking about," he said.

"Don't you? What about you, Ramsey? Will you admit you know what I'm talking about? It would save a little time if you would." She could feel the blood running down her side.

"Sorry, Cass. I guess you'll have to spell it out," answered Ramsey. He exchanged glances with his father. They could see that she standing by willpower alone. She might be a fast draw, but she'd be shooting with her left hand, and she was weak. It wouldn't be long before she dropped. Then they'd have her.

"Don't you remember what happened, Ramsey? I do. As if it occurred yesterday. You and your men came to my place and slaughtered my family. I didn't know it was you until the other day, the day Bobby Fleet put a bullet in me. I saw the sun on your bracelet that day, Ramsey, and I remembered. The sun reflected off your bracelet the day you murdered my family, too. I thought it was a silver gun handle. I searched for five years for a man with a silver gun, and all the while it was you." She chuckled, a sarcastic sound that gurgled in her throat.

"We don't know what you're talking about," said Hunt.

"You lie very well, Mr. Tylo. You've been doing it for years. But I don't believe you anymore, so why don't you tell the truth for once? It won't make any difference, of course. I'm going to kill you either way, but wouldn't you like the chance to tell the truth just once?"

Hunt laughed. "Maybe you're right," he said.

"Father . . ." Ramsey warned.

Hunt shrugged. "What could it hurt? She says she's going to kill us anyway." He started walking around behind the desk.

"Stay where you are," Cass ordered.

"Or what, you'll shoot me?" Hunt laughed again. "Look at her, boy," he said to Ramsey. "She can barely stand. In a few minutes she'll be dead. And this is the woman you were so hot to marry."

Cass narrowed her eyes. "Why?" she asked.

"For the land, Cass," Ramsey admitted.

"Just the land," she murmured. "Our land wasn't so valuable you had to kill for it."

"Access to the water was. Your father threatened to keep my cattle from the Losee," said Hunt.

"You have access."

"Not good enough."

"You killed my family for the sake of convenience."

Hunt raised his shoulders in a blasé gesture.

Cass's heart burned with rage. "But you missed me," she said.

"That was Ramsey's error. He was supposed to make sure everyone was there before he started the killing."

"And afterward?"

"He promised he'd finish you off, but it turned out he didn't need to. You left town to chase after the poor fools who'd been paid to do a job. With you gone and your uncle on the bottle, I ran my cattle across your land whenever I chose."

"And then I came home," Cass said, feeling her knees begin to quake.

"Yes. So I sent for Ramsey. He was supposed to come home and finish the job he'd started. Instead, he persuaded me to give him a chance to wed you. Either way, I'd have your land."

"But your plan didn't work. I didn't fall in love with Ramsey."

He rose as she spoke. "Not for lack of my trying, Cass," Ramsey said. "I think if it hadn't been for the marshal I would have won your love."

Cass thought a minute. "I could never love you, Ramsey."

Cass felt herself losing her battle for strength. She leaned against the open door. "And what about Rosie?" she asked.

"Rosie was just a little fun on the side," Ramsey said, raising an eyebrow in his father's direction, indicating that Cass was weakening even more.

Cass felt the darkness tugging at the corners of her mind again. The blood that dripped down her side was now soaking the top of her trousers. The pain throbbing through her shoulder and down her arm was the only thing keeping her conscious now. "You'll both burn in hell for what you did."

Hunt laughed again. "I don't worry about hell, Cassidy. Do you? You've killed six men. Doesn't it worry you that you'll spend eternity burning in the fiery pit with Satan?"

"I did what I had to do," Cass said, her voice growing weak. "I'll let the Lord judge me as he sees fit. At least I'll know my killing was for a good reason. I brought justice to cold-blooded murderers." She glanced from one man to the other. "And now I'm going to do it again." Her head drooped for a second.

Ramsey glanced at his father and whispered, "Her eyes are glazing over. I can take her."

"Didn't you say you've never seen anyone faster with a gun?"

Ramsey nodded.

"Then why risk it? She's about to fall over," whispered Hunt.

"What are you two saying?" Cass demanded.

"We're concerned about your health, Cass. You don't look too good," Hunt said with false sweetness. Leaning over slightly, he slowly pulled open his desk drawer, revealing his revolver.

Cass knew she had only a few minutes of lucidity left. Forcing herself to stand straight again, she focused her gaze on Ramsey. His gun was strapped to his thigh. He would be her first victim.

Ramsey saw the intent in her eyes. "Whenever you're ready, Cass," he said, sure he could beat her now that she was so weak.

Hunt began to move slowly. Bending his knees only a little, he was able to get his fingers around the butt of his gun. Jerking it upward, he aimed and fired in one motion.

Cass saw him move and drew her gun like lightning, pulling the trigger at the same time, sending a bullet to rip a hole through his heart.

"Noooo!" screamed Ramsey as he saw Hunt fall. Turning insane eyes toward Cass, he shouted. "You can't be that good!" He pulled his gun and tried to fire, but the bullet that split his skull hit him before his finger touched the trigger. He stumbled backwards, surprise registered forever as his last emotion.

Cass saw them die and slid to the floor. Dropping her gun, she began to cry. It was over, really over.

Brett heard the gunshots and yelled in anguish. "Cass!" he screamed, riding up to the house and flying from the saddle, his gun drawn. Bursting through the door, he ran for the study. "Cass! Where are you?" he shouted, terror filling his heart.

Charging through the study door, he almost stepped on Cass where she lay. "Dear God, Cass," he moaned, falling to his knees beside her. Dropping his gun, he swept her up in his arms. She was covered with her own blood, and tears streaked her face. She was sobbing as though she would never stop. "I was afraid you'd be dead by the time I got here," he said.

"I told you I had to finish it," she reminded him.

He looked around the room. Hunt Tylo lay dead across his desk. Ramsey had left a wash of blood on the wall behind him as he slid to the floor. "You finished it."

"I thought I'd be happy when it was over," she said, her body racked with sobs, "but I just feel . . . empty."

Brett held her gently while she cried five years' worth of tears.

Epilogue

Four Months Later

C ass stood in the doorway of her new home and watched Brett riding toward her. She smiled as he entered the yard, glowing from an inner happiness she had never known was possible.

"How's my pregnant wife?" he called as he jumped from his mount. "Getting fat yet?"

Cass ran to him, throwing herself into his arms. Standing on tiptoe, she kissed him fully on the lips, savoring the taste and smell of him. "You just saw me this morning," she murmured after the kiss. "Do I look any fatter?"

Brett let his eyes roam over the still perfect figure of the woman he loved. "Maybe a little," he teased.

"You, Sheriff, are a liar. I wonder if the good people of Twisted Creek know they've elected a liar to such an important position?"

"Are you going to tell them?"

"I just might. Unless, of course, I'm paid a price for my silence."

"And just what price did you have in mind?" he growled seductively, squeezing her more tightly to his body.

Lady of the Gun

"I'll think about it and let you know tonight," she whispered breathlessly.

Brett kissed her again soundly, then released her, swatting her playfully on the backside. "You know, your bottom feels different in skirts," he observed.

Cass giggled. *"I* feel different in skirts. I'd forgotten how cold the wind can be when it blows up under my petticoats."

Brett laughed. "I never thought about that aspect of it." He put his arm around her shoulders and began walking toward the house.

"Did you ask Buster and Rosie if they'll have Thanksgiving dinner with us?" she asked.

"Yes, and Buster said they'll be here with bells on. I guess Rosie's already started baking pies."

"But Thanksgiving's not until next week."

Brett shrugged. "I know, but you know Rosie."

Cass smiled. "Yes, I know Rosie."

"And Mrs. Wettle will be here?" Brett asked.

"Of course. Uncle Darby wouldn't have it any other way. They're so cute together."

"Love is a wonderful thing."

Cass smiled lovingly up at him. "You're right."

They stopped before entering the house, and Cass's mood changed slightly. "Did you get it?" she asked quietly.

Brett stopped walking and looked down into her eyes. "Yes, it's official."

"Let me see it."

"Are you sure you want to?"

"I'm sure."

Brett reached inside his jacket pocket and pulled out a folded newspaper clipping. "Here it is," he said, handing it to Cass.

She looked at the words and began reading aloud: " 'Cassidy Wayne, the notorious gunslinger known as the Lady of the Gun, was killed last week in a gunfight in Texas.' " She looked up at Brett. "Why Texas?"

"Sounded good," he answered, shrugging.

She kept reading. " 'The lady gunslinger was known to

have killed at least eight people, several of whom were suspected of murdering her family. She will be missed by the people who knew her well.' " She sighed. "It's finally really over," she breathed.

"No one else will come looking for you."

"The Lady of the Gun is gone forever."

Brett watched her eyes. "Are you glad?"

Tears filled her eyes. "More than you'll ever know."

At just that moment, Mirabelle and Pork Chop streaked across the yard, screeching and clawing, feathers and fur flying. Cass began to laugh. "See? I told you if Mirabelle ever figured out she was the one who was supposed to be doing the chasing there'd be hell to pay."

Brett laughed with her, wrapping his arms tightly around her waist in a loving embrace. "That chicken is definitely paying for her sins."

Judith McNaught
Jude Deveraux
Jill Barnett
Arnette Lamb

❈❈❈❈❈

A Holiday
Of Love

❈❈❈❈❈

*A collection of romances
available from*

POCKET
BOOKS

1007-02

A Gift of Love

Judith McNaught
Jude Deveraux
Andrea Kane
Kimberly Cates
Judith O'Brien

A wonderful romance collection in the
tradition of *New York Times* bestsellers
A Holiday of Love and *Everlasting Love*,
A GIFT OF LOVE is sure to delight
romance fans and readers alike.

POCKET
B O O K S

**AVAILABLE IN HARDCOVER
FROM POCKET BOOKS**

1093-04

The enchanting new novel from the
author of the *New York Times*
bestseller *Until You*

JUDITH MCNAUGHT

REMEMBER WHEN

Judith McNaught creates an unforgettable world
filled with her "very special brand of dazzling wit,
passion, and tender sensuality."—*Romantic Times*

COMING SOON IN HARDCOVER!

POCKET
B O O K S

The Best Historical Romance Comes From Pocket Books